ONE FOR THE
BLACKBIRD,
ONE FOR THE
CROW

amazon publishing

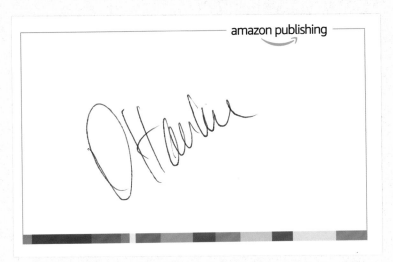

ALSO BY OLIVIA HAWKER

The Ragged Edge of Night

Writing as Libbie Hawker

Tidewater
Calamity
Baptism for the Dead

ONE FOR THE BLACKBIRD,

a novel

ONE FOR THE CROW

OLIVIA HAWKER

LAKE UNION
PUBLISHING

This is a work of fiction. Names, characters, organizations, places, events, and incidents are either products of the author's imagination or are used fictitiously.

Published by Lake Union Publishing, Seattle

www.apub.com

Amazon, the Amazon logo, and Lake Union Publishing are trademarks of Amazon.com, Inc., or its affiliates.

ISBN-13: 9781542006910 (hardcover)
ISBN-10: 1542006910 (hardcover)

ISBN-13: 9781542091145 (paperback)
ISBN-10: 1542091144 (paperback)

Cover design by Rex Bonomelli

Printed in the United States of America

First Edition

For my mother and my sister, who have seen the spiral.
And for Paul—my bluebird, my crow.

1

After He Took Himself Off to Jail

I was leading the cows to the milking shed when my pa shot Mr. Webber. It was the end of the season for blackberries, and the fence beside the shed was thick with the vines my ma had planted years before. The evening air smelled of berries, rich and sweet in the way that makes you close your eyes when you breathe in the scent. You can't help but do it; the smell takes ahold of you and calls to your heart, and it makes you think of all the good things that have passed and all the good things yet to come, so you close your eyes to shut out everything else that's real, everything that's drab or sorrowful, all the things that hurt you like the thorns. That's what I was doing when I heard the shot—standing with one hand on the gate and my eyes closed, thinking about those berries and how, after milking was done, I'd pick a whole basketful and share them with my brothers and my baby sister, sweet and good with cream on top, the cream still warm from the cows.

But the moment the shot cracked the air, I opened my eyes and my hand. The pail of grain fell, and the cows pushed me aside to lip up what was spilled. I knew right then that something terrible had happened, something that would change us all forever. And I knew it was my fault—at least some—for I'd been the one who told my pa that the calf was missing, and he'd gone off to search for it. If I'd never told him, if I'd gone to find that calf myself, it would have been me who seen what no one should have seen, and I would have left it all alone. Never said a word, just drifted off like a ghost through the dusk, with no one any wiser.

But instead, it was Pa who found them, under the poplars by the river, and now Substance Webber is dead.

I can't say just how I knew it was trouble when I heard that shot. Pa fired his Henry rifle all the time, at coyotes and eagles who came for our stock, and at bears to shoo them away from the places where my brothers and sister played. Maybe I heard a new sound in the rifle's voice. Maybe it was like a shout of pain torn from my father's throat, worse than the time his horse slipped and fell on him, and his leg was broke in two places. Maybe it was just because my ma had been missing all evening, and I finally wised up enough to think it strange. She slipped off toward the river once she saw that all her children were fed and the chores were underway. It was a thing she'd done for days now, but until the rifle sounded, I'd never thought twice about it. I was big enough to care for the little ones without being told.

As soon as I knew deep down in my heart that something had gone awry, I slapped the cows on their backsides to hurry them into the pen, and then I ran to the house, where the little ones were putting on their nightdresses. I said, Everybody into the bedroom, and don't come out till I say so. They complained, because they always do, but they did as I told them. They always do that, too. I wanted them shut safely away when the trouble came up from the riverside to our little gray house. I didn't want them to see the look on our pa's face when he returned.

When Pa came back through the twilight, he was paler than a bad-omen moon. He walked with a stagger, like he was struck by some illness, and his eyes seemed to see nothing that lay before him—only what lay behind, what had caused him to raise his rifle and pull the trigger before he could think any better. He held the gun as if it was a foreign thing, and too distasteful to bear, one-handed by its stock with the muzzle dragging through tall grass. Behind him came my mother, hair unbound and weeping into her hands.

I went outside to meet them both. I was scared all at once for them—afraid one of them should fall, like they were fragile, breakable things. The sight of me brought Pa from his daze. He stared at my face for a long time, and it was hard not to look away, for I'd never seen such agony in him before, and I knew right then that he was only a man, and mortal. No girl likes to realize that her father will die someday. Much less does she like to know that grief could be enough to kill him.

Beulah, he said, I done something wrong.

I said, I know it, Pa.

He nodded. Pa never questioned this way I have—the knowing that comes to me from the movement of wind or the scent of blackberries, or the sound of a gunshot by the river.

He said, I got to go now, over to the Webbers' place, and tell them what all happened. And then I got to ride to town and turn myself over to the sheriff. It's the only righteous thing to be done.

My mother wailed at that and staggered toward him, but Pa stepped back. He held up his free hand, a wall between them. It only made Ma weep more piteously.

I said, I'll saddle Tiger for you, and he answered, No, not Tiger. He's a fast horse. I can't say how long I'll be gone, Little Mite, and you may have need of a fast horse, by and by. You'll need the saddle, too. I don't know if the sheriff will return my horse to my farm and my family. I've never done this before. Could be a man forfeits his right to his horse when he . . . when he does what I just done. Put a bridle on Meg; I'll take her to town bareback.

I still liked to hear him call me Little Mite, even though I was thirteen and not little anymore. And I had never felt older or steadier than I did in that moment, when I stepped away from my parents to pull the old, slow mare from her paddock and ready her so she could carry off Pa to his fate. My mother was still weeping, her cries loud and long like the peal of a bell.

The pain in her voice was heavy to bear. I would have cried, too, if I'd had the lee, for I already felt the badness of it all, the distance between my mother and father opening wider like a crack in the earth. You'll fall into that cold, damp darkness if you aren't careful where to set your feet.

But there was work to be done, and no time for crying. Not if we hoped to get by without Pa.

In time, my mother stopped weeping and huddled on the doorstep. In the first silver creeping of moonlight, she looked smaller and frailer than she ever had before. She hugged her body and rocked as if it was a baby she held in her arms, not herself—and she stared at my father, hungry, desperate for one look from him, one word. He gave neither.

I handed Meg's reins to my pa, and he passed the gun to me.

You know how to use the rifle, he said.

I nodded. I wasn't handy with a gun—I never had needed to be—but it was simple enough. That much I knew.

He said, I'll send word, soon as I'm able. It's up to you to think of something to tell the little ones, something they'll understand.

I said, Is there anything you want me to tell Ma?

He stood listening to the crickets in the long grass. He wrapped Meg's reins around his fist and tightened it till his knuckles blanched white. Then he took a deep breath, savoring the smell of his homestead and the coolness of a soft Wyoming night. He closed his eyes and stood like that for a long while.

When he opened his eyes again, Pa said, In time, I'll want you to tell your ma how sorry I am, and that I love her still. But that time ain't come yet. Not yet.

I watched him ride away down the rutted path through our pasture, east toward the Webber farm. When night's gray shadows hid him from view, I turned my back on Pa and faced the house, and my mother wilting on the steps.

I went to her and unwrapped her hands from around her thin body, and pulled her to her feet, where she swayed. We didn't speak, for I knew she had no words yet, and wouldn't for days to come. That's the way with

Ma. Whenever a sorrow or a fear comes along to put a crack in her heart, she goes quiet—the only time she ever does. I knew she would say nothing while she was shrouded in grief and remorse, just as I knew that after he took himself off to jail, my pa would send word and forgive her.

But until forgiveness came, I had to run the farm on my own. There was no one else who could do it. I wasn't afraid. I haven't found anything yet in this life that's worth being afraid of.

CLYDE

After he took himself off to jail, there was nothing left to be done about Ernest Bemis. Clyde stood beside the window, the one next to the front door, looking out across the orchard and down the two-rutted road. He watched Mr. Bemis ride away, slowly, shoulders hanging as if the weight of all the world were pulling him down into the swayed back of his gray mare. The mare was old enough that she had paled up nearly to white, so her rump stayed visible even through the darkness, and Clyde could see her tail wringing with every other step. An old horse, and ill tempered. The sight of her rippled through the window's warped glass even after the drooping and regretful form of Mr. Bemis had merged with the darkness.

He heard a sudden clatter from the kitchen—one of the pewter spoons falling to the plank floor—then a hasty step and the soft metallic whisper of the spoon being picked up again. A moment later, the chiming of the spoon against the sides of one of her drab brown cups as Mother stirred her tea.

Stop thinking about horses. Clyde scolded himself because there wasn't anyone else to do it now. *You ought to be thinking of Mother, not some damned old mare.* That was the way with Clyde. Horses were easier to understand than folks ever were. There never was a time when he preferred to reflect on the nature of people rather than the nature of horses. People—men especially—hid their thoughts and their hearts behind thick, stoic walls, a dense blank-white nothingness, a silent room, a distant stare. Men hid what they couldn't control till the burden of that featureless mask grew too much to bear, and then they threw it off and broke it with a shout or a swinging fist. Or a rifle shot at the riverside. Then they picked up the pieces of their unreadable disguise and fitted them back together and donned the mask again. That was never the way with horses. Once you understood their language—the flick of an ear, the stamp of a hoof, a ripple running down sun-hot hide from withers to flank—horses couldn't surprise you. No horse disguised a worry or a fear or even its deepest hatred from anyone who cared to listen. If men were more like horses, things never would have gone this far. It never would have come down to Ernest Bemis, the only neighbor for twenty miles in any direction, appearing at the front door while the last trace of the gone day's blue still colored the western horizon, confessing he had just shot Clyde's father dead.

He ought to be thinking about Mother, not horses. Mother wasn't crying. She never cried, but that didn't mean she didn't want to cry. All the same, there wasn't a sniff from the kitchen, only the sound of stirring—a small, self-contained noise that barely broke the silence. Mother was the strongest person Clyde knew. She had always been stronger than fear, stronger than Father's fists when he got into his black moods and swung them, thoughtless as you'd swing an ax at a leg of firewood. She was stronger than the winds that blew down the Bighorns, scouring leaves from the cottonwoods, stripping soil from the earth and sheeting it against the windows till the house went black in the middle of the day. She was stronger than the Wyoming range, and what was more powerful than that?

He ought to be thinking of Father, who was lying out there beside the river, dead and unburied. He would remain unburied till Clyde did the work himself, for there was no one left to dig the grave.

There was no one left to scold Clyde into what was proper or to beat him bruised and sore onto a righteous path. Mother never scolded;

that wasn't her way. Silence was her way—silence and the stony, hard-angled face that she never washed with tears. Her face must have been beautiful once, before this life stole all the color from it and the prairie winds stripped her down to dry skin and sharp bones.

Clyde would be awake all night, digging that grave and rolling his father into it, covering the man with earth. Morning would find him bone weary and sleepless from what he had seen. Clyde knew that much already; he could sense it, the way you feel the presence of an animal in the darkness even when you can't see it—the quiet slink of a furred, feral body, the hush of its live flank brushing between tufts of grass. He was afraid of what more the night would bring, even though it had already brought the worst.

At least when he faced what was to come, he would have Joe Buck for company. The gelding was big and watchful, as warm as Father had never been. Whatever moved unseen in the darkness never dared come too close to Joe Buck, who was quick to kick at danger. It was time Clyde got out to the paddock and saddled his horse and went about this unexpected business. The sooner he finished the night's work, the better.

He took his felt coat from the peg. Mother heard the familiar sound, heard just where his foot landed on the floor boards, a step in front of the door.

"Where are you going?" she called from the kitchen. There was tension in her voice—almost fear. Understandable enough, given all that had happened this night.

"Someone's got to bury him," Clyde said. To his surprise and shame, tears came to his eyes and his voice trembled. He turned his back to the kitchen, so at least Mother wouldn't see him cry, even if she heard.

"Not you," she said. There was a sharp, glassy clink, her teacup meeting its saucer. "You're too young for that, God have mercy."

"There's no one else to do it, Mother. It's got to be me."

"We'll get the sheriff."

"When? In the morning?" The animals would have done their work by then, tearing him apart, spreading his bones. "And what if the sheriff can't come for days? We're miles off. It's got to be me, and it's got to be now. You stay here. There's no reason why you should see him."

It was cold outside. It was September; snow was not far off. He could almost smell it in the air—the sharp, clean chill, a faint smoky drift of coming winter. The sky offered just enough light for Clyde to see his way around the vegetable patch with its haphazard fence, built high to keep the deer away. The footpath to the paddock was almost invisible, but he had walked it so many times he knew the way by feel. Joe Buck smelled him coming and whickered in the darkness. Clyde went a little faster then, and he reached the paddock fence just as his horse did. Joe Buck's golden color was dulled to flat gray by night, but there was no mistaking him: fat, upright neck and small ears turning this way and that in a knowing fashion. The other horses milled in the darkness, unseen—the heavy black mare who hauled the plow and a pair of bay fillies Clyde had just broken to harness. But Joe Buck slung his head right over the top of the fence in greeting. Clyde wrapped his arms around the gelding's neck and pressed his face against the warm hide, and the smell of dust and hair and sweet grasses surrounded him. Clyde hung there for a long time, with the black wire of Joe Buck's mane falling over his shoulder. He let his tears fall freely then, let sobs shake his body. It was shameful enough for a boy to cry, Clyde knew, but for a man to do it was something close to sin. And he was a man now. Suddenly, violently, torn from what remained of his childhood in a blink, in a burst of gunfire.

Joe Buck was a patient soul. He would have stood at the fence all night and allowed Clyde to soak him in tears, but there was work to be done, and weeping wouldn't make the task any easier. After a time, Clyde pushed himself away and said, "I'll go fetch your saddle and bridle, Joe. We got to go out to the river tonight. Got no choice but to do it."

When the horse was tacked up and ready, Clyde led him past the new harness shed, the one he and Father had built that spring. The split shingles still smelled of pine sap when the wind blew the right way. A spade leaned against the door frame; Clyde took it and swung up into the saddle, then laid the spade behind the pommel as he rode.

The horse knew the river trail, and he carried Clyde through the dark without shying or stumbling. Clyde let his feet dangle alongside the stirrups, let the reins slide loosely through his cold fingers. He kept his other hand clenched tightly around the handle of his spade. Its weight across his thighs seemed more than a boy of sixteen ought to bear.

The voice of the river came to him first, its endless hiss, the whisper of water over stones. Then he heard the scuffle of night animals retreating—scavengers—and he knew he'd found the place, even before Joe Buck snorted and threw up his head, offended by the smell of blood. Clyde didn't dismount straight away. He feared wolves; there was no one to protect him if a wolf should come. He stared into the darkness for a long time, down at the shadows in the tall grass, the deepest black that clung low to the earth, until at last the weak moonlight revealed the body of his father sprawled across the ground.

Substance Webber had never lived up to his name. Clyde had always known it, since he'd been little more than a tyke—since he'd first learned to see the shift in his father's moods, the narrowing of his eye, the freezing over of what little kindness stirred inside the man. There was even less substance to him now. He seemed flat as a sheet of ice and every bit as colorless. The stillness of the body struck Clyde with a terrible significance; that stillness was more frightening than any thought of wolves.

The long grass, touched by night breezes, moved gently, and Joe Buck's ears flicked back and forth. The horse's flanks rose and fell with his steady breath. Even the river's quiet voice was evidence of its movement. But Substance Webber did not move. His eyes were partway open, staring up at the sky with the dry vacancy Clyde had seen countless times before in the deer he had shot and the sheep whose throats he cut when the time came to cull the flock. You can know your father will be dead someday, just as you know the long, bleak months of winter must follow the harvest, but nothing truly prepares you for the sight of him, fallen and unmoving, left where he was dropped among the shadows of the grass.

Clyde shuddered with fear and disgust, with a superstitious revulsion for this scene, this reality. This was never the way life was meant to be—a son so young, not really a man, burying his own father. But it would disgust him more to know that he had left his father's remains to be scattered by the coyotes Substance had always hated.

He swung down from the saddle and turned his back on his father's body, so he wouldn't have to see its stillness while he worked. Clyde stabbed his spade down deep into the tight sod of the prairie and dug and bent and sweated till his thoughts fled, till everything fled except the rhythm of the work, and only when the grave was ready and the wind bit cold through his sweat-dampened shirt did he look at his father again.

Clyde stepped carefully through the night. He stood above the body now, looking down at its blackness and whiteness. The face had blanched in death, pale as the sleeves of his shirt, and his beard and trousers and the patch of wet ruin that had been his chest were all the same deep and final shade of darkness. Clyde thought he should close his father's eyes, but when he moved to touch his face, nausea clutched at his stomach and he withdrew. He thought, *I should check his pockets for valuables. In case there's anything we can sell up in town for a little money, something to keep us warm and fed through the winter.* But he had a dreadful, dizzying fear that if he reached into the pockets, the body would move—the arm snaking out suddenly to strike at his hand—and then he would scream, and screaming would be a shame worse than crying.

11

Yet he had to move the body to its grave. The hole was only a few feet away; it would be the work of a moment. Clyde told himself as much, bending to take his father by the wrist, by one outstretched arm. He gasped when he touched the body. It was cold and hard, the stiff limbs unyielding, like no dead thing he had handled before. Clyde gritted his teeth and pulled, clung with both hands to his father's arm and dragged that stubborn, resisting weight through the grass to the spaded-up earth, and then he stepped across the narrow grave and hauled his father into the pit behind him. The legs fell down into the depths, but the rigid, outflung arms kept the body leaning ghoulishly up out of the hole. He seemed to stare at Clyde, his only living son, with heavy-lidded reproach.

"I'm sorry," Clyde said frantically, though his father couldn't hear him. "I'm sorry, I'm sorry," though he knew he had nothing to be sorry for.

Then, as gently as he could manage, he braced his foot against one of his father's shoulders and pushed until the joint cracked and the corpse gave way, and Substance Webber subsided into his grave.

Clyde turned away and heaved into the tall grass. Nothing came up from his stomach, but he couldn't stop. Choking and coughing, his guts spasmed so hard his whole body rocked, and a pressure built behind his ears that roared louder with every heave. When he had control again, he shoveled dirt over his father's corpse, quickly so he could leave and forget what he had seen and done. The body didn't lie in neat repose; it was an undignified heap in the black earth. But it was the best Clyde could do. He had never buried a man before.

When the work was finished, he thought perhaps he ought to pray. That was the way a proper burial was done; Clyde felt sure of that. He recalled the small, sober funeral for his sister Anna, who'd died not ten years before. And before Anna, his brother Luther—what seemed ages ago, when the Webbers had still lived in Nebraska. He could remember something of the burial of his three-year-old sister Alta, too—years before Luther died, when Clyde had been a small boy. And before Alta, when Clyde had been younger still, he had stood beside a tiny grave and watched as Mother and Father had laid to rest a baby boy who had lived only a few days, not even long enough for Clyde to feel as if the baby had truly been his brother. He remembered each time clasping his hands and lowering his head as Mother told him to do. He remembered Father speaking the words, a toneless recitation of grief, and *In Jesus' name, amen.* But now Clyde could think of nothing to say, no words to commemorate his father's life, and nothing to excuse his death. He hung his head, but instead of praying, he cried—great, racking sobs that shook his body and raised the sick feeling up to his stomach again. He cried, and pulled his fists up inside his sleeves and bunched the fabric from the inside so he could wipe and wipe at his face, his swollen eyes and running nose. He mewled like some weak, small thing until Joe Buck moved closer, blowing gently through the darkness, and rubbed his forehead against Clyde's shoulder.

It was time to return home. Mother would be worried with Clyde out there in the darkness. She needed him now. There was little love lost between his parents—Clyde had known that for a long time—but Substance had been the mainstay of their lives, the force that had kept them tethered to the prairie. What would Mother do now that her husband was gone?

Working by feel, Clyde straightened Joe Buck's reins. He swung up into the saddle and laid the spade once more across his lap, then turned his horse away from the river, back toward home. Joe Buck found the trail and moved slow and steady through the darkness. His hooves fell softly enough that Clyde could hear the rustle of the coyotes moving in again, searching for the death that had drawn them. But they would find nothing tonight. Substance was gone and buried now. Only his son remained.

CORA

After Ernest took himself off to jail, the world became a place of hollows and omissions, of yawning, empty spaces where he should have been. Cora sank onto the settee beside the hearth and watched as the bleak world ceased to turn around her. She was aware of nothing—not the rising of the sun by morning nor the singing of crickets by night. Not her children's voices nor the feel of their soft and trembling hands as they came seeking comfort Cora couldn't give. She heard only silence, even when the wind moaned down the chimney, and somewhere below and behind that silence, the voice of guilt scolding her, mocking her, filling her heart with the weight of blame and loss.

Cora had never felt any particular fondness for Substance Webber, though she supposed his undeniable show of strength—of grim, imposing power—had attracted her interest if not her heart. Substance was everything Ernest was not: firm in his every decision, commanding and sure, a bulwark against the numberless uncertainties that shaded every day, that marked life out there on the range. When their carryings-on had first begun, Substance had made Cora feel important again—the center of what little society their two families could claim, isolated as they were in a sea of grass, the gray-brown vastness of seclusion. But every time a tryst ended, Cora parted from Substance plagued by guilt, gnawed by its sharp teeth. Ernest had always been a kind, good husband, even if he had brought her to the foot of the Bighorns where there was nothing to do or see, nothing but nothingness for miles around.

Nothing. Substance had meant nothing to Cora; she had known it all along. He was only a change, a different face, different hands after almost fifteen years of marriage and eight years of the cruel prairie. She had ruined her life and the lives of her children—ruined Ernest's life, too—for nothing. She had gotten Substance Webber killed for nothing, made Mrs. Webber a widow for nothing, left the neighbor boy father-less—for what? A distraction. For an act that held no more meaning to Cora than the dust she swept from her kitchen floor.

Through the long days and nights after Substance was killed, while Cora remained mired in regret, her girl Beulah shepherded the younger children, feeding them and marshaling them, keeping them safe. Beulah put porridge in the children's bellies every morning and stew every night, with a good slice of buttered bread in between. At night, Beulah saw that their faces were scrubbed. She tucked the boys into the bed they shared and sang songs for the baby, Miranda, until she fell asleep. And all the while, Cora did nothing more than sit, wrapped in a blanket, shivering even beside a warm hearth. Astonishment over what she had done consumed her, and all that was left was a skeleton of grief, dry and brittle, rattling with blame.

Cora couldn't help but relive the moment it had happened. The memory returned ceaselessly and repeated inside her head, a zoetrope spinning faster and faster, turned by the hand of her conscience. She had been lying in the grass, watching the cottonwood branches move over-head, while Substance had his way. The branches were a net of graceful black lines against an autumn sunset, that depth of color one saw at no other time of the year, and what leaves remained on the cottonwoods were still bright. The leaves turned in the river wind, shivering, spar-kling like gold or like the delicate crystal drops of the chandeliers she had seen at the dances in Saint Louis when she was a girl. She thought of the dances while she watched the cottonwood leaves, while Substance took what he wanted. All those balls in grand society homes, and the dresses she had worn—not as fine as the other girls' gowns, but better than her prairie calico. How Cora had longed for a coming-out ball of her own, even though she had known her grandfather hadn't the money to host one. She had resolved herself to be content as a guest, taking her fun at the other girls' parties, going with a sweep of her skirts and a charming giggle into the arms of young men. How splendid they had all been—the men in their coattails with perfumed silk squares bright at the edges of their pockets, the girls colorful and intricate as flowers. Cora had felt precious while she danced, while one man after another held her small waist between his hands. She was delicate, breakable, something to be cherished and protected, and her own desirability had excited her. The men with whom she danced had always asked Cora if the rumors were true—was she really General Grant's niece? *I am,* she told them all, because it was the truth. And when the girls laughed behind their hands, whispering as Cora passed, she promised herself that someday she would have a house as fine and beautiful as any in Saint Louis. She would have a ballroom with a chandelier and a parquet floor, and parties whenever she felt like dancing, and life would be gentle and lit by happiness and she would never feel lonesome again.

Then Ernest had appeared on the riverbank, shattering the color and the memories. Substance lurched up, yanking up his trousers. He roared something foul at Ernest while Cora covered herself with her petticoats and crawled away into the grass, weeping with sudden shame. She never saw Ernest raise his rifle and take the shot, nor did she watch Substance fall. But she knew, when that blast split the air, that she had destroyed what little sweetness still remained in her life.

Cora had lurched to her feet, ears muffled and ringing. She had run past Substance's body and had seen from the corner of her eye the redness all around him, the slick sheen of blood, the arc of droplets sprayed out behind him. She had gone to Ernest with hands outstretched, pleading, but the look on his face had been terrible, and he had turned away before Cora could touch him. That was when she'd known Ernest was lost to her forever—that even if the sheriff up in Paintrock didn't hang him as a murderer, Ernest would be not a presence in Cora's life but a void—another part of herself irrevocably gone, never to return. Then a desolation came upon her, worse than she had imagined any sorrow could be. It was worse by far than the loneliness that had haunted Cora for eight years on the prairie, so far from Saint Louis and the joyous, easy years of girlhood.

The hearth and the blanket and the settee became the whole of Cora's world, the safety in which she wrapped herself so she wouldn't hear the shotgun blast again and again, wouldn't see the bubble and flow of blood pouring from Substance Webber's chest. She pulled the blanket ever tighter around her shoulders. She must take the blanket's embrace in place of Ernest's forgiving arms.

For three days Cora remained that way, content to shrink from her thoughts, glad for the emptiness of silence. When, now and again, she came up from her dark musings like a fish rising to the surface of a murky pond, she found Beulah—her girl, the first child Ernest gave her—managing the farm without complaint, with a quiet steadiness and patient acceptance that seemed to say Beulah had expected this sorry turn of events all her young life and was shocked by none of it. Not even disappointed.

Without Beulah, Cora never could have managed the younger children in those dark days. But after all, Beulah was only a girl, and she had always been more inclined toward daydreams than work. By the third evening after Ernest's departure, Beulah was falling behind on chores. The children were gathered at the table—Charles and Benjamin, their trousers muddy to their knees, and Miranda with her hair a nest of yellow snarls.

"Ma," Miranda said plaintively, "we're hungry."

17

"Shush," Charles answered. "Ma won't feed us. Only Beulie makes supper now."

Cora loosened the blanket around her shoulders. Cooler air came in, rousing her senses. She looked beyond the children, through the window to the farm outside. In the south-facing yard, Beulah was moving back and forth across the trampled grass. Wet garments hung heavily in her thin arms. In the weak autumn sunshine, the girl pinned shirts and aprons and stockings one at a time to the drying line. The cows bellowed in their pen, crying out to be milked, aching with the pressure. Beulah couldn't keep up the homestead alone—not by herself.

For her sake, I must wake up and face the truth of what I've done.

Cora pushed herself up from the settee. Her legs scarcely remembered how to hold her, after all those days crippled by grief and fear, and she paused to lean on the table, breathless amid the chatter of her children. She left them waiting at the table and went to the door, limbs tingling with the pain of movement, determined to take over hanging up the wash so Beulah could get on with the milking. She must show her daughter that she was not alone—not even here, where God had made nothing but loneliness.

When she stepped out onto the porch, Cora saw a man riding up the lane. He was mounted on a sorrel horse, and for a moment, her heart leaped with the lightness of her spirit, for she was certain it was Ernest, come back to forgive her. But then she remembered Ernest had left on the gray mare. She had seen him go, watching through her parted fingers as tears spilled down between her cheeks and her palms, leaving her skin roughened by salt. In the next moment, Cora recognized the sheriff out of Paintrock, and her stomach welled with terrible dread.

Beulah had seen the sheriff coming, too. She hung up whatever bit of cloth she'd been fussing with and started toward the gate, moving with the same unhurried peace that seemed to bless her in all times and seasons. For a moment, Cora hung back on the step, content to let her daughter shoulder this burden, too. Then a black gout of self-loathing rose up inside her, and Cora made herself walk out to meet the sheriff herself. She wouldn't leave everything to the girl. She would do this one thing right, if nothing else.

Cora reached the gate a few steps ahead of Beulah. They stood silently side by side as the sheriff reined in and dismounted, sweeping off his hat to reveal thin, graying hair slicked against his pate by the sweat of a long ride.

"Mrs. Bemis," the sheriff said—then, with a glance at Beulah, "young lady. I suppose you know why I've come."

Cora nodded. She tried to speak, but she had no strength for words. She went on nodding, waiting for the news to come.

"He's not to be hanged, is he?" Beulah said. There wasn't the barest hint of fear in her. She seemed to know the answer before the sheriff spoke.

"No, not hanged." The man loosened his collar. "Since he turned himself in and was properly remorseful—and seeing as how it was a crime of passion, not of malice—the judge didn't think hanging was necessary. Everyone in Paintrock knows Ernest Bemis, and can swear he's a good man."

"Want some water?" Beulah asked. "You look thirsty."

The sheriff blinked at her. Cora could all but hear his thoughts: *Your father has just killed a man. Shouldn't you be upset, child?*

"Go fetch a cup of water," Cora told her daughter. When Beulah had drifted off toward the well, Cora said to the sheriff, apologetically, "Beulah is peculiar, but she's a good girl." *And better than I deserve.*

"I'm afraid your husband must remain in the Paintrock jail for two years, Mrs. Bemis."

"Two years!"

"It's hard, I know, but surely you see that it's a lenient sentence, considering he killed your neighbor."

Cora could only shake her head helplessly.

19

"I wanted to bring you the news myself," he went on, "seeing as how Ernest is so well liked. It didn't seem right to send word by letter."

"We don't get letters here, anyhow," Cora answered dully. "Ernest goes to town twice a month and fetches the mail."

Beulah had returned by then, holding the blue tin cup that normally hung by its handle at the back of the pump. Cora could smell the water from their well, the familiar iron tang, a metallic crispness. When the sheriff took the water from Beulah's hand, Cora wrapped an arm around her daughter's shoulders. The girl was strong and upright, her wiry body unshaken.

The sheriff drained the cup and handed it back. "Thank you, young lady. You're a right hospitable girl."

Beulah only watched him in silence, and after a moment, the sheriff turned away and swung up into his saddle. The leather creaked as he settled his body for the long ride back to Paintrock.

"If there's anything I can do to be of aid, Mrs. Bemis, send me word." He touched the brim of his hat with two fingers and then wheeled his horse and trotted back down the long, dusty lane.

Beulah laughed softly. "That's a foolish thing to say. Send him word? What kind of word could we send? We got to ride all the way to town if we want to post a letter."

Cora tightened her grip on the girl's shoulder. The September day was colder than it ought to have been. Now that she was up from the settee and moving, talking, thinking again, she could imagine a hundred different ways the sheriff—or any other man—might be of aid. But Paintrock was twenty miles north. The sheriff and everyone else in town might as well be in California or Boston for all the good they could do Cora and her children.

"Winter is just around the corner," Cora said.

"I know." The cows were calling frantically from their pen; Beulah shrugged off Cora's hold on her shoulders and turned toward the work. "I got to do the milking, Ma."

"Wait, Beulah. Wait a minute longer. We need to talk. We need to think—think it all through—what we're going to do about everything."

Beulah looked back at her, smiling. The girl's distant hazel eyes were full of laughter. "We'll do what we need to do, of course."

Cora had always admired her daughter's flights of fancy before— what a relief it must be, to find oneself transported from the bleakness of prairie life by a convenient daydream. But now her palm itched with a sudden desire to slap the girl. Couldn't Beulah see how dire their situation was? Cora tightened her fist and hid it in the pocket of her stained, wrinkled apron. She had visited enough evil on her family already; there was no use compounding her children's sorrows by slapping them.

"That's just the trouble." Cora's voice rose with the first trace of panic. "I don't know what we need to do."

"We must go and see the Webbers, of course. Clyde is there—the boy. Between our house and theirs, I think there are enough of us to see us all safely through the winter together."

For a long moment, Cora couldn't speak. She stared at her daughter, disbelieving what she had heard—and knowing, too, that Beulah was right. No other sensible choice lay before Cora now. She might take her children to Paintrock, but what then? Her nearest family were in Missouri, days away by train, assuming she could get the children to the nearest train station in Carbon—which would take a week by wagon if luck were on her side. But what family she had in Missouri were distant relations with no desire to grow any closer. Even if she had the money to buy passage back to Saint Louis, there was no one waiting there to welcome her or her brood. The grandfather who had raised Cora was long dead, and the only place she held in the thoughts of her cousins and aunts was as a curiosity—the family shame, mercifully married off and lost to the great unknown range of Wyoming Territory.

The only thing to be done was to turn to her nearest neighbor—her only neighbor—for aid. Cora stared across the Webbers' sheep pasture to the dark, square-shouldered house: a two-story sod-brick monument to austerity built by Substance when he'd been a much younger man. The house was as bleak as a gravestone even with a thread of woodsmoke rising from its chimney. Cora shivered.

"Do you want me to do the asking?" Beulah said. "I'll go over after milking, but I should see to the cows first."

"No," Cora said at once. "I'll do it. I'll ask." The very thought left her weak and trembling, but facing Nettie Mae Webber was nothing more than the penance Cora deserved. This was what came of being foolish, of having a fool's heart. This was the price you paid for giving in to a man you didn't even love.

NETTIE MAE

After he took himself off to jail, Mr. Bemis's wife came over the pasture like a damned soul, wringing her hands, with a face as desolate as Judgment Day. Nettie Mae let the dish she'd been washing fall back into the tub of water and stared at the sight—the pale, pretty ghost stumbling over clods of earth, her skirt caught and torn by claws of autumn sagebrush. Cora Bemis was holding herself in that despicable way she had, cradling her own body in her arms as if she were too frail for this life. Those soft, womanish arms, wrapped around a body that had remained slender and firm even after birthing at least four children. The body that had tempted Nettie Mae's husband into infidelity.

Long before Cora reached her door, Nettie Mae could see that the woman's face was red from crying. That angered her all the more. It was Nettie Mae who ought to cry—she who had a right to tears. Who had been betrayed? Not Cora Bemis. Who had been forced to allow her sixteen-year-old son to bury the man of the house, and in the dark of night, no less, because there had been no one else to do it? It was Nettie Mae who staked a claim on sorrow, but weeping never did a bit of good. Cora had even stolen Nettie Mae's tears. What could God have in store next? She shuddered to think of the possibilities.

She retrieved the dish from the wash water and cleaned it again, then wiped it dry and turned away from the window, away from the sight of Cora—intruder, usurper, neighbor turned thief in the night.

Nettie Mae put the dish away in her cupboard and went to the door before Cora could knock. She couldn't allow it; the sound would be an intrusion on the silence Nettie Mae favored, the solace of her own thoughts. She didn't want Cora to have the pleasure of taking away her silence, too, so Nettie Mae swung the door open quickly, with enough force to make Cora step back, stifling a gasp.

Nettie Mae said nothing. She stared into Cora's eyes—a clear, beautiful blue, made livelier than ever by the shine of her tears. When Cora blinked and lowered her face, red with shame, Nettie Mae felt a little thrill of triumph. The emotion was petty. It would do nothing to bring Substance back from the dead. All the same, the victory gave her momentary comfort.

"What do you want?" Nettie Mae said coolly. "I'd think you've done enough already."

Cora didn't lift her eyes from the step. "I—"

"I know what you did. Your husband told me all about it—everything—how he found you on your back with your legs in the air like some common hussy, rutting with Substance."

"He said that? Ernest said—?"

Nettie Mae cut off Cora's tremulous question. "Why have you come?"

Ernest had not used those words. He had been far more delicate, calmer than the situation had called for, but it pleased Nettie Mae to allow this woman to believe otherwise.

Cora drew a shuddering breath, which made her bosom lift in a slatternly way. It was little wonder Substance had been lured by this creature, this Jezebel. She flaunted herself with every movement, every thoughtless twitch. The Bemises had been their neighbors for more than seven years. Why had Nettie Mae never noticed how earthy Cora was, how lustful?

"I've had word from the sheriff," Cora said, wavering. "Ernest will remain locked up for two years."

Nettie Mae laughed, short and hard. "Two years? Not nearly long enough."

Cora covered her face with her hands, convulsing with the force of her silent weeping. *Does she think I'll put an arm around her?* Nettie Mae wondered. *Comfort her—there, there?*

"Stop crying," she said. "It isn't dignified, given the circumstances. At least you have a husband. Mine is dead now."

That only seemed to pain Cora further. She let out a high, thin wail and swayed so that Nettie Mae thought for a moment she might tumble down the steps.

"I'm sorry," Cora said. Her voice was made thick and ugly by her weeping. She never removed her hands from her face, too ashamed to look at Nettie Mae directly. Good. She ought to suffer with that shame. "I'm sorry, Mrs. Webber. I never meant for this to happen. I never thought—"

"One wonders what you did think, carrying on with another woman's husband. And now you have the gall to snivel because Mr. Bemis has gone to prison. For murder. Two years—I've never heard of such a thing. It should have been longer. They should have hanged him." She added that last, a relentless barb, and felt a swell of satisfaction when Cora recoiled.

"I'm sorry," Cora said again. "I wanted to tell you . . . I'm sorry. I can't ask you to forgive me, but—"

"Pretty words. I guess you should have thought of how sorry you'd be long before you had to do with a married man. And now, if you'll excuse me."

Nettie Mae turned away, making to close the door, but Cora found her strength. She blocked the door with one hand. When Nettie Mae pushed, Cora resisted, and those tear-polished blue eyes locked with Nettie Mae's own. There was an insistence to Cora's stare—a desperation—that Nettie Mae found both surprising in such a fragile woman and unsettling.

"Please, Mrs. Webber. I must speak with you."

"I should think you've said everything you need to say. Now take your hand from my door, and—"

"No. Listen to me; I beg you."

"I will not listen to you." Nettie Mae glanced past her neighbor, out to the lower pasture where Clyde, mounted on his buckskin gelding, was bringing the sheep to their stone-walled fold. He was too far away for Nettie Mae to call to him, too far off to help.

"Mrs. Webber, I know you dislike me. You have every reason to hate me now, and I don't blame you for it."

"That's generous." Acid words were all she had left at her disposal.

Cora pressed on. "But winter will be here soon. What are we to do, with two farms between us? This land is too much for women to work alone, and I've got young children to care for."

"That's no concern of mine. Clyde is sixteen; he's big enough to do his share of the work, and sensible enough to keep our place running through the winter. We will be fine, Mrs. Bemis. Whether you and your brood will suffer any hardship is not a question over which I shall fret, I can assure you of that. I might have done, once, when we were still friendly neighbors. But given our present circumstance, I see no reason to trouble myself over you and yours."

Nettie Mae pushed more forcefully on the door.

Cora redoubled her resistance. "We aren't as fortunate as you, Mrs. Webber." That admission seemed to cost Cora something; her tearful flush paled for a moment, and her lips trembled. Nettie Mae sensed this was a different sorrow—far older than the turmoil newly to hand, more deeply embedded under Cora's skin. "My eldest child is a girl, and only thirteen—and dreamy, at that. I've no hope of seeing all my children through the winter on my girl's work and mine alone."

Nettie Mae jerked the door more widely open. Cora lost her balance and stumbled forward, catching herself against the frame.

"What, then?" Nettie Mae said scornfully. "You expect me to share what I've put by to feed your brats? You expect me to work your land for you, bathe and clothe your children? You've already taken my husband. Now you come begging and weeping, expecting me to give you more?"

"I know what I did was wrong." The trembling had returned to Cora's voice. Her eyes fell again to the floor. "I don't ask you to forgive—"

"Don't expect me to forget, either."

"Surely, Mrs. Webber, you're a Christian woman!"

"I needn't ask whether you are. Any Christian woman knows her Commandments."

She managed at last to close the door. Before it slammed shut, Cora bleated out, "Please!" But it was too late now for begging, too late to play on Nettie Mae's moral sense. Substance had never been much of a husband, but he had been Nettie Mae's. She was left with nothing—nothing but Clyde, the one child God had allowed her to keep.

Nettie Mae returned to her washing. The water was cold now, and greasy, but she plunged her hands in and worked with the cloth until the joints of her fingers ached from the chill and the pressure. She watched the Bemis woman stagger back across the pasture toward the distant gray house—a house that had always been full of life, the laughter of children. Nettie Mae's hands grew too clumsy to keep up her work, so she put the kettle back over the fire to heat more dishwater. She wrapped her hands in a length of towel, drying and warming them. But as she waited for the kettle to steam, she never took her eyes from Cora, that slim figure vanishing through dry, brown grass. Four children—the same number Nettie Mae had lost.

"Your children aren't mine to worry after," Nettie Mae said to the woman's distant back. She thought with time she might convince herself it was true.

2

WHAT NEEDS DOING CAN'T BE STOPPED

I was taking down the wash from its line the day Clyde came over the fields. He had a scythe slung over one shoulder and a small clay jug at his belt, and the braces he was wearing had already pressed dark patches of perspiration into the cloth of his dust-gray shirt. He was leading the lost calf by a rope around its neck, and he paused to turn it loose through the pasture gate. As he came on toward me, I could tell by the look of him that he was tired from working his own land all that morning. But still he came. He crossed our yard, making for the stand of corn out back of the house, and I could hear him whistling. At first, I thought it was a proper song—a hymn, maybe— but I couldn't place it, though the notes and rhythm caught at my mind and pulled at me, willing me to remember. Then I realized it was no song man ever made, but the call of a sage thrasher. Only Clyde did it wrong; the trill was too slow and not high enough in pitch, so no birds answered from the pasture. I thought it amusing, so I stepped back behind the hanging sheet where he wouldn't see me laughing. And then, for a moment, I could see myself through his eyes, or the outline of myself, a shadow blue against the yellow of a sunlit sheet, the shape of me rippled and broken by a wind that stirred the line.

Clyde may have waved at me—I can't recall—but he never paused, only leveled his scythe at the edge of our cornfield and set his feet wide apart, and then he began to swing the blade. There was a fluid beauty to the way he worked, the smooth turning of his body and the gentle arc of the scythe, the cornstalks tipping and falling with every sweep. I dropped the last sheaf into my basket, then I stood and watched him for a while. The watching made me realize why I had felt no surprise at Clyde's coming. The corn patch was his natural place, for he was tall among tall stalks and browned by the sun as the plants were browned. The cornstalks called to him. They beckoned him to the harvest because he was their kin, grown to maturity, on the point of harvest himself. Since his father's death, the boy had changed like the ears change in their season. Now, in the final heat of autumn, when even the small, secret flush of green had been sapped from the joints of grass stems, now was the time for a seed to drop to the earth's bed and sleep through the snows and sorrows of winter. And the seed will put down roots, even in the shadow of the plant that made it. Even while the old stalks, exhausted of their green power, bow before the sickle and fall.

I had come up behind him to watch him work before he knew I was there. He drew a dripping whetstone from his clay jug and ran it along the blade, and it made a high, thin sound like larks in the morning. When an ear broke from a fallen stalk and rolled into a rut of earth, I watched him pick it up and brush it clean. His hand moved slowly, as if in worship, lingering over the ribs of husk, over the tangle of silk, dark brown with age but still faintly damp with the lifeblood of the plant. That was how I knew him true—how I understood that he was of the land, like me, though he didn't yet realize his own nature. When he had tucked the ear of corn into the back pocket of his trousers, he took up the scythe again and went on swinging. He didn't seem to understand how much he loved the corn, or the season, and he didn't hear the stalks calling to him, saying, We will gladly fall, but only by your hand. Maybe grief over Mr. Webber's death blinded Clyde to his own feelings and stopped up his ears to every sound except the whisper of the blade. It had only been a few days, after all, since he had put his father in the ground.

Hello, I said, and he started and almost dropped his scythe, but he recovered himself and turned to face me, leaning on the long handle, panting to catch his breath.

He said, Miss Beulah. I never heard you come up behind me.

You don't have to call me miss, I said. And I have a way of coming up behind without nobody hearing. It ain't something I mean to do. Just the way I'm made.

What I didn't tell him was this: he had never called me by name before. In fact, we had been neighbors since I was six years old. His ma and pa settled below the Bighorns a year after my family did, building that fine two-story sod-brick house near the only good source of sweet water for miles around, the place where Tensleep Creek flows into the Nowood River. Clyde and I had crossed paths plenty often before. Sometimes he had come over with his father to help my pa mend a fence or patch a hole in the barn roof, and I had carried hot biscuits and fresh cream to the men for their lunch. But in all those years, Clyde had never said my name aloud, nor I his, except to my ma when no one else could hear. I was surprised and glad to find out that he knew my name after all. I liked the sound of it in his mouth. I liked that his hair was the same color as the dried-up corn silks, too—not golden, not brown, but somewhere in between. I could see his hair at his temples below the sweat-soaked brim of his hat. He kept it cut short.

He said, I've come over to help you bring in the harvest, since your daddy's off to jail and all. Can't just let the corn rot in the field. That would be a waste.

Sorry my pa killed your pa, I said.

The skin between Clyde's eyebrows pinched together for a second and he smiled, but with only one side of his mouth. He said, You don't sound awful sorry about it.

Neither do you, I said.

He wasn't inclined to speak more about his dead father or my living one, so we let the subject drop.

I said, Your ma's real angry that you've come over to help.

How d'you know that?

It just makes sense that she'd be sore over what all happened, and wouldn't like you coming around, I said.

Sore don't hardly go far enough, Clyde said, but quietly, under his breath, so I couldn't be sure he intended me to hear.

Your ma don't like me much.

My mother doesn't think twice about you.

There was something wary in his voice when he spoke those words. He meant them, and they were the truth. But he could sense what I already felt coming. There would come a day—and soon—when Clyde's mother would think of little else but me. Every seed puts down roots in its own time and grows to its greenest power.

I bent and gathered the first cut stalks, arranging them in a sheaf.

What are you doing? Clyde asked.

Since he had eyes to see, I didn't bother to answer. I went on gathering until Clyde found a stalk that was still green enough to bend. He handed it to me, and I twisted it around the waist of my sheaf and stood it upright in the field. We went on working together, Clyde cutting the corn and me gathering the sheaves. That was the way it had to be—the two of us joined together in our work, doing what our mothers couldn't bring themselves to do. For there were too many small lives now that depended on us alone. My brothers and my little sister; the sheep and cattle, the horses, the hens. Even the seeds relied on us. It was our work to gather and put by. It was we who would plant when the time came, and we who would tend the crops as they grew.

Clyde was one who did what needed doing, even when grief sought to drown him. And I labored beside him in the cornfield because I was like he was—just as he was like the corn—ready to be twisted free of my cob and dream through the dark of winter, ready to rise up green and new to a life that was my own.

The scythe swung in long, smooth arcs, flashing in a perfect rhythm. When I wrapped my arms around the sheaves, the stalks felt dry against my cheek. They rattled in my ear. You can't just let the corn rot in the field; what needs doing can't be stopped. The seasons don't cease to change because we haven't the time to plant or tend or harvest, because grief like a hailstorm comes up sudden and frightens us with its noise. Once the storm rolls on, the fields remain, and life goes on, whatever we prefer.

CLYDE

What needs doing can't be stopped. Clyde leaned on the stone wall of the sheepfold, watching the flock as it milled inside. The animals were dust gray, and blocky and thick beneath a crust of sage twigs and barbed seeds. They crowded at the gate, bleating to be let out to feed. It was the first truly cold morning the Bighorns had seen in months; summer had reached its end, and soon the rains would come, followed quickly by the first of many snows. Each time a sheep called out in protest, a plume of silver steam rose from its muzzle to hang above the fold, and the early-morning light refracted within that cloud, so the air just above the animals' backs glowed in the rising sun.

Clyde and his father had worked hard to split the flock evenly, breeding half to lamb in spring, half to give birth in the fall. The breeding flock had finally matured enough that there was never a lack of good, fresh meat, except in the depths of winter. Now he could see that the fall-lambing ewes were almost ready to drop. Their bellies hung low and distended. White fissures showed through cracks in their dirty outer fleece, and deep hollows had formed at their flanks where the lambs within had turned. In a matter of days, the first lambs of autumn would arrive. He must shear the mothers now, before their offspring came. There was no time to mourn for his father—no time for contemplation, nor even for anger. There was time only to sharpen his shears and set to work. What needs doing cannot be stopped.

When the shears were ready, Clyde climbed inside the pen and opened the gate just enough to allow one sheep through at a time. The herd ran one by one toward the pasture, but the fat ewes Clyde kept back. They gathered in a far corner, pawing at the ground, their breaths rising in a rapid spate. Dark eyes rolled to watch him as he moved—as he reached for the shears and tucked them under one arm. The ewes darted away when he stepped toward them, no matter how slowly he moved. The animals circled their pen, heads high and defiant, scolding in their deep, harsh tones.

Substance had had a way with sheep. Not in the same sense that Clyde had a way with horses—the quietness of movement, the watchful eye, the comfort of mutual understanding. Substance's way was to stride and grasp, to capture. Dominate. When he would lay hold of the ewes for shearing or the young lambs for castration, the animals would strain and scream. Their eyes would turn to bloodshot half moons; flailing hooves would churn the ground; but there was never any escape. There was only a froth of desperation at the creatures' mouths, tongues showing pale—so pale they were almost white. But the work would be done, quick and efficient, over in a moment, and each sheep would be released to stagger back toward the fold.

Clyde had helped with the shearing, of course, but he had never caught the ewes himself. He tried to imagine the task: Bulling in among the frightened animals the way his father had done. Reaching out to find only fleece; digging fingers in, as a hawk's talons locked in the soft belly of a rabbit. The sheep's pain as her fleece was wrenched this way and that—or her leg, her ear, whichever part came readily to hand.

There must be a better way, he thought as he watched the sheep watching him. They were gentle creatures, as horses were, and the mistrust they gave him now was not without reason. They had suffered much at Substance's hands. You could earn a horse's trust through slow touch and quiet speech, through never concealing your intentions—loading every gesture with honesty. Why shouldn't the same be true of sheep?

Clyde stretched his hands to either side, palms out, as far as he could reach with the shears tucked beneath an arm. He took one slow step toward the ewes, then another. They shrank back into their corner. As he drew nearer, one cautious foot at a time, the ewes jostled and bleated, fighting to be the first to break away. The slower Clyde moved, the more easily the ewes evaded his hands. But they were also beginning to settle; Clyde could tell that much. Now when their dark eyes tracked his progress around the pen it was with calculation, not fear. One ewe stood still enough that Clyde touched her back. His hand rested there, palm down and open, just long enough to feel her trembling.

"Are these ready for lambing?"

Clyde started and turned, and found his mother standing beside the gate. The ewe he had touched cried out and ran.

"Any day now."

Nettie Mae shielded her eyes with one hand and watched the horizon for a moment, the weak sun rising in a thin, cold sky. "It's early for it yet."

"Maybe so, but the lambs are coming all the same. I got to get these sheared up before, or the fleeces will be ruined."

Nettie Mae kept her silence, watching Clyde as he stood there, as he waited for his mother to say something more, to do something. But she only looked at him, then at the sheep—dispassionate, with the faintest air of offense at the ewes' audacity, this inconvenient business of lambing weeks earlier than expected.

When he thought his mother would say nothing more, Clyde adjusted the shears under his arm and turned to his sheep again. But Nettie Mae spoke up at once.

"You know, that Cora woman came over to talk at me yesterday."

Across the pasture, at the base of a foothill dry and brown from the summer heat, stood the Bemis house. It was small and pale, cladded in old, fading pine, but the peak of its roof shone brightly in the morning sun. No one moved in the garden outside, nor around the sheds where the animals waited.

After a moment, Clyde said, "Did she?"

"Can you imagine—she asked me to care for her children. To share our food and our goods with her, to see her through the winter. She took what was mine by rights, and got my husband killed in the bargain. Now she comes begging for my charity."

Wary, Clyde said, "Maybe she does need help, Mother. After all, she's got three small children to look after."

"And a big girl to help care for them—though that Beulah isn't much good, I dare say. Always mooning about the pasture, picking flowers and doing Heaven knows what in the hills. Anyway, that woman's worries are none of mine. If Cora Bemis wanted an easy ride through the coming winter, then she shouldn't have helped herself to another woman's husband."

"Mother, maybe we ought to lend a hand over at the Bemis place."

Nettie Mae's face hardened; Clyde knew he had overstepped.

"Only till their harvest is in," he added. "What can it hurt?"

"I promise you, that woman didn't stop to ask herself *What can it hurt?* before she went prowling after your father."

"How do you know Father didn't go prowling after her?"

"Don't you backtalk me, Clyde."

She narrowed her eyes at him over the stone wall—a hard stare, cold as the oncoming season. It sent a shiver of sickness right down into Clyde's middle. Nettie Mae had never looked at him that way before, with such open hostility that he felt suddenly disoriented. The mother he had always loved and respected had never given him reason to believe that she hated him. But hate was what he saw in her now, hanging around her head, impossible to ignore—like the steam and the morning light glowing above the pen, an emanation fiery enough to blind him. Clyde would have flinched from the presence of his mother's anger or slunk to the horse shed to cry from the shock and fear of it— this realization that the woman who had soothed and nurtured him all his life could look at him that way, as if she would sooner spit on him than suffer him to speak. Then he remembered that he was the man of the homestead now, and sixteen at any rate. Too old for crying and carrying-on, too wise to believe his mother never hated and couldn't be made to despise her only living son.

Clyde made himself stand his ground. He watched her calmly, saying nothing, patient and still while the ewes circled his legs and moaned with the pressure of the life inside their bellies. It was Nettie Mae who looked away first, she who stooped to pick up the basket at her feet. It was her harvesting basket, wide and shallow. The familiar knife hung from its rim, short, curve bladed, tied with a leather string. Nettie Mae turned her back on Clyde abruptly and stalked away to the garden, where ripe squashes weighed down the drying vines.

Clyde considered the Bemis homestead again. Across the yellow pasture, he could see their garden, ready for the harvest as the Webber garden was. But no one moved inside the high deer fence—nothing moved but the broad leaves of pole beans wreathing their willow towers, stirred by the wind. There was a patch of corn out back of the house; Clyde could see the edge of it between house and cowshed, the tall stalks faded of their color. That corn needed harvesting within days, or it would surely spoil. Rain would come soon, lifting the strong, flat hand of heat that had pressed down upon the prairie all summer long. But when the rains came, they would lace the ears of corn with rot beneath the skin of their husks, and then the crows would follow.

Clyde finished the shearing well before noon and carried the heavy fleeces to the long shed. Soon his mother would pick and wash and card the wool, and then she would sequester herself at her spinning wheel, the only place in the world where Clyde ever saw the hard parts of

Nettie Mae soften. He paused in the shed's pleasant darkness—despite the cool morning, the day had rapidly gone to heat—and breathed in the sharp, close odor of fleece. It hung in the dim space of the shed: lanolin, oily and forcefully present, a compelling reek still rich with the warmth of the animals' bodies. The smell flooded him with grief and a strange, salient anxiety he couldn't understand. That was the smell of his mother at peace, in the rare moments when she laid down the burdens of her life—a scent of wheel and treadle, the whisper of wool sliding through her callused fingers. Lanolin was the smell of Substance Webber, whose hands never touched but seized and took and held in an inescapable fist. The wool of frightened sheep clutched in Substance's fingers, the steel trap that was his living flesh, the pain of being caught by him when your legs flailed and your eyes rolled white and you knew you were helpless to stop him. Clyde remembered a spring rain, some two years before, when he had pulled on a new sweater his mother had knitted and gone out to see to his chores, and the drops of rain had raised a smell of raw wool from his shoulders, so the odor followed him from the coop to the horse paddock and back again. Thoughts of his father had chased him, too, and he had stood in the rain smelling like an animal, stilled like an animal that knows it can't escape the slaughter. He had thought, *If I am ever a father someday, I won't be a father like you.*

The scythe hung from its pegs, spanned above the door. He took it down and found the leather belt that held his jug and whetstone. Outside, he pumped water into the animals' trough and allowed the last gush to fill the clay jug to its brim. Then he sank to his knees and caught the final trickle of water in his mouth. It was tepid and tasted of earth, for the crisp snows of the Bighorns had long since melted and the river was running low.

When he straightened, Clyde saw his mother in the garden. She had already taken in all the squashes from the vines and now she stood there, staring back at him, a bundle of long weeds trailing from one hand. Even across a great distance, Clyde could read the same hardness in her eyes that he had seen that morning. *She must understand what it means,* he thought. *The belt, the scythe, the whetstone. Well, let her seethe. I won't see little ones go hungry if I can help it.*

Clyde led the Bemises' dun calf out of the barn, where he had shut it up the previous night. The runaway heifer had come foraging through the sheep pasture the evening before; it had been the work of a moment to catch it from Joe Buck's back and lock it up where his mother couldn't see, with a good armful of hay to keep it quiet until morning. Then he slung his blade over one shoulder and headed across the pasture. The Bemis homestead had come alive while he'd been occupied with the sheep. Cora, in a faded rose-pink dress, was sweeping out the hen coop while the little children played in the yard, chasing the chickens to and fro. The girl was hanging wash on a line to dry.

The two families had never been especially close—Substance and Nettie Mae were both inclined to keep to themselves, and the Bemises had always seemed content with the distance between the farms. Even so, they were the only people for twenty miles in any direction, and a handful of friendly encounters couldn't be avoided entirely—a benign routine of *How do you do.* Clyde had grown familiar enough with the sight of the girl to notice that she had changed since the last time he'd seen her at close range. That must have been months gone by, when Clyde had passed the girl on the river trail, he heading toward the shade of the cottonwoods, she returning from a wade in the shallows with her skirt still tied up around her knees. The girl was thin, as ever, but she had grown a little taller and there was something carved and set about her features, as if her chin and cheeks and nose had made up their minds about how they ought to look and were committed now to their purpose. As she bent to take a wet, heavy sheet from her basket, her wrist slipped free of its calico sleeve, showing itself pale and refined to Clyde's startled eye. He looked away, embarrassed by his own interest, the keenness with which he longed to study that wrist, its slender shape and the slight curve of bone along its side. He whistled to distract himself—a birdcall, though no birds called back from the sage.

He went straight to the corn patch as if he had worked the Bemis land a hundred times before. The corn fell easily to his scythe. The stalks were thoroughly dry, and Clyde's blade was sharp. He had always enjoyed scything. It was easy work, a pleasant task with a simple, soothing rhythm—the turn and turn of your body, the momentum of the tool's arc. The frequent pauses, with sweat cooling on your brow, to draw your whetstone down the blade.

After a time, when plenty of stalks lay felled around his feet, the girl spoke from the edge of the corn patch, and Clyde jumped in surprise.

"Hello."

Heart pounding, Clyde turned to face her. She stood with her hands behind her back, so he couldn't see those fascinating wrists, for which he was grateful. She watched him with a curious zeal, an eager, upturned face that shone with something akin to triumph. Clyde couldn't think what the girl ought to be so nervy about. Her hair was lank and rather thin, but he liked the color of it, even though he couldn't exactly name it. Not brown, not yellow, not ash gray. It was like the dun hide of a deer or the soft feathers on a sparrow's belly.

"Miss Beulah. I never heard you come up behind me."

"You don't have to call me 'miss.'" She stepped out into the corn patch. Her skirt of blue calico and the pale-green pinafore she wore over it were damp from her efforts at the clothesline. Beneath her feet, dead corn leaves crackled and sighed. She said something more—something about sneaking up on people, and the way she was made, but Clyde was distracted by her nearness and he didn't really hear the words. All at once, he smelled raw wool again, and remembered the feel of the ewe holding still beneath his hand.

"I've come to help you bring in the harvest." Clyde stepped away from her, for the fact that they were alone together frightened him suddenly. He had no cause to be afraid of a girl, yet he was, and couldn't say why. "Since your daddy's off to jail and all."

He had meant that last to stall her, to discourage her advance. But Beulah was unfazed by the stark absence of her father. She didn't stop. She came very near Clyde, so he could see the redness of the skin between her fingers, the chafing from lye soap and hot water. She bent and began gathering cornstalks and bundling them into sheaves.

"Sorry my pa killed your pa."

She didn't sound sorry, and Clyde told her so, but he wasn't exactly sorry, either. Mostly he was disoriented by the change and tired from the extra work, tired from Nettie Mae's anger. And the memory of his father's grave still clung to him, the dark place in the earth and the smell of heavy soil, the murmur of the river. The way Substance had locked his arms out to the side and resisted going down to his finish. The grave had upset Clyde; the grave upset him still. That was all—or at least, that was the better part of his anxiety.

Then Beulah spoke of Nettie Mae while she bundled the sheaves. The girl never looked up but went about her work methodically, as if Nettie Mae's hatred for Cora mattered less than a spilled cup of water. As if a woman's anger was of no consequence, or as if the girl thought Nettie Mae would forget all about it and let go of her rage with time.

Is she simple? Clyde wondered.

He watched Beulah lay the cornstalks out neatly on the dusty red ground, side by side. No; the girl wasn't simple. She was dreamy and odd, no doubt, but Clyde perceived no lack in her wits. If anything, Beulah possessed an air of too much seeing, too much knowing. The girl seemed perfectly content with their situation, not, Clyde thought, because she was too foolish to understand the hardships both families faced, now that their fathers were gone. Rather, Beulah seemed to believe that despite the trials lying just ahead—the harvest yet to be gathered, and winter looming cold and barren, mere weeks away—everything would work out precisely as it should. The girl seemed so content, Clyde almost caught himself believing that everything had already sorted itself, just as it ought to have done from the very start of the year, from the start of his life.

Clyde shook his head in cautious wonder. Then he helped her tie the first sheaf with a green twist of cornstalk. They went on harvesting together—he cutting, turn and turn, pause, slide of stone along blade, and she placidly picking up stalks with the ears still attached.

It took Clyde half the corn patch to grow accustomed to Beulah's presence. He had spent precious little time around girls, though he often encountered them in Paintrock on the days when he drove the cart to town to fetch the post and visit the general store. The girls in town giggled when Clyde walked by, and if he met their eyes or smiled at them, they would blush, or sometimes they would bunch together in little circles and whisper. Town girls had always put Clyde in mind of hens panicking when a hawk flies overhead, so after the first handful of baffling encounters, he had made it a point never to meet their eyes, so he wouldn't feel obliged to smile. Sometimes it only made the girls giggle more when he didn't smile. Beulah did not laugh, though, nor did she blush. Maybe town girls were different from prairie girls, Clyde thought—fundamentally different, the way the wild sheep up in the foothills were different from the docile creatures he bred on the farm. Still, though Beulah's silence was easy and pleasant enough, somehow her calm acceptance of fate's recent turn put Clyde on edge. He thought he might prefer town girls after all, if prairie girls were so immovable.

But by the time half the corn was cut and tied, Beulah had become familiar to him. He moved around her—with her—effortlessly, the same way he moved around Joe Buck and the other horses he trained. No need to look up. He could sense the other, feel her movements and her pace. She calmed him with her steady presence, just as he calmed his horses when a snake moved in the grass or when a sudden wind ripped down the steep flank of a mountain.

When most of the corn had been cut and the full heat of afternoon hung in shimmers above the pasture, the little children wandered over to watch Clyde and Beulah working. There were two small boys, both under the age of ten but too old for short pants, and a girl barely big enough to run. They stood toeing the edge of the field, shy of Clyde but visibly burning to come nearer.

"Keep your sister away from the scythe," he told the boys. "But you can try it out, if you want to, one at a time."

He showed the boys, one after the other, the right way to hold the scythe's handle and how to swing the curving blade above the soil. How to keep the sweep of your blade level so you wouldn't leave pointed stalks behind, which dried sharp enough to punch through the sole of a horse's hoof. The boys weren't any good at scything yet, but they would learn with time.

The woman Cora hung back, vivid and lovely with worry. Her face was colored like her dress, delicate rose-petal pink, and when she wrung her hands in fear for her children's safety—in fear of Clyde, too, who after all was a Webber—the gesture was compellingly fragile. She wouldn't approach the field, and when Clyde looked at her, Cora shifted on her feet this way and that and threw up her head in fright, as if she wanted to run.

"You'd best go back to your mother now," Clyde said to the little children. "Beulah and I will finish up with the corn."

The children scampered away.

Beulah called after them, "Benjamin, you bring us some bread and butter and water. We're proper starved 'cause it's all past noon."

While he waited for the meal to arrive, Clyde swung his scythe again for some minutes, but he sensed a stillness behind him. Beulah had ceased to work. He let the blade fly to the end of its arc, then grounded it against the soil. He turned, panting, and found her on her knees beside a half-assembled sheaf. She had peeled back the dry husk of a loose ear of corn and was turning the ear in her hands, absorbed in the sight of those small, hard kernels.

Clyde lowered himself beside her, squatting on his heels. "If you don't keep a-gathering, we'll never finish the job."

Beulah didn't answer. She only raised the ear for Clyde to see. Her thin face was solemn with wonder, as if she were offering him a treasure of immeasurable value.

Clyde frowned down at the corn. The kernels had dented and begun to separate, showing the spaces between, the papery redness of the cob.

"Look," Beulah said, almost scolding.

Somehow, Clyde had disappointed her. He had failed to see.

Confused, he shook his head. "I don't—"

"You don't see," Beulah said, agreeing.

Slowly, she ran a finger down one row of kernels. Clyde tracked the movement of her finger, and wherever she touched, the kernels seemed more vivid, as if she had swept away a film of dust, revealing the luster of gold. Now he could tell that some kernels were minutely flecked with white, and some speckled with red as deep as garnets. They were beautiful.

"They're alive," Beulah said softly. "Isn't it strange? Every one is alive, though they don't look it, dried up as they are. And every one is different. Look at this one, here. See how the white and yellow are swirled together?"

Clyde couldn't see the markings. At least, he couldn't understand why the pattern on a corn seed ought to fascinate a girl so completely.

"There's a whole stalk inside every kernel." Beulah's voice was low and soft, barely more than a murmur. "A stalk, and roots, and leaves, and another cob with its own seeds. And all of those seeds have more seeds inside of them. How far back does it go, do you think? Or how far ahead?"

When she looked up, her eyes shone with tears. They were tears of wonder, Clyde saw—not of sorrow or pain.

Had she never felt pain or sadness? Was suffering a foreign thing to this odd prairie witch? It was intolerable, that the girl should escape the confusion, the hurt of what had happened between their fathers, their families. The unfairness of it struck Clyde like an ax blow. Beulah's loss was not as great as his, yet it was still a loss. Why ought she to be exempted from suffering, while he . . . he had been forced to plant his boot on his father's chest and push him down into his grave.

"What you said earlier, about being sorry your father killed my father . . ."

Beulah nodded, waiting for Clyde to go on.

"It ain't true. You ain't sorry; I can tell. And it's terrible wrong-headed to say things that ain't true."

"Should I be sorry?"

"'Course you should. A man's dead. And it was your father as killed him."

"Your pa wasn't a good man."

Clyde stood so fast that his head spun, and he had to lean on the handle of his scythe to keep from pitching over. "How do you know whether my father was a good man or not?"

Beulah twisted the ear between her hands. A few dry kernels slid from the cob so easily they might have been eager for it. Seed corn had never come loose so readily for Clyde; the cobs always blistered his fingers and left his skin cracked and stinging.

"I just know it," Beulah said. "I also know you ain't sad that your pa is gone, either."

"I am, too."

"You ain't sad the same way my ma's sad about my pa being locked up in jail."

"Your pa'll be back after two years."

She smiled up at him and said with a tolerant little laugh, "Your pa ain't gone either, Clyde."

He stepped back—stepped away from her—gripping the handle of his blade. "You're crazy, girl. Plumb crazy."

"No I ain't, and you know it." She brushed aside a few fallen leaves of corn till the bare earth showed, dry and flat and waiting. "Come and see."

Clyde didn't want to go near her again. He didn't want to look at her wrist or the certain, newly determined angles of her face. But she was watching him, waiting for him, and he felt foolish and weak for being afraid. He laid down his scythe and knelt near Beulah, but not so near that she could touch him.

The girl rested her hand on the soil for a moment, palm down, as if feeling summer's remnant heat rising from the earth. Then she pushed a finger down deep into the dryness. Dust rose in a tiny puff, and it made Clyde recall incongruously the smell of lanolin hanging about his shoulders, the smell of springtime rain. Beulah dropped the kernel of corn into the hole she had made, then patted the soil flat.

"Buried," the girl said, "just like Substance Webber. When the time comes—when the time is right—it will sprout again, like him, and live."

NETTIE MAE

What needs doing cannot be stopped. The vines in the garden had dried, coils of green and gold. The time had come for Nettie Mae to gather the squashes and cure their skins before the rains arrived. Hard, smooth rinds could withstand any weather and would keep in the darkness of the long shed until spring. The drying down had come early this year, as with the fall-bearing sheep's readiness for lambing. It was more work piled onto the usual chores of summer's end, which was always the busiest time of year. But the seasons turned when they would, without regard for human preference.

As she cut the heavy striped squashes from their vines and laid them in her basket, Nettie Mae thought of Substance lying somewhere out there by the riverside, underneath the soil. The rot was on him now, surely, moving doubly fast—invading from the outside, seeping out from the inside of his heart. She might have mourned over the fact, might have felt fear at the image of the man she had married decomposing, softening and weeping like the bruised skin of a fruit. The terrifying abruptness with which life changed to death, integrity to decay. But Nettie Mae had known Substance far too long—endured him too long—to weep over the loss.

When she had harvested the last of the squashes, Nettie Mae hauled her heavy basket to the back stoop and sat in the morning sun to wipe down the fruits with vinegar. The light felt paler and weaker than it had for weeks. Dew still clung to the grass, filling the morning with an easy coolness that would be crushed and smothered by noontime. Beside the outhouse, the hollyhocks had faded. Drops of water gathered in the dimples of their leaves, sparkling as the sun climbed higher, treading its routine path across the sky.

From her place on the back stoop, Nettie Mae could see the Bemis homestead waking—finally, hours after any proper family ought to have been up and out of doors. The three little children tumbled out and ran about the yard, unruly as a pack of wolves. Nettie Mae could almost imagine she heard their shouts across the wide sage-dotted pasture.

Then Cora emerged. Even from far away, Nettie Mae could see that woman's beauty. She wore a gaily colored dress, cut to show off a neat figure. But the woman's timidity was plain to be seen, too. She took up her chores in a subdued manner, moving with hesitation even in her own yard, and Nettie Mae watched with avaricious interest. The slump of Cora's shoulders, the slowness of her step, the incapability of managing and directing her own children—it all came to Nettie Mae across the fields like the smell of baking bread. Hungry, she watched as Cora grasped weakly at a life that slipped farther from her hands with each passing minute. She doubted whether Cora could see her. The colorless brown gray of Nettie Mae's dress—undyed wool—blended with the sod bricks of the Webber house. She allowed her knees to ease apart as she worked, and lowered each squash into the depression of her skirt where it would be hidden from view, where Cora wouldn't notice the flash of gold and orange and green and look across the fields to find Nettie Mae there, watching.

Each time Cora stumbled or moved too slowly to intercept a running child or a hen escaping from the yard, Nettie Mae's face tingled with a flush of pleasure. She might have had no love left for Substance, and no inclination to weep over his grave, but he had been her husband. The Bemis woman had had no right to take him, no right to deprive Nettie Mae of whatever small comfort she received from the man she had married. The theft had made a permanent fire in Nettie Mae's soul, and now, with the weight of the farm pressing down on her shoulders as well as her son's, she had no intention of extinguishing that blaze. Like an engine, she needed the heat and the pressure to keep working, keep moving, keep living.

She never took her eyes off Cora unless it was to trickle a little more vinegar from the old yellowware jug onto her rag. Nevertheless, Nettie Mae was sharply cognizant of the Bemis children. Like fish in the shallows, they darted into view and away again, lively and small. Only three of Nettie Mae's children had lived to that age, when they might frolic and play and know whatever small joys life permitted. It was one reason more to hate the Bemis woman.

The knuckles of Nettie Mae's right hand stung with sudden force. She lifted her hand and examined it. The skin, always hard and rough from endless toil, had cracked. Through the pale gray of the callus, lines of vivid pink opened and burned. A minor wound, but vinegar had gotten inside, so it hurt big enough for a more serious injury. She pressed a dry corner of her cloth against the place and clenched her teeth, watching the children chase one another around and around the distant gray farmhouse.

It isn't Christian, Nettie Mae thought with a surge of bitter guilt. *It's not Christian, to let a family in need go without.* She knew it was wrong to leave her neighbors hanging at a loose end. But if the fire didn't burn, then the steam would die back, and the engine would come shuddering to a halt. And if Nettie Mae couldn't keep moving forward, what would become of her? What would become of Clyde? He was the only child God had allowed her to keep.

In time, the squashes had all been wiped clean. Nettie Mae tore herself away from the sight of Cora struggling over the chores, carried her basket inside, and lined the squashes up on the kitchen mantel. A few days resting above a nighttime fire would toughen their skins, making them resilient enough to last through the winter. Now the apples needed picking. The trees Substance had planted some seven years before had borne well this year, the first time they would yield a proper harvest. The putting by of cider and preserves, of dried apple rings and thick apple butter, would keep Nettie Mae occupied for days yet to come.

By the time she'd carried the ladder and her bushel basket from the long shed, the day's heat was beginning to encroach upon the pocket of coolness that hung around the base of the foothills. She could smell afternoon coming. The oaten heaviness of the air, the thick-porridge density of it, the way its odor of dryness and limpness sank down among fresher scents of green and dew and lay there, immobile as a dead thing. The insects had already begun to drone in the pasture, a long, unbroken hum of weary resignation.

She pulled her long skirt and petticoat up between her legs, tucked them into the waistband of her apron, and climbed up among the branches of an apple tree. The air was still soft and cool there, faintly damp, sugared by the apples' ripeness. When she picked the apples from their boughs, the fruits parted easily from their stems, as if the tree were giving Nettie Mae what it had worked all spring and summer to create. *Here, take it; take it all. The apples are yours now.* They were generous things, those apple trees—peaceful and serene, sheltering, as the man who had planted them never had been.

She tossed the apples she gathered down into the bushel, listening to each round, solid strike of sound. Then her hand rested for a moment on the curve of a branch, and she froze. The bough was twisted there, forced down at a tortuous angle by some old slight, some unknown injury—the weight of winter snow or the ceaseless torment of wind. Nettie Mae looked around her in the filtered green light, following the route of each branch in turn as it angled suddenly, breaking from a smooth, easy path to bend this way or that. The angles were like scars, she realized—marks of agonies long gone by, the tree's flinch carried out over months and years of growth, a memory of pain set permanently in the body of the living plant. All at once, her blood ran cold with anxiety. It was Substance who had planted the seeds, Substance who had tended the saplings as they emerged from the earth. Perhaps the saplings had retained some sinister trace of the man who had planted them. Taking him up like their roots took up water, exhaling his hateful words like vapor from their leaves. A breeze stirred the branches, and the tree whispered around Nettie Mae's head. The hiss of it sent a dark and hopeless chill up her back.

When the breeze died away, she could hear Clyde in the sheepfold, talking to the ewes as he sheared them. She couldn't make out her son's words, but the sound of his voice was gentle. That was not the way Substance had ever gone about shearing. He had thought it a great foolishness to speak to animals as if they understood words. They knew nothing of words, Substance had told Clyde once, when he'd caught the boy murmuring to his buckskin horse, pulling tangles from its mane. *They know nothing of words, and speech is wasted on the dumb. Kindness is wasted. The way to run a farm is to move with authority; see how that damn horse shies away from me when it sees me coming? That's all you need to know, son: how to walk with purpose, how to hold yourself and move as if you mean to be obeyed. That's what a man does. He doesn't fawn over his horse like he's in love with it, nor coddle his sheep in the fold.*

And what of Clyde, the only one of Substance's seeds that had never withered? Had the boy already taken up his father's poison? Was Substance, gone as he was, still contorting Clyde's limbs, still bending the arc of his life? Gripped by a desire to see her boy, to watch him for any sign of a sinister twist, Nettie Mae climbed back down to the grass and let her skirts fall free. The apples would keep on the trees for a while yet to come.

Nettie Mae returned to her garden and began pulling up weeds, but only in time to watch Clyde release the last ewe from the pen. The animal skipped toward the flock as lightly as its full belly would allow, and Clyde followed the animal across the yard, fleeces piled high in his arms. He disappeared into the long shed, but when he emerged some minutes later, it was with Substance's good scythe propped across his shoulder. The boy headed over the pasture toward the Bemis place, as Nettie Mae had known all along he would do. Clyde had a better heart than his mother, thank God. Neither heat nor pressure had ever driven the boy forward. Whatever powered the engine of his soul, it wasn't hatred. Perhaps that was sign enough that Clyde had evaded his father's foulness. Perhaps Nettie Mae could rest assured that her son would be nothing like his father when he came into his own.

When Clyde reached the Bemis farm, Nettie Mae went to the edge of the pasture and stood watching the sheep. The ram had called the newly shorn ewes to his side; he nosed at their swollen flanks, exploring the novel shortness of their wool, the paleness of their bodies. When the flock settled in to graze, the ram caught sight of Nettie Mae and wandered closer. He turned his attention to some cropped, dry grass. Whenever his great coiled horns brushed against sage, the small gray leaves scraped and hissed and released their warm, intoxicating late-summer scent into the air.

Nettie Mae had always felt a strange affinity for the ram, a respect— or perhaps an affection—she could neither understand nor explain. While Substance had lived, she had felt rather embarrassed by how strongly she had taken to that animal. It was foolish, she knew, to make pets of one's stock. But at least Nettie Mae had never been fool enough to tell Substance how she felt. Substance would certainly have mocked her. If a good breeding ram weren't so valuable and so hard to find, he probably would have shot the creature dead, just to teach Nettie Mae a lesson.

But here you are, she said silently. Her favorite moved at his ease in the sagebrush, calm in her presence. *Here you are, alive, and where is Substance? Rotting in his grave. Leaching into the river. Drunk up by the roots of thirsty plants and breathed out like a curse into the air.*

As she stood quietly in the ram's company, his many wives came toward him and settled in a circle of peace. Cicadas chirred in the pasture. Substance, Nettie Mae thought, had wrung fear from the sheep the same way he'd wrung it from people. And from horses and chickens and apple trees. The deer that crossed the fields at dusk, the coyotes slipping silent and blue between shadows, all had feared him, all shied away from his presence. It had always been hard to watch Substance work the sheep—gentle animals, giving as the trees gave, without much fight. But worst of all was Substance among the flock at culling time. Twice a year, the day came when the older lambs had to be slaughtered, and on those days, Nettie Mae went to the sheepfold and stood beside her ram. The high stone walls hid from her sight what went on in the small corral down by the smokehouse. But nothing could disguise the sound of the yearling lambs crying for their mothers or their last thrash as life drained hot from their throats. Nothing could quiet the grunts from Substance, his hard shouts, the way he spat his resentment at the young sheep even while they died in his hands.

The ram understood what was happening down at the corral. Somehow, Nettie Mae had always known that the ram understood. She could read acceptance in his calm, dark, saddened eye. His children were dying, but he kept his peace and comforted Nettie Mae with his nearness. What was the place of the sheep in this world if not to fall, to die? To give and give—their wool, their milk, their children, their lives—so that others might go on living. The ram let his offspring go to the slaughter without any fight. And even he would die someday, like his children before him. There were times when the ram's complacency, his very air of wisdom, had made Nettie Mae so angry that she wanted to hurt the dumb beast—kick him, throw stones. More often, she wanted to wrap her arms around his neck and weep into his burr-studded coat, as she had sometimes seen Clyde do with that tall yellow horse he loved.

Now, without the sound of Substance to fracture the still air, Nettie Mae stood and allowed the flock to come nearer. Sheep surrounded her. They filled the afternoon with their scent of dung and dust, with the quiet tread of their small hard feet, the rhythm of tearing grass.

My children are dead, too, she told the ram, but without words, for no animal understood words; no animal cared.

The ram went on grazing, unconcerned by Nettie Mae's pain.

She lurched toward him, reaching with hard hands, fingers hooked like claws. The way Substance did it, grabbing because he had a right, because he was human, and they were only sheep.

The flock scattered, darting away across the pasture, leaving Nettie Mae alone among the sage.

CORA

What needs doing can't be stopped. The children were dusty from their play, and hungry now, too, as afternoon faded to a hot evening, dense and muggy with the feel of distant storms. She must make their supper before the hour grew late. Cora had managed to sweep out the hen coop and scatter fresh straw across the floor. She had also taken down and folded the wash that Beulah had hung, for it had dried quickly in the late-summer glare, the hard, unforgiving heat. But there was still the garden to tend, with its crops waiting to be brought in and preserved for the winter ahead. There was still the chicken flock to cull, meat to smoke, drafts in the house that must be found and stopped up with rags. Winter was not far off.

That thought made Cora pause on the porch step as the children ran inside, clamoring for jam and bread. Winter. The snows that piled up against the house, drifts taller than the windows. Cold so brutal, breath burned inside your chest, and even the running river turned sluggish and lost itself under a hand's breadth of gray ice. It was the kind of cold that brought months of deprivation, months of long white nothingness glaring under a weak and distant sun. Winter killed in this place—cattle and horses, wild animals. It could kill a person, too. Every spring, when the roads finally thawed to red mud and Cora made the journey up to Paintrock with Ernest and the children, they learned which lives the winter had claimed. How many men and women had frozen or starved out there on the prairie, imprisoned by the drifts, isolated in a sea of white. Women and children, dead every season. Cora didn't mean to hear her children's names added to the annual litany.

She glanced at the shed beside the hen coop. The pile of firewood was half as wide as it had been that spring, when Ernest had gone up into the foothills with his hatchet to replenish the store. The pile stood waist high now; Ernest had cut enough wood in April to fill the shed from ground to eaves. How much longer would the present supply last? Cora ran the grim calculation in her head. Three weeks, perhaps four, if God was merciful and the mild weather held out a little longer.

There was nothing for it; someone had to go up into the foothills and cut wood—enough to see the family through the deep snows until April or May, when the mornings would be warm enough that Cora need no longer shiver under her blankets, fearful that if she stirred and rose from her bed, the ice-teeth of winter would take her and she would be swallowed down into the gullet of the prairie. But who?

It must be me, she realized, and shivered. *If I don't go up into the hills and find the pine forests myself, the cold will take us—all of us.* The cold would take the youngest first. Little Miranda, the bright and sunny child, the greatest joy of Cora's life. Miranda first, but the others would follow. By spring, she would have no children left.

Cora stared up at the great hill that towered above the homestead, its long flank sere and brown, dotted here and there with pockets of sage. Rainfall and runoff had sculpted smooth troughs into the hillside, and the shadowed tracks of those ravines fissured and fanned toward the hill's crest. They seemed innocuous now—gentle lines and impressions. But when the rains came, the ravines filled with water, and the water gushed down the hill, impeded by nothing, until it met the plain below with a roar—a wall of brown water moving fast enough to overwhelm a grown man. Then the river would rise, rapid and indifferent, cavalier, as if it had all the right in the world to overflow its banks and come up over the fields, come up to where Cora or her children might be taken by the current and consumed.

Above the foothills, the sharp white peaks of the Bighorn Mountains cut into the sky, so near they seemed poised to stride out with great feet of stone, crushing whatever huddled helpless on the prairie below. That was where firewood could be found: beyond the first hostile range of foothills, in the mountain gorges sheltering unseen on the leeward side. How long was the trek to the forest? It took Ernest all day to gather wood in the spring, but he was well experienced; he knew where to go, how to split logs quickly. And he was far stronger than Cora.

I must plan for two days away, she told herself. *I must sleep outside. Up there in the hills.*

Cora tried to swallow down her fear. She gripped the porch rail and stared at the blue granite spires, willing herself to calm, struggling to puzzle out the most sensible course of action. She hadn't hitched a wagon or driven one herself since before Beulah was born. But horse and harness were simple enough, surely. Ernest took the same trail every spring; she would follow the faint double-rutted track, driving where her husband had driven before, until she found the pine groves, the source of her salvation.

And the children—ought she to bring them along? Beulah would be a great help in the hills, for Cora had never wielded an ax in all her life. Nor did she know how much wood she must gather. Beulah would have some idea; the girl had an uncanny instinct, a way of knowing, which Cora had never understood and resolved never to question. But if she took Beulah into the hills, she must take the boys and Miranda, too, for there was no one else to mind them. Nettie Mae Webber would not take up the task; she had made that much clear to Cora already.

Tears stung Cora's eyes and tightened her throat. There was nothing for it, no sensible option but to leave the children under Beulah's care and venture up into the hills alone. She fetched up against her own helpless nature and clung to it, dug her fingers into an edifice of fear. The hills terrified her with their solitude, their muffled silence far from her children's voices, far from the isolated yet familiar world of house and farm. But the thought of winter's murderous cold frightened Cora even more. She would go and do what must be done, no matter how she quaked at the thought, for watching her children sicken and die was a torment she could never endure.

Beulah's voice drifted from the barn behind the house—laughing, or singing one of her nonsense songs. Cora seldom could tell the difference between her daughter's laughter and singing. Beulah and the boy, Clyde, had cut down all the corn in a matter of a few hours and had carried the sheaves to the shady barn. Now they were shelling the dry seed into bushels and casting the cobs out into the yard for the pigs to find.

Clyde Webber. The boy wasn't much like his father—not that Cora had truly known Substance well. The man had been a distraction; a novelty, nothing more. Substance was a novelty Cora sorely regretted now, and casting her weary mind back, she couldn't remember why she had given in to his attentions in the first place. She had spoken to Substance but little, even after their shameful carrying-on had begun. Now she wondered whether she had acquiesced for the sake of the act alone, not out of any affection or even familiarity. Indeed, Cora had wondered more than once why Substance had professed such a keen interest in her. He had never offered sweet words nor made any attempt to soothe her spirit. He had taken what he wanted simply because he'd had the strength to take it, and Cora had given—why? Something about their exchange must have excited her. She had made herself the prey, had reveled in the hunt, and even Substance's flat, dark predatory stare had thrilled her, for it had seemed to Cora that when she surrendered to Substance's passions, she could tame—for a short time, at least—that which was untamable. The wolves, the bears in the foothills. The flash floods and the river surging beyond its bank. Any of a hundred perils waited on the prairie or up among the hills; any of them might claim

Cora or her children in an instant. Substance, at least, Cora could predict and control.

But though his father had been a hard and frightening man, there was nothing malign in the Webber boy—not so far as Cora knew. True, once the sinful affair had begun, Cora hadn't been able to bring herself to speak with Clyde. She still found herself silenced by his presence, hot faced and unable to meet his eye, though she had been moved by his aid with the corn patch and impressed with his vigor. What could she have said to the boy? How does one apologize after one has broken a marriage, destroyed a family, condemned a young man's father to death? Cora could only stand at a distance and watch as Clyde cut the corn and Beulah moved along behind him, bundling up the sheaves as if she'd been born to the work. But in that watching, Cora had discerned a certain difference between father and son. Substance would never have called on his neighbors merely to offer help. Substance surely would never have walked onto their land and taken up whatever work needed doing without being asked. As if he had been hired—as if it was his own land. The boy was free of his father's darkness. Cora hoped he might remain free for good.

She left Clyde and Beulah to their work and fixed the children's supper: bread with jam, and a bowl each of the soup Cora had simmered since that morning, onions and carrots with an old smoked joint of elk's leg to hearty up the broth. She had to chide Miranda and Charles to make them eat their soup; they always complained about onions.

With the children well into their meal, Cora cut several thick slices of bread, buttered them generously, and scraped the pot of blackberry jam to spread the last of it atop the butter.

"Who's that for?" Benjamin asked.

"For young Mr. Webber. He was very kind to help us with the corn." *Without him, it surely would have rotted in the field.*

"I gave him biscuits already." Benjamin sounded rather sulky. He didn't seem to like that the dregs of blackberry jam should go to young Mr. Webber.

"That was for lunch," Cora said. "It's supper time now."

She carried the bread outside before the children could distract her further, or worse, clamor for more jam. Clyde and Beulah had finished the work by then; the girl drifted toward the house, brushing the tips of long grasses with her fingers, moving slowly in the golden light of evening. Clyde had couched the scythe on his shoulder once more, and was headed more briskly toward his home.

Cora watched him in frightened silence for a moment, uncertain what she ought to say. Then she surprised herself by calling out, "A moment, please."

Clyde stopped and turned, waiting for her.

Quickly, Cora closed the distance between them. Better to get this over with. She still couldn't meet the boy's eye, but she looked at the brim of his hat, the strap of his braces, his fist on the handle of the scythe.

"This is for you." She held out the bread, stacked jam sides together.

Clyde took her offering with a solemn nod. "Thank you, ma'am. I did work up a hunger."

"I . . . I would pay you if I could, but—"

He shook his head. "No need for payment. I'm glad to help a neighbor. And I think you've got plenty need for help, with Mr. Bemis off to jail."

The frankness of those words seemed to strike the air, a mallet to a bell. The reverberation hung all around them, freezing Cora to her place.

"I . . . I'm sorry," she said.

Clyde shifted uncomfortably. The hand that held the bread lowered to his side, and for a moment Cora thought he would drop the slices in the grass—throw them away. But he said only, "It was a tragedy, all that happened. Now it's best if we move on. Nothing else to be done but move on."

She nodded, watching the setting sun wink and slide along the curve of his sickle. After a pause, when it was clear to both of them that Cora would say nothing more, Clyde touched the brim of his hat with the crust of his bread—an attempt at a polite farewell—and turned back toward the sod-brick house.

Cora thought she might call to him again, might beg him to go into the foothills and cut her winter wood. She might pay him for the work somehow, though she had little money and few possessions of any real value. But she couldn't make herself speak, let alone raise her voice. She had used up all her strength forcing out that pathetic apology. There were no words left to her now—not today—and after he had so kindly seen to her corn, Cora couldn't presume to ask the boy for more labor.

When Cora had eaten, she took her sewing basket outside and sat on the porch steps, picking now and then at her mending. The last flush of light spread across the prairie, golden and slow. It shifted to rose and then to violet as night's impending chill honed its edge against the foothills. The cicadas ceased to hum, and the brief silence they left behind was soon filled by the calls of birds—meadowlarks and finches, thrushes and bluebirds, all settling for the night's roost. Crickets began singing when the blue-gray dusk descended. The sky had gone deepest purple, pricked here and there by the pinpoints of stars. Across the field, the Webber boy led his sheep toward the stone fold. Now and again, Cora could hear a faint bleat coming gently over the sage. The sounds were distant and small, contained by the vastness of night.

"Ma?" Beulah had opened the front door and was leaning against the frame—swinging on it with one thin arm, carefree and unconcerned. "Time to get the little ones tucked into bed. Do you want me to do it?"

"No." Cora stood with her sewing basket. The light was all but gone from the sky now; there was no point in trying to mend. "No, I'll do it. It's my work, after all."

The children were sleepy enough that they made no protest while Cora led them through the nighttime routine of washing faces and dressing for bed. She helped little Miranda into her long flannel nightgown, then pulled out the trundle bed while the boys climbed beneath their blankets and snuggled down together.

"Say," Charles said, "wasn't that scythe fine? I swung it better than you, Benjamin."

"You didn't neither."

"Either," Cora corrected. She had always been determined that her children would speak with the culture of city folk, not with the careless drawl of the Wyoming plains. It was a fight she would lose in the end, she knew.

"Pa never let us swing the scythe," Benjamin said.

They all fell silent, then—Cora, the boys, even Miranda on the trundle bed. The boys looked at one another, and something jumped beneath the blankets, Charles slugging Benjamin on the arm, Cora supposed, as punishment for breaking the taboo. No one had spoken of Ernest since the event, the tragedy. *All that happened*, as Clyde had said. Beulah must have done it, Cora realized—must have sat the children down and explained what had happened, told them all that their father was up in Paintrock, in the jailhouse, and would remain there for two years. A strange lightness struck Cora in her middle, a lifting, pulling sensation that rose up into her chest and toward her throat. She clenched her jaw tightly, for she wasn't certain what would happen if she opened her mouth and tried to speak. She would either sob or break into wild, hysterical laughter, and she was resolved to do neither in front of her children.

"Now go to sleep," she said when the unruly feeling subsided a little. "There's work to do in the morning. You boys must pull weeds in the garden."

The boys groaned in protest, but all three children settled, nearly asleep by the time Cora blew out their candle.

She found an oil lamp burning in the kitchen, the flame dancing within its glass shade. Beulah had hung a kettle of water over the fire to heat for her bath, and steam was already rising from its spout.

"Do you want to wash first, Ma?"

"No, dear. I won't bathe tonight. I've mending I must see to."

Cora sat at the kitchen table, close beside the lamp, and worked at her stitches while Beulah took out the tub and filled it with hot water. Then she stripped off her dress and stockings—both dirty from her day's work—and stepped into the tub.

"Corn's all in, in one go," Beulah said. She stooped to saturate her rag, then squeezed it over her shoulders, careful not to splash the floor.

"You made a fine job of it."

"Clyde made a fine job of it. It was right kind of him to help, for I don't think I could have done it all by myself. I'm not strong enough yet to swing a sickle."

There was something in Beulah's voice that made Cora look up from her sewing, needled by sudden caution. An eagerness, a breathless excitement.

"Don't forget to wash behind your ears," Cora said, and nothing more. But she watched her daughter bend again to the surface of the water, noting the long strength of Beulah's coltish legs, the shape of the muscle at the top of her arm, rounding into the shoulder. When the girl straightened, Cora could see the faintest flair to her hips, and noticed for the first time that the flat, ribby chest of childhood had begun to swell. Beulah was fast becoming a woman. There was an undeniable latency in the girl—something supple and powerful waiting to bloom, a fern ready to uncoil from its fiddlehead, a sapling extending its first true bough.

We can't stay here, Cora realized with a pang of helpless need. *The prairie is no place for a young woman. She needs to be in the city—any city.*

Even the nearest town would do, if Cora couldn't see Beulah safely back to Saint Louis. Paintrock—twenty miles north, inhabited by no more than three hundred people—was a far cry from a city. But three hundred souls was a great improvement over this unsettling isolation. A girl of Beulah's age needed society. Friends. From who else could she learn to be a proper woman?

Not from her mother. That much is certain.

How long did Cora have before Beulah became a woman in truth? One year, perhaps, two at the most. Ernest would be freed from his cell by that time, and when he returned to the homestead and saw his eldest daughter—a child no more, grown to womanhood—he would understand. Cora would make him see then. There was no hope for any of them here on the prairie, here in this wilderness. If they didn't return to civilized life, Beulah would suffer, and Cora would surely die. She had been dying already, slowly enough, for eight long years.

Cora's needle went astray, stabbing deep into her forefinger. At her gasp, Beulah turned to look over a dripping shoulder.

"You all right, Ma?"

"*Are* you well, *Mother?*"

The girl only smiled at Cora's correction, her grin wide and mischievous.

Cora sucked the blood from her finger. It tasted hot and metallic, like Substance Webber's kiss.

Little wonder Substance died, Cora thought. She took her finger from her mouth and pressed the pad, squeezing another drop of blood from the wound. *The prairie is no place where anything may truly live— not a girl, not a woman, not a man.*

The prairie was nothing but death, season in and season out. Dry grasses, gray sage, the hawks falling from the sky to seize whatever small lives struggled in the thin shadows below. Wolves howling at night, eager for the hunt. The brown water racing down a hill face, the sterile winter snow six feet deep.

Cora was resolved to get her children back to Saint Louis, even though she could no longer claim a place there—if she had ever truly had a place in Saint Louis society. But she had to do it, had to go. She understood that now. With or without Ernest, she would return to Missouri, and take her children with her.

Beulah especially, before it was too late to save her from the corrupting influence of the wild.

3

GRAY AGAINST GRAY

That year, the rains didn't sweep in all at once. Nor did they come in from the west as they had done all the years before, when banks of cloud piled up along the white ridge of the distant range across the basin, black and dense and sudden as if a new crop of mountains had grown there overnight. That year, the rains were early but shy. They lingered far to the south, across the plain. I watched them while I led the cows out to pasture or cut cabbages from their stalks, clouds of deepest purple, stretched in long bands, obedient to far-off winds. Banks of cloud so vast, so endlessly mobile, they turned the world as I knew it on its head, so the sky became reality—the solidness, the wholeness—and the earth below was ethereal, shifting through veils of color, parting light with shadow and shadow with light, all the way out to the horizon where a sheet of rain slanted between Heaven and earth, its edges indistinct, swallowing prairie and sky in a motionless blue mist.

Day after day, the clouds came nearer till at last they found us. I felt the first drops fall, saw them fall in the garden, raising a smell of renewal from the parched earth. The drops fell upon leaves wilted and exhausted by heat—a light, hollow drumming. Rain left circles of shine on faded green. Circles in a coating of dust. I closed my eyes and tipped my face up to the blurred and purple sky. The rain struck my cheeks, my forehead, my shoulders. When a droplet ran from the edge of my nose and down to the corner of my lips, I put out my tongue to catch it. The rain tasted of a summer season that still hoped it might last. It tasted of fast currents rushing down ravines, a rising river, a long winter that would all too shortly arrive.

Clyde and I had worked together plenty times more since that day in the corn patch. Every afternoon, in fact, when the most pressing chores at the Webber homestead were finished, Clyde came across the sheep pasture to meet me at the edge of our cow pen, and together we fell into whatever work needed doing, sometimes without either one of us saying a word about it. Most days, there was something tense and distant in Clyde, as if he wasn't altogether comfortable with my nearness or with my talk. But he kept coming all the same, kept lending his considerable strength to our farm. I stayed quiet out of gratitude and worked alongside him, just as hard as I'd ever worked before—harder, in fact. But the day I tasted the first rains of autumn, I knew I had to tell him what was weighing so heavy on my poor ma's heart.

Snow's gonna be real early this year, I said.

How do you know?

I shrugged. He wasn't apt to like the answer to that question, and wasn't apt to believe me if I told him the truth.

I said, We don't have enough firewood to see us through. I ain't sure how to get more. I already picked up all the cottonwood branches I could find alongside the river. And the cottonwood trees are too big to cut down without one of those special-made saws. Ma says a body has to go and cut firewood where the trees are smaller and easier to fell, but the nearest pine forests are on the western face of the foothills. I don't suppose I can get as far as that. Not easily, anyhow.

Clyde said, There's no sense in a girl going up to the foothills to cut wood. A bear'd eat you, like as not.

I laughed at him. A bear wouldn't eat me.

Clyde shrugged and went on working. After a minute, I said, I think my ma's going to venture up into the hills herself for our firewood.

No sense in that, Clyde said. It's a dangerous trip for a woman alone. You can get wood up in Paintrock. Lots of fellas cut it and haul it in from the pine forest, and folks can buy it or trade for it.

But we don't have a penny to spare, I said. And I don't think we have much for trading.

I'm going to town tomorrow for the post. Mother needs more sugar and some other things from the general store, so I'm taking the wagon. If you ain't got money or goods for trading, then I'll buy the wood myself, Clyde said.

He was half turned away, pulling at a board on the cow-pen fence that was loose and needed mending, but I could see the quick, shy smile that came over his face and vanished again. The thought of buying our firewood pleased him, in a secretive way. I couldn't make out why.

I said, That's about the kindest thing you've ever offered to do, and you've done a heap of kind things for us already.

I wouldn't be very neighborly, if I was to let a lone woman and her four children freeze to death.

I'm not much of a child anymore, I said.

I know.

I said, Let me come over to your place, Clyde, and work for you the way you work for us. You know I can work hard.

He didn't look up as he pulled the loose board away from its posts and examined the rotted ends. I know, was all he said, and then he tossed the board over his shoulder.

Then let me lend a hand.

He did look at me then, so sharp and direct it fairly cut me. You know my mother wouldn't take kindly to having you around, Beulah.

Neither of us said any more. We both knew it was true. Nettie Mae harbored a powerful dislike of the Bemis name; she made no exception for me. Clyde and I rummaged in the barn till we found nails and a good plank for mending the fence, and I held the wood in place while he drove the nails deep into the post. The post was still damp from the last rain, and

I could see taffy-colored hairs caught in the cracks and in the grain of the wood from where the cows had rubbed against it.

After the fence, we scraped slime from the insides of rain barrels, readying them for the wet season to come. We didn't speak then, either. I thought maybe Substance and the corn seed were still weighing on Clyde's mind. He didn't like the idea of his father buried, I thought—or maybe he was frightened of what might rise up to take his father's place. Clyde couldn't see that Substance had already grown again. There was nothing to fear in the sprouting. Seeds don't always breed true; sometimes they bring up a better crop than the one that came before.

When the work was done, and Clyde departed with my ma's usual offering of buttered bread, I took my leave of the farm and walked out to the river alone. The rains had been light that day, but a heaviness of indigo clung to the edges of an overcast sky, and I knew the night would be loud with storm and the next day too cold and wet for walking. I intended to get my peace while I still could. I followed the old trail through waist-high grass. Every sort of plant had responded to the rain with a passionate effort, and the way had become a thicket—long, bladed leaves reaching out to obscure the path—for no one had walked there since the night my pa left. No one but me, and I didn't go to the riverbank often.

When I got there, I could sense the fullness of the river, the water running high and fast among the huge old cottonwoods. They were talking among themselves, the trees—their newly turned leaves whispering together, speaking of the water soaking cold and good down among their intertwined roots.

Substance was there, too, restless yet tethered to his place, like the cottonwoods.

I took what I had brought for him out of my apron pocket. It was a great splinter of half-rotted wood, long as my hand, broken from the board Clyde had pulled free of the cow-pen fence. I laid it carefully on Substance's grave, among the other things I had given him: feathers weighed down by flat river stones; a chip of agate I'd found in the creek, white swirled with red; an old horseshoe; the skull of a crow, picked clean by other crows, its beak still dark pigmented and smooth as night. Short grass and the thin, wiry vines of bindweed had begun to cover the grave, but I could still discern the rise where his body lay, and of course my gifts to Substance marked the spot.

I had never really known Substance in life, but I knew him now, in death . . . and a more stubborn man the world had never seen. No one who died stayed put together afterward quite so long as Substance—no one I'd ever encountered, anyway. But there he was, a presence hanging over his own grave, aware, knowing, furious in the face of his fate. The hens I killed for our soup pot fell apart the moment their wings stopped flapping—those quick, curious, darting little spirits bursting like sparks from a campfire, dispersing out into the world. My ma had cherished a pet cat some years ago, and when it had died suddenly, I sat beside its body and felt the cat's awareness linger for half an hour or more. The cat had been amazed by its sudden weightlessness, pleasantly drawn to all the silver strands of light that reached for it, thirsty for its spirit, the threads of all the lives that continued on: me and my family and the hens in the yard and the cattle in their pen, the squash vines and carrots in the garden, the insects trilling on the prairie— the prairie itself. Sheep seemed to consent to their dissolution even before their bodies had died, and most plants, too, as if the great unraveling was a sacredness for which they had always lived. But Substance Webber refused to do what other spirits did. He would not be dissolved. He would permit no other life to touch him, to take him, to use him. He didn't yet know that we can't remain whole forever, but he would learn the truth soon enough. No one escapes the great unraveling; no thread is unspooled and escapes the weaver's hand. I knew the roots of the newly sprouted grasses surrounded Substance's body. The bindweed thrived on his rich flesh. A few yards away, the cottonwoods were already reaching toward him, delving through the soil with ancient hands. Before much longer, the earth would take every last bit of Substance Webber, whether he consented to be taken or not.

But he wasn't gone yet.

Hello, Substance, I said, standing over the feathers and the crow skull.

He greeted me, but not with words. Substance spoke with feelings— images. Quick impressions I felt like thumps inside my chest.

Clyde is an awful good boy, I told him. And then I felt foolish for calling him a boy. I said, Clyde is a good man.

Substance felt the roots wreathing his body, what was left of it below the soil. I felt those filaments surrounding me, too, pale and cold, never still, growing and growing, thirsty as Indian summer. He seemed to say, I'm a man, and I should be living still.

No, I said. That's not the way of things. None of us lives forever. We don't get to choose when our time comes.

I always chose, Substance said. Not with words—with a tightening in my throat, a clenching of my fists, a welter of rage rising in my stomach.

I told him—as I always told him—You ought to let go now. Feel how light you are. You can fly, if you want to. You can go up and join the birds. You can be a bird. You can be anything you like, and all things you like at once. All you have to do is let go of yourself. Allow yourself to fall apart.

Substance wouldn't do it. He brooded, refusing to tell me any more. He lay beneath the soil, or lingered somewhere just above it, hard and resentful of death as he had been of life.

What I didn't tell Substance was this: You've renewed already, so there's no use staying as you are. Your son has taken your place. It's he who will carry on without you. Without your anger, without your hate. There is a future, Substance—but though it isn't yours, you can be glad for those who will shape it.

I didn't say those words to him because he wasn't ready to hear. Instead I patted and smoothed the soil of his grave between the relics I'd brought to amuse him, between the leaves and stems of the plants he nourished. There was no use trying to convince some folks of anything. They only accepted the truth when the truth caught up with them, and the truth was coming for Substance, inexorable as the roots of the cottonwoods. He wouldn't evade the weaver's hand much longer.

None of us could. The loom was ready, the shuttle already moving. I saw the pattern forming itself the next morning—a colorless dawn, still smelling of the rain that had scoured our two farms overnight. A morning sharp with cold and too still for my liking. I waited for Clyde to cross the pasture and join me in my work, but nothing stirred at the sod house except a thin line of smoke rising from the chimney, gray against a gray sky. It was only then I realized the barn door was open and the wagon was gone. And so was Tiger, our only horse. And so was my ma.

NETTIE MAE

Gray against gray, the hours had passed featureless and unchanging. But morning had come at last, and in its weak and hesitant light, Nettie Mae had found her resolve. She kissed Clyde's brow, praying it wouldn't be the last time in this life. But he was hot, and his hair was damp with sweat; his eyelids, thin and tinged with blue, scarcely flickered at the touch. Certainly, he did not wake.

Nettie Mae turned her back on her child and descended the stairs, clinging to the railing, for her legs trembled with weariness. She hadn't slept a wink the whole night through. Fear shook her, too, but deep in her belly, low down below her heart. She ignored the fear. She had always ignored it, even when it howled its loudest, when storms of grief had battered her, and God had tested the mettle of her spirit with one unbearable loss after another. If Clyde could be saved, it would be by Nettie Mae's strength alone. She would only give in to fear and weep and tear at her hair and shake her powerless fists at the blank gray Heavens if Clyde were lost. Then they all would be lost, every child she had borne, every person she had loved. Only then—when no one was left to rely on her cold and stoic presence—would Nettie Mae surrender to fear.

She wrapped herself well in two shawls, pulling the corner of one up over her head, for a light, misty drizzle was still falling. It hadn't abated the whole morning through, but at least the rains no longer pounded as they had done the previous day. She caught Clyde's favorite horse, the buckskin gelding, and heaved a saddle up onto its back. Then she fussed with its placement on the horse's withers, lurching the saddle forward and back, trying to recall exactly where it ought to rest. She had been an enthusiastic rider in her youth, but those years lay far behind her now. She hadn't tacked up a horse since she'd been a young bride—long before Clyde was born. But at last she reached below the horse's belly and caught the dangling cinch. The animal's hide rippled and twitched, which caused Nettie Mae to step back, wary. When she felt reasonably certain the horse wouldn't snake its neck around to bite, she tightened the band around its ribs, then coaxed the bit between its teeth and clambered up into the saddle.

The seat wasn't meant for a woman; there were no leaping heads to steady her posture and cradle her legs in comfort. The saddle was built for a man—astride and clad in trousers. Nettie Mae was obliged to sling her right leg over the pommel, crooking her knee around the leather-capped horn. The horse shifted, flicking its ears in confusion, reconciling itself to the unexpected distribution of weight, and as it stepped to the side, the world lurched and swam around Nettie Mae. Gravity dragged at her skirt, her body. She glanced down only once; the earth seemed impossibly far below and hard, and studded with stones.

You've ridden countless times before, she told herself. *There's nothing to fear. The feel of it will come back to you. Soon it will seem as natural as walking.* She prayed it was true.

Nettie Mae turned the horse toward the Bemis farm and set off over the pasture, stiff and awkward with the sway of its gait. The light rain had begun to chill her cheeks and nose, and her knee already felt cramped and strained, caught up as it was over the horn of the saddle. Twenty miles would make for a long ride in the rain. The sooner she took to the road, the better off she and Clyde would both be. But she couldn't leave the farm without first calling on her neighbor.

The Bemis house was surrounded by a four-foot split-rail fence—goodness knew why, for it did nothing to keep deer or other wild animals away. Someone had left the gate open, for which Nettie Mae was grateful. The prospect of dismounting to open it and then climbing up into the saddle again was enough to make her quail. She pressed on toward the house and thought to raise her voice, to call out for that Bemis woman to come and speak with her. But the girl Beulah appeared on the porch before Nettie Mae could open her mouth.

"Good morning, Mrs. Webber." The girl didn't seem the least bit surprised to find Nettie Mae mounted—perched in a graceless sidesaddle—in the front yard. She just watched Nettie Mae with those strange, heavy-lidded eyes. Nettie Mae never could make up her mind whether the girl's eyes were dull with stupidity or turned so far inward, gazing at a vista she alone could see, that they had lost the spark and brilliance of an ordinary child. There were times when Nettie Mae was half-convinced the girl saw more clearly than any mortal had a right to see.

"I must speak with your mother," Nettie Mae said. Her voice failed her then, but only for a heartbeat. There was no time for delay, no time for pride or anger. She forced out the next words. "I must ask a favor, and I'm afraid it's urgent. Go and fetch her for me."

"I would, Mrs. Webber, but my ma is gone."

"Gone?" A wave of dizziness struck Nettie Mae; she twined her fingers in the horse's mane, fearful she might drop from the saddle.

"Yes, ma'am. I got up this morning to feed the hens, and our horse and wagon had vanished."

"She has driven to town, then."

Something hard and hot struck Nettie Mae in her chest—her heart, giving one desperate and futile beat. If she had known the Bemis woman had intended to drive to Paintrock, Nettie Mae might have ridden with her. The journey would have been strained and bitter—nigh on unbearable. But the doctor might already have been speeding on his way to Clyde's bedside, too. Nettie Mae would endure any torment, even the company of the Bemis woman for twenty long miles, if her son's life could be saved.

"I don't think she went to town, Mrs. Webber." The girl came to the porch rail and leaned her forearms against it, peering down into the grass with those veiled eyes. Her limp hair fell down over her face. Nettie Mae could have slapped the girl for such casual unconcern. "I think she drove up into the foothills to look for firewood."

"Firewood? What a foolish errand. A woman can't cut firewood on her own."

Beulah shrugged. "I would have said as much to my ma, if she'd asked me, but she never did. She just up and left."

A wave of despair filled Nettie Mae's gut. A sour taste rose to the back of her throat even as her breath came short and hard—an onslaught of weeping she struggled to master. The girl looked up sharply then, at precisely the right moment to catch Nettie Mae in her fleeting weakness. The heaviness was gone from the child's eyes, vanished like a pebble dropped down a well. Beulah fixed her with a stare so direct, so suddenly piercing and clear, a current of superstitious dread rushed along Nettie Mae's spine.

"What's the matter?" Beulah said. "Something is wrong. What's gone wrong? Why did you ride over to speak with my ma?"

"I . . . I must ride to town." Nettie Mae floundered among her weary thoughts, her useless words. There was nothing to be done but tell the girl everything. "Clyde has fallen ill. He's in a terrible state. Fever—delirium—I must bring the doctor at once."

"Oh." The girl relaxed again, staring into the grass, watching beads of rain travel down the long green stems. "Clyde will be all right, Mrs. Webber. There's no cause for fretting."

The girl's lack of concern sickened Nettie Mae as much as it infuriated her. There was no doubt now: Beulah was as close to witless as any child Nettie Mae had ever seen. It was a wonder Cora had driven off and left her younger children in the care of this vacuous creature—but then, the Bemis woman had scarcely more sense than her lazy, dull-eyed daughter.

Breathless with outrage, Nettie Mae struggled for a rebuke. Beulah spoke again before she could marshal her words. "Clyde will be well, but I can tell you're just about in a fit with worry. If you like, I can go over and tend to him while you're away."

Nettie Mae pressed her lips together. Her hand clenched the horse's mane.

"It would be better," Beulah said, "if you would stay here, Mrs. Webber. There's no need to rush off after the doctor. But I can see there's nothing a girl like me can say to convince you to stay. So I'll go on over and tend to Clyde, and you can put your mind at ease till you get back."

"Your manners are very shoddy." Nettie Mae's voice sounded small, insignificant, even to herself.

Beulah ignored the admonishment. "But I must care for my brothers and my sister today, as well. I'll have to take them over to your place."

"Do what you must," Nettie Mae said. "Only don't allow the children to disturb Clyde's rest."

"No, ma'am, I won't. I guess you'd better get going now. It's an awful long ride to Paintrock."

∾

The road was as endless as the night had seemed. An hour into her desperate ride, Nettie Mae's hands had lost all feeling, thanks to the cold and damp, though a certain slowness and stiffness persisted, a reminder of the winter yet to come. Her back and legs ached and burned with a devilish fire. She had no way of knowing how far she had traveled and how many miles she had yet to ride. Rarely did she visit Paintrock—and she had always made the journey by wagon in the past, with Substance or Clyde driving and some small bit of needlework to occupy her hands and while away the empty hours. The road was unfamiliar to Nettie Mae. Landmarks held no meaning; all she could do was fix her eyes to the northern horizon and strain for that first sight of Paintrock in the distance.

She had tried all night to convince herself that there was no real cause for alarm. People took fevers all the time. Clyde had been working hard of late, toiling on their own land as well as the Bemis farm. He had spread himself too thin; the sudden change of weather had overcome him, weary as he was. The chill of autumn had come, and Clyde had scarcely stepped inside to warm himself. But he was a strong boy. Young and strong. He would soon turn the corner and be right as rain once more.

But when Clyde's breathing had begun to rattle just before sunrise, Nettie Mae could no longer convince herself that this was a routine fever. As she rode north, hunched against the chill, she remembered that morning—the dawn of bleak fear.

Morning light had come gently through the window, filtered through layers of cloud, through the cutwork curtains that hung limp and unstirring in the close air of Clyde's bedroom. Nettie Mae had stitched those curtains years ago, sitting exactly as she'd sat that morning, on a comfortless chair that was hard enough to keep her alert through days of exhaustion and hopeless, endless prayer. But it had been Alta's bedside then, not Clyde's.

Alta hadn't been the first child Nettie Mae had lost, but she had been the first to die beyond her infancy. The girl had been but three years old when she had slipped away from Nettie Mae and fallen into the creek. Substance had found Alta quickly and pulled her out of the water, thank God, but though the child didn't drown, the water still did its worst. Nettie Mae never slept in the two days she spent at her daughter's bedside. She had remained awake, praying all the while, never ceasing, even while she took up her needlework. Endlessly, Nettie Mae had begged the Lord to spare her daughter's life. When her eyes grew heavy with weariness and her shoulders began to slump, she drove the needle into her finger or wrist until she gasped with pain and sat upright again, wide eyed, resuming her prayers, sucking a drop of blood from her skin. God would hear her plea. God would answer, Nettie Mae knew, if she only prayed enough, if her faith remained unshaken.

Indeed, God had answered, in His time. Two days after Alta had been pulled coughing and screaming from the water, she was laid to silent rest beneath the earth. By the time the girl drew her final breath, it almost came as a relief to Nettie Mae. At last, she no longer had to listen to her daughter's struggle for life—listen, unable to help, unable to save the precious life she had so cherished. But the memory of Alta's tortured breath stayed with Nettie Mae. The sound had never left her in peace. The long rattle of each desperate inhalation, the slight pause before she breathed out again, the crackle in her lungs. How large that sound was, filling the room, yet Alta had been so small. The hole Substance had dug to bury the girl was scarcely wide enough to hold a yearling lamb. They had laid their child to rest beneath a lilac tree. Nettie Mae had chosen the place, thinking how Alta would like to smell the blossoms in the spring, if only she could. And then, the following summer, the Webbers had moved away, and Nettie Mae had never seen those lilacs bloom again.

Four graves behind her. Four graves at four different farms, faded marks on the map of her life, tracing the route of her forced march out into this bleak wilderness. From Wisconsin to Minnesota to Nebraska, then to the eastern plains of Wyoming and finally here, under the merciless eye of the Bighorns. One Webber grave lay here already—the fifth monument to Nettie Mae's losses. She had never deigned to visit Substance's final resting place, but she could feel its nearness.

Let there not be another grave, Lord. If You take my son, I will have nothing left.

She dared not pray for much beyond that humble request. God in His power, in His infinite and bewildering caprice, might take Clyde all the faster if Nettie Mae drew too much divine attention. That had been her mistake at Alta's bedside; Nettie Mae was sure of it.

The wind shifted and came down from the north, bearing the smell of ochre and mud with a faint, far-off musk of rain-soaked animals. Nettie Mae breathed deeply, trying to capture the scent, hoping to discern through some instinct long disused whether Paintrock lay just ahead. She had been riding for hours now, surely, though it was impossible to track the sun through a density of cloud. If it was a ranch she had smelled—a herd of cattle—then the worst leg of her journey might be nearing its end. She prayed it was so. Clyde's horse was gentle and sure footed, but the monotony of its gait had long since sent a biting pain into Nettie Mae's lower back. Her knee had gone numb from the pressure of the saddle horn, and her seat bones throbbed with a terrible, tingling agony each time the horse set a hoof upon the road.

The pain doesn't matter, she told herself, resolute, clutching her shawls tighter with one hand. *Nothing matters but Clyde. I can't lose him—I won't. Not my last son, my only child.*

There on the road, with no one to witness her weakness, Nettie Mae gave in to the pain of her body, the weariness of her soul. Tears blurred her vision, then spilled over to mingle with the rain on her cheeks. Weeping brought a curious release—an immediate clarity, a peace she hadn't thought to find. How long had it been since she had wept over anything? She hadn't even shed a tear for Substance; there had been no time, in the wake of his death, for the harvest was upon them with winter just ahead.

Substance. If you were here now, you could have ridden for Paintrock and left me at our son's bed. If you were here now, Clyde wouldn't be forced to work like a whipped mule. He never would have taken this fever.

Merely thinking those words sent a shudder through Nettie Mae. One did not speak harshly to Substance Webber. One did not accuse him of any wrongdoing; one did not even imply. The man was dead, yet still Nettie Mae felt a tremor. She turned in the saddle, wincing at the pain, half-convinced she would find her husband's shade striding up the road behind her, fist clenched and face set in the flat, hard stare that meant his ire had been raised.

Their lives hadn't always been that way—she small and quiet, cringing to avoid Substance's rage. Nettie Mae had loved her husband, once. Long ago, back in the rosy sweetness of Wisconsin, where she recalled every day as a lingering summer sunset, flushed and warm. She had been a girl of seventeen, smitten at the midsummer dance. Substance had looked so fine in his waistcoat and John Bull hat—and how he had danced! Never had Nettie Mae imagined a fellow as tall and broad as Substance Webber could move with such grace. When he took her hand for the reel, he had grinned down at her, and she had liked the mischief glinting in his eyes.

They were married six months later, and Nettie Mae had never dreamed of such bliss—the simple, comforting ease they found in one another's company, the pleasure of keeping house for a good, appreciative man. Substance had always made her laugh. He was a great one for humor and clever little jokes, and because he was so jolly, he and Nettie Mae were invited to every party in the county. Never could she have believed, in those blushing, summery days, the turn her marriage would take.

The change in Substance had come slowly, as the change had come slowly in herself, Nettie Mae supposed. It was Alta—the second child taken cruelly by a callous God—who broke something open in Substance. He had pulled Alta from the water, but he couldn't save her life. Nor had he the power to lift Nettie Mae from the eddies of her grief. What did Substance's strength matter if he couldn't save his daughter's life or spare his wife from suffering? What use were broad shoulders and capable hands in the face of death?

We might have found our joy again. The road unspooled beneath Nettie Mae, mile after painful mile. *We might have found some comfort in one another if we had been granted a few years of respite, a few years to grieve.*

But God had withheld His mercy. Nettie Mae bore one child after another, praying each one would grow and thrive, and mend the holes in her tattered heart and in her threadbare marriage. As each babe was lowered into another tiny grave, she had sunk further into the depths of her pain until the current of grief caught her and swept her far beyond her husband's reach. By the time they left Nebraska, headed for eastern Wyoming, Nettie Mae's girlish warmth was all washed away. The bones of her spirit lay exposed, and those bones were hard as granite, cold and immovable.

Perhaps that's why he turned so brutal, she mused almost lightly, for the pain of the long ride and worry for her son had eclipsed all fear of Substance. What was there to fear in a memory? *Perhaps he thought he could beat the coldness out of me—break the stone of my determination with his fists.*

Something inside Substance had broken open beside Alta's grave, and a foul darkness Nettie Mae had never seen before had come trickling out. What was inside Nettie Mae couldn't be shattered, not even by her husband's strength. But he did dash her love to pieces, and she had come to despise Substance long before they settled in the shadow of the Bighorns. Many a time, Nettie Mae had entertained the thought of leaving him—taking Clyde and whatever few possessions she could fit inside a saddlebag and riding away in the dead of night. Riding off in search of mercy, if any was to be found. But Substance was so damnably strong, so certain of his own mind. He always knew precisely what to do when Indian traders came nosing around the farm or when the floods came or when wolves descended on the sheep. The world beyond the Webber homestead was untamed, unknowable. In his anger, Substance was as terrible as a brush fire. But when he and Nettie Mae were at peace, Substance proved a better bulwark than God—protective, infallible.

Nettie Mae's tears dried with time, and she settled into a grim acceptance of the ride: the ache that plagued her body, stabbing everywhere at once; the clumsy stiffness of her cold hands; the hunger that gnawed at her belly, for she had eaten nothing since supper the night before and hadn't thought to pack so much as a crust of bread. After another weary hour, acceptance caved, and she wept again with sheer frustration, for it seemed as if she had ridden for a season—a year—and still Paintrock was no closer. Then she noticed that the road had widened. It sloped around its edges from use. Rainwater ran off to either side, so the going wasn't quite so muddy; the middle of the road was firm enough that she asked Clyde's horse to pick up its pace. Her left foot in the stirrup was so cold and stiff—and the muscles of her leg so cramped—that she couldn't rise to the rhythm of the trot. She bounced in the saddle like a baby dandled on a knee, weak and precarious. But Paintrock emerged from the rainy haze ahead—brick buildings, wide and low, solid and blue with distance. Relieved, she rolled her shoulders to ease the tension of the long and solitary ride.

The sheriff's building stood on the southern edge of town—corrals and horse sheds out back and the tall, flat-topped jail butting up against the road. Nettie Mae watched the front of the brick jailhouse as her horse jogged past. Ernest Bemis was somewhere inside, pacing out two years in a narrow cage.

What might happen, she wondered, if she were to go on inside and speak to the jailer? What if she could find the sheriff and plead the case for her neighbor? *Release Mr. Bemis early. Give him a shorter sentence.* The Bemis family must have their man returned to them, or Clyde—assuming he survived this fever—would go on helping his neighbors. He would wear himself to the bone because he thought it the right thing to do. But the work would only grow harder as the rains carried on and mud piled up to one's knees.

Clarke's General Store was the next building after the jail. Its red-painted walls were dark with rain; a continuous strand of silver fell from a corner of the roof, splashing on the hard-packed street below. Three women had clustered together on the plank sidewalk outside the store, where a shingled awning offered shelter from the rain. The women had been admiring the bolts of silk displayed in the store window, but one of them glanced over her shoulder at the sound of hooves. When she spotted Nettie Mae, jouncing like a rag doll in the saddle, she dug her elbows into her friends' sides. They all turned to stare. Nettie Mae's face went hot, and the flush prickled against the cold. Surely by now the whole of Paintrock had heard the news. Nettie Mae was a widow; Substance Webber had been shot dead for having to do with another man's wife.

Pointedly, Nettie Mae turned her face away from the women under the awning. *Time enough later for shame. My son's life is in danger. Let those cats gossip as they will; I care nothing for them.*

The doctor's office stood in the heart of town. Nettie Mae reined in with a shudder of relief and slid from the saddle. Her feet hit the ground, but her legs couldn't hold her; gravity dragged at her heavy skirt, her rain-soaked woolen shawls, her exhausted bones. With a startled cry, she clutched at the saddle horn and hung from it, supporting her weight with a trembling arm, wincing at a thousand needles of pain.

Her heart raced with a fresh new fear. *I've damaged my legs. I'll never walk again. I'll be helpless—an invalid!*

"My goodness. Nettie Mae Webber, is that you?" A stout woman with a graying braid had opened the doctor's door. She hung half inside the office, half out, watching Nettie Mae with wide eyes. Nettie Mae had met her only once, years before. She was Abigail Cooper, the doctor's wife.

"Yes, Mrs. Cooper. Is Dr. Cooper in?" The possibility that he might be away brought tears to her eyes again, but Nettie Mae refused to weep now. She had come this far on her own; if the doctor had gone elsewhere, tending to some other patient, she would find the man and drag him by his ear to Clyde's bed.

"Land sakes," Abigail said, hurrying out into the rain. "You're shaking. Are you ill?"

"I'm only tired and weak from a long ride. And I . . . I'm afraid I can't walk so well. My legs have gone numb."

Abigail tied the horse to the doctor's fence, then pressed herself under Nettie Mae's arm. "Lean on me."

Nettie Mae shook her head. Her arm felt almost as weak as her legs, but she couldn't let go of the saddle. She would fall for certain; she had never been strong enough to hold herself upright against the agonies of life. That had been Substance's duty.

"Come now." Abigail wrapped an arm around Nettie Mae's waist and tugged at her insistently. "Your full weight—lean into me, my dear. I'm stronger than I seem."

"But my legs—"

"They'll be right as you please in a few minutes. Though I'm afraid you won't much enjoy the thawing out. Let's get you inside. One foot in front of the other—that's the way."

Abigail guided Nettie Mae into a tidy parlor and eased her down into an upholstered chair. Nettie Mae couldn't suppress a groan of relief; the softness of the velvet cushion seemed to wrap itself around her entire body, soothing the relentless ache in her seat and the small of her back. The respite was short lived. As Abigail bustled away down the hall, calling for her husband, Nettie Mae's legs began to tingle—then to sear. A thousand individual pains crackled along her limbs, each clamoring at once for her attention. And the pain worsened with every frantic beat of her heart.

Nettie Mae willed herself to stillness as the doctor emerged from the hall. She clenched her jaw, determined not to cry out at the current of torment coursing up her legs.

"Mrs. Webber." The doctor took the chair beside her, adjusting a pair of spectacles on his broad nose. "What brings you here this afternoon?"

"Is it afternoon already?" She turned to a great wood-cased clock in the corner. "It's nearly three o'clock! God have mercy! I may already be too late."

"Now, now."

The doctor patted the back of her hand. Nettie Mae resisted the urge to jerk from beneath this touch. There was no time for sympathy, no time for conversation. At this rate, she wouldn't return to the farm until well after nightfall.

"Doctor," she said, rather breathless from the pain in her legs, "my son Clyde has taken a fever. I nursed him all through the night—I never slept a wink—but he's in a terrible way. His breath has begun to rattle."

"I see," the doctor said. "How old is your son?"

"Sixteen. You must come and help him. I've had to leave him alone, or nearly alone—"

"Ah yes. Your poor husband. My condolences, Mrs. Webber."

Nettie Mae shook her head impatiently. "That doesn't matter now. Substance—Cora—none of it."

"Cora?"

"Please, Doctor; you must come at once. I'm . . ." Her voice caught in her throat, and came out fractured and small. "I'm afraid my son will die."

"Very well," the doctor said, rising much too slowly for Nettie Mae's liking. "I'll hitch up my cart and we'll drive back together. You may tie your horse to the back." He raised his voice and called into the depths of the hall, "Abigail, my dear. You mustn't expect me for supper tonight. I'll be down at the Webber farm, and I suppose I must stay the night, for it will be too dark to drive home after."

Nettie Mae sat for a long while in the silence of the parlor. The clock ticked out a mocking rhythm. The pain in her legs rose to a fierce crescendo and she conceded one small whimper, squeezing her eyes shut, begging God to bring her some relief.

The next moment, relief came. The agony abated—not entirely, but enough that Nettie Mae settled back in the chair, sighing. Her legs still quivered with weakness, and the stabbing pains still burst like the sparks of a campfire. But she no longer feared she had ruined herself for good.

By and by, she felt brave enough to lever herself up out of the parlor chair and take a few experimental steps across the room. Every step was clumsy and halting, and her thighs and calves burned from overuse. But some of her strength was returning, and she found it felt good to walk after so many hours in the saddle.

Nettie Mae slipped outside, impatient for the doctor's cart, ready to strike out for her son's sickbed. The rain had finally ceased and the sky had lightened, spilling a wash of yellow light across the town. Nettie Mae patted the faithful buckskin horse, stroking its sodden hide, silently thanking the animal for its strength.

You're Clyde's horse, aren't you? I know he loves you; I've seen how he cares for you. If we get to him in time—if we manage to save his life—I'll tell him how well you carried me today.

A thin call from across the street took her attention away from the buckskin. The post stood opposite Dr. Cooper's office. The postmaster had come out below his eave, which still dripped rainwater; he waved at Nettie Mae with obvious urgency, summoning her closer.

Nettie Mae frowned. She had no time for distractions now. But the doctor still hadn't appeared in his cart, and she would gain nothing by standing about waiting. She hobbled across the road and nodded a greeting to the postmaster.

"You haven't been up to fetch the mail in far too long, Mrs. Webber."

Nettie Mae had no appetite for a scolding. Not this day, of all days. She replied with a hint of acid. "Perhaps you haven't heard the news, Mr. Fields. I am newly made a widow. I've had other matters on my mind."

The postmaster swept off his hat and pressed it against his chest. "Indeed, I had heard. Terribly sad news. You have my sympathies, Mrs. Webber."

"Do I?"

The man pretended not to notice her sting. "Since you are here in Paintrock now, I must ask you to carry a parcel south."

"I'm afraid that's impossible. I've come on an urgent errand, to fetch Dr. Cooper."

"But this is a very special parcel. Come inside; let me show you."

Nettie Mae glanced over her shoulder, but the road remained empty. Clearly, the doctor felt no urgency in hitching up his team. Nettie Mae clenched her teeth at the postmaster's audacity, but she followed the man inside. She might as well while away the minutes, and the postmaster's grand parcel was as good a distraction as any.

Mr. Fields had installed a jaunty new bell on his door, and it rang and bounced on its long steel spring as Nettie Mae entered. The postmaster vanished at once behind an oak counter, ducking through a set of twin half doors that swung wildly on their hinges. He reappeared before they had stopped swinging and beckoned to Nettie Mae.

"Step right behind the counter. Don't be shy, now, Mrs. Webber."

The man was grinning like a fool, eager as a child—itching to reveal some great surprise. Nettie Mae's stomach clenched; she had no taste for such foolish games.

"I wish you'd come right out and tell me what you find so very important."

"It's a delivery," Fields said, "though not for you and yours, I'm afraid. There has been a rather sizable shipment intended for the Bemis farm. It's been taking up space in the back room for two weeks now. I'd intended to send a rider to Mrs. Bemis, to inquire when she meant to fetch her parcel. But I find you here instead. I call that fortuitous. Seeing as how you live so near to the Bemis farm, I thought—"

"I will tell Mrs. Bemis she has a delivery waiting," Nettie Mae said, turning back toward the door. "Good day, Mr. Fields."

The postmaster cleared his throat with a small, rather nervous-sounding cough. "I had hoped, ma'am, that you might be willing to deliver the parcel yourself. That is, if you've brought the wagon. And if you've enough space to carry it. It's a large crate, you see. It certainly can't be carried like a letter or a small package. Yes, it's most fortunate you've happened in today—most fortunate."

"I haven't brought my wagon, but I will be riding home with Dr. Cooper." She placed special emphasis on the doctor's name, hoping to impress upon the man how silly his parcel was when set against matters of life and death. "It's possible the doctor may have room to carry it in his cart. How big is the crate?"

Fields gestured to his swinging doors. "Suppose you step back here and have a look. You can tell me whether you'll be able to take it with you."

Nettie Mae stifled a curse. She stepped around the oak counter, following Mr. Fields to the back room. It was a modest space, already dominated by several tall wooden stacks, each partitioned into countless slots, each slot labeled with the names of the families who lived in or near the town of Paintrock. Some held letters or small parcels wrapped in brown paper. A long table held packages too big to fit inside the slots. And standing before the table, jutting haphazardly into the meager space, was a wooden crate almost four feet to a side.

Fields gestured at the crate with all the gusto of a showman revealing his most astonishing and wondrous act. "The post fee has already been paid. Paid by the sender. I'm sure I can't guess what might be inside that crate. But just look at the return address, will you?"

Nettie Mae crept forward. The crate—its sheer size, its unexpected appearance in her life—left her feeling distinctly cautious. Bits of straw and a few wisps of cotton batting showed in the cracks between boards. She read the words painted on the crate's top, neatly stenciled in dark green.

MRS. CORA BEMIS

PAINTROCK, WYOMING TERR.

RETURN TO:

1600 PENNSYLVANIA AVENUE NW

WASHINGTON, DC

Nettie Mae could feel the postmaster's agitation. She couldn't understand why the man ought to shiver so, why his hands clenched so tightly in his trouser pockets. Nettie Mae shook her head vaguely and looked at Mr. Fields in hopeless confusion.

"Don't you recognize that address, Mrs. Webber?"

"I'm afraid I don't."

"1600 Pennsylvania Avenue. It's the White House, by Jove! The president of the United States has sent this crate here—to Paintrock, of all places! To Cora Bemis, a humble prairie wife. What do you think about that?"

Nettie Mae straightened, still staring at the damnable box with its tidy green address. The last of the pain dissipated from her legs. Her trembling stilled.

"I will certainly tell Cora about this parcel," she said, slow and cool. "It seems a very important delivery indeed. And now I must be going, sir; the doctor is waiting."

Nettie Mae hurried back to the street, where Abigail was securing Clyde's horse to the rail of a smart black hooded carriage. Dr. Cooper was waiting in the driver's seat, and he stretched out a hand to help Nettie Mae clamber up beside him. The carriage springs creaked as she settled back in the seat, and Dr. Cooper urged his pair of grays into a hasty trot.

If God was good, Clyde would survive. And even if he did live— even if she was granted one gift to keep in a long life of deprivation— Nettie Mae resolved never to speak a word about the crate. A gift from the president! Of all the absurd, unacceptable things. Cora had everything already: living children, a living husband, even Substance's affection. Nettie Mae wouldn't allow her to also have the president's gift—whatever it might be.

CORA

Gray and gray, and grayer still. That was all Cora saw when the wagon finally lurched to the crest of the ridge and the lee-side valley opened below. She had never traveled so far into the foothills before. Indeed, she had always avoided the rutted track that snaked up into the high, sage-covered slopes, fearful of Indians and wild animals. Cora hadn't known what she might find on the other side of the ridge, but she hadn't expected this. A bank of cloud had gathered against the mountains' flanks, obscuring the Bighorns from view, and a dense mist fell heavily from the hidden peaks into the valley, gray like vast swags of some heavy, stifling fabric draped and slung among the pines. She could scarcely discern the trees themselves through the mist, and all color was robbed from the scene—evergreen trees dimmed to flat charcoal and the borders between mountain and sky erased as if they had never been.

The persistence of so much gray unsettled her; the mist wrapped around the wagon, rolling across the ridgeline in slow tumbles and torpid spirals. Could she see the farm at all, if she turned now on the wagon seat to stare back down the trail? Or had autumn swallowed the farm, as it had consumed the ridge? Cora did not look back the way she had come. She already felt weak and isolated—insignificant. No good would come from proving her fears well founded.

The drive up the hill had taken far longer than Cora had expected. The horse was reluctant and ill tempered—possibly Cora hadn't fitted its harness correctly, for she had never done the job before—and every foot she ascended above the prairie felt hard won, gained only by her insistent command, lashing the horse's rump with the ends of its reins. She paused on the ridge, surveying the gray forest below. The pines seemed thin from her vantage—slender enough to fell with a hard shove. But there were so many trees. Even with the better part of the valley obscured, still the wall of pines made Cora shudder. How far into the foothills did the forest extend? Shadows clung beneath the pine boughs, menacing and cold. The bleak woodland might stretch on into eternity for all Cora could tell. And God alone knew what beasts were watching from the shifting fringes of the fog, wily and hungering, patient as only predators can be.

The horse snorted, impatient to be off—to finish its work, to be free of Cora's poorly fitted harness. The sound rang loud and hollow along the ridgeline. Cora winced, then shifted her boot against the wagon's footboard—carefully, so as not to draw the attention of mountain lions or the great bears with heads like boulders, whatever gape-jawed things waited among the trees.

Her heel found what it sought: the solid weight of her husband's rifle, stowed beneath the seat, precisely where she had placed it that morning. Cora had almost left the gun behind, for she couldn't stand to touch it, could hardly force herself to look at the thing, the instrument of Substance's death—as much a cause of this present misery as Cora herself. But there were animals in the foothills. The bears were busy fattening themselves on huckleberries; this was the time of year when they were most belligerent, except when the sows emerged from hibernation with new cubs on their heels. Cora knew if she came face-to-face with a bear, the rifle would be her one slim hope for survival.

The horse stamped its hoof. Cora watched the border of the pines, searching patches of red-stemmed dogwood and the spent flower spikes of fireweed, keen for any sign of movement. But nothing stirred. Cora pushed her fear deep down into her chest until it was nothing more than a ripple of nausea. Then she flicked the reins and guided the horse to the downward slope of the trail.

Cora stopped the wagon at the edge of the forest. She remained for a moment in the driver's seat, staring up at the flat gray clouds. The ridge from which she had just descended was partially lost to view already; the mist was moving on a slow current, dropping tendrils toward the earth, suffusing the valley with the scent of wet stone. The day's light seemed to come from every direction at once, filtered through banks of cloud. Cora couldn't begin to guess where the sun stood in the sky, and she had lost all sense of time on the difficult ascent.

I had best get to work, she told herself stoutly. *For all I can tell, night may already be on its way.*

She climbed down from the seat and paced a cautious circle around horse and wagon. The trees had seemed slender from the ridge, little more than saplings. Now, standing among the pines, Cora noted their girth, their staunchly upright power.

You thought you could push a tree over, you fool.

Cora located the slimmest pine in her vicinity and retrieved the ax from the wagon bed. It was heavy; the weight dragged at her arm and slowed her, so she moved like a woman imprisoned by a dream, lagging and perplexed. She took the haft in both hands and swung the blade back over her shoulder, then hacked at the chosen tree.

The ax blow bounced from the trunk. A few chips of bark flew off into the fireweed, exposing a slash of pale wood, but the cut was small. Cora allowed the ax head to drop to the earth. She trembled, listening to the echo of that single strike reverberate from the valley walls. She glanced toward the wagon—the gun, just out of sight. How many blows would it take to fell a single pine? And then she must cut the trunk into smaller pieces.

God help me, I'll never do it. The bears and mountain lions will find me before I can drop a single tree.

Cora's chest quivered. She ignored her mounting despair and lifted the ax again, but the heavy blade dropped back into the loam almost immediately. Cora leaned on the haft, shuddering and gasping as she tried in vain to ward away her sobs. But the weeping came, heedless of her will. She had thought her life hard and mean all the years before, ever since she and Ernest left Saint Louis behind and settled on the prairie. But now—now, Mother of Mercy—she would learn the meaning of hardship. Winter stalked closer with each passing day. Cora could smell the cold coming; she could feel the chill, the bite against her cheeks as the mist moved through the valley. Winters past had frightened her, every year, for the snow piled up against the house, higher than the window panes, and made of her home a prison cell—a tomb. It was Ernest who had kept Cora in good spirits through the long winters. Ernest, laying in a store of wood and smoked meat to last the season. Ernest patting Cora's hand, reassuring her that the snow wouldn't last forever, and when the thaw came, the prairie would burst with color— the flowers of spring opening to welcome the warmth.

The house would become a tomb indeed this year. Cora had no strength to protect her children, to provide as their father had done.

You did this. To yourself, to your children. It's your doing, all yours, and now God will see to it that you suffer for your sins.

The thought stabbed deep into Cora's breast, bringing a sharp pain and a curious satisfaction—a sickening confirmation, as when one overturns some small dead creature's body to find white maggots writhing among the fur.

Cora would have made any sacrifice, except to lose one of her children, if only Ernest would return before winter set in. Not only for his strength, his easy capability, but for his company. The comfort of his presence. He had been the very paragon of a man from their earliest days together—gentle, patient, without the least tendency toward violence. Ernest seldom even shouted; he had no temper to speak of, being all good humor and kindly tolerance.

Cora had been fortunate in that respect, for she hadn't even known Ernest when she had agreed to marry him. She had accepted a farm boy's proposal on a girlish impulse—the sort of thoughtless flight that would have landed an unluckier woman in a lifetime of entrapment and misery. A lovestruck stranger, dropping to his knee to ask for Cora's hand. He could have been anyone, any foul-tempered, hard-eyed brute, but God had proved merciful back then, when Cora was still young, and the Lord had given her a worthy husband. Not a rich man, as Cora's grandfather had wanted, but a good man, a respectable man, and Cora had known herself blessed.

And she had wasted that blessing—tossed it on the rubbish heap—for nothing.

Something crackled in the brush, a swift movement, passing too near for Cora's liking. She ceased crying on the instant; before she realized she had moved, Cora found herself beside the wagon, heaving the ax up into the bed. It clattered as it fell, and Cora seized the rifle from beneath the seat. She held it out before her, extended like some crippled limb, and turned in a stiff half circle, staring hard into the forest. She could see nothing—whatever animal had crept nearby was gone now, or was frozen in place, watching. All the world seemed to stare at her: a thousand unseen, unblinking eyes, peering with dispassionate interest from the formless shadows between the pines.

Cora's hand trembled on the rifle stock. She had as little experience with guns as she did with axes or harnesses. The rifle was heavier than she'd expected, too; the weight weakened her arms and made the muscles of her back clench until they ached. Perhaps it was the burden of guilt she felt more than the burden of steel and wood. She couldn't help but imagine herself in Ernest's place—the last person to hold this gun, the last one to fire it. Cora could see herself, sprawled on the riverbank with Substance over her; she could feel the sudden rush of anger, of pain at the betrayal. The vision lasted only a heartbeat, then she saw nothing but the pines. Yet a shameful heat lingered on her cheeks, and a foul taste rose to the back of her throat.

Impossible that Ernest should have fired that rifle at another man, even considering the circumstance. Neither violence nor rage had lived before in Ernest's heart. Hate was as foreign to his character as strength was to Cora's. If she hadn't heard the rifle blast herself—if she hadn't seen, from the corner of her eye, a dark river running from Substance's flesh—she never could have believed it. Not of Ernest, her gentle, worthy husband.

Perhaps that was why she'd felt herself drawn to Substance Webber. That man had exuded power, even brutality, breathing out his strength like some formidable poison. A more disparate pair of men could scarcely be imagined. After fourteen years married to Ernest—coddled by his essential goodness, wanting for nothing—perhaps Cora's heart had yearned for a change.

Or perhaps Cora had found in Substance all the strength and certainty she herself had never possessed. Substance was all power, all swift and unerring decision. Against the ceaseless danger, the routine terrors of life in a vast, unfeeling wilderness, Substance had proved to be an even greater bulwark than Ernest had been.

And yet it had been Ernest who had seized the ultimate staff of power. Ernest who had killed.

I never really knew him, Cora realized. *All these years, my husband remained a stranger to me, for I had thought him too gentle and Christian to do murder.*

Then another thought struck her—nearly felled her with its blow. *Ernest killed because of me. I pushed him to it. It's my fault that he committed the unforgivable sin. I have damned the man I love.*

Cora reeled on her feet. She lowered the gun, heedless of the thousand eyes, but the forest had gone silent. The chill crept in around her thoughts—the flat, gray expanse of guilt and self-loathing. The valley still smelled of winter, of rain yet to come, of the tombal dark of the year. There was work yet to be done; Cora would accomplish nothing by pointing that instrument of violence into the underbrush. She returned the rifle to the wagon and set about her business once more.

There was no sense in trying to cut down a tree; Cora could see that now. She hadn't enough strength to wield the ax, nor had she time to split the trunk before nightfall. Instead, she moved through the underbrush, gathering whatever fallen limbs she could find. She hauled branches from forest to trail, then hacked at the branches with the heavy ax, tossing manageable pieces into the wagon bed. She worked steadily until her wool dress was soaked with sweat and the muscles in her arms felt useless—insubstantial—quivering like the jelly aspics that had been so stylish at parties back in Saint Louis. Her dampened clothing raised a shiver whenever she slowed or paused, so Cora kept on doggedly, wading into the underbrush with only a prayer to defend her against the beasts of the forest, dragging heavy limbs up the slope until her hands were blistered and raw.

The light had begun to dim. Then droplets of rain splashed on her face and shoulders, and pattered among the trees. Cora leaned against a wagon wheel, panting, and scrubbed the sweat from her brow with the cuff of her sleeve. She must return to the farm now, for if she were caught out in darkness and rain, she might lose the trail—and she hadn't anything more substantial than a shawl to protect herself from the weather. She flexed her hands, wincing at the sting of her blisters. Then she turned to survey the wagon bed, to take in the results of a hard day's labor.

Cora froze in disbelief. She had toiled for hours, yet the bed was far from full. Indeed, she had collected no more than a few sticks—or so it seemed now—scarcely more than an armful. How could she have worked so hard for so little gain? The shock of failure rooted her to the spot; the rain pelted down, falling harder by the moment, soaking her hair and running in rivulets down her scalp, under her collar, down her stiff, cold back.

God help me. My children will freeze for certain. Unless . . .

Cora saw the only path left to her, the one way she might hope to bring her children safely through the dark and cold of the year. She must go to Nettie Mae—as she had gone once already. She must abase herself before the woman she had wronged, must plead for help, for charity.

The mere thought soured her gut and set a terrible pressure of anxiety beating inside her head. But she would do it. Cora would do whatever was necessary, make of herself a spectacle, a shameful fool. Without wood—without charity—her family wouldn't last the winter.

CLYDE

Gray against gray. All colors in the world had settled, one into another. There was nothing left to distinguish between dreaming and waking. The fever was deep and dry as a summer ravine, and Clyde moved warily through its passages, one hand on the high stone wall of conscious thought, even as his weary feet slipped in the sand and all that was once true and solid around him—everything he had known to be real—shifted and flowed like dust through his fingers.

His mother's presence was constant, and sometimes Nettie Mae's nearness comforted Clyde. Sometimes she only made him feel weaker, for now and then he could hear her weeping, the sudden catch in her breath, the shuddering inhalation, the pause and the silence when she refused to breathe out again till she could do it without wailing. He wanted to speak to his mother—offer her comfort in turn. But this sudden illness had drained all the strength from his body and deprived him of his will. He could do nothing but lie in his bed, eyes closed, clinging to a small awareness of the world while he slipped easily, fluidly, in and out of consciousness.

The border between dream and reality was nothing now, transparent, dark with shadows. There were fish in the river. In the springtime and in autumn, he would stand ankle deep in the shallows and look down into the water. On the river's surface, and seeming to hang just below it in a hand's depth of water, the cottonwoods made a pattern of green so deep it was almost black. The edges of treetops showed ragged, frayed as torn paper, haloed and shot through by a white or yellow sky. And among the dark reflections, trout glided against the current. They came near to Clyde's bare skin if he held still enough, and if he was still, his feet sank down into silt softer than velvet. Under the silt—through it—the water flowed more sluggishly, and it was warm from the sun. In the fast-moving currents just above, cold as the mountain snows from which the river ran, the trout drew so near he could feel their tails stirring the water. A slow and gentle shift, a subtlety, the heightened nerves of his cold-shocked skin aware of the nearness of the fish before his eyes could pick out their spotted backs against a green-and-amber dappling of stone. That was the way he moved between the mundane world, the world of his farm and the Bemis homestead, and the world of his dreams—or if not dreams, then spirits. His mind, his awareness, his heart beating steadily, all moved as the trout moved through a cold shadow realm. Slow, side to side, slipping from the cover of deep-green reflection into the shallows and back again, never still long enough to be sure of where he was.

The pure, demanding whiteness of morning light glowed through his eyelids. He turned his face away, then lay exhausted by the movement. His mother was gone. He couldn't feel her presence anymore—not in his bedroom, not in the house. Outside, he could hear his sheep bleating. They were still shut up in the fold. Someone must let them out, but who? The fall ewes would begin lambing soon, but the timing was bad. Early as the ewes were, the rains had come earlier still. It might be that no lamb would survive, unless Clyde could reach every ewe before her labor began. He would bed them down in the barn with deep straw to keep their young ones warm and dry.

It doesn't matter, Substance said. Clyde could hear his father's voice very near, ringing just over his right shoulder, though Clyde was lying flat in his bed. No one could truly be standing there behind him, menacing him.

If any lambs die in the rain, then they were too weak to survive. God's will.

They're helpless things, Clyde protested. *Shouldn't we give them a chance to survive, if it's in our power to do it?*

Substance seemed to laugh—the short, cruel chuckle that had always made Clyde's backbone feel as if it had been set on fire. Once, the day after he and Substance had burned a pile of brush, Clyde had walked past the charred circle and found tendrils of smoke rising from the earth. He had dug into the soil with the heel of his boot and exposed a tree root, gnarled in its long, secretive, ancient course. It had carried the heat of the fire underground, where it still burned, unseen. Now the root was a long, twisted core of ember, white ash cracked by thin lines of glowing red. That was how Substance's laugh had always made Clyde feel.

Substance said, *If you care so much about pampering sheep, then you're weaker than a woman, and no son of mine.*

The anger and hurt those words roused gave Clyde just enough strength to open his eyes. He was looking at the wall of his bedroom, whitewashed, blurred, and there were footsteps receding, somebody walking away from him. Out the door, down the hall, descending the stairs. He followed the sound and discerned that the tread was light, the stride short. Not his mother, then. He knew the rhythm of those feet after so many days working at Beulah's side. Where had his mother gone? Nettie Mae had sat beside him for hours—for days, as far as Clyde could tell. A familiar stillness, her long habit of watchful waiting. Clyde shut his eyes again; the whiteness of his room pained him. He recalled Nettie Mae's hand resting on his brow, brushing back his hair. Then she had walked away—out of the bedroom, out of their home.

You're weaker than a woman, and no son of mine.

I'm the only son you have, Clyde said to his father's memory.

Substance made no answer. He was gone now, if he had ever really been there. Gone, but the terrible heat remained, throbbing down Clyde's back. He could all but see it, the whiteness of his bones, each small bit of spine spaced as evenly as the seasons. And the black lines between, and the embers glowing within, threads of red against the darkness.

There was one way to be a man—only one. Any other way a man had of being was wrong, all wrong. Substance had taught Clyde that much. You do not pamper sheep; a man does not coddle his flock. You let God take what He wishes to take, and you shut your ears to the crying of the ewes when they stand over the lifeless bodies of their lambs. They are animals, nothing more. They do not think, do not feel. To go tender for the sheep, to balk at taking a rooster's head, to feel pity for the deer you fell with a single shot from your rifle—these things are weak. To be weak is to be womanish. To be like a woman is to be unlike a man.

That was why Substance had been all the things he had been: fist and boot, hard eye and hateful mouth. Because he had been a man, and a man was not a woman.

The heat lurched up Clyde's backbone. Up toward his neck, his throat. Down into his gut, where it made him feel so sick he wanted to heave and spit it from his mouth, no matter how it might burn coming up. But to gasp and choke in the grip of illness was to be weak and womanish, too.

You aren't here anymore, Clyde said to his father. *You're gone now—gone forever.*

Substance said nothing. He wasn't there.

There were other ways to be, Clyde knew. The ram in the fold was not a man, but he was male. Clyde could see him now, leading his flock out into the sagebrush to feed, patient and steady as he walked into the low summer sun, though it was autumn now, and rainy. The ram defended his own, but he didn't brutalize the ewes. He never harried his young nor drove them away. And Joe Buck. How many times had the horse stood in quiet acceptance, allowing Clyde to hide his tears in the coarse, dark hairs of his mane?

Once, Clyde had gone to Joe Buck and hidden his face against the horse's neck. And after a time, when Clyde's tears had run dry, the horse had whickered in surprise, and Clyde had looked up, more curious now than he was hurt. A few yards away, in a patch of trampled grass, he had seen three young jackrabbits playing. Clyde held so still at Joe Buck's side that the rabbits hadn't known he was there. He watched them chase one another in the sunlight, in the drone of cicada song. Running, skipping, boxing with their paws. He could see the jackrabbits again now, but from above, like a hawk gliding over the plain. Dark bodies sharply defined against the white glare, brown and distinct as figures carved in wood. The rabbits ran in a circle, faster, faster still, until their rapid legs blurred and then their bodies, until all Clyde could see with any clarity was the creatures' long ears. There were three rabbits; Clyde was certain of that. Yet he could count only three ears. There should have been six. He blinked—the hawk blinked—and then he understood. If he narrowed his eyes and focused, he could pick each rabbit out of the blur of motion, see each animal whole. Every jackrabbit in the circle sported two long ears, after the usual fashion, but as each ear tapered to its point, that point merged with the skull of the next rabbit, so that every animal shared its body with the others. There were three rabbits, and yet not three. What seemed an individual, whole and distinct, was tied inextricably to its neighbors. You couldn't separate one rabbit from the circle. If you did, you broke the chain, deprived the remaining lives of wholeness. The jackrabbits were more than merely connected; none could have existed without the others.

Someone entered Clyde's bedroom again. His mother—or the memory of Substance, brooding, hanging near the threshold. Clyde shifted on the mattress. The bedstead squeaked when he moved, and the sound was far too loud. He winced, squinting toward the window. His eyes watered heavily, but he could tell that the light was thinner and higher. The morning had grown late, so suddenly. Or perhaps he had slept without dreaming.

"Who?" Clyde's voice was so thin, so dry, he could scarcely hear it.

"It's me. Beulah."

She stepped away from the door and moved to Clyde's bedside where he could see her. She was holding a pitcher of water with both hands, and she set it on the small table near his pillow. A stack of clean cloths waited there, too. She dipped a rag in the water and wrung it out, then laid it, cool and soft, on his forehead.

"Can you sit up?"

Clyde attempted it, but his arms were trembling—weak. He fell back on his pillow.

"Never mind."

She soaked another rag and held it to his lips. Confused, Clyde drew back.

"You're powerful dried out," Beulah said. "You'll have to suck on this rag to get a little water in you. Like a baby sucking pap. Come on, now; don't be shy. We were all babies once."

Clyde knew it was shameful—the greatest shame—for a man to be coddled so, treated like a delicate infant. But thirst racked him, searing the back of his throat. All at once, he could feel the thickness of his own blood, its sluggish, labored pounding in his veins. He took the dripping rag into his mouth and sucked. The first mouthful of water was such a relief that it made him giddy. It tasted sweet and green. The river was full, fed by autumn rains, and the well was generous.

Beulah soaked the rag again and held it while Clyde drank. When she made as if to dunk it in the pitcher a third time, Clyde shook his head, and she lowered herself to the bedside stool.

"The sheep," Clyde said.

"I've let them out to graze. I'll bring them in again at sundown."

"The ewes."

"None have lambed yet. There's time still."

But not much time. Clyde must get up, must spread new straw in the barn, no matter what Substance thought. Joe Buck would be watching from the corral while he worked. A yellow horse standing stark against a heavy blue sag of rain cloud.

"You'll need more water and some food before you're fit to get out of bed," Beulah said, as if she could hear Clyde's thoughts.

"What happened to me?"

She answered lightly. "Caught sick by all the rain, I guess."

"Am I . . . am I bad?" He felt as if he must be. The burning in his back was relentless, the thirst still demanding, though he wanted answers now more than he wanted to drink. He must get up, yet the mere thought of doing so hollowed him out.

But he had asked the question he'd feared to ask. The thing was done. All that remained now was to hear Beulah's answer. Whatever it was, Clyde would accept it. He had little choice.

"Heavens, no," she said with a laugh. "You ain't bad; just weak from not drinking all night long. Your mother should have made you drink, but I guess she was sore afraid for you and couldn't think straight. She loves you a powerful lot, you know. I can tell by the way she looks at you."

"Mother is downstairs," Clyde said. It wasn't a question, but he did seek reassurance, for he couldn't hear her moving down in the kitchen, couldn't feel Nettie Mae at all.

"No," Beulah answered. "She rode to town. Thought you needed the doctor, though I told her you didn't. You'll be all right, and she'll see for herself, once she returns. Come on, now; suck up more of this water till you're strong enough to sit. I put some chicken soup on the fire. It'll be ready soon."

Clyde turned his head on the pillow, so he could see Beulah clearly. Her hair fell loose around her shoulders. There was a tiny leaf caught in one sparrow-brown lock, a dry autumn curl from an apple tree. Clyde wanted to pluck it out of her hair, but his hand was too weary to move. He wanted to take that leaf from her hair and hold it, enclose it in his fist, never let it go.

When she held the rag to his mouth again, he drank; and now, at last, some of his weakness gave way. Clyde struggled up till he was leaning against the headboard.

"Good," Beulah said. She poured water into a clay cup and placed it in Clyde's hand. "You sip this, real slow and easy, while I go down and check on the soup. And on the little ones. I had to bring them all over with me, for my ma's gone today, too. I told them I'd scald their backsides if they made a sound. You need your rest."

She vanished a moment later, so quickly that Clyde would have thought her a part of his fever dream if he hadn't heard the girl's feet on the stairs and then, low and tense, the murmur of her voice admonishing the children.

Distant sounds drifted in from outside, too, blending with the wordless rise and fall of the voices downstairs. The ram calling to his ewes, thin and small at the far end of the pasture. Birds chittering in the lilac trees out beside the barn. Far across the fields, at the Bemis homestead, the milk cows lowed, rising on an emphatic note, and Clyde thought he could hear the light, fleeting sounds of a sage thrasher singing by the river. He could hear the river itself, far away though it lay—a low, constant sigh of unending movement. Clyde sat with the cup gripped in both hands, steady on his lap, and listened. Beulah and the children, birds and sheep and river, he heard them all, each voice distinct. And then, as he listened to each in turn—to every voice at once—the sounds blended and merged. They stretched, reaching beyond their respective boundaries, the walls of the house or the bodies of the animals, and suddenly Clyde lost the distinctive notes. All became one vast, concerted hum. Everything he heard, he heard as a singular voice, and the voice sang in harmony with the heat that still flowed up and down his back, the ember that burned inside him.

He closed his eyes, but he still saw Beulah's face and the hair hanging down across her shoulder. The leaf caught up in those thin brown strands. She was downstairs in the kitchen, but she was also beside him, and her voice was one of many singing an endless chord. Clyde and Beulah were a part of the whole—two limbs of one body—as were the others, the blackbirds trilling beside the barn and the river breathing down the long, smooth course of its banks. There were two families, two farms, but the lines drawn between them were dissolving now, just as the trout in the shallows dissolved the boundary between light and shadow, between water and fish. There was but one land, one reality, and everything that moved beneath the boundless sky shared itself with its neighbors.

The cup tipped on Clyde's lap, and he tightened his grip before the water could spill. He opened his eyes and drank, lifting the cup to his lips with both trembling hands. When he leaned back against the headboard, he could feel the water at work inside him, cooling what remained of the fever, returning strength to his body.

I'm not going to die yet, Clyde thought defiantly.

He half expected Substance to answer, but it was Beulah's voice he seemed to hear, asserting itself over the chorus of life just loud enough that Clyde could pick out her words.

Not yet, she said. *It's not your time to fall apart.*

He heard the kitchen door open, then close, and heard no movement below. Beulah and the children had left the house. Clyde pivoted carefully on his sweat-damp sheets, slung his legs over the edge of the bed, and stood, clinging to the bedstead with both hands. After a few moments of uncertainty, his legs firmed and held his weight.

Clyde shuffled to the window, still holding the bed for security. He brushed back a curtain and peered out at the world. The sky was still heavy, but the clouds had thinned enough to admit a diffuse, pearl-white glare of late-morning light. He looked down from the height of his window to the patched yellow and green of autumn pasture. Sheep were moving out near the hedge that held them back from the riverside, small and pale, square amid countless ripples of bending grass. The children played in the yard below, chasing one another through the wet grass, leaping over Nettie Mae's herb patch. Beulah stood watching their game, hands on hips, unwearied by a long day's work. She turned to face the barn. An instant later, the blackbirds sang.

4

Root and Branch

Just before sundown, my ma returned, rounding the shoulder of the hill in our rattly old wagon. I watched from Nettie Mae's kitchen window— watched the wagon pick up speed, for Ma was eager to leave the dreadful lonesomeness of the forest behind her. But she drew up short outside our barn, and even across the pasture, I could see a new tension take her, a kind of fear. It took me a moment to realize what had upset her. She had expected the little ones to come running out to greet her, but our gray house was silent except for the hens darting and fluttering in the yard.

Come on, I said to my brothers and sister. Ma's come back with the wagon, and I bet she'll be powerful hungry. Let's all go over and I'll fix us a bite of supper. Then I must come back and see to Clyde, for I promised Nettie Mae I would stay with him till she gets back from Paintrock.

By the time I'd rounded up the little ones and guided them out of the Webbers' yard, Ma had abandoned the wagon with our horse still cross in his harness; I could see him lashing his tail, vexed and sore. Ma was hur- rying over the pasture toward the Webber house. I could tell by the way she ran that she was near-about frantic with worry. When I appeared with the little ones, she stopped in her tracks. Her shoulders sagged, and she tipped her face up toward the heavy sky. I could all but hear Ma's prayer of gratitude.

When we reached her, Ma gathered up the little ones and hugged them so tightly the boys became embarrassed and twisted away. She wrapped me in her arms, too, and I could feel their trembling, the bone-deep exhaustion that had wrung her out like a well-used rag.

Thank God you're all right, Ma said. When I came home to an empty house, I thought . . . Never mind what I thought. You're all safe; that's what matters.

I explained about Clyde's illness and how Nettie Mae had come riding over that morning to plead for my help.

Nettie Mae, asking our aid? Ma shook her head. Wonders never cease. How does Clyde fare?

He's dandy, I said. He never was in any danger, and I told Nettie Mae so. But she wouldn't listen.

No, Ma said, I suppose she wouldn't. She doesn't know you the way I do, Beulah dear.

Then Ma clapped her hands and shooed the children toward the house, promising them supper, though I could see she hadn't the strength to fix it. I didn't mind. There were biscuits and cheese in the pantry, and a good smoked ham for sandwiches. Ma would be glad of my help.

The little ones ran ahead, but I hung back and walked at my mother's side—slowly, which seemed the only pace she could manage. I noticed how her hands clenched and flexed, as if she were testing their mettle. Her dark hair was wild, locks pulled out of the tight bun and blown askew by the mountain winds. I could smell her sweat, too—a sour smell, thick with desperation.

Did you get a good load of wood? I asked.

No—oh, no, I should say not.

There was a dreadful catch in her voice. In another moment, I knew, she would begin weeping.

Beulah, it was a miserable day. Alone up there in the hills, in that sinister forest. I worked until I could scarcely stand, until I was all but done in. But I hardly gathered more than a few sticks of wood.

She raised her hands, pressing them to her face, and I caught a glimpse of the blisters on her palms—angry, white, already leaking their stinging honey.

Oh, what are we to do? Ma wailed. This rain . . . Snow can't be far off. We must have wood—we must! But I cannot gather it myself; that much is plain to me now.

You can buy firewood up at Paintrock, I said. Men go out into the foothills to cut it. They sell it by the wagonload.

But we have no money. Ma whispered those words, for shame at her plight—and, I suppose, shame at her weakness—robbed her of breath.

I said easily, Then we must trade for our wood.

What ought we to trade? I've nothing of any value, and I don't dare trade away any food. Not with an early winter looming just ahead.

We had reached the porch steps by then, so I patted my ma on her weary back to brace her up and quiet her. I didn't want her frightening the children.

I'll work something out, I said. Don't you worry.

But I knew she would go on fretting, for my mother had never learned to trust in the land to provide.

Nettie Mae returned with the doctor long after dark. I went out with a lantern to greet them and to take in the doctor's horse, and when Nettie Mae hurried inside, she was pleased and startled to find Clyde lounging on the parlor settee, bundled up to his chin with good, thick blankets. I had fed him on soup and boiled potatoes, and he was looking fine and sturdy, as thoroughly out of danger as the doctor pronounced him to be.

Once she had settled the doctor in for the night in an upstairs room, Nettie Mae stood awkwardly before me, shuffling her feet and failing to meet my eye.

I must thank you, she said, rather grudgingly. I'm grateful for your help, and . . . and for the good care you gave Clyde.

It ain't worth mentioning, I answered.

But Nettie Mae insisted. She said, *Without you, I might have gone mad with fear. But Clyde is well; that's all I care about. You were very neighborly, girl. Your mother could learn a valuable lesson by emulating her daughter.*

The rain stayed on for a few days more, sheeting down relentlessly, both day and night. Ma and I ventured outside only to tend our animals, who were restless and cross from the small choice we'd given them: stay shut up in their coops and barns or venture out to feed in the downpour. Ma was terrible afraid the cows would catch scald, for we had no tar left to treat their wounds if they did. We lost two young pullets to rattlers who found their way into the coop, sheltering from wind and wet.

My brothers and sister were every bit as restless as our animals, for they weren't allowed to step foot out of doors under any circumstances, not even to visit the outhouse. Ma made them use their nighttime chamber pots; she went out to empty the pots herself, and came back each time looking as if she'd been soaked in the laundry kettle and run only partway through the wringer.

I kept the children occupied as best I could with stories and games. But when my stories lost their luster, I fell to braiding straw, fashioning bracelets and necklaces with intricate weaving, which the boys used to play Indian chief and Miranda mostly sucked on. I kept one of the bracelets for myself, and when the rain broke at last and the skies were more forgiving, I ventured out to the riverbank to visit my neighbor's grave.

The grasses of the prairie had flushed out with green, recovering from months of parched heat in only a few days' time. Every blade and stem had been beaded with raindrops, and the land was like one great expanse of velvet, green on one side of the nap, silver on the other. When a breeze stirred, the grasses shifted, rippling from silver to green and back again, as if some vast, invisible hand were brushing the fabric of the prairie this way and that. As I walked through the cow pasture, sweeping the dark line of my path with my wet and heavy skirt, I watched the colors shift all along the field, down over the Webbers' land below, out to the twin ruts of the road. And even beyond, to the endless flat forever of the untouched prairie, where a flock of blackbirds had risen, black against a gray sky, all of them twisting and turning high above the earth, a dance of gladness in the brief respite between the storm that had passed and the storm yet to come.

I found the river high and vigorous, as I had expected, with the water encroaching on the cottonwoods, seeping up in wide puddles beside the trail and gleaming mirrorlike between small stones pressed into the soil. I wondered if we'd see enough autumn rains that the river would escape its banks entirely, and wash away the bones of the man buried so close to its shore. Maybe Substance would prefer that, I thought. Since he still insisted on remaining whole, stubbornly maintaining himself in defiance of death's natural order, he might at least enjoy a change of scenery.

When I reached his resting place, I saw that the wind and rain had put some of my gifts out of order. Many of the feathers had come dislodged from their stones and had blown into the nearby grasses, where they clung bedraggled and sodden. Some were gone altogether. The crow's skull had toppled down the shallow curve of the mound. I righted it, placing it on one end of the grave, where I thought Substance's head probably lay. Then I slipped the straw bracelet over my hand and set it among the other offerings.

You won't believe all that's happened, I told Substance. My ma actually went up into the hills alone. Can you imagine her doing such a thing?

His only response was a general feeling of contempt.

You needn't try to scorch me, I said. However little regard you held for my mother, she thought you ten times worse. She was only amusing herself, same as you were, but she's alive and you ain't.

Substance had no answer for that. I let the stillness exist between us for a while, blank and monotonous like the sound of the river running. I thought it might be good for him, to know that stillness. I thought it might inspire him to go. But after a time, I could tell he was still there, waiting for me to say something, hungry for the sound of a human voice.

I can tell you've got something more to say, I told Substance. But you'll have to say it without insulting my ma, for I won't hear a word against her.

She's a good woman—just lonesome and sad, for she thinks she's isolated here on the farm.

I didn't expect the answer I received. I felt what Substance had been feeling, those long days of rain when he'd lain there, immobile in the tight fist of earth while the new wild coldness of rainwater pressed down from above.

The grave is cold, he seemed to say. It's colder than I can bear.

Then don't bear it. All you need to do is unbecome.

And then such a mournful misery swept over me that I fell to my knees beside his cold, green-blanketed bed. He was waiting, Substance told me. He must remain where he was because he didn't know. He couldn't see what his son would become—whether Clyde would be safe, whether Clyde could survive without him.

I left my boy too soon, Substance told me. Though it was none of my doing, none of my choice to die when I did. My boy, my only son, the last child left to me. What will he become without me? And if he is to die—if he's too small to manage on his own—then I must shepherd him in death, for I failed to shepherd him in life.

My mind went blank and flat then, a slate wiped clean. I reached out into the world with every sense I had—sight and smell, the feel of rainwater soaking through my skirt to my bare knees. And all the senses besides, the ones for which there are no names, the ones that guide the birds in migration and tell the frogs to wake in spring and tell me all the things I need to know. I reached and waited and opened myself to the knowing. And then I saw Clyde as Substance saw him: a small boy, no taller than the prairie grass, wide eyed and quiet with fear. Clyde had always been this fragile, precious thing in Substance's reckoning, a child as easily lost as the rest had been. The final refrain in a litany of sorrow.

So that's why you were always so mean and hard, I said to Substance. That's why you hurt Clyde, and Nettie Mae, too. You wanted to make him stronger. You wanted them both to be strong. But you know now, don't you? You know you treated them rotten all those years. You were afraid for them,

Substance—afraid you would lose them both and be left with nothing, no family at all. So you hardened yourself and hoped the fear couldn't touch you. But once you've turned yourself to stone, love can't reach you, either.

Substance had no answer save for a terrible, writhing pain that sickened my stomach and loosened my bowels. There was a taste in my mouth like ash, dry and grim, yet strangely compelling. I had to take slow breaths and press my hand to my middle so I wouldn't be sick, and through the waves of nausea and shame I came to understand that I was feeling Substance's love. Or at least, I felt his regret over never having shown love properly before.

That's why you won't leave, I said. That's why you won't let go. You're hanging on till you know Clyde and Nettie Mae are safe. Or is it forgiveness you want? If it's forgiveness you're after, then I ain't sure you're entitled to it. The way you treated your son and your wife—was that what you called love? Darkening your hearth, making your family live in fear of your anger? And never allowing a kind word, nor any smallest affection?

He was angry with me. He didn't like to have it all laid bare—his weakness, his failings. Especially not now, when he couldn't get away.

I said, It ain't love to rage and lash out like a rabid dog. You didn't really love your wife, nor Clyde, either. You made them to worship you, same as they worship God, with fear and trembling. What love you had was all for yourself, not for anyone else. Not Nettie Mae, not your son, and not my mother, either. My good, kindly ma—you wanted her to love you, too. You wanted her to give and give of herself for your gratification, because you thought you deserved everything, all the time and attention and tenderness of everyone within your sight. But now here you are, caught like a pebble under the ground. Now you see you're as small and insignificant as any other man. Now you see how ordinary you always were.

Substance met my tirade with silence, but there was a calmness to it, a peace I'd never thought to find beside his grave. I was right, and he knew it. The coldness of the earth, its undeniable weight, had humbled him at last. He would make no more argument—at least not that day.

Help me, he seemed to say. Or if you won't help me, then help Clyde. He's but a young thing. He hasn't had his life yet. And now that I'm gone, and he's got a real chance for happiness, it'd be an injustice for him to die so soon, to fall prey to this wilderness. Help him, please, girl. I can do nothing.

I will, I said. The memory of autumn rain still surrounded Substance and chilled him, made him eager to hear my words. If I can be of any help to Clyde, in anything, you can rest assured I will. But not for your sake. I'll do it for him, and for me—for the sake of what we will become.

I could see it then, what we would become. Not only Clyde and me, but everyone, everything—all that lived and breathed and grew on our two farms, reaching roots and branches across the boundary lines, merging into one. The fragmented parts we once had been could fit so easily together.

CLYDE

Roots and branches and chips of pine, roughly split from the log—Clyde took every stick, every sliver George Crowder had for sale.

"It isn't the prettiest load of firewood I've ever hauled down from the foothills," George said, pulling the felt cap from his balding head. He mopped the sweat from his pate with a grimy rag that he extracted from a trouser pocket. "By rights, I ought to have cut sounder pieces. But it's bitterly cold up there in the hills already. I feared if I drove any higher up the trail, I would run into snow, what with all the rain we've seen of late."

"Doesn't matter what it looks like." Clyde tossed another armful of wood into his wagon. "Only matters that it'll burn."

"As to that, this wood must be seasoned, or it won't burn at all. Or at least, not much."

Clyde grunted, nodded, and went on stacking the jumble of branches and gnarled pine roots as best he could. One piece tumbled from the top of the pile and rolled down the side. Clyde paused, cautious, waiting to see whether the heap of pine would hold or whether another cascade would break loose. He had lost count of how many times those uneven scraps of wood had clattered and rolled along the wagon bed already. Clean, well-cut logs would have stacked much more securely, tight and sound against the long miles that lay between Paintrock and the Bemis homestead. But George Crowder was the only fellow Clyde had found who had plenty of fuel for sale. Beggars couldn't be choosers, as his mother often said.

"Do you have a good spot for seasoning wood?" George asked. He passed another bundle of pine up to the wagon bed, and Clyde did his best to position the pieces. "Someplace dry, and out of the wind?"

"Yessir. There's plenty of space in the barn. I've seasoned wood every year since I was knee high to a frog. Don't you worry about me none, Mr. Crowder."

George flushed. "Of course you have. Look at you; a big, strapping . . . er . . ."

The man turned away for another load of wood before Clyde could see his blush deepen. He had very nearly called Clyde a boy. *That's how he sees me. Too young for common sense, and helpless now that I've lost my father.*

Clyde's first impulse was to make some smart retort, but he thought better and let Mr. Crowder's comment pass. He wasn't likely to find another source of wood today—and with the weather taking such a quick and decisive turn, he might not have a chance to return to Paintrock till the spring thaw came. *And anyway,* Clyde thought, *I guess every fella who ever lived has been where I am now. No longer a boy, but not exactly a man.* There was no sense in getting sore.

"I sure am grateful to you," Clyde said, by way of smoothing over the rough patch between them. "This wood might not be the prettiest a fella ever cut, but it'll keep a fire going in the hearth all winter long."

George straightened from his woodpile with a sheepish grin. The smile faded when he met Clyde's eye.

"Say, Clyde. You're looking peaky. Are you well?"

"Had a bit of a fever, few days past. I'm dandy now, though."

Clyde still felt hollowed out by that dreadful illness. His legs trembled; every load of wood he accepted from George Crowder's arms seemed to weigh twice what the last had. He had found his chores slow going since rising from his sickbed but had comforted himself with the knowledge that strength and vigor would soon return. Now, however,

Clyde's certainty was fading. The quiver in his limbs and the strange void in his middle had lingered unabated. He feared he might remain as useless as a toddler all the rest of his days.

George and Clyde wedged the final pieces of wood in the wagon bed. The load filled all but the last few feet of space, and Clyde felt he had packed the ill-fitting pieces tightly enough that the weight wouldn't shift on the long drive home. George helped him stretch a piece of oiled canvas across the bed, from wall to wall, and secure it with a few frayed pieces of rope. Then Clyde reached into his pocket.

"How much did you say, again?"

"Thirteen."

Clyde wouldn't allow himself to wince. The price was high—especially for branches and poorly cut pieces. But the Bemises couldn't hope to survive the winter without that supply. There was nothing for it but to pay. He counted thirteen dollars into Crowder's palm, then shook the man's hand and climbed up into the seat. The sooner he made for home, the better. The sky was a patchwork of blue and gray; God alone could tell whether the rain would come drifting back that afternoon, catching Clyde cold and exposed on the lonesome road.

At least the two bay fillies would pay no heed to the rain, if foul weather caught them on the homeward journey. Clyde had spent the summer training the pair and breaking them to the harness—and now, on their first drive to Paintrock, he felt certain he had chosen the fillies well. They had already proved both sensible and biddable, for Clyde had put them through the most rigorous of paces since recovering from his fever. True, the fillies were still young, so Clyde kept a sharp eye out for signs of flightiness. But even driving rain hadn't upset them. The bays had worked eagerly around both farms, despite the pall of weather that had dulled recent days, and he took no small amount of pride in them. If his strength—his very worth as a man—remained a matter of question, at least no one could say that his reputation as a horseman had suffered from the fever.

Clyde put George Crowder's acreage to his back. The road broadened, revealing Paintrock just ahead. The bays stepped out smartly when Clyde flicked the reins and clucked for a little speed, though their ears turned and their tails lashed in protest at the new weight of the laden wagon. Clyde soothed his fillies with sweet words, and they settled at once, trusting to his voice and his hands. He would hate to part with them someday, when they were fully trained, broke to the saddle and tested in their mettle. But what a fine price they might bring. With two households to care for—at least till Ernest Bemis was let out of jail—Clyde would need every penny he could get.

Wind rippled over the prairie, bending sage and spent grasses, moving in arrowhead waves of silver and palest green. A band of cloud stretched overhead, shadowy and ash gray, and a scatter of stray raindrops fell across the road. Each drop seemed to hang in isolation, golden and luminous, struck by a sideways slant of light. The rain drummed on the brim of Clyde's hat. A few drops ran around its edge, gathering in a fat globe that hung for a moment at the corner of his vision, glinting and blue. Then the drop broke under its own weight, spattering on the wagon seat beside him.

He looked at the place where the drop had fallen, a circle of darkness on aged wood, the edges splayed and reaching. Like the soil darkened and wet under his father's body.

Clyde swallowed hard, willing his heart to steadiness within his hollow chest. All that morning, well before dawn, as he'd hitched the bay fillies to the wagon and taken to the road, Clyde had felt thick and stupid, burdened by more than the weakness that trailed in the fever's wake. Fear had followed him then. It trailed after him still. A terrible, stark certainty that now, at last, grief or anger over his father's death would overtake him and he would weep. But out there, below a patchwork of cloud, Clyde found nothing more terrible waiting for him than a blunt, easy acceptance. His father was dead. Substance was as gone now, as absent from the world, as the cicadas were absent from the wet sagebrush, as the birds from the weeping sky. And in the suddenness of Substance's departure, Clyde had done what needed doing. There was no reason to grieve, no reason to rail. The sun rose farther to the south each day. The year, like life, carried on.

One of the fillies tossed her head, shying at a rut in the road. Clyde steadied both horses with the reins, but the wagon lurched and bumped, striking the rut at a shallow angle. Something rattled around Clyde's boots, jumping and scooting with the vibrations of the road. He glanced down. A corn seed shivered between his heels. The seed must have fallen into a crack and wedged itself there . . . and all at once it was Beulah, not Substance, who sprang up in his mind. The girl appeared as if she were really there before him, as if she sat astride the near filly, backward, watching Clyde with those solemn, knowing, inescapable eyes. He blinked and told himself not to be a fool. He was still under the grip of fever. He stared hard at the bay filly's back—naked save for the harness, no rider, no girl, hide dappled by the light rain—and he wished he were at home instead, breaking his back over double chores with no time to stop and think, no time to dwell in the undergrowth of his mind.

But Clyde wasn't at home. He was twenty miles away, and his team didn't offer much in the way of distracting conversation. Soon he could see Beulah's wrists again—couldn't escape the memory—then the curve of her back as she stooped, picking up cornstalks. Her back was like a sapling bent toward the earth: lively with all its young strength, quick to spring up when you let go your hold. He shouldn't be thinking of Beulah that way, not after what her father had done. And his mother would never forgive him if she found out he'd taken a shine to the Bemis girl. But he had taken a shine; there was little sense denying it now. That odd girl with her dreamy habits, her way of seeming half cut loose from reality. Beulah had taken up residence in Clyde's imagination. There seemed no point in telling her to leave.

I guess it's only natural, he told himself. He was a young fellow, and didn't young fellows always go staring and mooning after girls about their age? The corn seed skittered from one side of the toeboard to the other. Clyde kicked it away and sent it flying out into the grass.

There was more to this business with Beulah than mooning and staring, though. Clyde could admit that much. Something about the girl both haunted and compelled him, something beyond the mere fact of her femaleness. She had a *way*. With the farm, the animals, with Clyde himself. Beulah's calm demeanor didn't seem quite natural—her unflappable acceptance of all things. Men and women alike struggled through life, struggled *for* life. Wasn't the fight life itself? The force you needed, the sudden bearing down, to sink a plow into hard soil. The sweat and the strain as you held a ewe for shearing. Even in winter, when the land hid itself beneath snow, a body was obliged to fight against the chill and the dark. There was the daily toil of rising from your cold bed to a colder morning, then a march through snow, knee deep or waist deep, to tend your shivering animals. There was the soreness in your hips at the end of every winter day, that tight, particular pain from lifting and placing each foot among the deep drifts, left then right, left then right, every day a drawn-out agony, nights never restful enough. That was the way of life. That was the struggle.

The fact that Beulah did not or would not struggle filled Clyde with mistrust equal to his wonder. It wasn't as if the girl didn't work. She had labored beside him from the first day, when he had cut the corn behind the Bemis house, and he had come to rely on her strength—surprising, in a small, slight, female body—almost as much as he relied on his own. Beulah was tireless, too. She never complained, never slowed, though her natural pace was never hasty. Amid the uncountable tasks of running a farm, she left time for what seemed to be her real occupation: watching, seeing, knowing. The beauty of the corn seeds, distinct and individual on their papery cob. The way the meadowlarks called and answered across the expanse of the Webber pasture. One bird would call, then pause, and Beulah would point to the other end of the pasture just in time for another lark to answer. As if the birds sang to her well-timed cue.

The girl knew something about the prairie. Or perhaps the prairie knew her. Beulah saw what none of them could understand—not Clyde or his mother, not Cora, not the rest of her ordinary children. What Beulah saw and what she knew both attracted and repelled him, for he could see and comprehend none of it himself. Now that he found himself alone with his own mind, at leisure to mull over Beulah, Clyde was disturbed by the girl. She wasn't even there beside him—and yet she was undeniably, forcefully present, coloring his thoughts like a view through tinted glass. Neither the patter of sporadic rain nor the sound of his fillies' hooves on the muddy road could drive Beulah from his head.

What would Substance think if he knew? Somehow, if Substance saw—looking down from a Heaven to which he was not entitled—what would he say, knowing his only son was helplessly drawn to that Bemis girl? Clyde entertained a sudden fantasy that Substance did know, and the possibility made him shiver. The memory of that man still stood like a monument everywhere, looming over the two homesteads, vast and dark as the Bighorn Mountains—and Clyde couldn't help but feel that his father still saw everything. He could all but hear his father berating him for foolishness, for weakness. Substance wearing that cold, unyielding expression, mocking Clyde for setting his sights on such a worthless female thing.

Clyde talked back to his father's shade. He'd never dared such a thing while his father still lived, but Substance was dead now and couldn't retaliate. *You wouldn't think any girl was worth a fella setting his sights on.*

The Substance of Clyde's imagination had no answer. The shade of memory departed from the wagon—flew off into the grass like the corn seed—and the wagon drove on, and Clyde was alone once more.

The wagon rolled into Paintrock. Clyde let out a long, slow breath, for the town offered plenty of distractions, and he welcomed the reprieve. He tipped back his head, studying the sky, trying to discern through the racing clouds exactly where the sun stood, how long he could allow himself to linger. It would be good to speak to other folks, to learn what news they had to tell. Maybe he'd find one of his friends, the fellows of his own age, and play a hand of cards or have a cup of sarsaparilla, and there would be neither need nor opportunity to humor the two ghosts who haunted his every thought—his father; the girl. The firewood hadn't left Clyde entirely destitute. He still had a few dollars in his pocket, which he had earned that summer by breaking two fine young colts to the saddle and selling them to the Paintrock sheriff. He could spare enough coin for a stop at the saloon, for that sarsaparilla—or maybe, now that he was the man of the Webber farm and there was no one to check him, he'd try a bit of ale. Clyde had been meaning to drink his first ale for a long time now. His father had always said he'd skin him alive if he caught him at it before he turned eighteen. But there wasn't much Substance could do about it now.

The wagon approached a white church surrounded by a fence of pointed palings and the headstones of the cemetery. Three girls lingered beside the gate, swinging folded parasols and murmuring over a paper box that one of them held. Clyde was gripped by a familiar compulsion, an urgent need to stare at the girls and a paradoxical shame at doing so. He kept his face turned toward the road, but his eye traveled back to the church gate—to the bright dresses and lively sway of their bodies. The girls had fixed their hair, and each was wearing white gloves and holding a paper box. Attending some party, Clyde assumed. One girl lifted the lid of her box; the others peered inside, then looked up grinning. Their eager smiles plucked at something in Clyde's stomach, and he didn't know whether he wanted to laugh or be sick over the side of his wagon.

One of the girls noticed Clyde. He looked away quickly, but she called out to him.

"Well, if it isn't Clyde Webber. Don't be a stranger, Clyde. Stop and say hello."

Against his better judgment, he drew rein. The bay fillies halted, snorting at the girls' colorful dresses.

"Hello," Clyde offered. He didn't know what else to say, and couldn't recall the young ladies' names, so he tipped his hat and prayed it was enough to satisfy.

"There's a baking contest at the church today," said the one who had called his name. Her hair was chestnut brown. "Why don't you come in and be a judge?"

"I . . . I can't tarry. Got to get back home before dark." He jerked his thumb over his shoulder and added, "Firewood."

The girls looked at one another. A wordless understanding passed among them.

"Don't you remember my name?" said the chestnut girl. "It'll just about break my heart if you've forgotten me."

"Oh, I . . ." Clyde swallowed. The reins felt sticky in his hands. "It's been a long spell since I came to town last."

The girl lifted something out of her box—a tart hardly bigger than a silver dollar, bright red at the center. "I'm Elsie Schoen. Land sakes, Clyde; one would think a gentleman would remember the girl he danced with at the spring jubilee." Elsie stared at Clyde, and he found he couldn't break her gaze. Her eyes were very large and blue, bluer than chicory flowers, and they seemed to pin him to the wagon seat. She bit into the tart, then licked a crumb from her lip. Clyde's face burned.

Giggling, the other two girls fell upon Elsie's shoulders. That quickness girls had, to whisper and laugh—it had always confounded Clyde. Now, after so long in Beulah's company, the feminine reaction of giggling struck him as repellent. He had to make his excuses and get away from Elsie and her friends. Somehow he felt sure he would meet some grim peril if he lingered in their company.

"I'm powerful sorry if I offended, Miss Elsie. You do dance lovely, though. Now I must be off, or I won't make it home before dark. Good day to you all."

He tipped his hat again and clucked to the bays. But another girl shouted after him.

"Wait, Clyde. You'd best stop in at the post."

He turned in the seat; another girl was hurrying along beside his wagon.

"You don't recall me either, I guess," she said, "but I'm the post-master's daughter. My pa is about ready to curse your mama's name."

Clyde stopped his horses again. "My mother? Why? What has she done?"

"Stopped in to see him a few days ago," the girl said. "He's had a big shipping crate taking up space in his back room for weeks now. Can't find a soul to take it down to the Bemis farm. Your ma said she would send Mrs. Bemis up for the crate, but Pa hasn't seen hide nor hair of anyone from down south at Ten Sleep. You'd better go get that crate, before Pa sets it afire."

"I ain't heard a thing about a shipping crate. Mother never mentioned it."

The girl shrugged. She offered up her paper box. "Want a tart? They're made with raspberry jam. I'm going to beat Elsie's cherry tarts in the competition. I do every year."

Clyde helped himself to a raspberry tart, but he hardly tasted its sweetness, for talk of his mother had raised a new swell of anxiety in his stomach. He guessed by now Nettie Mae had found his note on the kitchen table. He'd left it under the saltcellar, then crept from the house before dawn.

Dear Mother,
I've gone to town to buy a load of wood to see Mrs. Bemis
through the winter. I know you don't love her any, but I
can't let a woman and small children suffer and maybe
die, even if that woman got my father killed. You can be
sore at me when I get home, but my mind is made up. I'll
be home by dark, or maybe a little after.

Clyde suspected he might be rather sore himself, when he finally returned to the farm. What was his mother thinking, allowing a delivery to languish at the Paintrock post?

If I can't find some way to reconcile my mother and Cora Bemis, we'll
all of us have one Hell of a miserable winter.

CORA

Root and branch, she had found her family tree. And the confirmation, after so many long and desolate years, was enough to make Cora weep—with gratitude, with shock, with the knowledge she had been vindicated at last. Vindication had come too late to preserve her life in Saint Louis, too late to save her from the prairie, but it was a measure of justice all the same. That small scrap of justice was the most valuable thing she had, and she clung to it like a treasure.

"Go on and open it, Ma," Beulah said. "Don't make us wait!"

Cora pulled a kerchief from her sleeve and wiped her eyes. She stared for a moment at the sealed crate—a moment more, just a moment to savor the sight of it, solid and undeniable, those perfect green words painted on the lid. The wood was damp from the long drive, the day's scattering of rain.

Clyde had been so good, to haul the heavy crate all that long way, which was to say nothing of the firewood he had provided. That young man's generosity was enough to make Cora weak with gratitude—and with shame, knowing how her careless ways had changed the course of his young life forever. Every kindness Clyde offered only drove the blade of regret deeper into Cora's middle, and every kindness made her love the Webber boy all the more.

Clyde came in from the yard. Evening had settled, but a thin gray light still hung above the prairie, caught between the clouds and the land. The boy had fetched an iron crow from the barn. He offered it to Cora while the children skipped around him, unruly with excitement.

Cora shook her head. "I don't think I'm strong enough to pry it open. Will you do it, please?" She still felt shy, inadequate even to speak in the Webber boy's presence.

"Yes, ma'am, if you like."

Clyde stepped forward, into the ruddy hearth light where he and Beulah had set the heavy crate just a few minutes before. He worked the end of the crowbar beneath the edge of the lid and leaned his weight against it. The lid gave way with a loud squeal, nails sliding through wood. Bits of straw packing lifted into the air as the lid came away. They settled at once to the floor.

"What is it, Ma?" Beulah approached the crate. The children followed, tearing at the packing; they thought it an excitement equal at least to Christmas Eve.

Clyde pulled Charles and Benjamin back. "All right now, you two rascals. Let your mother be the first to see. Whatever's inside this crate was meant for her, after all."

Cora came forward, tentative, reluctant, half-afraid that now this would all prove a dream. She would wake suddenly in her cold bedroom, in her half-empty bed, and she would still be herself—only Cora Bemis, a woman of no account, the farm wife who couldn't even manage her own farm. No place in the city that Cora could claim, and no real place in the wilderness, either. Then Beulah brushed aside a little more straw, revealing a wax-sealed folio. She handed it to Cora. The moment Cora touched the paper—substantial, every grain of it lively beneath her fingertips—she knew it was real. She opened the letter and read.

> *Dear Mrs. Bemis,*
> *It has come to my attention that a great wrong has been*
> *done to you and to your late mother by a certain member*
> *of the Grant family. This is a fault that must be duly*

*corrected. I hope you will accept this set of fine china as
my apology, on behalf of all the Grants, for any suffering
you may have endured on account of certain unsavory
elements within our family.*

I hope this letter finds you well and thriving.

With sincerity,

President Ulysses S. Grant

Relief scoured Cora, so strong, so sudden, it was more than she could bear. A great hollow place opened between her ribs and filled with rising warmth, as water fills a trench, flooding up from below. She took up her kerchief again, pressed it to her eyes, and wept into it with great, racking sobs. She felt Beulah take the paper from her hand. There was a long pause while the girl read, for distractible as she was, she had never been a strong reader. Then Beulah asked, "What does all this mean, Ma?"

Cora swallowed her next few sobs and blew her nose as delicately as she could manage. She took a few deep, shuddering breaths to calm herself. Beulah had, by then, passed the letter to the Webber boy. He read it by the light of the hearth, shaking his head slowly in puzzlement.

"They've finally acknowledged me." Cora's voice was small and frail, even to her own ears, even in her moment of vindication. "The Grant family. And to have it come from the president himself . . ."

"You're family to President Grant?" Clyde said.

He passed the letter back to Cora; she folded it carefully and ran her thumb over the wax seal. The seal bore the impression of the White House. She had only ever seen a few engravings of the White House in papers back in Saint Louis, but it looked exactly as she remembered, with the pillars and the high-arched dome.

"I'm President Grant's niece," Cora said. "I *am*."

How many times had she insisted as much at the parties, the balls, while the well-bred ladies of Saint Louis laughed behind their hands, and the gentlemen—among whom she had always hoped to find a husband—shook their heads in pity and looked the other way? Now she could say those words, *I am his niece, I am*, with conviction, not with desperation. *Our family,* the president had written. Certain unsavory elements within *our family*. She was one of them. She belonged to the Grants—and to the man who had been the great general, hero of the war. Now he was more than a general, even more than a hero. Grant had become something greater than anyone in Saint Louis had imagined he could be. And he was Cora's uncle. His family and his glory were also her own.

The truth had finally been acknowledged. It was enough.

"I never knew that about you, Ma." Beulah sifted through the straw and cotton again. She found a sauceboat and held it up to the light. The gloss of its white body, the rounded belly, shone like a beacon in the dimness of the kitchen. A delicate tracery of blue flowers and leaves ran around the lip of the sauceboat, along with an unbroken line of gold. "Would you look at that," Beulah said.

"Set it on the table there. You and I can unpack the lot." Cora wagged a finger at her unruly boys and little Miranda, who was sucking her thumb while she eyed the crate with suspicion. "You little ones keep away. I won't have you breaking anything with your carelessness."

Together, Cora and her daughter delved into the crate, uncovering one gilded treasure after another, stacking the plates and teacups on the kitchen table. How strange they looked together, the elegant china and the rough-hewn table with its pitted surface, its cracked wood stained by blackberries and hen's blood. Cora told the story while they worked.

"My mother's name was Lydia," she said. "Lydia van Voorhees. She came here from Holland with her father when she was a young girl, and they settled in Saint Louis. My grandfather had been a man of some means back in Holland, and he had always meant to rejoin better society in America. But he fell on difficulty, and was obliged to work so hard that he never found a chance to rise above his lot. But he always held great hope for Lydia's prospects. She was a pretty girl—that's what Grandfather always told me. Pretty as a picture, and so sweet tempered, one would think she was an angel come down to earth."

"You talk as if you never knew her," Beulah said.

"I did not know my mother."

It was strange, that Cora's voice should catch a little now, for she had never dwelt on her mother's story before with any particular sadness. Lydia's fate had always seemed the origin of Cora's own, a blunt fact that couldn't be altered, and Cora had faced up to it with the same resigned acceptance with which she had faced the other grim events of her life. But now, working beside her own daughter—who was not many years younger than Lydia had been when she'd fallen in love—the tragedy of female frailty struck Cora with its stark injustice.

She set a gold-rimmed plate atop the others and pressed on. "I never knew her, except through my grandfather's stories, and he didn't speak of Lydia often . . . though whenever he did, I could tell how much he loved her. She had been his only child—all he had left after his wife died back in Holland. Grandfather had hoped Lydia would marry well in America and become a woman of status. She would have made a fine wife for any gentleman—sweet, beautiful, and kind. And she was a trusting soul, I'm afraid. Too trusting, really, for her own good.

"When Lydia was fifteen, Grandfather began sending her to parties and dances. He didn't have much money by then, but whatever he had, he put into Lydia, buying her the most beautiful dresses and seeing that her hair was always fixed well. He had hoped she would attract the attention of a good suitor, you see—a man who would court her and marry her, and care for her as Grandfather found himself unable to do.

"One night at a ball, she did meet a man—but not the sort of man Grandfather had wished for. His name was Samuel Grant. He talked sweetly to Lydia, I suppose, and coaxed her into . . ." Cora glanced from Beulah to Clyde and back again, then busied herself brushing flecks of cotton from a teapot. "He coaxed her into iniquity. Lydia thought her-self in love. She was young and foolish enough to believe that scoundrel loved her in return, and would do right by her and marry her. I'm sure my grandfather hoped for the same, but all too soon, Samuel fled Saint Louis, leaving my mother to face her shame alone. What more is there to say? I was born soon after, but Lydia died of a fever days after I came into the world.

"My grandfather raised me as if I were his own daughter. He poured all the love and hope he had once given to Lydia into me. I had the best of everything—the best he could afford, at any rate—but as I grew older, we both came to understand that I would find small welcome among the upper crust of Saint Louis. You see, Samuel Grant had a brother, and that brother had distinguished himself in the war with Mexico.

"When I was born, Saint Louis was agog at the heroics of one Ulysses S. Grant. The Grant family had some business ties within the city, although they came from Ohio. That explains how Samuel found himself in Saint Louis, despoiling trustful young girls. And when I reached the age of fifteen and Grandfather deemed me old enough to debut, Ulysses Grant was considered an upstanding citizen—well respected, well liked. The Grant name soon became one to reckon with.

"Grandfather put it about that I was the niece of our own war hero, Ulysses. That was his biggest mistake, I suppose. Society didn't take kindly to my grandfather's story, though it was the truth. The gen-eral feeling was that old van Voorhees was trying to put a dark mark on the good Grant name, or trying to skim off some of their fortune. Grandfather knew the truth, though, and he persisted. He sent me to all the best parties and picnics, all the dances that spring and summer, and I was left alone, a girl of fifteen, to face the aspersions of my neigh-bors. Saint Louis society now knew me to be illegitimate, you see, and so they thought me to be grasping—reaching for a place in the world to which I was not entitled, or worse, trying to glean some of Ulysses Grant's well-earned comfort for myself with these tall tales of being his natural niece."

Cora paused. She braced her hands in the small of her back—always aching; it had ached for years, since moving out of the city—and stared down at the china, the stacks of delicate gilded things that had no business being here, twenty miles from Paintrock in the shadow of the Bighorns.

"Well?" Beulah prodded. "What happened then, Ma?"

What happened next was foolish—ridiculous. Cora's face burned at the thought of recounting the rest of her story. But she could feel them all waiting, hanging on the unfinished tale—Beulah and Clyde, even the little children.

"I hardly think you'll believe me if I tell the rest. But it is true. I was walking home from church one Sunday. Grandfather had been ill—the first signs of a sickness that would later kill him—so I'd gone alone that day. It was a beautiful, fine afternoon, and I decided to take the long way home, which led through a farmer's back field and over a little brook. I liked to linger beside the brook, when time permitted, and pick flowers along its bank. There was a young man working in the back field, harvesting potatoes. He had black soil up to his knees and covering his hands. He called out to me, which was terribly bold—I should have turned away in scorn. A proper girl would have turned away. But I stopped and let him approach, for I was curious, and I felt as if nothing could go wrong that day. Everything had gone so dreadfully foul all that spring and summer—the girls at the dances and parties mocking me, the gentlemen turning away whenever I walked by. I felt as if I was owed a good turn, and somehow, I madly believed I was about to find something good, something I deserved, right there in that potato field. Well, the farm boy—he was a little older than me, but it wasn't his farm—sauntered up to me grinning. He fell on his knees in the dirt before me. He was only jesting, but he said, 'You're the prettiest girl I've ever seen. Won't you take pity on my ailing heart and marry me?'"

Silence hung in the kitchen. Cora watched the firelight moving along the golden rims of the dishes. Stretch and flicker, glitter and fade. No one spoke, but still she could feel their waiting.

"I did marry him." When she could speak again, her voice was very small. "I surprised him by saying yes, for I didn't know his name—didn't know a thing about him. He gawked at me and then climbed to his feet. He said it had only been a freak, a game. But it was no game to me. 'Marry me,' I said. 'You told me you would, now make good and do it.' I had grown so weary, you see—not yet sixteen years old, but already weary. Tired of being the girl whom gentlemen tried to avoid at the dances, and tired of weeping each night into my pillow. At least this farm boy, whoever he was, would look at me without pity or scorn. At least he spoke to me. I figured it was more than I could hope for from any other man in Saint Louis."

"That's how you met Father?" Beulah sounded delighted.

Cora nodded. She couldn't meet her daughter's eye.

"It's late," Clyde said at length. "I had best get home. My mother will be expecting me."

"Thank you," Cora said. "For bringing me the president's gift, and for the firewood."

"Think nothing of it, Mrs. Bemis. Good night."

When Clyde had gone, Cora turned to her daughter. "You had best get Miranda washed up and dressed for bed. Charles, Benjamin, you run along and wash your faces, too. In the morning, you boys must move all that firewood young Mr. Webber gave us out to the barn. Otherwise it will never dry out again."

The boys went off grumbling, and Beulah picked up her little sister, propping Miranda on one slender hip.

"I can take the ax and break up this crate tomorrow, too," Beulah said. "It'll make fine kindling, and so will all this straw."

"No." Cora rested her fingertips on the crate protectively. "No, don't break it up just yet."

"Why not?"

"It might prove useful."

Beulah took Miranda away without another word. Cora was left alone in the kitchen, listening to the pop and crack of the fire, watching as the light played over the curves of teacups and slid along the rims of plates, those stacks of sudden, unlooked-for gold.

NETTIE MAE

Tangled root and broken branch. That was all Cora Bemis was. Nettie Mae shook her head at the news Clyde brought. She refused to believe. She turned the rumor aside as stubbornly as her dead husband had turned aside kindness or mercy or affection, all the marks of weakness Substance had despised.

"It's true, Mother," Clyde insisted. "I saw it all for myself. I read the letter, too."

He was bolting down the stew Nettie Mae had dished up, and she never liked to see him talk while he ate; it was plumb uncivilized. Nettie Mae would rather have scolded him for his half-witted stunt. Imagine taking to the road—in the rain, no less!—after one has been sick in bed, after one has almost expired from fever.

Nettie Mae buttered a few slices of bread and cut a small wedge from the last remaining wheel of cheese. She set the whole lot on a plain pottery dish—no fancy president's china for her—and slid the dish across the table toward her son. Clyde bit into the cheese at once. Nettie Mae hadn't touched that damnable cheese since Substance's death. She had got it from the Bemis woman earlier in the summer; traded good yarn for it, too. She would rather have had the yarn back now. It felt like some sort of bedevilment, an insidious, lurking witchcraft, to have anything the Bemis woman had made beneath her roof.

"Slow down," Nettie Mae said. "You don't want to take a stomachache from bolting your food. That would be all you need, on top of the fever."

Clyde scarcely restrained himself. "The china is real pretty. Blue and gold—real gold. And I read the letter, like I said. It came straight from President Grant. Can you imagine such a thing? For anybody to get a gift from the president is plain unbelievable, but it's our own neighbors—"

"You can't call that woman a neighbor. She hasn't got a neighborly bone in her body."

Clyde slowed at that, finally. "Come now, Mother." He let his spoon fall back into the stew and frowned across the table at Nettie Mae. "I know Mrs. Bemis did you wrong, but she is still our neighbor."

"Don't expect me to be giddy over her presidential china; that's all." She pulled the loaf of bread closer and cut herself a slice, buttered it slowly. Without looking at her son, she said with a casual air, "What did the letter say?"

"It was short. I can't remember every word exactly, but the general thrust was *Here's a gift to make amends for how the Grant family has wronged you.*"

"Wronged her? That woman?"

"And her mother. The letter mentioned her mother, too. I remember that part."

Nettie Mae laughed suddenly. Even to herself, it sounded like the bark of a wary dog. "You see! That explains everything."

Clyde shook his head slowly, dunking his bread into the dregs of his stew. "I don't see. What do you mean?"

"A wronged mother and a wronged daughter. Think about it, Clyde. Cora Bemis has no paternity."

Clyde dropped his bread in the dish and stared at Nettie Mae. He had stilled his face carefully, thinking to hide his thoughts. Had the boy learned that trick from Substance, she wondered—or from Nettie Mae herself?

"Cora Bemis's mother was unmarried," Nettie Mae insisted, all but crowing with excitement, with vindication. "It's obvious now. I should have guessed before, since only a person made in the worst kind of sin would think to inflict such a shame upon others. So, was it the president who occupied himself with that woman's mother, I wonder?" Nettie Mae shrugged, answering her own question before Clyde had a chance to speak. "No, I suppose not. If he had, he would hardly have sent the china himself. He would have instructed someone else to do it on his behalf. I suppose presidents have no end of servants and employees who might handle such distasteful business for them."

"I don't guess it makes a lot of difference who did the sending," Clyde began.

Nettie Mae didn't allow him to finish that thought. "But make no mistake, that woman will lord her treasure over us. You see if she doesn't."

"How can she lord anything, Mother, when you won't even look at her, let alone speak to her?"

"Why should I look at that woman, or speak to her? God knows, I see visions of her in my head every time I close my eyes. Sights I'd rather be spared."

The boy sighed deeply, resuming his supper. Nettie Mae watched him with a new flush of intensity, a sharpness of fear. Clyde had grown too thin this fall, too pale, and the sickness had been far worse than he knew. Shadows lay heavily around his eyes. He had acquired a droop to his shoulders that had no business on the frame of a sixteen-year-old boy. She remembered, with a cruel and sudden vividness, the way her third boy, Luther, had looked just hours before his death. Luther had succumbed to his fever—carried off to his grave at ten brief years of age. And hadn't Luther looked just this way, with darkness like bruises circling his eyes, the young body sagging like an old man's?

No, she told herself. *No, it won't happen again. God spared Clyde from that fate. He wouldn't be so cruel as to strike my son ill again. He can't be cruel enough to take them all—my little children, and Substance, and my last remaining son, my good, strong Clyde. It cannot happen. It won't.*

Clyde was only tuckered out from a long day. And all that extra labor he'd performed, this nonsense of carrying a heavy crate full of dishes for that woman. That creature born of sin, that Jezebel.

"The gift must be intended to buy her silence," Nettie Mae said.

Clyde looked up from his supper, dull and confused. "What now, Mother?"

"The china. President Grant sent it to keep that woman quiet. It's payment for a service, and her service will be to keep her mouth well and truly closed. She must have been rutted into existence by some brother or cousin of the president."

Clyde gaped at Nettie Mae's coarse language. "Mother!"

"Don't pretend shock. You've lived on a farm your whole life. You know how animals are born."

"Mrs. Bemis isn't an animal, however you may hate her. And you'll only do your own soul harm by saying such things."

"Planning to become a minister?" Nettie Mae said dryly.

"Don't make me cross, Mother. I work hard to keep you; you know I do."

Rebuked by the weariness that still clung to her son, Nettie Mae subsided. "I know it," she said quietly, almost remorsefully. A strained silence filled the house. She could hear the wind moaning across the top of the chimney. After a moment, she added, "I'd be real proud of you, though, if you were to become a minister someday."

Clyde's laugh was short and bitter. "God knows, I got no plans to be a preacher." After another pause, he added rather meekly, "But can't you see your way to mending things with Mrs. Bemis—just a little? The girl who lives over yonder, Beulah, has been real grateful for the help I've given. She wants to come and work our land in exchange, Mother—help me with the chores over here, and help you with your work, too. I could use her. She's stronger than she looks, and she works steady without no complaints."

"You mustn't even think such a thing." A fresh, new fear pricked at Nettie Mae. "Now we can all see what sort of stock that child was bred from. There are generations of sinners in her family."

"You can't blame Cora for the way she was brought into this world. She had no say in the matter."

Nettie Mae folded her arms, sat back rigidly in her chair. "Like mother, like daughter." Then, thinking of the strange, eerily detached Bemis girl—her too-calm face, her habit of drifting from place to place like a spirit caught half in, half out of a dream—she leaned forward and repeated with emphasis, "Like mother, like daughter. If you know what's good for you, you'll keep yourself well away from that little sinner, Clyde."

"Beulah never sinned in her life."

"She will, soon enough. She will when the time comes. And it's coming soon, you mark my words."

Clyde's face and neck flushed. He pushed back his chair, rose slowly from the table. "Time I was for bed. Got a terrible lot of work to do in the morning. Pity I can't call on that little sinner across the pasture to lend me a hand. Might make the work go easier on me."

With that, he turned away, shuffling toward the stairs and his bed.

Nettie Mae watched him go, fighting down the pressure of fear that struggled to rise up from her middle. Clyde moved with the wincing tenderness of an old man, her young and healthy son. She remembered the smallness of Luther's hand in her own, the darkened skin around his closed eyes—skin that glistened with the damp of fever. Luther's hand going cold and colder by the minute.

Better to go to your grave untouched by sin than to die tangled in a web of corruption, she told herself.

But then Nettie Mae shuddered, though the fire blazed in the hearth and the kitchen was warm enough. She couldn't help feeling as if God had heard the private thought, and was even now calculating, working out the time and specifics of Clyde Webber's death.

5

THE WARP AND WEFT

Even after Clyde was back on his feet, I couldn't help but worry. He was pale and moved a little slower than he ever had before, tending to his work with a strange deliberation, a careful placement of foot and hand that put me in mind of the old men I'd seen lingering on crates outside the Paintrock general store. Long past their strength, trembling with palsy, sinking day by day into the quiet inutility of age. Apples still remained on the branches of the Webber orchard, and the garden hadn't yet been tilled under. The far corner of the horse-pasture fence was sagging, the boards loose and rotted with rain. I knew this bout of weakness wouldn't hamper Clyde for good. I also knew a body couldn't rush itself through healing—and the harder Clyde worked, the longer his recovery would surely take. Before his fever, Clyde would have had the whole farm buttoned up and ready for winter in a week's time. Now I wondered whether snow would take the Webbers unprepared and mire them in hardship—or worse, condemn them to near starvation.

I couldn't help but feel guilty. Clyde had worked himself to the bone for my family's sake, even fetching our firewood from town. I didn't like the sensation of guilt. It crawled like a chigger under the skin, an itch that could never be satisfied. I would have lent my own strength to the Webber farm, for the president's china had brought a steadiness or purpose to my mother, steeling her to every task. I knew I could safely slip across the pasture and work for Nettie Mae without Ma or the little ones sliding into trouble. But Nettie Mae wouldn't have me. She was hard as granite and every bit as unmovable, resolved to go on hating the Bemis clan till her dying day.

I didn't mind the hate so much. But if the fences fell down and her stock ran away, or if her garden failed come the spring, I fretted that Nettie Mae's dying day would come much sooner than she expected.

On a blue-gray morning, windy enough to drive away the clouds and cold enough to make my nose run, I set out from the gray house bundled up tight in my shawl and followed the muddy trail out toward the riverbed. The pasture was empty; Clyde hadn't turned the sheep out of their fold. I could hear them calling from the Webber farm, a distant chorus of distress. For a moment, I worried that Clyde had fallen sick again. But then I spotted him away in the corner of the horse corral, busy with the sagging fence. He hadn't yet gotten to the sheep—that was all. But the days were growing shorter, the nights long and harsh. Those sheep needed their grass while the grass was still green for the taking.

When I arrived at the grave, I took the offering from my apron pocket and set it in its place. I had brought Substance a gnarled piece of pine root, little bigger than my thumb—a scrap I'd salvaged from the great stack of firewood Clyde had carted down from Paintrock. I pressed the chunk of pine into the wet red soil of the mound and waited for Substance to collect himself, to gather the separate currents of rage and affront and disbelief.

I felt the drifting parts of him converge, felt his unseen eye focus on me. Then he said, What do you want from me, you pest, you gnat of a girl?

Clyde is safe, I told him. He was down with a fever, but he's up again. He'll survive.

Substance said nothing, but something lifted a little inside my chest—a weight I hadn't known I carried. It was Substance's fear, settled deep down in my own spirit since the last time we'd spoken.

I said, Clyde won't expire from the fever, but things are looking bad for your farm, Substance. Nettie Mae can't handle all the work on her own, and Clyde hasn't regained his strength. Who can say whether he'll be fit by winter? I'm powerful worried for both of them. I guess you must be worried, too.

Substance seemed to rise then, surging up above the earth, as if he remembered—for one fleeting heartbeat—what it felt like to be a man, to move your limbs in powerful concert, to stride out in dominion. Then the fist of his grave closed around him. He fell back, seething, hating me for my living flesh, for the freedom and the power I held—to do and act and be.

You can't help them, I said. You can't be of any aid, dead as you are. I'm sorry to be so blunt, but that's the way it is.

Go away, girl, if you can't bring me anything more than words. News of my family's suffering. Premonition of their deaths. Worthless, powerless words.

I said, That's why I've come to see you today. I don't look like much, I know, but I'm strong and hardy, I swear it. I can do the work Nettie Mae and Clyde can't do. But Nettie Mae won't tolerate me, since you took up with my ma.

Don't remind me of that wanton whore, Substance said. That temptress you call a mother. She has no more worth than the dire news you bring.

She's the niece of the president, I sauced back, so I guess she's a damn sight better than you are.

After that, Substance didn't try to insult me or my ma again. But he was still there above his grave, knit together, listening.

I said, Nettie Mae is an awful stubborn woman. I guess you know better than anyone how to make her yield. I wish you'd tell me how it's to be done. How can I make her come to her senses? How can I prove to her she's got no choice but to work with me, even if she hates me and wishes me dead in my grave?

Something dark and cold moved through me then, a ripple of black humor. I realized it was Substance's laughter. I pulled the shawl tighter around my body, but it couldn't protect me from the answer Substance gave.

I felt it—the flush of triumph rising to my face, and something blunt and solid inside, like a wall rising without a mason. My hands made fists of their own accord. The fists knew how to swing.

A stubborn woman, Substance agreed. And cold. Cold, and heartless since the children died. There was only ever one way to make my wife see sense. One way to bend her to my will. Force is all she understands. Give her no choice, and she will do as you say.

I left him then without saying good-bye, for I didn't like the way his power felt inside my spirit. I feared I wasn't strong enough to resist that intoxication, the rush of brute force, and I knew it would ruin me forever if I once gave in.

Yet I could also see that Substance was right—or at least, he wasn't altogether wrong. If I hoped to bring Nettie Mae to her senses, I must bend her to my will. I mustn't allow her to choose, for wounded as she was, and frightened by her own pain, she would retreat into isolation, like any injured creature.

I was not Substance Webber. I had neither size nor strength to force my will. I was obliged to work by subtler means—tugging Nettie Mae and my ma in the proper direction with a feather's touch, with a cryptic hand, disguising the warp and weft of my design.

And if a tug wouldn't suffice, then I was prepared to shove.

NETTIE MAE

The warp and weft of life had come loose in Nettie Mae's hands. The weave of the farm was unraveling. The sheep still moaned in their pen; Clyde hadn't found the time to turn them loose to pasture. He and Nettie Mae had awakened that morning to the two bay fillies loose in the pasture, and only a heel of old bread in the pantry to break their fast. Clyde had caught the fillies and set to work straight away, mending the corral fence, while Nettie Mae mixed the dough she ought to have prepared the day before. When had time grown such rapid and vigorous wings? The day already felt as if it were slipping away, and she knew she had little hope of catching it.

Nettie Mae craned her neck while she kneaded the dough, straining to keep one eye on her son. She could see him through the warped glass of the kitchen window, there at the far corner of the horses' pen, crouched over the boards. Even at a distance, and distorted as he was by the glass, she could read the tension in his body, a certain stiffness in the neck and shoulders. Clyde was strained, bent almost double by the weight of work unfinished and by the weakness that still plagued him, the remnant tremor of his illness.

I ought to have let the sheep out myself, Nettie Mae thought. But she had already begun working the dough by the time she realized Clyde had slipped behind on his chores. *I oughtn't to have been so careless, either. A mother should notice these things. A mother should keep better watch over her son.*

Some new sound caught at Nettie Mae, pulling her briefly from the hopeless reverie. The sheep were still murmuring, but softly now, without their indignant note of demand. She heard the quick, lively tattoo of their hooves, and then heard it dissipate. The animals were running from the fold, Nettie Mae realized with dull shock. The sheep were headed toward their pasture. Had Clyde finished mending the fence already? Surely not. Even if he had, he couldn't cross the pasture as quickly as that. Not unless he'd sprouted wings and flown.

Nettie Mae scraped as much dough as she could from her fingers and crossed to the kitchen window. She rolled her wrists as she went, wincing at the stiffness and pain. Kneading was such tedious work, and of late, it seemed the drudgery of every mundane task had settled deep into her bones. She stared out across the yard. The pane of glass was bubbled and warped, so the world beyond bent and distorted around the window's flaws. Even so, Nettie Mae could make out the flock receding, plunging eager and pale into the sage, the regrowth of autumn grass. And there, swinging the sheepfold gate closed with an unhurried air, she saw the Bemis woman's daughter. Nettie Mae could discern little of the girl; through the imperfect window, she was nothing more than a blur of subdued color against the monotonous red brown of hard-packed earth. But there was no mistaking those lazy movements, the slow, stupid way she drifted from the fold toward the two-story sod-brick house.

Nettie Mae spun away from the window and dunked her sticky hands in the dishpan, scrubbing frantically to remove the dough. The water was bitterly cold, and did nothing to soothe the ache in her wrists. She dried herself on a bit of linen towel, then ran her hands down her apron, smoothing away its wrinkles and dusting off the flour. Why did she care all at once what the Bemis girl might think of her? Unease prickled along the back of Nettie Mae's neck, creeping up her scalp.

She looked weak and tired, overwrought, and she knew it. She didn't like that the strange girl child should see her this way, pale and strained from weeks of struggle, stiff with lingering fear.

Don't be stupid, Nettie Mae told herself bluntly. *Send the girl away. It's nothing to you what she sees, and nothing what she thinks of you. Assuming that half wit thinks anything at all.*

Nettie Mae turned back to the kneading board and the waiting dough. She wouldn't open the door when the Bemis girl knocked. Let that chit waste away on the kitchen steps, for all she cared. What went on in this house, in this family, was of no concern to that useless wisp of a neighbor child.

The girl did not knock. Nettie Mae heard the door squeal open behind her and then the unmistakable tread of hard-heeled boots stepping over the threshold.

She whirled, cheeks burning with indignation, and fixed a glower to her face. The girl lingered in the open door, one careless hand lighting on the iron handle, limp as a half-dead bird.

"What are you doing in my home?"

The Bemis girl blinked slowly, then offered a laggard's smile.

"Get out," Nettie Mae said. "Don't you know it's wrong to enter someone's house without knocking? But I suppose your mother never taught you as much. She seems unable to understand what boundaries are, or where they lie."

The girl smiled again, wider this time, as if Nettie Mae had told an amusing story. She advanced into the kitchen.

"I said get out. You can't come in. You aren't welcome in this home."

"I've come to help you, Mrs. Webber, for Clyde's sake."

"I don't need your help. Now clear out. I've work to do; I can't spare any time for your foolishness."

"I let the sheep out of the fold," the girl said, as if offering something of great value. "I'll bring them in again before sunset, too. May I come in?"

Nettie Mae folded her arms, but the gesture felt defensive, as if she were shielding the soft parts of her soul from the girl's heavy-lidded eyes. "It seems to me you're already in. What use is there in asking permission now?"

The girl moved again, one slow step and then another, delving deeper into Nettie Mae's realm. *No,* Nettie Mae wanted to tell her. *Turn back. Leave my house at once; you don't belong here.* But the girl's very presence—the eerie calm of her demeanor, the inexorable rhythm of her stride—drove Nettie Mae back against the table as if in dread.

The girl came to stand beside Nettie Mae. She looked down at the kneading board, the bread half-finished upon it. She surveyed the unswept hearth, the fire dying down to useless embers, the empty kettle hanging from its hook. Then she turned on her heel, facing about. The motion was so sudden, Nettie Mae scarcely choked back a cry of alarm.

"I can do plenty here," she said. "I'll get supper going now, so it's ready by midday. You won't need to fret, and neither will Clyde. You can finish the bread." The pale stare slipped down to Nettie Mae's hands, still tucked protectively around her body. "No; you're aching from the work, aren't you? I'll finish kneading. You go and fetch some liniment for your wrists."

"I'm not aching. What do you know? Who are you, anyhow? Only a stupid girl of twelve years."

"Thirteen years," she said with a little laugh, as if Nettie Mae were foolish for not discerning her age on sight.

"Don't knead it too much, or you'll overwork the dough."

With a surge of some nauseating emotion, half wonder, half caution, Nettie Mae asked herself, *When did I become resigned to this dirt-stained hussy standing beneath my roof, and taking over my kitchen as if she has a right?* But she went to the pantry for her bottle of liniment, and she sighed with relief when she rubbed it into her aching wrists.

"Clyde looks fit and fine," the girl called from the kitchen. "Though I noticed your fire is about to go cold and the kettle is empty. Clyde needs a good strong broth if he's to regain all his strength. You look as if you could use some broth, too, Mrs. Webber, if you don't mind my saying so."

"I need nothing. Now get away from that dough and let me finish. I won't have you ruining my bread with your careless ways."

"You oughtn't to work the dough now, or it will taste like liniment. Why don't you sit down, Mrs. Webber? You look as peaky as they come. Take a rest. I'll finish up here."

Nettie Mae surprised herself by sinking at once into a chair while the girl went on kneading. Her back fairly sang a chorus of praises at the relief, but a voice chided inside her head. *When did you agree to take this half wit's advice? This spawn of sin, this future harlot?* Her hands rested in her lap, and Nettie Mae examined them. They were clasped together, knuckles white with strain, bones hard and sharp beneath her skin, the clenched claws of some terrified bird. *Lord have mercy—when did I begin to look so old?* If she had remained as youthful and fair as Cora, surely Substance never would have strayed.

Light pressure on her arm, just above the elbow. She started and looked up from her lap. The Bemis girl had stepped silently to her side, to lay one hand upon Nettie Mae. Her immediate instinct was to flinch, recoil from that strange creature's touch. But the girl smiled easily, and Nettie Mae exhaled—a long, unsteady sigh. Relief came as a sensation of warmth, rising from the soles of her feet up her aching legs and settling in her middle. The sensation was so unfamiliar she wanted to flinch back from it, too, even as she reveled in the comfort.

Then a chill fell over her, eclipsing all relief. What had the Bemis girl done to her? She had quieted Nettie Mae's mind with a touch. Nettie Mae had always assumed the girl was simpleminded. What else could explain her lack of haste and her slow-blinking, fearless eyes? Now she wondered if something sinister lurked behind the girl's uncanny demeanor. She leaned back, removing herself from the girl's reach.

The girl shrugged and turned away, as if she hadn't noticed Nettie Mae's obvious repulsion. Perhaps she truly hadn't noticed. That child seemed to see only what she wanted to see.

"Bread's good and ready now. I'll cover it and let it prove. Let me fix you something to eat."

The girl ducked into the pantry, as confident as if this were her mother's home. She reappeared carrying a tin plate laden with the last two pieces of bread from the old loaf. Plenty of good pale butter was smeared over each slice. She had trimmed the hardened skin from the last small chunk of cheese—the cheese Nettie Mae didn't like to eat—and had cut up an apple, too. Evidently, the girl could move quickly and see to her tasks when she chose.

"Just you tuck in, now." She laid the plate before Nettie Mae. "It'll bring back your strength. You and Clyde both need some good broth to pep you up again, but I'll need to build the fire and scrub out the kettle. I'll see to everything, Mrs. Webber; don't you fret."

Nettie Mae watched as the girl piled tinder and sticks of firewood in the hearth. Within moments, new fire blossomed from the coals. The girl fed it carefully, and when she was satisfied with its strength, she lifted the kettle from its hook and poured its dregs into the tin pail beside the door.

"I'll go and throw this lot to your shoats later," she said cheerfully. Then she disappeared outside.

Nettie Mae looked down at the plate. Her stomach ached suddenly, cramping from a hunger so powerful it almost made her feel ill. But she hardly dared touch the food the Bemis girl had prepared. Nettie Mae was half-convinced the girl had performed some strange enchantment on her with a touch. What foul transformations might she effect with food? There were stories, Nettie Mae recalled—tales her mother had whispered when Nettie Mae had been but a small girl. Tales from the old country, from Wales, the far-off land her mother's mother had called home. The legends came crowding back into her mind, though she hadn't thought of her mother's stories since she had grown up and married. She recalled every detail now with vivid clarity, with stark and brutal force. Ethereal, shining, long-haired women who lived in the forest and drew unwary travelers into traps—circles of mushrooms or stones. If you ate the food the shining ones gave you, you couldn't step out of their circles again till a hundred years had passed, or three hundred.

Foolish, Nettie Mae scolded herself. *Stories for children, and nothing a Christian ought to fear.*

She picked up a slice of bread and bit into it, chewing with deliberate care. Her mouth watered at once and her stomach growled; it was all she could do not to tear into the bread with both hands and gulp it down in a few ravenous bites.

The girl returned to the kitchen. That easy smile hadn't left her face. She had pumped fresh water into the stew kettle, and it now swung heavily at her side, while in the other arm she cradled two onions and a few small turnips. She had helped herself to Nettie Mae's root cellar, it seemed.

"I found a good smoked mutton bone in that box in the pantry." The onions and turnips thumped onto the table. The girl hauled the kettle to the fire and replaced it on its iron hook. "I suppose it's all right if I use the mutton for broth, ain't it?"

Nettie Mae only stared at the child as she worked.

She seemed to take the silence for assent. Moments later, the smoked mutton joint fell into the kettle, and the girl busied herself with knife and roots. The sharpness of cut onions filled the room, pricking Nettie Mae's eyes.

"Won't take more than an hour to get a good simmer going," the girl said, dropping handfuls of onion and turnip in the pot. "A shame you didn't have any carrots in the cellar, though. We've got some still at our place. I can run over and fetch them, if you like."

Nettie Mae still held her tongue, but by now the simple needs of her body, neglected through days of frantic toil, had taken hold. She picked up the second slice of bread and ate steadily. The force of her hunger receded a little.

"You ought to have something bracing to drink," the girl said. "It'll help you recover. Have you got any fruit wine or liquor?"

Nettie Mae found her words at last. "No," she said firmly. "I have never thought it proper to keep strong drinks in my house. I suppose it's a matter of course under your roof."

The girl grinned, though she was stirring the kettle and didn't look up from her task. "I wouldn't say it's a matter of course, Mrs. Webber, but my ma has always kept a bottle or two of wine about the place for warming and perking up. It comes in handy now and again."

"I'm sure it does," Nettie Mae said dryly.

The girl lifted the ladle from her broth and eyed its contents critically. "I don't think that lone joint of mutton will do after all. You and Clyde both need a more fortifying broth if you're to perk up properly. It's my fault, I guess, for using too much water. We've got to have a chicken, to make the stew good and rich. Shall I kill one of your chickens or one of mine?"

"I've got too many roosters anyhow," Nettie Mae said. "They've been fighting, and I've meant to kill a few and smoke their meat or salt it, but I haven't had the time lately to do the job properly. With Clyde so often occupied at your farm," she added, with pointed force. "You may go out and kill one of my roosters. Any except for the redheaded one with black wings. He's a useful bird; I won't lose him to the stew kettle."

Nettie Mae continued eating as the girl left the house again. She finished the last slice of bread, and then, before she realized what she was doing, picked up the cheese and bit into it. At once, Nettie Mae froze. The tang of it sat brightly upon her tongue, savory and intoxicating. That damnable cheese had been made by the Bemis woman. It might as well be ashes, then, for all Nettie Mae cared. Scowling over her carelessness, furious that the Bemis woman had gotten the better of her again—albeit in a small and insignificant way—Nettie Mae finished the cheese with the grim concentration of a soldier forcing himself toward the battlefield.

It was only then that Nettie Mae realized the yard outside the kitchen had fallen silent. Usually, the chickens set up a ruckus whenever anyone approached the coop. The redheaded rooster would sound his call and the hens would come running from all corners of the farm, eager to pick through kitchen scraps. But there was nothing to hear—no clucking, no crowing. Had the girl forgotten her task and wandered away?

Nettie Mae stood and crossed to the kitchen window, expecting to find the yard empty. What she saw froze her to the spot with a flush of superstitious fear. The girl had not wandered away. She was standing in front of the coop, gazing down with her accustomed languid, unconcerned air. The birds milled around her. The redheaded rooster hadn't called to his flock, yet there he was among the rest, gathered calmly at the Bemis girl's feet. The girl turned her head this way and that, considering each fowl in its turn—assessing the animals, observing them.

Then she bent and picked up a young rooster. Lifted it as easily as one might pluck a flower from its stem. The bird was placid in her grip. Nettie Mae watched with growing unease, and no small amount of fascination, as the girl lifted the young rooster and pressed its folded wing against her cheek. She leaned into the bird, feeling the softness of its feathers, the warmth of its living body, and even through the imperfect glass, Nettie Mae could read the girl's expression—lips pressed tightly with regret, a tension of loss around closed eyes. Then the girl took the bird's feet in one hand and held it upside down above the earth. Wings hung loose from the dark body, spread wide above the flock. The rooster still lived, and yet it didn't struggle. It had already surrendered to its fate. With her other hand, the girl stroked the glossy mane of feathers, the ruff around the creature's neck. Her lips moved in prayer or in words of gratitude—Nettie Mae couldn't hear the Bemis girl, couldn't possibly know what she said, and she was grateful for the silence, the lack of knowing. And then in a heartbeat, with the flick of her wrist, the child snapped the rooster's neck. Its wings stirred briefly and then hung limp, with none of the usual flapping and commotion, the last fitful burst of life that usually accompanies the distasteful necessity of killing a bird for the pot. The flock paused in its scratching and pecking, looked up at the girl and the bird she held. She spoke a few more words to the animals, slow and quiet. Then she pulled the rooster's head from its body and allowed the blood to run down, down to the bare-scratched earth.

The girl turned and walked away. The redheaded rooster led his flock back to the garden, where they returned to the business of gleaning and pecking through the dry remains of the harvest.

Nettie Mae reeled back from the window. The flavor of the cheese she had eaten was forceful in her mouth, sharp and accusatory.

What in the precious name of Christ did I just witness? God forgive me and protect me.

Nettie Mae retreated to the kitchen table. She sank back down on her chair, trembling, her body gone cold. Now and then, dark feathers drifted past the window. The girl was plucking her kill, preparing the carcass in the yard. Nettie Mae was grateful for that small mercy, too. She didn't think she could watch the Bemis girl at her work now, going about her task as dispassionately as one might sweep a floor or wash a dish. Yet though she couldn't see it, Nettie Mae couldn't help but imagine the work being done in her yard. Ropes of innards pulled from open flesh, still warm with life. Her mind dwelt again on what she had seen out there beside the coop. The slack way the rooster's wings had unfolded just before the twitch of the girl's hand. The calm acceptance, an inevitable death. And that stream of blood pooling on the hard-packed earth. Substance must have bled, too. A hot red flood cooling, congealing around an unmoving body.

The kitchen door swung open so suddenly, Nettie Mae gasped. The girl smiled as she had done when she'd carried in the water. Nettie Mae turned away so she couldn't see the rooster's carcass—the frank whiteness of the stripped body, the limp bounce of useless wings. The girl made quick work with her knife, and when Nettie Mae heard the soft splash of meat and bones falling into the kettle, she exhaled with relief and allowed herself to look at the Bemis girl once more.

The girl stood at the drain board, wiping her hands with a damp towel. Without looking up, she said, "Soup's coming up to a nice simmer already, and with that chicken meat, it'll be good and hearty. But if you're still feeling shaky, some nice hot tea with sugar or honey will be just the thing. Tea will be ready before the soup's done, anyway. Have you got a teakettle and some leaves? I can go out and fetch more water—"

"I can do it myself," Nettie Mae snapped. "I don't need you hanging about. Meddling."

"I ain't bothered." The girl hung her towel over the drain board to dry. "You've been busy for days now, Mrs. Webber. You might as well rest for a spell. Let me carry the burden."

"I can accomplish more than you can even when I'm tired out. I've seen you out there in the fields, mooning and daydreaming instead of doing a proper share of work on your family's farm. You're lazy. Good for nothing. Don't think I haven't noticed your sloth, girl, even if your mother hasn't."

"You don't like me much, do you?" The girl sounded amused.

"I can't think why I should."

"I can think of plenty of reasons why you should."

Nettie Mae drew herself up, cheeks hot with indignation. "Count on you, girl, to speak to an elder with such appalling disrespect."

"Don't you know my name, Mrs. Webber?"

Nettie Mae blinked, startled out of all her anger. Would nothing put the child off? Had she no instinct for fear? It was unnatural, the way she simply *looked* at the world—observed it and accepted it, without reacting to its ceaseless affronts, its endless dangers.

Nettie Mae could think of no response.

"You never call me anything but 'girl,'" the girl said.

"Of course I know your name." Nettie Mae forced herself to speak it. She wouldn't be bested by this layabout chit—not in her own home. "Beulah." And as soon as she'd spoken the Bemis girl's name, the fear lifted, replaced by scorn. "If you want to know why I dislike you so, maybe that's the reason: your name."

"What's the matter with my name?" Rather than waiting for Nettie Mae's response, Beulah took a broom from the pantry and began sweeping the hearth—without haste, with an unfocused, hazy smile. The same way she did everything. "My name's from the Bible. Did you know that, Mrs. Webber?"

"Oh, I know it, all right. If I were the type to gamble—which I'm not, I assure you—I'd wager that I know far more about the Bible than you do."

She would also have wagered that this fearless child had had little in the way of religious schooling. What else could one expect from the daughter of Cora Bemis? And what else could explain Beulah's uncanny confidence? It was plain the girl feared nothing—not even death, as her unnatural display at the chicken coop had proved. The first thing the Bible taught was to fear God, and once a body feared God, the remainder of proper human cautions flowed down like water. Nothing could preserve a soul from fear or sin but the salvation of the Lord Jesus Christ.

"My pa named me," Beulah said. The broom scratched patiently across the bricks of the hearth. "He always told me it's a name from the Bible, but I never found my name in my ma's Bible when I went looking for it."

"You don't open a Bible to search for names. You read it to learn God's word."

"Well, Beulah is a word I ain't found yet, but my pa said it means 'married to the land.' Or maybe 'the wedded land'; I can't exactly recall."

"Your father sounds as foolish as I expected him to be," Nettie Mae said. "The word—and your name, girl—comes from Baal, the name of a false god. Enemy of the true and living God. It's a name for a sorceress, a witch. A necromancer."

Beulah glanced up from her sweeping. "What's a necromancer?"

Nettie Mae thought of the rooster's limp wings and suppressed a shudder. "Someone who meddles with what they shouldn't: The unholy. The dead."

Beulah tipped her head to one side. That look of dull surprise amounted to more emotion than Nettie Mae had ever seen from the girl. "Are all dead things unholy, Mrs. Webber?"

"Yes, of course."

"But why? Everything dies, sooner or later, as a matter of course. Why would God decide that a matter of course is unholy?"

Bread and cheese sat like millstones in Nettie Mae's stomach. Everyone died, sooner or later, just as the girl had said. And Nettie Mae had seen more death than any woman ought to see. Yet mundane as the end was, still her heart pounded at the thought of her own death. Staring back at Beulah—who leaned at her ease on the upright broom, waiting for a reply—Nettie Mae couldn't help but feel that her own death was perilously close. Reaching for her with cold black hands.

She swallowed, struggling to quell a rising tide of her fear. Despite her faith, despite her hope for salvation, a dark and featureless eternity struck real terror into Nettie Mae's heart. For there was some part of her, she knew—she had always known—that couldn't quite believe what the Bible said about death, or the peace of Heaven waiting just beyond its inscrutable threshold. The promise of Heaven couldn't be true, couldn't be real; for if it was true, then God was unjust. There had never been a man who had lived his life so assiduously as Substance Webber. He was a paragon of virtue, meting out his every action, his every thought, in strict accordance with Scripture. Except for his dalliance with Cora, Substance had never sinned. Nor had he suffered the least affront to order, to perfection, to God's laws in his home or in his presence.

And God had never made a man less deserving of eternal peace than Nettie Mae's dead husband. If Heaven had thrown open its gates to Substance, then the very idea of Heaven was a mockery of justice.

Trembling, Nettie Mae said, "Don't you know it's very bad to speak of the Lord so vainly? If I were your mother, I'd wash your mouth out with soap."

Beulah shrugged and resumed her sweeping. "Anyhow, Mrs. Webber, you needn't be afraid that Clyde will die."

"I'm not afraid of it. Not anymore."

The girl peered at her through a hanging lock of her limp hair. Another smile—she seemed to have an inexhaustible supply of them—passed fleetingly over Beulah's face. It stung Nettie Mae. There was too much sight in the girl's confidence, too much knowing. Beulah possessed far more wisdom than a girl of thirteen years was entitled to. And Nettie Mae didn't like to think that the girl saw more of her soul than Nettie Mae saw herself.

She snapped at Beulah, "You're just a stupid child. A witless prairie rat. You know nothing of me—or my heart, or my fears. And you certainly know nothing of Clyde. How can you say whether he is safe from harm?"

Beulah straightened, grinning, almost laughing. She faced Nettie Mae without a twitch of concern. "I'm a sorceress, ain't I? That's what my name means, so you said. Maybe I talked to the dead, and they told me Clyde wasn't to come and dwell among them. Not just yet, anyway."

Chilled and sickened by the girl's audacity, Nettie Mae leaned back in her chair until it creaked under the strain.

Beulah swept ash and crumbs into a neat pile, returned the broom to the pantry, then took the slop pail from beside the door and went humming out into the yard to feed the pigs. Nettie Mae was left alone to wonder whether Beulah was being impudent or merely speaking the truth.

CORA

The warp of the homesteading life was monotony, isolation its weft. The prairie was never silent, for the wind moved ceaselessly, moaning hollow and cold around the chimney and shaking an endless sea of grass with a low, sinister hiss. During warmer months, crickets and cicadas filled the air with their monotonous drone, a sound that worked its way down into a body, filling the limbs with leaden weight and deadening the mind with its hypnotic hum. Fall rains roared against the house. Hailstones beat the earth in winter, even when deep snow should have deadened all sound. In any blessed respite, any short spell of what should have been silence, the cattle issued mournful cries or the thrushes sang, loud and relentless, just before the sun rose, depriving Cora of sleep. It was always the same, season in and season out, day after long and weary day.

Of course, the city was never silent, either. But the noises of Saint Louis were different. The rattle of wagons, the clamor of human voices, the distant churn of industry all combined into one agreeable chorus, a music of fellowship and life. Cora could still recall the church bells ringing out the hour, melting long and mellow across the town. She had often stood on the covered porch of her grandfather's home, a girl on the verge of womanhood, one arm wrapped around a turned post, counting the tolls of the bell and listening to the city's voice rise and fall in the spaces between the notes.

There was neither rise nor fall to the sounds of the prairie. Its murmur was constant, obtrusive, and cold, even in the summer when the sun beat down so brutally it hardened the soil and crazed it with fissures and cracks. Cold because it was the voice of the wilderness, an untamed vastness to which mankind did not belong—the borderless breadth of nature, unmapped and unmarked, the indifferent mire into which Cora had been sinking for eight long years. If only the prairie would swallow her at last, she would be grateful. Close its sinister weight over her head and allow her to finally suffocate. This drawn-out agony was no sort of life—this dull and relentless struggle. She had been dying by inches from her first sight of the unpopulated grassland. She would much rather die by yards and have it over quickly.

Since she couldn't have the sounds of the city, Cora would have given almost anything for silence. An hour or two during which she might retreat into her own thoughts or simply lie across her bed, mind blanked by relief, forgetting for a while the limitless expanse of scrubland, its emptiness, its changeless form.

The rains had ceased after nine long days, but wind was still howling from the dark throat of her kitchen hearth, and the panes of her windows ticked now and then as the prairie hurled sage twigs and grains of dust against the glass. Cora had bundled the children up in their warmest clothing and sent them outside to pull up the last of the weeds, dried stems of squashes, and spent bean vines in the garden. She had no doubt that they played more than they worked, but she gladly seized the opportunity to send them out of doors to run off their tireless energy while the chance presented itself. For her part, Cora sat beside a window taking down the hem of one of Miranda's dresses. But it was slow work, picking at a stitch here and there. The endless lamentation of the wind pulled her away from her task and led her, time and again, into a labyrinth of bleak thoughts from which there seemed no hope of escape.

Cora watched her two young sons chase one another down the long furrows while Miranda picked late-blooming chicory flowers, faded and frail along the margins of the garden. Beyond the wattle fence, the wilderness gaped like a greedy mouth, ready to swallow the children and Cora along with them.

I can't do this without Ernest.

Cora had avoided admitting her own vulnerability even in the privacy of thought, but she could no longer deny the truth. She was weak. She understood nothing of this life—the farm, the Bighorns, the restless sea of grass—for all she had lived in the small gray house for nigh on a decade. In all that time, she had thrown herself into motherhood, a distraction and a shield against the prairie's hostility. For eight years, she had been content to leave to Ernest whatever happened beyond the walls of her home. Cora seldom ventured farther than the hen coop or the garden if she could avoid it. Farm and prairie alike had been her husband's concern, her husband's realm.

I can't go on this way. I must have help if I'm to survive. If my children are to survive.

Beulah never shirked her duties, but she was a young girl, and distractible besides. Cora needed the aid, the presence, of grown men and women. She needed community, human voices to drown out the hungry wind. She needed the order and reassurance of industry.

I will return to Saint Louis.

It was the first determined thought she'd had since accepting Ernest's proposal in that field so many years ago, the first decision she had made on her own in a long, desolate time. It surprised her, that certainty could arrive as easily as that—naturally, as the blackbirds came down to roost in the cottonwoods at sunset.

It would take some doing, to travel so far with four children and the family's worldly possessions. Cora must find some money if she hoped to make the trip. She must pack up the children's clothes and the few things she wished to keep—family portraits, her good quilts and linens, the most useful tools from her kitchen. Would she find enough boxes and bags in the house and barn to carry everything away? If not, she must purchase crates in town. Then would come the task of hiring a wagon, preferably one in a train. She would not attempt to drive the family's humble cart herself, for she must go all the way to Carbon—days to the south—if she hoped to find a train. Her recent foray into the foothills had disabused Cora of any notion that she was a skilled driver. And a woman traveling alone, with small children—Cora shuddered to think of it. The Indians would fall on her like fire from the sky. No, she must hire transport to Carbon. From there, they could take the train to Saint Louis.

And assuming I do make it back to Saint Louis, what then?

Dress, needle, and thread lowered to her lap as Cora stared unseeing through the window. She had no work, no skills, no trade. And no relations still living in the city—at least, none who would be glad of her presence. Ulysses Grant might have acknowledged her in his roundabout way, but Cora hadn't any reason to believe the Grants of Saint Louis would accept her as one of their own, even with the letter. No one would care for her in Missouri, just as no one cared for her now on this wind-blasted plain. But surrounded by people once more, she might hope to find some work—caring for a wealthy woman's children, perhaps. Surely she could earn enough money to scrape by.

If God was merciful, Ernest would forgive Cora, and once he'd been set free, he would follow her to the city, where they could resume their lives as husband and wife. They could put everything—Substance and the prairie—far behind them. Cora had no earthly reason to believe Ernest would return. But for now, she knew, the possibility that he might forgive her someday must serve as fortification. There was precious little hope elsewhere to steel her spine.

She turned on her chair, eyeing the president's china. It was still stacked on her kitchen table, for Cora hadn't yet determined where she might keep the fragile cups and saucers in safety. They were beautiful, those gleaming plates and serving dishes with their gilded, finial lids. It had been a chore to keep the children away from the china these past few days, when the rain beat down so hard Cora felt certain God had decided to flood the earth again, and she had confined her brood to the house for fear they might be swept away or catch pneumonia. The dishes looked so refined, so elegant. They wanted no part of prairie life. It was little wonder Cora had found no suitable location to store them; the president's china set couldn't live comfortably in this dismal landscape, with its scouring wind and Biblical rains.

It was well I never broke up that shipping crate for firewood, Cora thought. *I'll need it, if I'm to carry those dishes up to Paintrock.*

Surely Cora would find a buyer in town. Paintrock was in no way a wealthy place, but enough cattle ranchers surrounded the community that Cora could hope to raise the money she needed. If she was lucky, she would find an eager buyer—someone willing to pay enough that Cora could give the Webber boy a few dollars, too, in gratitude for his help. The load of firewood he had donated to the Bemis farm might be all that stood between Cora's children and the deadly cold of winter. That alone was a priceless gift, and it was to say nothing of the countless hours Clyde had labored in Cora's garden and fields, driving her cattle, harvesting her corn, and keeping her barn and sheds in good repair.

For a moment, she considered leaving the land and the house to Clyde. She would have no use for them once she had gone. Perhaps the acres of farm and pasture would make some small restitution for the Webber boy's fatherless state. But this land belonged to Ernest, and though Cora nursed a shrinking hope that her husband might still love her, she knew only God could say whether Ernest would take her back after the shocking way she had wronged him.

I must send Ernest a letter, Cora decided, taking up her needle again. *I will tell him the truth: that I've returned to the city in disgrace, and he is free to come and find me—or not, as he chooses—once his sentence has been served.*

If Ernest refused to join her in Saint Louis, then Cora knew she must live as a widow lived, humbled, forever on the verge of penury, raising her children on the charity of churches and ladies' aid societies. It was well that her grandfather was long since in his grave. How his heart would have broken to see Cora now. Grandfather had sacrificed everything—his reputation, his business—so that she might marry a wealthy blue blood and be kept securely, a proper wife, a proper woman.

I failed you, Grandfather. Can you ever forgive me?

But even as she thought those words, Cora's newfound determination steadied her heart. The decision was made; she would go as soon as the china was sold and throw herself and her children on the mercy of city folk. Living in poverty within a city could scarcely be harder than scraping out a miserable, mean existence on the prairie.

Outside in the garden, Charles called, "Hullo, Beulah!"

Cora looked up from her stitches. Beulah was returning from the Webber place—she had gone over earlier that morning to offer Clyde some help with his morning chores—but the girl was not alone. Nettie Mae accompanied her, striding through brush and stands of tall grass like a bull charging a matador. Her arms were folded, tight and impenetrable, just below her flat bosom. Nettie Mae and Beulah hadn't reached the garden fence, yet already Cora could read the marble of her neighbor's face: hard, cold, deeply etched by hate.

Blood rushed in Cora's ears. She stuck her needle into a fold of fabric, put the dress in her sewing basket, and lurched up from her chair, smoothing her skirt and patting her coiled braid with frantic hands. Standing so quickly rendered her dizzy, and she clutched the back of her chair, heart fluttering, wondering if she was on the verge of a faint.

She heard Beulah and Nettie Mae ascend the porch steps, and a moment later, the door swung open. Cora had only enough time to swallow some of her fear—not nearly enough of it. She stepped away from the chair on which she had been leaning. The last thing Cora wanted was for Nettie Mae to see her propped up like some corpse posed for a photographer. She hoped she didn't tremble visibly as her daughter and the neighbor came into the sitting room.

"I've brought Mrs. Webber over to speak with you, Ma," Beulah said brightly.

"You . . . you ought to call me 'Mother,' not 'Ma,' Beulah." What must Nettie Mae think of Cora's children, unschooled, unrefined?

Beulah did not acknowledge the correction, but that was no startlement to Cora. The girl was not malicious; neither was she slow. Beulah simply paid more heed to her own thoughts than to Cora's scolding and cajoling. The same had held true for most of Beulah's life, since she had been a tiny girl of five years. From the first day the Bemis family had set out for the Bighorn Basin—leaving the town of Carbon and its train station behind, rolling out into the endless grass in their newly purchased wagon—Beulah had been her own child, governed by a secret heart, following a compass only she could see.

Well did Cora remember the moment when that peculiar change had come over her daughter. Cora had been perched on the driver's seat, close beside her husband, with Beulah in her lap, held securely in her arms. Benjamin, only a few months old, slept swaddled in a basket at Cora's feet. As Carbon had dwindled behind them and the steady vibration of the wagon's wheels had settled into their bones, Beulah had gone silent and still. Her daughter's face had been hidden by the starched brim of a bonnet, but Cora had felt a shiver of awe rack the girl's frame. Beulah had stared straight ahead for hours, unspeaking, watching the place near the northern horizon where two dark ruts of the wagon track vanished in a glare of sunlight. Beulah's silence had frightened Cora, whipping to new heights the anxiety she had already carried for weeks while she and Ernest made their plans and set their affairs in order, preparing to venture out into the unmarked blankness of the prairie.

Cora had wondered whether Beulah might have taken ill, and if so, what in the Lord's name she could do about it, so far from help and home. But that afternoon, when they paused beside a stream to water their animals and have a bite to eat, Beulah had gazed up at Cora speechless with happiness, wide eyed and shining of face. Cora lifted her daughter down from the wagon seat, admonishing Beulah not to venture out of sight. The grass was so tall, waving high above the girl's head—a jungle teeming with hidden ferocities, its countless cryptic eyes alert and watching. But Beulah seemed unafraid. She had plucked a stem of grass and run its bristling seed head across her lips. Cora had never forgotten the way her daughter's eyes had closed at the feel of it, as if she had found the bliss of Heaven.

"Go on," Beulah said to Nettie Mae, encouraging, "you can speak to her, you know. She's a real friendly sort."

Nettie Mae's mouth tightened. Her thin, pale cheeks turned whiter still until her complexion seemed almost blue. "I know how friendly she is," Nettie Mae muttered. Then she shut her eyes briefly, and Cora had the impression that Nettie Mae was steeling herself for an especially odious task. When she opened her eyes again, Nettie Mae's words came rapid and hard, like the hailstones of winter. "My son took ill a week ago. On the day you drove up into the hills, in fact."

"Yes," Cora said rather faintly. "Beulah told me Clyde had sickened. He seems much stronger now."

"Thank God, he survived. The next time, he may not be so lucky. Clyde simply worked himself into a dangerous exhaustion. That's what Dr. Cooper said. Things can't go on as they have done, Mrs. Bemis."

"Please, call me Cora."

Nettie Mae's shoulders twitched, as if the prospect of familiarity made her skin crawl. "I can't dissuade Clyde from working on your farm—he is the man of the house now, and it's right that he should make up his own mind. But I fear the extra work will kill him. The next time he works himself to exhaustion and takes to his bed, he might never leave it again."

Cora clutched the back of her chair again. "The poor dear boy. I certainly wouldn't like to be the cause of any harm to you or to Clyde,

Mrs. Webber." Her own words struck her then, and Cora lowered her face, blushing with shame at her own foolish tongue.

"Helpless as you are," Nettie Mae said, "Clyde surely will work himself to death, looking after your affairs and your children, though I can't think why he ought to care."

Cora risked a timid glance at her neighbor. Nettie Mae did not acknowledge Beulah, who stood half smiling, unconcerned, to the woman's right. But the right side of Nettie Mae's mouth twitched—once—and Cora had the impression that the woman restrained herself from glaring at the girl only by force of her considerable will.

"We are all so grateful for everything the young Mr. Webber has done for us," Cora said. "I feel simply terrible, to know that we have caused him to suffer. Please, Mrs. Webber—tell me what my family may do to help."

Nettie Mae sniffed sharply but said nothing. She stared into a corner of the sitting room, her flat cheek pulsing with a furious rhythm. Cora realized the woman was clenching and releasing her jaw.

Beulah looked from the neighbor to Cora and back again. Then she said, "I've had a talk with Mrs. Webber over at her place. You remember what you suggested once, Ma, a few weeks ago: that we all should work together and run our two farms as one. Well, Mrs. Webber has agreed. It's for the best; she sees that now."

Cora spoke before she could think better of her words. "Do you?" The surprise was evident in her voice, and it pleased Nettie Mae none too well.

"I *don't*," she said. "Sharing my days with you, Cora Bemis, is nearly the last item on my list of desires. There is only one eventuality I would find less agreeable, and that is losing my son. For Clyde's sake, I will do it. Only for him. Don't make the foolish mistake of believing your sins are forgiven."

Cora folded her hands and lowered them meekly to the pocket of her apron. She lowered her face again, too, hoping she looked as contrite as she felt. Nettie Mae was the last person Cora would have chosen as a helpmeet, but God had granted the aid she needed—another grown woman to help manage the unmanageable, to keep the wilderness at bay. Cora was often reckless, to her eternal sorrow, but this time she was determined to be more sensible. She needed Nettie Mae. Very probably, neither she nor her children could survive the coming winter without Nettie Mae's assistance. From where else in this vast, cold wilderness was salvation to come?

I need only soldier through what's left of the autumn and one winter ahead, Cora told herself. *By spring, the weather will be mild enough that I can take the china to Paintrock and find a buyer. And from there, I will set out for Saint Louis.*

What were a few months at Nettie Mae's side? Cora had already survived eight years on the prairie. Saint Louis was but two seasons away. Her long trial was almost at its end. She could muddle through until spring.

"Very well," Cora said softly. "I will be glad to help you in any way I can, Mrs. Webber, and will be most grateful for your help in return."

"I don't know whether you'll be of any use, particularly," Nettie Mae said, "but this girl of yours is strong, even if she doesn't look it. She's lazy, and probably rather stupid, but strong enough to share in the chores."

Beulah laughed brightly, as if Nettie Mae had told a clever joke rather than insulting her.

Nettie Mae narrowed her eyes at Beulah. When the girl had mastered her laughter, Nettie Mae continued. "I have one condition, though, Cora Bemis."

"Of course. I will agree to anything you say."

"We will live together under my roof, and on my land. All of us—your brood of squalling brats, your cows, the rest of your animals. No more of this scuttling back and forth between two plots. It's too much strain for Clyde to bear."

Cora kept her gaze fixed to the floor. She nodded acceptance.

"Under my roof—and by my rules. My household is a well-ordered one; I won't have you and yours interfering with my ways."

"Of course," Cora said. "It's a generous offer, Mrs. Webber. We are all grateful for your charity."

"My charity." Nettie Mae's murmur was dark, tinged with amusement. But she said nothing more, only turned her back on Cora and strode toward the door.

"I will need some time," Cora said timidly, "to make the children ready and to pack up our belongings."

"Tomorrow, then," Nettie Mae answered. "But you, girl—Beulah. You'll come over tonight, straight away. I'll need your help, if I'm to spare Clyde the extra work before the autumn lambs arrive."

Nettie Mae saw herself out and shut the door rather firmly behind her. The fact of her departure hung silent and heavy in the Bemis house. Only when Cora was certain Nettie Mae had truly departed did she lift her face and meet her daughter's eye.

Beulah grinned back at her, and Cora could almost see the bristle of a grass head passing across the girl's lips.

6

YOU CAN'T DO A THING TO CHANGE IT

My ma and my brothers and baby sister followed me back over to the Webber place the next day. It was clear to all of us—even little Miranda, I think—that Nettie Mae had no great liking for our presence in her house. But Clyde's illness had frightened her enough to open her door, if not her heart. She was tougher than my ma by far, but there was a limit even to Nettie Mae's great stoicism. Clyde's fever had burned hot enough to melt the coldness of her will. For his sake, she was ready to endure the Bemis invasion, at least till winter had passed.

Nettie Mae cleared her sewing and spinning out of one of the upstairs rooms, and I helped Ma carry her bed, piece by piece, over the pasture and up the stairs to our new accommodations. Ma and I would sleep together in that bed, with Miranda on the trundle below us. Nettie Mae had planned to set up a couple of cots in the kitchen near the hearth, where it was always warm, and there Benjamin and Charles would bunk each night like hunters in a cabin. Instead, Clyde gave up his room to the little fellas, as he called them, by reason that they might be frightened in a strange new house and miss the nearness of their big sister and their mother. He took a cot in the kitchen for himself, and never objected when Nettie Mae loaded his arms with quilts and coverlets, admonishing him to stay warm lest the fever return with all its force and fury. Nettie Mae kept to her own devices each night behind the pointedly closed door of her own bedroom. My ma warned all her children, even me, to stay quiet as mice in the evening and do nothing to disturb the peace of Nettie Mae's home.

Ma was as humble as a servant whenever Nettie Mae entered a room. She kept her eyes lowered and spoke softly, but only if Nettie Mae addressed her first. She was obedient and helpful, always first to rise from the supper table and start the washing up and first out of bed each morning to begin kneading dough for our daily bread. Any weight she could take to lessen the burden on Nettie Mae's shoulders, my ma picked up and bore without complaint. She had never been so industrious on our own farm. But then, on our farm, my mother had never felt obliged to prove her worth to anyone.

Despite Ma's hard work and amiable temper, the air fairly crackled around Nettie Mae whenever she laid eyes upon my ma. Spite surrounded her in a thick cloud, buzzing minutely in a harsh tin voice like the deerflies that descend in summer's heat to bite and drink your blood. So hard was her scowl, so frigid her voice, that even Miranda reasoned it was better to be seen than heard when Nettie Mae loomed nearby. I taught my little sister how to hold an embroidery hoop and how to thread a needle, though she was far too young to make good fancywork and tangled her thread in a dreadful mess more often than not. But stitching—or trying to stitch— kept her occupied and distracted in some far corner of the house, where she couldn't inadvertently stray into Nettie Mae's path and be frightened by our benefactress's stare.

Discord, scarcely controlled, pervaded the Webber household. But beyond the sod-brick walls, among the pastures and barns our families now shared, Clyde and I worked in agreeable harmony. He still hadn't regained all his strength after the fever's ravaging, but nevertheless, each morning after we'd filled up on my mother's porridge and a few slices of smoked ham, Clyde led me out to the sheepfold or the long shed or the paddock where Tiger, my pa's last remaining horse, switched his tail alongside Joe Buck, the bay fillies, and the other horses Clyde had taken in for training. With hardly a word exchanged between us, we would set to work mending fences, tending the sheep, bringing my milk cows across the field and installing them in the newly repaired pen alongside the Webber barn. I could sense Clyde's weakness—the shaking of his exhausted legs and the feeble grip of his pale hands. I took the brunt of the physical work, for I always have been stronger than a body would guess just to look at me. Clyde guided and directed my work and made what decisions needed making. There was no tension between us. Like the river and its bank, we flowed as one.

I guess that's the privilege of the young. Age roots a person, grounds a body to its habits. Our mothers had each learned to hate or fear the other, depending on which woman you asked. More than that, they were powerful set in their ways. Nettie Mae wanted her household to run as it always had; she expected to despise the Bemis woman and her children for their inconvenient presence even more than she despised us for the wrongs my family had done. My mother expected her life to be difficult, bordering on unbearable, and so it was. Each had learned their own sort of stubbornness. Each had taken up the truths they had trained themselves to see, drinking anger and hate or loneliness and despair as eagerly as the summer-parched prairie drank the rain. I ain't fool enough to think I'm wise, exactly, but I have learned one scrap of wisdom, at least: whatever a body expects their life to be, that's what they'll make of it in the end.

The fall ewes began dropping their lambs on my third night under Nettie Mae's roof. I had finished my supper, helped my ma wash up, and was leading the children upstairs to ready them for bed when Clyde came into the house, bringing with him the sweet and dusty smell of rain on the sage.

Beulah, he said, come on out to the fold if you can. That red-faced ewe has passed her water. The lambs are set to come.

I'd seen calves born, of course, but I'd never seen a sheep come wet and fresh into the world. Clyde had already told me that lambs were most often born in pairs, and after patiently enduring the thunderheads of Nettie Mae's temper, I was eager for the delight of greeting not one but two new and hopeful lives.

I cast a questioning look at my ma, who was drying Nettie Mae's drab plates with a towel.

You may run along, Ma said. She struggled to hold back a weary sigh. She had run herself ragged already, after only a couple of days, but she could see the enthusiasm shining out from me, and she never liked to trample on anybody's joy. Benjamin, you must get your brother and sister ready for bed, and see that they wash their faces in the basin. Dress warmly, Beulah. It's still quite damp outside. I won't have you taking ill.

Up in the cramped room I shared with Ma and Miranda, I pulled on an extra set of stockings and tied my warmest shawl around my body. Then I hurried back down the stairs and out into the fading light with Clyde close beside me.

He carried a lantern. Its tin sides were pierced by tiny stars and half moons, and spots of light scattered wide all around us, sliding and rippling through wet grass, gray as moths in the dusk. The smell of rain still lingered heavy across the land and I breathed it in deeply; it compelled me to inhale, to savor its presence and its rarity. The sheep rustled in their fold. They could sense that one of their number was about to give birth, and it made them anxious. Night was the time of predators, and they had only their hooves and the ram's horns to protect the vulnerable among them.

We eased the fold gate open and then shut, moving slowly to soothe the flock's worry. At the far end of the enclosure, against the stone wall, I could see the red-faced ewe. Night had grayed her, stealing the whiteness of her short wool, recently shorn. The ewe's forelegs had knuckled under her body. She seemed to be kneeling, shoulders against the earth and haunches in the air, as if praying to an unseen god.

That's good, Clyde whispered. They usually bear their lambs in that position. See how her sides have tightened?

The ewe's flanks were tense and trembling, and the great ripe roundness of her belly lifted as she strained.

Come on. If the lamb is stuck, we have to turn it. But Clyde didn't move toward the laboring sheep. He only raised his lantern, setting the stars and moons to dance among the milling flock.

What's the matter? I asked.

I . . . I guess I ain't so good at handling sheep.

But you handle them every day. You have since you were a little boy.

I did it my father's way then. Clyde sounded as if he were making some dire confession, one that might damn him. *This is the first time I've ever presided over the lambing by myself, without my father.*

What of that?

I don't want to do it his way—rough and mean. It just don't seem right to me.

I could understand his reservation. The hour of birth was a sacred time, holy as the hour of death. It wouldn't do to desecrate the moment with violence.

So don't be rough, I told him. *There's no law says you have to.*

Still he hesitated. The flock seemed to bleat with one urgent voice as it circled the pen.

When he finally answered, Clyde's voice was small, almost drowned out by the sounds of his sheep. *I don't know how to be any other way. Whenever I've tried to hold the sheep for shearing, they thrash around and slip right out of my hands. I have to hold them tighter and . . . and frighten them. Force them. Or else they don't keep still.*

Along the western horizon, the last trace of fading light—blue gray, gathered in a close, concentrated band—surrendered to the cold black dominance of rain clouds. Night had truly come. I watched Clyde's face for a long spell; even in the darkness, I could see the sharpness of his features, made stark by uncertainty.

Then I'll show you how, I said at last, and walked across the pen, through the flock that shied away and the darkness that enfolded us all.

I trusted that Clyde would follow, and he did. I went slowly, and told the laboring ewe with my quiet, deliberate movements that I was a friend. Her head jerked up on a stiff neck at my approach, but I paused, waiting for her to settle. She did, as I knew she must. I knelt beside her shoulders, stroking the shorn hide. With a sigh, she accepted the comforts I was murmuring. Specks of light from the lantern moved over the ewe's body, playing along the edge of the stone wall. I could feel Clyde standing behind me, hanging back, still caught in the web of his fear.

You can come up now, I said to Clyde without taking my eyes off the ewe. She's calm; she won't struggle.

He shuffled forward, step by cautious step. The ewe remained as she was, hindquarters up, back feet stamping with pain and impatience. Her breaths came short and harsh.

What do you see? I asked Clyde.

He leaned forward, peering at the ewe's backside. The first lamb's feet are showing. I can see both feet, too. When she has another pain, she'll—

The ewe's contraction came upon her then. She grunted and strained, and the corners of her mouth turned white with foam. But when the straining halted, Clyde shook his head.

The lamb is stuck. I've seen this before; its neck is turned, and that's stopping it from coming.

What shall we do?

He didn't answer with words. Instead, he sank to his knees and reached into the sheep's body. She cried out in alarm, and I spoke to her softly, running my hand from the crown of her head down to the broad, strong span of her back.

There, Clyde said, I've pushed it back up toward her womb. Its head ought to be facing the right direction now. Let's see if it doesn't come.

The sheep's next pain came upon her soon enough, and this time, Clyde declared that he could see the lamb's nose lying between its knees. He laughed with relief as he spoke. He sounded so young, so startled by his own capacity.

You see, I told him, you can be gentle after all.

The ewe required but three pains more, and the lamb slid to the ground. It hit the hard-packed soil with a wet smack and struggled for a moment, tearing its caul, lifting the sharp, newly carved V of its nostrils high into the cool night air. The small mouth opened on a thin, indignant cry. As the dark afterbirth followed, Clyde pulled the caul away from the lamb's body and set the newborn in front of its mother's head. I could hear the excited rush of the ewe's breath as she sniffed her lamb. Then she began to clean it, licking the tight, wet coils of its coat.

Will there be another? I asked.

Yes; it'll come soon.

The second lamb was born without any trouble, and Clyde placed it beside its brother. Her work finished, the ewe rose to all four legs and stood trembling and panting. The new lambs had struggled to their feet; Clyde and I guided them with gentle taps toward their mother's milk. Both suckled at once, and the ewe seemed to calm herself, letting the last of her uncertainty drift into the darkness with the soft plumes of her breath. The flock drew in around the mother and her newborn young, ready to defend them all against the dangers of the night.

We ought to bed her down in the barn, Clyde said. Lambs don't usually come so late in the evening. They'll be stronger by the morning and able to run, but till then, they might bring coyotes or wolves down on the flock.

Clyde paused. Over the tread of the sheep, I could hear his throat working as he swallowed. My father didn't approve of such things, you know.

What things?

Shutting up new lambs in the barn. He always said if a coyote took the lambs, then it was God's will, and anyway, those lambs weren't strong enough or smart enough to survive.

I guess he was right, in a way, I said. But he ain't here anymore, is he? This is your farm now, Clyde, and these are your sheep. It's your own will you ought to follow, not God's.

He stood in a long silence, mulling over my words. Then he nodded— only once, and abruptly at that. But he nodded.

I said, Will any other lambs come tonight?

No; that red-faced one is usually the first of the fall lambers to give birth. But the others will follow her lead. By morning we'll have our hands full, you and me.

Good. I like being a midwife for sheep.

You did a fine job of it, Beulah. There was admiration in his words, and more than a little awe. I accepted both as my natural due.

We left the fold and headed for the barn, Clyde's lantern swinging between us.

I said, How many more ewes will drop their young this fall?

Five more. If we're lucky, we'll have a dozen good lambs by April, when they'll be ready for butchering. Of course, it's ordinary to lose a few to weather and coyotes. That can't be helped. Even so, we ought to make out well next spring.

Inside the barn, Clyde opened the wind screen of his lantern, and the red flicker of candlelight illuminated the space. We set to work, strewing a stall with a deep bed of hay. Clyde was still weak from his fever, near as shaky as the lambs. The next few days would be demanding, with so many births to oversee in addition to the chores Clyde and I had to share. I hoped he would sleep well in his cot by the kitchen fire.

Five more ewes, Clyde had said. But that wasn't so. There were six sheep waiting to give birth. I had noticed the other shorn females in the pen, of course, but there was another ewe, round bodied and hollow at her hip, just as a cow was before she dropped her calf. Her fleece was still long and heavy with its crust of dirt and seeds; Clyde had mistaken her for a maiden and had left her unclipped. The sixth ewe was smaller than the rest—young, I assumed; this could well be her first season as a mother. Her belly wasn't as big as the others', but even so, the new life she carried was ripe and ready to come forth. She would give birth soon, along with the rest of the autumn flock.

I pondered for a spell whether I ought to correct Clyde and tell him about the sixth lambing yet to come. But though I had noticed the young mother only for a moment—she had vanished again among the pressing bodies of her flock almost as soon as I'd glimpsed her—I thought it better not to mention the ewe at all. Brief as my encounter with that ewe had been, I had seen with vivid clarity the sacred shadow hanging over her back, darkening the curve of her poll. Death was waiting, already drawn close beside her. I couldn't yet see whether she or her newborn would die—maybe both—but weak and uncertain as Clyde was that night, I thought it better not to mention the matter to him. Death comes when it comes. You can't do a thing to change it, once the great and final decision has been made. And Clyde had enough to trouble him, with a farm of his own to run—and his own will to hear and obey.

CLYDE

You can't do a thing to change it. That was what Clyde told himself, and told his mother silently, with the hardness of his eyes and the set of his shoulders, as Nettie Mae laid out her expectations for the strict order she intended to maintain beneath her own roof.

"This house is already too crowded for my comfort." Nettie Mae never looked up from her spinning, but her foot beat the treadle faster, and the spokes of the wheel blurred before Clyde's eyes. "It's bad enough that I must have that woman's children all around me. I won't have her belongings cluttering up my home, too."

"The children are well behaved," Clyde said. "A nest of mice would make more racket inside the house."

"It's fitting, that you should compare them to vermin."

"Mother, don't." *You can't do a thing to change this.* Why couldn't he bring himself to rebuke her, to speak those words aloud? "Cora is doing the best she can to keep out of your way and please you."

"She should have thought of pleasing me—"

"Before she dallied with Father," Clyde said wearily. "I know. Listen, Mother; Cora has a loom at her house. She can weave. I've seen the cloth she makes; it's good and sturdy. Seems it would be useful to have plenty of cloth on hand. Winter never gets any warmer, and sewing goes much faster than knitting."

"Well and good; *Cora* may go across the fields and weave at her own house." Nettie Mae never said that name if she could avoid it. When she did deign to speak it, she loaded those two syllables with all the venom of a curse.

Clyde suppressed a sigh. "Well, we must at least bring more of her blankets and clothing for the children. You know there'll be no chance for laundry once the snows come."

"That can't be helped, I suppose," Nettie Mae conceded, glowering at the thread as it slipped from her fingers and wound itself around the bobbin. "But I won't have you carting over any more than the bare essentials." She looked up suddenly, fixing Clyde with her forbidding eyes. "Those dishes of hers—the china from the president. They must remain where they are."

"Mother—"

"I won't hear any argument, Clyde. The china is a bribe, payment for her silence, a reminder of her sins."

"Cora had no say in her own birth."

"Nevertheless, I won't have any reminder of her sinful ways in my home. It's bad enough having the sinner herself. I will admit, she seems humble and contrite . . . for now. But you mark my words: If she were allowed to bring that frippery with her, it would soon go to her head. The woman would strut and preen and think herself higher than the sun in the sky. The dishes stay at her house. That's all I have to say on the matter."

Clyde knew better than to argue with his mother when she had declared her final word. He nodded and left her to the spinning, then hitched Joe Buck to the float and drove across the sage to the Bemis place. The morning had presented high, thin clouds, which scattered the yellow glow of diffuse sunlight across the basin. There was no sign of rain. Cora had led her children back to the little gray house for a day's work, packing up the rest of the belongings they intended to bring to the Webber farm for the long winter ahead. When he reached their

179

garden fence, the little fellows came tumbling out onto the porch to wave in greeting, and Joe Buck threw up his head and whickered.

"You boys tie my horse up to the rail there," Clyde said, stepping down from the float and handing the lead rein to Benjamin. "I'll go on in and speak with your mother."

He found Cora and Beulah in the kitchen, nestling the last pieces of the china set in their crate, covering the cups and saucers with handfuls of straw.

"Afternoon, Mrs. Bemis."

Clyde's mouth had gone dry. He didn't like being the conduit between his mother's anger and its target. Cora struck him as a small, frail, infinitely frightened thing. Life itself was terror enough to her, or so it seemed to Clyde, without heaping Nettie Mae's endless scorn upon her head. But he couldn't change this either—couldn't dodge this task, no matter how bitter the words would taste upon his tongue. Cora had agreed to abide by Nettie Mae's rules, and this was one of them.

"We've finished packing up," Beulah said, "more or less."

"That's good—that's good." Clyde shuffled his feet, hid his hands in his pockets, and glanced around the kitchen rather than meet Cora's eye, or Beulah's. "Mrs. Bemis, I'm sorry to be the one to tell you this, but . . . but my mother said there's no room at the house for the president's china. I'm afraid you must leave it here."

Cora withdrew her hands from the crate. A few wisps of straw fell from her fingers. "Oh, I see." She breathed in, long and slow, and Clyde understood that she was steeling herself. She knew full well the decision was nothing more than Nettie Mae exercising her power. After all, the china could have been stored in the Webber barn. Only pettiness required that it be left behind.

"Your loom, too," Clyde said. His cheeks prickled with embarrassment. "I tried to convince her otherwise—honest, I did."

"It's all well and good, Clyde. We owe you and your mother so much. More than we can ever repay. I'll gladly do as Mrs. Webber asks.

We're an imposition already; let us not make ourselves more of a bother than needs must."

"No harm can come to the china or the loom here at the house," Beulah said. "There's no cause to fret, Ma."

"Everything left here will be safe enough," Cora agreed. "But the loom would come in handy during idle times. I'll have plenty of empty hours once the snows set in. And the china . . . I had thought to keep it close, for if by chance I should find a buyer before the spring—"

Clyde and Beulah spoke up together. "A buyer?"

"Of course." Cora shrugged, turning lightly away from the crate. A basket stood unlidded on the kitchen table, and she placed a few folded cloths inside. "I mean to sell the whole lot."

"You can't, Ma!"

"Beulah, we need the money. What else ought I to sell? We've nothing of any real value."

"But President Grant himself gave you these dishes!"

Cora cut a brief but sharp glance at her daughter. "I'll hear no argument, Beulah. It is what it is."

"We don't need money, Ma. We get by all right."

Clyde could see the furious flush rising to Cora's cheeks, the tears of humiliation gathering in her eyes. He laid a hand gently on Beulah's shoulder. "Leave her be. It can't be an easy decision to make." To Cora, he said, "I'll load up the bags you've packed and those quilts you've folded up in the sitting room. The little fellas can come across with me and help me unload at the big house. Is that good for you, Mrs. Bemis?"

"Yes." The word was brisk and composed, but Clyde didn't miss the way her hand darted up to wipe below one eye. "Thank you, Clyde. You're a good neighbor—a good man."

Clyde led Beulah into the sitting room. They gathered up the quilts, hugging them against their chests.

"How are the lambs faring?" Beulah asked.

"They're strong. I've let the red-faced ewe out of the barn. She's back with the flock, and the new lambs with her."

"Will more ewes drop today, do you suppose?"

"None look as if they're ready just yet, but the rest will come any day now."

Beulah moved toward the door, making for the float cart tied outside. Clyde found himself suddenly apprehensive. He remained rooted to the spot.

The girl looked back and saw his hesitation. "What's the matter, Clyde?"

"Today I've got to . . . I've got to cull the flock. Butcher the older lambs and make way for the new."

Patient, Beulah nodded.

"I'm not sure I can do it, Beulah." Clyde's voice sank to a whisper, through no will of his own. "I don't know how."

"That's nonsense. You've done it plenty times before."

"But not since . . ." Clyde didn't know how to finish the thought, what excuse he could offer that wouldn't brand him as weak. He hadn't killed anything since his father's death. The mere thought of taking the young sheep's lives, of cutting their throats and watching the blood spill hot and red onto the soil, filled him with a nauseous tension, a restless stirring of dread. He remembered the stiff arms of Substance Webber flung out from his body in defiance. He remembered the feel of it, his father's cold, hard chest under his boot, the pressure he'd had to exert to force Substance down into his grave. He couldn't be the one to dole out death now. He couldn't take the lambs' bodies apart and hang the pink things up in the smokehouse as if the work were as ordinary as picking Joe Buck's hooves or shucking corn. Clyde had no more dispassion for death. He had touched death too intimately for it to remain ordinary and isolated, a thing beyond himself.

Beulah softened. She seemed to hear the words he had left unsaid. "I'll be there to help you."

"You've never butchered animals before. Have you?"

"More chickens than I can count."

"A chicken is different from a sheep."

She laughed. "Is that what you think? There ain't no difference between them, as far as I can tell. Except that one has feathers and the other has wool. One lays eggs and the other births lambs. They're both alive; that's what matters. Come to that, the corn and the cabbages are alive, too."

She stepped through the door and disappeared. Clyde heard her out on the porch, scolding Charles and Benjamin to stop their fooling and get back to work; there was so much left to do. Clyde still found himself unable to move. He gripped the folded quilts tighter till his arms quivered with the force. If Beulah saw little difference between a cornstalk and a hen, between a hen and a sheep, then did she discern any separation between a sheep and a man? Clyde didn't want to know the answer to that question.

God made man different from the animals, he told himself. *There is a difference. There must be. Surely Beulah sees that much. Surely she can't believe otherwise.*

But God was a distant, unfocused being. What had He to do with life on the prairie, with survival out here among a living sea of grass? The sheep, the hens, the cornstalks discarded and rotting behind the barn— all were nearer than God. The earth was nearer still. Clyde could feel it, somewhere down below the floor boards on which he stood, helpless and stunned. The earth pulled at him and held him to this place. And God in His Heaven was far, far away.

~

A few hours of daylight still remained by the time Clyde drove the laden float back across the pasture and helped the Bemis family carry their belongings inside. When the last basket had been toted into the house and the little fellows had taken Joe Buck to the barn to unhitch him and rub down his hide, Beulah turned to Clyde, silent with expectation. The task could be delayed no longer. The time had come to cull the flock.

Clyde and Beulah drove the sheep back to the fold with its hard stone walls. There was no need to speak; they worked together with the same strange understanding, the feeling and knowing that flowed between them as easily, as naturally, as if they shared one heart, one river-branched current of blood. When the sheep were contained, Clyde stood mute at the fence, gripping its upper rail with a hand so cold he might as well have laid his palm against ice. He watched the flock as they circled desperately, bleating and crying. They seemed to know what must follow. And they wanted to live. Didn't every living thing want the same?

"I can't choose," Clyde finally managed to say. Who was he to decide which lives should end? Who was he to take what the prairie had given? Pressure built in his throat. It stung; it burned. It choked off his words, and he was grateful for that mercy. If he could have said anything more, he would have confessed his emotions: Sorrow at the deaths he must dole out, pain and regret over the shortness of the spring lambs' lives. Fear of the blood—an instinctive fear, one all people shared when they saw how fast and hot it flowed.

Men didn't feel fear, or pain, or sorrow. Men did not regret. Wasn't that what Clyde's father had always told him? That was the reality Substance had worked to create: A son who was a man. A son who did not feel those weak and shameful things.

Beulah climbed up and over the gate. "Then I'll choose for you."

She walked into the center of the fold and stood unmoving, with her back to Clyde. The sheep circled her once, twice. They slowed. Their voices quieted; the dark eyes ceased to roll. Now there was only the sound of their breath, soft as water over stones.

Beulah lifted her hand as one of the spring lambs passed. She touched its back. The lamb slowed, stopped, and stood close by her side. She touched another, but it kicked up its hooves and ran. It lost itself among the flock, and Beulah made no move to pursue it. She went on that way, waiting, watching, touching one young sheep and then another. Some stilled beneath her hand and remained at her side. Others fled, and she left them to leap and shove, left them to the fast heat of life. Soon seven spring lambs stood docile and ready at Beulah's back. Clyde shuddered to see it—the ease with which Beulah chose, the lambs' calm acceptance of their fate. The proceeding was unnatural, or at least, not a thing done before. It seemed to Clyde as if Beulah had silently asked for the spring lambs' lives, and they had consented to face the knife. She turned and made her way back to the gate. The seven chosen lambs followed quietly in her wake, committed to their terrible purpose.

For a moment, as he watched the girl and her sheep crossing the pen, Clyde despised the lambs. Why didn't they fight for their lives? Why didn't they flee back into the crowd, as their brothers and sisters had done? *I would never go so willingly to my death.* He thought of the grave by the river, its yawning darkness, the smell of freshly dug soil. He thought of Substance's arms, outstretched. *That's the right way. The man's way.*

Resist the end until the end comes, till its jaws gape wide and it takes you, whole and fighting.

NETTIE MAE

You can't do a thing to change it.

By the time midday gave way to afternoon, Nettie Mae had lost track of how many times she'd repeated those words to herself. Every time she looked up from her spinning, she found more evidence of Cora's intrusion. A wooden soldier one of the Bemis boys had dropped behind the chairs and forgotten. The frayed end of a snipped thread, discarded by the small girl—scarcely older than a baby—who seemed intent on learning how to embroider, even though her fingers were childish and clumsy. Now one of Cora's hairs had found its way to Nettie Mae's skirt. Long, dark brown, curled upon itself like a deceiving serpent, it could only have come from Cora's head. Nettie Mae's hair was pin straight and softer in color.

She took the hair gingerly between thumb and forefinger, pulled it from her knee, and let it fall to the floor. She very nearly crushed it under her heel, too, just for good measure. Nettie Mae had hardly seen the Bemis woman all day, praise God for His mercy. Cora had taken advantage of a break in the rains to lead her brood back to her own home, there to finish all the necessities of invasion.

Even when she's gone, she is still here. Nettie Mae scowled down at the floor. The hair had vanished against the dark wood, but she wasn't fool enough to believe it was no longer there merely because she couldn't see it. She tempered herself again. *You can't do a thing to change it. Not if you wish your son to survive the winter.*

Now that the little children were established in Nettie Mae's home, she could admit a grudging acceptance of them. They were well behaved, a fact which startled Nettie Mae, considering the loose morals of their mother. Although they were young, the two little boys and the baby girl seemed earnestly determined to acquit themselves well. They said "please" and "thank you" and "may I." They took to their few small chores and duties without being told twice. They were children, so a certain amount of fussing was to be expected, but on the whole, they kept quiet and took pains to yield before the mistress of the house. The girl, Miranda, even smiled shyly at Nettie Mae now and then, when she happened to catch the child's eye, and more than once, Nettie Mae was startled to find herself half smiling in return.

Pleasant children. It was far too late for their mother to redeem her sins and her soul. Beulah, with her casual disregard for propriety and her unsettling ways with animals, seemed bent on making of herself a sinner equal to her mother in infamy if not in specific offenses. Nettie Mae had little use for either Beulah or Cora, save for the work they did. They were beasts of burden, nothing more—good for nothing other than to ease the weight of responsibility Clyde must carry until the spring thaw came. But perhaps Nettie Mae might hope to redeem the younger Bemis children. If God proved merciful, then she would stand as an influence in their lives, a pattern of righteous womanhood they might look to for a better, more suitable example. A mother's sins might pass down to her offspring, generation after generation, but perhaps in these tender years, when the mind was still as malleable as freshly dug clay, there was hope that one might break the patterns of iniquity.

Nettie Mae allowed the last of her wool to wind upon the bobbin, and the wheel slowed and creaked to a stop. She stood, knuckling and arching her back, stifling a groan as she stretched the morning's stiffness from her muscles. Hunger had left her feeling more on edge than usual;

she hadn't had a bite since breakfast, just after sunrise. She headed for the pantry, where she had hidden a few jars of potted spiced chicken and jackrabbit in a dim corner, behind a large, heavy box of curing salt. It was rare that Nettie Mae's store of potted meats lasted into the winter. The delicacy would vanish all the sooner if Cora and her brood found the jars. But as she entered the kitchen, Nettie Mae glanced out the window and found Clyde driving his low-slung float across the pasture. The little girl was perched on the seat beside him, while the remainder of the Bemis family trailed the cart on foot.

No time for more than buttered bread, then, to take the edge off her hunger. Not if she hoped to protect her private stores.

By the time Nettie Mae finished her hasty meal, the float had pulled into the yard, and the whole crowd of Bemises busied themselves with unloading its contents. Nettie Mae was relieved to see that they had brought only the most urgent necessities—baskets of clothing, extra quilts for cold months to come, preserves and sacks of grain, salt, and sugar from Cora's pantry. They had even loaded the contents of her root cellar into a few heavy crates; Nettie Mae stood on the front step of her sod-walled fortress and surveyed the onions in their papery red skins, the squashes bearing pale, raised nets on their yellow rinds. The Bemises had evidently dug up what roots still remained in their garden; there was a crate heaped with turnips and another full of parsnips, all still dark with soil.

"This will never do," Nettie Mae said. "You've dug the parsnips far too early. They'll be bitter, not sweet."

"Oh, I know," Cora said in that meek, apologetic tone—that show of feminine frailty that always flicked on Nettie Mae's nerves. "Sweet parsnips would have been much better, but we thought we ought to take advantage of Clyde's cart today, rather than making him drive over again after the frost arrives."

"I don't like bitter roots."

Cora tried a smile, designed to placate. "The children and I will eat these, if you prefer. We won't complain."

Nettie Mae grunted. "Nonsense. There's twice the work in cooking two separate meals. We shall just have to settle for bitter suppers."

Cora came toward Nettie Mae, displaying her most sycophantic mildness. She climbed one step of the short porch. Only one. Nettie Mae halted her with a stare.

"Let me cook, Mrs. Webber," Cora said. "You do enough work already."

"Isn't my cooking suitable?"

Cora was quick to amend her thoughtless commentary. "Of course it's suitable! Why, it's better than suitable; your cooking is delicious. We all love it, don't we, children?"

Solemn and quiet, the Bemis brood nodded.

"But I know you've been meaning to preserve those apples you've stored in the barn," Cora went on. "With the weather so damp, we oughtn't to wait much longer. They might begin to rot. If I were cooking and you were preserving—"

"Then we would both be in the kitchen together."

There was no need for Nettie Mae to say more. Cora lowered her eyes. Those smooth, girlishly rounded cheeks colored. Nettie Mae wanted to slap them, left and right, until they turned redder still.

Ordinarily, Cora held her tongue once she knew she had pushed Nettie Mae too far. But it seemed she had dug up a backbone in her garden that morning, along with those inadequate parsnips.

"Would it be so terrible," Cora ventured, "if you and I were to work side by side? There is much I might do for you—many burdens I might ease."

It was the wrong thing to say; Cora seemed to understand that at once. She swallowed hard and half turned away, waiting with the air of a cringing dog for Nettie Mae's reply.

Nettie Mae obliged with the answer Cora seemed to expect. "My greatest burden of all is you, Mrs. Bemis, as I'm certain you know."

Clyde spoke a few quiet words to the boys, and they led the horse and cart off to the barn, while Beulah picked up her sister and carried the child around a corner of the house. Nettie Mae and Cora were left alone on the stoop.

"I see little you might do to ease my real burden," Nettie Mae said, "until you've departed from my house. I'm not like you; I have no need for useless chatter. I need no 'company' while I work. Such notions are better left in the cities where they belong—with the idle, sinful women who fritter away their lives in shameful ease, pretending all the while that they live the lives of honest ladies."

With the children and the horse gone, silence pervaded the yard. Nettie Mae could hear the thick, abrupt sound of Cora swallowing.

She didn't care whether she hurt Cora. In fact, Nettie Mae rather felt herself righteously entitled to lash out and wound. Wasn't that satisfaction the least of what she was owed? Cora had made these tremulous overtures of friendship from her first day occupying the Webber house. What offensive presumption—what hubris! That woman was shameless in her pursuit of attention. Cora seemed to believe the world owed her admiration, sympathy, happiness. Never had Nettie Mae passed the Bemis woman in the upstairs hall or drifted past her while she sat sewing by the hearth but Cora looked up hopefully, undeterred by all Nettie Mae's countless past rejections. Cora thirsted for idle conversation as a drunkard thirsted for whiskey. She required friendship, fellowship—and the stark bareness of that need disgusted Nettie Mae. The woman had no self-control. She was lust and gluttony and weakness, all pressed into one perfectly formed, rebukingly feminine mold.

She has lived here just as long as I. Longer, in fact. Eight years for her. Hasn't she come to understand by now what the prairie is?

Cora almost seemed to hear Nettie Mae's thoughts, for at that moment, she turned back to face her. Cora's eyes remained downcast, though, and Nettie Mae caught the impression that she had trapped the woman who had wronged her, pinioned her between two terrible ramparts. One was the prairie at Cora's back—its endless expanse of flat emptiness, its lonesome monotony, the sea of nothing upon which no friendly vessel sailed. The other was Nettie Mae herself.

Why should I be a friend to her—this woman who took from me the only life I knew? Let her go on thirsting for what she craves. She won't get a drop of society from me.

There might be nothing Nettie Mae could do to change her own circumstances this season, or the next. But neither would she change Cora's. The Bemis woman reaped all the isolation, all the cold rejection, she had sown.

"I regret, Mrs. Webber, that my children and I must be a burden to you. But know that I am grateful for your kindness and generosity in taking us in. Very likely you saved our lives. We are all indebted to you."

"Your children are no burden."

Nettie Mae startled herself by answering with that confession. Her heart pressed hard against her ribs and felt, quite suddenly and with a warm, strangling force, far too large for her chest. Unbidden, Luther's face leaped into memory with brutal clarity. Luther had been but two years older than Cora's Benjamin when the fever had taken him away. He had been a good boy—sweet tempered and mild. It was almost a mercy that God had taken Luther back into His arms before Substance could truly take the boy under his black wing. Luther never would have stood up to Substance's methods. None of her dead children would have survived their father long. Clyde was the only one who possessed adequate strength.

And it's for Clyde's sake I do this now. I mustn't forget that. No matter how I may hate this woman, I love my son far more.

For Clyde's sake—for the sake of the small and fragile harmony Nettie Mae knew she must construct if they were all to survive the winter under one roof—she said, "I must tell you, in fact, your children are quite good and well behaved. They seem sensible, considering their ages."

"Thank you." Cora sounded relieved, almost giddy with surprise at Nettie Mae's kindness.

"All except Beulah. She's . . ." Nettie Mae shook her head, scowling past Cora to a deep-blue slash of low-hanging cloud. It blanketed the southern horizon—more rain on the way. "Beulah is strange. Unnatural."

"She's only dreamy," Cora said. "Many girls of Beulah's age prove distractible. She'll grow out of those habits with time."

I've seen her take a rooster's life before the bird was even dead. Nettie Mae didn't dare speak those words aloud. She feared that if she did, the image would come crowding back into her mind—the bird's dark wings sagging in submission, the ease with which it had laid itself on the altar of death. She would never sleep again if those pictures took root and blossomed behind closed eyes. The clucking of her hens among the tall grasses seemed intrusive to Nettie Mae now. She folded her arms tightly across her middle and forbade herself from shrinking away from the sound.

Nettie Mae thumped a crate with the toe of her boot. "We had best get these roots cleaned off and stored."

Cora nodded eagerly. "Yes; you're right, of course. I'll fetch some rags, and together we can—"

"Together? No. You may brush them clean and take them to the root cellar. I've other work I must see to now."

"Very well," Cora said softly.

Nettie Mae opened the door, and the warmth of her house rushed out to meet her. The smells of woodsmoke and lanolin surrounded her, as they always did when she came in from the cold. For one heartbeat, one flash, she remembered the sound of Luther's voice. She had no recollection of the words he was speaking, but she could remember the tones, the sound of him, high and gentle and trusting, still years short of manhood. The memory came upon her so abruptly that Nettie Mae drew a sharp breath. It was almost a gasp of pain.

On the threshold, she turned back and fixed Cora with another stare.

Cora waited, trembling, for Nettie Mae to speak.

"If your children are hungry," Nettie Mae said, "you'll find some good potted meat in the pantry. In the far corner behind the big alderwood salt box. Only leave a little for me, will you?"

She stepped inside and shut the door firmly behind her.

CORA

There's not a thing you can do about it. Nettie Mae will never forgive you, and why ought she? If it were Nettie Mae who had lain with Ernest, you wouldn't forgive her.

Left alone on the bare, unsheltered stoop of the Webber house, Cora raised her eyes from the ground at last. She rolled her head carefully, sighing with relief as the bones of her neck shifted and popped. No one could know what a strain it was, to hold oneself in submission. To debase oneself before the fury of another. Only the knowledge that Nettie Mae was righteous in her wrath kept Cora fixed to her purpose, committed to this meek abasement.

Months. There are months yet to go. I've only lived a few days under Nettie Mae's roof—not even a week. How will I survive until spring? A dull ache had settled into her neck and back, the cost of hanging her head in shame day in and day out. Cora repeated the litany of her distraction, the words she clung to during moments like these to keep her wits about her, to keep her will strong enough to last through the barren season that stretched ahead. *I have the president's china, and time enough to find a buyer. When the thaw arrives, I'll have train fare in my hand. We'll be in Carbon as soon as the mud is hard enough for driving, and Saint Louis only days later. You've survived eight years in this place, Cora Bemis. You can last a few months longer.*

Cora settled on the stoop and pulled a rag from the pocket of her apron. She took a parsnip from the crate and cleaned its tender ivory skin, beating at the caked red soil with the cloth as if she were whisking away flies, and the soil fell away in damp crumbs. Cora tossed the first parsnip into a nearby basket, which someone had forgotten in the shadow of the stoop. She cleaned another, and another, grateful for the easy work, allowing her thoughts to roam.

She must get a message to Ernest at the jailhouse up in Paintrock. She had packed her letter box with its ink and blotter, its carved bone pen, and a few remaining pieces of paper. The box was hidden under the children's clothes in the largest reed basket, which Beulah had already carried upstairs. Nettie Mae knew nothing of its existence.

Would she have refused me the letter box, too, if she had known I would try to bring it?

She would tell Ernest everything: That she and the children would spend the winter with Mrs. Webber, so he mustn't fear for their well-being. That she would take them back home, to the city, come spring. She would tell Ernest that if he didn't hate her too much, if he still felt any affection for his wife—any duty toward her and the children—they would reunite in Saint Louis and go on living there. But once the winter had passed, Cora could no longer remain in the cold shadow of the Bighorns. Let Ernest make of that revelation whatever he would.

Cora lifted her eyes from the parsnips in her lap and stared south, to where the last shallow slope of the foothills leveled into the eternal flatness of the prairie. It stretched forever, an unrelenting emptiness of grass and scrub, gray beneath a heavy gray sky.

It was the openness of the prairie that had always upset Cora the most. In a land so flat and unvaried, there was nowhere one might hide, no shelter from the storms of life nor from the beasts that came hunting by night. Whenever she stepped outside her house, whenever she looked out a window, there was the great expanse of the untamed world. How heartless it was, had ever been, from that day long ago when she and Ernest left Carbon in their wagon. It was too open to the sky above, a disorienting vastness of sky that arched overhead like the cupped palm of some unfathomable giant, a vast hand descending to trap a scuttling insect. The relentless heat of the sun by day, the violence of the storms that broke against the Bighorns—the prairie offered no shelter, no respite. It gave nothing but hardship. Each day was a battle, forcing the wilderness to yield a paltry sustenance. And well did Cora know that life was only possible here, where the two isolated homesteads crouched at the base of the foothills, because of the proximity of reliable water. Beyond the dark line of the cottonwoods, the only visible trees for miles in any direction, ran the Nowood River and its tributary creek, a rocky, red-silted tumble of water the Indians called Tensleep, or so Ernest had once told Cora. She shuddered to imagine what their lives would be like without the blessing of year-round water.

Such dark musings never entirely left Cora in peace, but now, in the silence of the afternoon, in the muggy warmth that plagued autumn just before evening fell, her own thoughts were too much to bear. She turned her face away from the southern prairie and concentrated on her work. It went quickly enough, once she quieted the fearful voice inside. The basket was half-full of cleaned roots and the cloth was smudged red by her efforts. By and by, Cora filled the basket to its brim, but the crate of freshly dug parsnips still held at least three-quarters of the harvest. She must take the roots to Nettie Mae's cellar and store them well against rot.

Cora stood, stretched her legs and back, then lifted the heavy basket and propped it on a hip. She carried it around the house and made for the earthen mound that served as the Webber cellar. Tassels of grass, their heads shaggy with seed, waved along the cellar's upper curve. On the eastern face of the mound, a small door of thick wooden planks and iron straps sealed shut the man-made cavern.

Cora set her basket beside the door and reached for its handle, but Beulah's voice caught her attention. She looked up and found her daughter emerging from the sheepfold. Clyde held the gate, and Beulah passed him with that familiar, drifting stride—how Cora envied the ease, the confidence with which her daughter moved through a hostile world. How proud it made her, to know that Beulah was a creature set apart from fear.

She never learned that courage from me.

Cora straightened in surprise when the sheep followed Beulah through the gate. There were seven of them, lambs grown just to the verge of maturity, and they moved with docility in single file. As the last sheep cleared the gate, Clyde swung it closed and tied it securely, then jogged to catch up with Beulah. They spoke as they walked together, heading for the big barn and, Cora now understood, the small round slaughter pen that stood beside it. Cora couldn't make out the words they exchanged, but the two young people were calm, glad in one another's company. No fear shadowed the space between them, no resentment, though they were Webber and Bemis, the scions of enemy clans. Their conversation made a muted sort of music, and Cora shut her eyes for a moment, savoring the rare sound.

"That girl of yours is trouble."

Cora started—she nearly screamed. She hadn't heard the kitchen door open, hadn't heard Nettie Mae striding across the yard toward the cellar. Yet there Nettie Mae stood, stiff with the fury that never left her, as close beside Cora as she ever deigned to come.

Nettie Mae was holding an old hemp sack in her hands, empty. She jerked her head toward the cellar door. "I've come for a few roots and things for the stew pot. Time to get supper cooking."

"Of course."

Cora seized the iron handle and pulled hard. The door opened slowly, grudging every inch. Cool air rushed across her forehead and cheeks, easing for a moment the thick and oppressive atmosphere of afternoon. The cellar smelled of damp earth, the spice and tang of harvest.

"Would you like me to—" Cora reached for the hemp sack, but Nettie Mae jerked it away. She brushed past Cora and vanished into the darkness below the mound.

Cora heard the bump of onions or rutabagas against some wood-sided crate, the rustle of Nettie Mae's hands sifting impatiently through straw. A moment later, she emerged with a scowl and a sack full of roots.

Nettie Mae's hard stare slid past Cora toward the barn. The skin below her dark eyes tensed, a sign of extreme displeasure, which Cora had already come to recognize in her neighbor turned reluctant savior. She turned to see what Nettie Mae had seen—to find out what had redoubled her anger.

Clyde and Beulah were leaning on the rail of the slaughter pen, side by side, talking as they watched the chosen lambs. Cora shook her head slowly, uncertain why the scene upset Nettie Mae.

"That girl of yours is trouble," Nettie Mae said again. "Trouble. You mark my words."

"Beulah isn't a bad girl," Cora said, almost pleading. "She works hard."

"She most certainly does not. If you call her shameful lollygagging 'hard work,' then I suppose it's no mystery why you ended up here, seeking refuge under my roof."

Cora held her tongue, waiting for Nettie Mae to say more. There certainly were more words coming, more accusations. Cora could sense them.

"You had best teach that daughter of yours how to be a proper woman—assuming you still have any inkling of propriety—and do it now, while you still can."

Silence fell between them, stretched on the pegs of Cora's sins. She didn't know whether Nettie Mae expected a response.

"What . . . what do you mean?" Cora ventured.

"You know what I mean. And heed what I say, Cora Bemis: If your daughter gets herself into trouble, you'll get no help from me. You'll have reached the end of my charity, and no mistake. I'll see to it that Clyde never claims the baby as his own. You must make up your mind to break the pattern of your family's iniquities, for if you don't, you'll only compound your miseries and destroy the lives of all who come after you. Clyde isn't the president, Cora. There will be no fancy tableware to buy the complacency and silence of a bastard child."

Nettie Mae spun on her heel and marched away before Cora could frame some hopeless answer. She swallowed hard, willing herself not to cry. She bent to pick up her basket again and carry it inside the cellar. Instead, she took a single parsnip and held it in her hands, turning it over, feeling the smoothness of its skin, the tiny hairs of its roots, the faint grainy texture of what little soil remained.

Then, for no reason she could name, Cora lifted the parsnip to her lips and bit off the thin, pointed tip. An acrid pungency filled her mouth, the flavor so powerful it made her want to spit. It was the bitterest thing Cora had ever tasted.

7

WHEN WE HEARD THE THUNDER

I felt winter drawing closer, coming faster than it had ever come before. We who had gathered in the sod-brick house worked against time, and the hours seemed to regard us with calculation, a swift and predatory intent. But before the harshest weather set in, we stripped our two farms of every stalk and grain. Whatever this menacing, early winter might bring, at least we could be certain none of us would go hungry.

Everyone, even the smallest, helped bring in the final harvest. On days when no rain fell, Benjamin and Charles climbed up into the Webber apple trees and picked the remaining fruit from the boughs. The shadowed interior of the barn was sweet—a bright, fresh scent of ripened apples. Nettie Mae and my mother took turns with bushels of fruit, cooking down sauce flavored with dark molasses sugar, pressing cider, and stringing up slices of apple, cheery as springtime flowers, on twine above the kitchen hearth, where the heat shrank the slices down to leather.

Miranda had the task of picking dried pods from the skeletal wisps of bean plants, saving those that had been left on the vine to mature into next year's seed. Miranda was small, but she did her work well, presenting me with baskets and bowls brimming over with the split brown pods and rattling with the seeds that had already dropped from their husks. I showed my little sister how to shake the beans free and lay them out on old rags in the cool solitude of the barn, where the memory of recent rains could dry from their plump, shiny skins. Then I helped her pack the seeds she had gathered into little clay jars, which we set high upon a shelf beside stores of corn, wheat, and barley, peas and squash and beet seeds. There the seeds would dream through winter till the season of sowing came again.

The root cellar was fragrant with the earthy bite of turnips and the sharp richness of onions and dried braids of meadow garlic. The smokehouse exhaled a constant blue breath through cracks in its plank sides and around the edges of its roof. A few late-ripening pumpkins, the last fruits of the vine, stood proudly on Nettie Mae's oaken mantel, orange skins plump and glistening with the vinegar bath that would drive away the rot. Even with winter's rapid advance, we had managed to bring in the whole harvest, right down to the cull of the spring lambs. If you considered only our food stores, you'd have thought us well prepared for whatever the harsh and eager season thought to bring.

But if you observed my ma and Nettie Mae together—the few times when their work forced them into one another's company—you would have shaken your head in dire prediction and prayed for peace between our families, without real hope of your prayer being answered. Whenever Ma and Nettie Mae crossed paths, the air around them seemed full of yellow jackets, buzzing and angry, bristling with venomous stings. They never shouted at each other nor exchanged any insults that I ever heard. But all the same, there was no mistaking their ire. It lived in both their hearts.

Ma hid her bitterness with unthinking ease—the cultured city woman, the president's niece, too proud and refined to lash out in anger. Nettie Mae had always been a woman of half-wild places, and she saw no purpose in tempering her rage. She never spared a word of thanks for my mother's help nor wasted breath on encouragement. Nor did she miss a chance to scowl when the opportunity came along. Her dislike for my ma was naked and unashamed, but Cora's distaste for Nettie Mae was at least as great as the guilt that still shrouded her heart a month after Substance's death. My ma had a natural talent for disguising her feelings.

But she had never been able to hide her feelings from me. Few people could, who I ever met. That was my talent, I guess you could say—my purpose in the world—to see and know. To see and know, even when everyone else had blinded themselves to the truth.

Ma had never loved life on the prairie. She couldn't help feeling fragile and bare whenever she looked upon the greatness of the world, for then she knew herself to be a small and helpless thing, and the blunt fact of her weakness couldn't be ignored. Before the power of Nature, its inescapable presence and fixed dominion, all men and women are as mice in the talons of the hawk. In a city, I could well imagine—surrounded by streets and commerce and carriages, everyone dressed Sunday-fine, with the forests and fields only a thin shadow on a distant horizon—a body might trick itself into believing that mankind held the world in its white-knuckled hand. But on our homestead, the wilderness ran right up to the front door. A few steps from the threshold and the prairie had you, stripping away the power of man, caging you under the dome of an endless sky.

A woman like my ma couldn't do a thing save cower before the inescapable vastness of the plains. That flat solitude of weak light and blue shadow, of grass and sage and cicada's hum, went on and on to every horizon, to every eternity that had turned its ceaseless cycles below the sun, back to the time before mankind existed. And the wilderness would go on existing long after mankind had fallen to dust and blown away on a rain-scented wind. That was why my ma refused to love the land on which she depended for her very survival: because the land never allowed my ma to deny her insignificance. The buffalo moved in far-off herds, darkening the distant plain, and she knew the great majestic animals had no care for her, a woman left to her own devices. The pronghorns ran before the wind, heads up and free, and Ma knew she didn't frighten them. She was nothing, in their estimation. The hawks dove into the tall grass and lumbered back to the air, dangling their prey. Ma watched the jackrabbits kick and scream as they were torn from the earth and carried into the sky. She knew that she would die someday, that mankind itself wouldn't last forever. She feared and hated the greatest truth, the greatest beauty Nature had to offer.

But as we put the harvest by in jars and crates and beds of straw, a spark of strength flared in my mother's breast. It was the first time in all my life I had ever known her to be so steady. At first, I thought it was Nettie Mae's nearness that had braced Ma up, in spite of the yellow jackets that swarmed between them. I thought the mere presence of another grown woman was a comfort to my ma, even if that woman was hard and cold, ever alert for the least excuse to throw Cora Bemis out of her house. Nettie Mae hated my ma, but at least Nettie Mae was society, of a sort. But soon enough, I came to see the situation more clearly. After Nettie Mae would rake Ma with her eyes or spit a few hard words of instruction and then storm from the room, my ma would smile to herself with her head down over preserves or sewing. It was the comforting smile she had used on us, her children, when we had skinned our knees or stubbed our toes and cried from the pain. It was the smile that had always said, You'll be all right. The pain will pass. By and by, you'll see.

I came to understand that my ma was brooding a secret. Some plan had taken root within her, and she was nurturing it with all the tenderness she gave to her children. It was as precious to her as I was, or Charles or Benjamin or my baby sister. And in the presence of that secret, sheltered by her private thoughts, the meekness fell away from my ma's demeanor, replaced by a clear-eyed determination I had never seen in her before.

I noted a change in Nettie Mae, too. For all she prided herself on her unbending hatred, her rigid adherence to the rules of moral life, she was softening, bit by bit. Oh, not to my ma; Nettie Mae was firm in her resolve to hate poor, tender Cora unto the very end of days. But as we settled into a new routine of life, the mistress of the big sod house grew a little less harsh with my brothers, and gentler with tiny Miranda's feelings.

Nettie Mae Webber was a natural lover of children, and there was nothing she could do about it. She had set her heart to despise every creature *that carried the Bemis name, and she still wore her dire frown whenever she laid eyes on Cora's offspring—me, most especially. Yet I noticed the way she would turn to watch my brothers as they scampered outside to their chores. The faint lean of her body, yearning after their boisterous energy. I saw, now and then, how she smiled over her spinning, and all because Charles and Benjamin were singing a soldier's marching tune in the low glow of an overcast afternoon, somewhere out beside the long shed. Miranda had solemnly presented Nettie Mae with a handful of withered chicory flowers, and I had thought Nettie Mae would toss them in the scrap bucket for the hogs. But later that day, when the call of a bird drew my attention away from my chores, I looked up from the wall of the sheepfold to find Nettie Mae standing at her bedroom window, holding back the curtain with one hand, watching with disapproval as Clyde and I counted the flock in the pen. There on the sill before her were the ragged blue flowers, soaking in a cup of water.*

It was Nettie Mae's native tenderness for children that brought her to the yard, running, panting, pale faced but flint eyed, when we heard the thunder. And it was she who acted in time to save Miranda's life. Hard as Nettie Mae was, tightly as she had bound herself to hatred, without her level head and steel command, my sister would never have survived.

CORA

When she heard the thunder, so close that it seemed the very Judgment of God come down from a vengeful Heaven, Cora bolted up from her chair. Her letter box, the lid of which converted into a small lap desk, flew from her knee and crashed against the floor, sending its contents clattering and rolling around the close quarters of the bedroom. Something hot and prickling rushed through Cora's body, concentrated in her throat and lungs. For a moment, she knew only that the sky had split overhead with a force so sudden and violent, so shockingly near, that reality itself must have splintered. Then she felt the fire in her throat, the fast pulse burning along her limbs, and she believed she must have been struck by the lightning. A heartbeat later, she scolded herself for a fool. How could she have been struck? She was in her cramped new bedroom, writing a letter to Ernest, safe behind the sod-brick walls of the Webber farmhouse. The heat and pressure in her chest were relics of her own terrified scream. As the roar of thunder quieted a little, leaving only its frantic, trembling echo in her ears, she heard the reverberation of her shriek, too, fading quickly in the confines of her room.

Cora gasped and turned to look at the spilled letter box. The inkwell had fallen, of course, but luck had dropped it squarely on Cora's green shawl, which lay crumpled beside the chair. She hissed through clenched teeth, struggling to hold back a curse, and fell to her knees, fumbling the inkwell with hands that would not stop shaking. Half the ink had poured out already. Her shawl would bear an ugly black stain; she must make another, assuming there was enough yarn to spare. But at least the ink hadn't spilled onto Nettie Mae's floor.

Cora scooped the rest of her writing implements back into the box and found the letter to Ernest, which had skittered beneath the bed. Cora whisked it out of the shadows and examined the page. The tumble hadn't damaged the letter, thank God, for Cora wasn't certain she could bring herself to write those words again. What little courage she had found would inevitably fail if she were to begin the letter anew.

> *I will leave Wyoming Territory by train in the spring.*
> *I will take our children with me. Come and find us in*
> *Saint Louis if, by the time you are released from prison,*
> *you can still think of me as your wife.*

She thrust the letter into her apron pocket and hurried from the room, down the stairs, and into the empty kitchen.

But for the memory of thunder—shocking and close, a palpable tightness in the air—the Webber house was silent and still. A fire crackled on the hearth, simmering the stew pot and sending tendrils of steam up the dark hollow of the chimney. Outside, the cattle called to one another, the pitch of their frantic voices rising to bellows of panic. Horses screamed in their paddock; the drumbeat of their hooves cut through the sod walls as they ran the perimeter of their enclosure, seeking escape. She could hear the sheep coming closer, too, bleating in fear as they abandoned the open pasture for the solid comfort of the stone fold.

Cora edged closer to the kitchen window and peered outside. The rear yard of the Webber homestead was dark as twilight, yet the day couldn't have been later than two hours past noon. The sky was so black with cloud that Cora could scarcely make out the ramparts of cottonwoods along the river.

Why hadn't Clyde or Beulah thought to mention the storm? Surely they had seen it coming; they had been outside all day, fortifying the cattle fences with the willow branches they'd cut from the banks of Tensleep Creek. Cora craned her neck, struggling to see the cattle pen clearly through the rippled glass. She could make out little of the scene, but there was no mistaking Clyde's strong, lean form running toward the house.

Has someone been struck by lightning? Her heart froze between one beat and the next. *Beulah. No, God, please!*

Cora flew out the kitchen door into the yard, already shouting for Clyde, dreading the news he would bring. But he ran past her, waving his hat in one hand, and Cora turned to watch him go. One of the horses had jumped the paddock fence; Clyde seemed to dance with the terrified animal, dodging this way, that way, dodging again to cut off its flight. When the horse finally recognized its master, it calmed just enough for Clyde to approach, though it still tossed its head and chewed the air. White spittle flew from its lips.

"Ma!" Beulah shouted from the barn, gesturing with one spindly arm through the partially open door. "Get inside, Ma! There's lightning."

Thank God she's safe. Cora reeled in the yard. The air was dense, choking, tight with the intrusion of the storm. Her body had gone frigid with fear, stiff and clumsy, as she braced for another hellish crack. That thunder had been like the voice of Hell itself—not the long, gentle roll, the mellow power of weather skirting the world at a distance of many miles. This storm had torn the sky directly overhead. Breathless, Cora looked up and found a flat slab of cloud, blacker than pitch, protruding over the crest of the Bighorns. The storm had come upon the two farms suddenly, then, from north and east—not the usual route for autumn weather. No wonder they'd had no warning; the mountain range had hidden from view the advance of that great, dark beast of cloud and wind and striking fire.

Cora turned back toward the house but had only stumbled a few steps when Nettie Mae erupted from the root cellar. She burst out so suddenly that Cora lurched away and almost screamed again. For once, Nettie Mae didn't bother scowling at Cora's proximity. Pale and shaken, she took the fabric of Cora's sleeve in a hard fist and would not let go.

"Lightning?"

Nodding, Cora swallowed hard. It was the only answer she could manage.

"Did you see it strike?"

Cora shook her head.

Nettie Mae, too, looked up at the bank of cloud. She watched for a moment, narrowing her eyes slowly, tracking the storm's pace as it sailed beyond the mountain peaks. The day gave up more of its feeble light. Cora strained against Nettie Mae's grip, desperate for the shelter of the house, yet unwilling to wrench her sleeve free of the other woman's hand.

Finally, Nettie Mae spoke. "It's not likely any of our buildings were hit. If they were, we'd see smoke rising by now. So the worst of the storm hasn't arrived yet, but it soon will. Look—do you see the rain?"

Trembling, Cora followed Nettie Mae's eyes. The jagged teeth of the Bighorns had caught the belly of the storm; black cloud ripped and sagged, bleeding a veil of charcoal gray and sickly, unnatural blue. In moments, the highest spurs of granite vanished behind a sheet of rain.

"Flash flood coming," Nettie Mae said grimly. She turned on her heel, still holding tight to Cora, and called across the farm. "Clyde! Flood on its way!"

Clyde had returned his horse to the pen. He nodded once at his mother's shout, replaced the wide-brimmed hat on his head, and sprinted to the sheepfold to shut the returning flock inside.

Cora still struggled for her breath. "Won't . . . won't the animals be trapped? If the water—"

"Likely not," Nettie Mae said. "We've had a few bad floods before; you remember two years ago, surely."

"Our farm is high enough on the slope that floods never threatened our animals. Or our home. But here, you—"

Nettie Mae cut her off again, pulling Cora along as she marched around the house. "We're high enough on the slope, too. I know it doesn't seem so from where we stand, but Substance was always particular about such things. He situated the house and the animals' pens just so, when he built this farm. Leave the sheep to Clyde; he knows what to do. We must account for the children and get them inside the house before the rains arrive."

"The children!" Cora hadn't forgotten her children, but neither could she bring herself out of that damnable fog of confusion and fear. Her mind refused to work as swiftly as Nettie Mae's. She swallowed hard, insisting that her nerves calm themselves, willing away the panic. "Where were they last? What chores did you give them today?"

"I sent them all into the orchard," Nettie Mae said, "to pick up the apples that had fallen and begun to rot. They were to feed the apples to the pigs."

The orchard lay ahead of the two women now. Long before they reached the trees, Cora could see two tin pails resting under the apple boughs, abandoned and forgotten. There was no sign of the children. Now, at last, she jerked free of Nettie Mae's grip and ran into the orchard, but there was nothing she could do, save turn slowly in a helpless circle, staring down at the half-filled pails and trampled grass. The cloying smell of rotted fruit hung heavy in the air.

"Did they go back into the house?" Nettie Mae asked.

"No; I was there when the thunder sounded. I came down from my room and found no one inside."

"Come along." Nettie Mae left the orchard and completed her circuit of the yard. As they returned to the back portion of the Webber farm, they found the sheep streaming past the long shed, crowding through the gate and into the fold. Far beyond the flock, Cora spotted Benjamin and Charles running toward the house. Charles tumbled, then disappeared in the tall grass as he crashed blindly into a stand of sage. A moment later, he regained his feet and pelted after his brother.

"God protect us!" Cora exclaimed. She ran toward her sons.

The boys met her at the far end of the barn and flung themselves into her arms. Tears streamed down their cheeks; they were red faced, choking on their spit, sobbing for breath.

"There, there." Cora tried to comfort them, even as she dragged them toward the barn door. The lightning might return at any moment; they mustn't be caught in the open. "There, there; you're safe now."

Suddenly, Beulah was beside her, thrusting open the door from the inside. She took Benjamin by the collar and hauled him into the cool interior.

"Land sakes," Beulah said rather casually. "That's some storm."

Nettie Mae pushed Cora and Charles into the barn and stood on the threshold, arms braced across the door as if to prevent their leaving. "Where is Miranda?"

Benjamin and Charles exchanged a stupefied look. Charles began to cry again, his red face falling into a mask of agony and shame. His little body heaved and shook as he struggled for his breath.

"She . . . she was with us in the orchard," Benjamin said.

Nettie Mae scowled. "And you left the orchard."

"But she didn't follow us."

"Are you certain? You must be certain, boy."

"I . . . I never saw!"

Beulah rested her hand on Benjamin's head. "Where did you go when you left the orchard, Benji? Tell me. I promise I won't get angry."

"To the riverbank. We wanted to skip stones."

"The river," Cora cried. "Mother of Mercy! The flood, Nettie Mae—the flood!"

This time, when Nettie Mae touched Cora's arm, she didn't seize her sleeve, made no demands with her strength. The touch was almost gentle. "You must remain calm, Cora. We don't know for a fact that Miranda went to the river. We'll spread out and look for her. No, not you boys; you'll remain here in the barn come what may, do you understand? There may be more lightning. You aren't to leave this place until I tell you it's safe."

Benjamin had taken Charles under his arm; both boys nodded, eyes on the packed earthen floor.

Nettie Mae caught Cora's eye and jerked her head toward the pasture. "We'll fetch Clyde, and together, the three of us will scour the entire farm. Very likely the thunder frightened Miranda and she's hiding somewhere. She may even be in the house, safe and sound, quiet as a mouse for fear of the storm. Don't despair, now; let's just bear down and do what we must."

Mute, numb, Cora followed Nettie Mae outside. A cold wind tore down the slope, whipping grit and fragments of sage against Cora's face. She flinched from the sting, squinting against the storm, praying that God would hold back the lightning until Miranda had been found and whisked off to some shelter. She followed Nettie Mae along the edge of the pasture. Nettie Mae spoke as she walked, murmuring her plan for searching the fields and orchard, or perhaps offering encouragement. Cora couldn't make out a single word over the rising howl of wind, but the low, soothing tone was like a rope stretched taut through a lightless passage, and Cora clung to Nettie Mae's calm strength with all her will.

Over the wind came the crash of the barn door slamming shut. Cora and Nettie Mae both looked around and saw Beulah running against the force of the storm, pushing across the pasture's weedy border, making steadily for the river.

"The fool girl," Nettie Mae snapped.

"Let her go," Cora said. "She'll be all right."

"Against lightning and a flash flood?"

"Beulah has good sense," Cora answered. "I trust her; you must trust her, too."

They reached the eastern edge of the apple orchard, the last place anyone had accounted for Miranda with any certainty.

"She may be cowering in the long grass," Nettie Mae said briskly. "I'll go to the other side of the orchard. On my signal, we'll both walk toward the house, calling her name. If she doesn't show herself, we'll look around the outhouse and the root cellar next, and then the horse shed."

Cora nodded. She was calm now—too calm, resigned to the truth. Miranda was a small, helpless child, and the prairie was vast as a raging sea. It was a wilderness of inhuman things, wolves and bears come down from the mountains, the unsettling movement of wind across the grass, that never-ending motion like the stirring of a great beast's flank, a steady inhale and exhale. She and her youngest daughter—all of her children—were no more than fleas on the prairie's hide. Another lightning strike, another slash of thunder, could shake any of them loose and send them falling out into the fathomless dark of the storm.

Cora pressed on through the orchard, calling Miranda's name, wondering why she didn't shiver when her terror was so great. Every moment, she waited for the separation, the terrible knowledge that would come to her—must come, now—that Miranda was lost forever. She would never see her youngest child again.

Nettie Mae rejoined Cora, striding under the apple boughs. There was no point talking; neither had found the least sign of Miranda. They turned as one and pressed on toward the outhouse.

Clyde had secured the sheep and returned to his circling horses. He was crouched on his heels in one of the three-sided sheds that served as the animals' shelter. The boy rose when he saw his mother and picked his way through the anxious, milling herd. He squeezed through the bars of the fence.

"You should be inside the house," Clyde said to Nettie Mae. "That rain—"

"Not just yet. Have you seen Miranda?"

"I haven't. Not since she went out to the orchard after midday."

"Someone must have noticed which way the girl ran!"

Clyde stared beyond Nettie Mae for a moment, toward the pasture. Then he thrust himself away, sprinting hard past the shed and barn, picking up speed with every leaping stride. Cora tried to shield her eyes with one hand, peering into the blowing grit to learn what had caught Clyde's attention.

It was Beulah. The girl was running back over the pasture, just as Benjamin and Charles had done. Her arms worked at her sides, pumping like the bars of a locomotive's wheels. There was no mistaking the urgency in her headlong dash.

Nettie Mae took Cora by the hand, pulling her across the yard. They ran together to meet Beulah. As the girl broke through the fringed edge of the pasture, Cora cried out with hopeless agony; Beulah was clutching Miranda's rag doll in her fist.

Panting, Beulah held up the mud-stained doll. "By the river." She heaved for a few more breaths, then said, "On the trail that leads to the ravine."

Cora covered her mouth with both hands, but she couldn't hold back a scream of loss. It tore at her throat, long and sharp, and left a taste of blood in her mouth. Someone was holding her now, pulling her into a tight embrace, pressing her mouth against a bony shoulder as she screamed again. She tasted wool and sweat, and dug her nails into the flesh of whoever had embraced her.

Cora drifted in a strange, formless unreality. She was dimly aware of Clyde's voice, muffled, as if he were speaking from a great distance.

"I'll bridle Joe Buck and ride after her. Beulah, get everyone into the house. The storm will be directly overhead in a few minutes. There's no time to lose."

And in that very moment, as if his words had called forth the fury of a vengeful God, Cora heard the hollow crack and scrape of stones displaced, of willows torn up by the roots, of water crashing down through the narrow canyon that reached like a fatal wound into the belly of the Bighorns.

The flood had come.

CLYDE

When he heard the thunder, Clyde knew it was no ordinary storm.

He and Beulah had been occupied for hours with the cattle fence, thickening its wattles against the snow he could sense was coming. Winter seemed determined to fall upon the homestead weeks earlier than usual. The day had been muggy, vexatious with flies, but the sky hadn't offered any greater threat than it had done for days, dropping its intermittent rains in daylong showers. The sudden crash of thunder shattered their quiet, contented work. It struck them as a physical blow first, the raw power of the explosion knocking Clyde and Beulah to the ground—or perhaps they both had thrown themselves down in a lurch of pure wild instinct. An instant later, the blast shook them. The thunder was more sensation than sound, a violent rending of the sky, a shuddering of the earth, a muffled whine in Clyde's ears that blocked, for a moment, the screams of the animals and the throaty roar as the thunder spread itself out from the mountains, out across the open prairie to the south.

As soon as he knew he hadn't been struck—indeed, he hadn't even seen the lightning flash—Clyde pushed himself up to his knees and stared around the yard. He raised himself from the dirt just in time to witness one of his bay fillies sailing over the paddock fence. Eyes rolling with terror, she galloped toward the house.

"Horse out," Clyde barked to Beulah. "Get in the barn where it's safe."

He ran after the filly, his arms thrown wide, speaking as low as he could manage with the white flare of shock still glowing in his chest. The horse tried to wheel around him and bolt, but Clyde reached toward her flaring nostrils, the hot jet of her fearful breath. The filly danced in place but allowed him to touch her neck. Stroking, soothing, he guided her back to the paddock and shut her in with the rest of the herd.

Clyde followed the filly inside and stood under one of the shelters, arms crossed over his chest in an attempt to still his quaking body. If he remained motionless, the horses would take notice and calm themselves, too—or so Clyde hoped. If any of his horses panicked again and collided with the fence, there would be precious little time to spend on another repair of the corral.

Clyde remained in the paddock for several minutes, willing the herd to settle even as his body tensed instinctively, cringing in anticipation of another burst of thunder. The midday sun faded more with every rapid heartbeat, lost behind a wall of cloud. He could hear the sheep calling, the tattoo of their hooves as they bolted from the pasture, seeking the comfort of their stone-walled pen. Clyde watched his anxious horses a moment longer. He didn't like to leave them untended—not when they were in such a state—but if he didn't see to the sheep himself, Beulah would take the excuse to leave the shelter of the barn. With lightning so near, Clyde couldn't allow her the risk.

"Stay quiet, you," Clyde said to Joe Buck. "Keep the rest of the herd calm, do you hear?"

Then he left the paddock and hustled toward the fold. Cora and Nettie Mae were crossing the yard. Both women looked pale and rigid with fright. "Clyde," Nettie Mae shouted, "flood on the way."

He held the fold gate wide and the flock crowded in, pressing their bodies together, craning their heads above one another's backs. Their eyes were white with terror. There was no time to count the sheep properly; Clyde had to trust that the entire flock had remained together.

He shut the gate, tying it securely, then returned to the horses, calling their names, speaking with slow and gentle words as they twitched and snorted and flung themselves into short bursts of flight down the length of the paddock fence.

By and by, Cora and Nettie Mae appeared again. They were both trembling, but Cora's eyes were glazed and she stared unblinking into the distance. There was no mistaking the vacancy of shock, the emptiness of tragedy. Clyde slipped through the fence once more.

"You should be inside the house," he chided.

His mother silenced him with a sharp, impatient gesture. "Not just yet. Have you seen Miranda?"

"I haven't." The white fear dissipated in Clyde's chest. A sensation far worse replaced it: the cold stab of knowing, a sickening pang of loss. No wonder Cora wore that fixed mask of helpless agony. "Not since she went out to the orchard after midday."

Something pale caught Clyde's attention, flashing against the dark, dense atmosphere of storm and shadow. He stared past his mother to the sheep pasture. Beulah was there, running through the waist-high autumn grass, as fast as her legs would carry her.

God in Heaven, she'll be struck out there!

Clyde left the women and ran for Beulah, his boots gouging the earth with the force and desperation of his stride. Every breath came sharp and hot in his throat, his lungs. There was no sense in going to the girl; Clyde knew that. His presence could be no shelter from the storm.

At least if lightning is to fall, it might hit me instead, and spare her life.

Clyde met Beulah at the pasture's edge. Her face was dark with the effort of running. The heavy-lidded, half-dreaming look was gone; her eyes were as bright as candle flames, burning with urgency. She lifted a hand. Miranda's rag doll dangled by one arm.

Cora's scream of pain, just behind Clyde's shoulder, was the first notion he had that the women had run after him. But he couldn't tear his attention from Beulah.

"By the river," she panted. Her thin shoulders rose and fell like a bellows as she struggled for her breath. "On the trail that leads to the ravine."

"I'll bridle Joe Buck and ride after her," Clyde said at once. "Beulah, get everyone into the house. The storm will be directly overhead in a few minutes. There's no time to lose."

Beulah nodded. She reached one slender arm toward the women— Nettie Mae had gathered Cora to her chest, holding her tight as she wailed with terror and grief. Like ewes obeying the calm command of a shepherd, Nettie Mae and Cora both stumbled toward the house. Beulah's hand rested on Nettie Mae's back, guiding and controlling. The girl called over her shoulder, "Benjamin! Charles! Come to the house at once!"

Clyde ran toward the paddock. A persistent rumble lifted from the slope above the farm, vibrating down the flanks of the foothills. For a moment, Clyde thought it was thunder, but it was too quiet, too sustained. Then he heard a hollow pop, the blow of stone against stone. It reverberated from the direction of the river, sharp as a rifle shot.

Only one force could dislodge boulders from the ravine. Only one force could hurl great blocks of sandstone as easily as Cora's boys tossed their leather ball in the yard.

Flood.

He threw open the tack shed door. Clyde had no need to pause, no need to adjust his eyes to the darkness. He knew just where Joe Buck's bridle hung, on the first peg inside. He scarcely paused long enough to retrieve it; as soon as his fist closed around soft leather, Clyde was running again, reins trailing behind and whipping his ankles. There was no time for the saddle. He must ride bareback, and pray he'd be fast enough to find Miranda before the floodwaters took her.

Clyde shimmied between the fence boards and called for Joe Buck. The gelding peeled away from the restless herd, trotting to meet Clyde. Joe Buck carried his head high; he snorted with every stride, fearful of the storm. But he had always trusted his rider, and Clyde knew there was no braver horse in all of Wyoming Territory. Clyde fitted the bridle quickly. Joe Buck kept his teeth clamped shut for one wild moment, dancing nervously where he stood, but Clyde pleaded under his breath and the bit slid into place. He led the gelding from the paddock, flipped the reins over Joe Buck's neck, and sprang up, pulling on the mane until he could swing his leg across the broad yellow back.

Clyde drummed his heels against Joe Buck's ribs. The horse lit out for the pasture and the cottonwoods beyond. Clyde didn't often ride bareback, and now, with no saddle between them, he could feel Joe Buck's fear, the twitching of his hide and the stiff reluctance of his muscles, the short and uncertain stride. Surely Joe Buck could hear the oncoming rain and the roaring flood far more clearly than Clyde. But he had never been the sort of horse to defy his owner. Clyde held him steady, demanding that he race toward the swelling river, and Joe Buck obeyed.

The gelding's hide had already been damp with fear sweat when Clyde had mounted. As they plunged into the tall grass of the pasture, Clyde urged greater speed, leaning as low as he could manage over Joe Buck's neck without the stability of his saddle, and his seat grew slicker. It was all he could do to rock with the horse's movement and keep himself astride; his body slid alarmingly from left to right or jounced back toward the horse's croup whenever Joe Buck's gait turned rough. Clyde entangled one fist in the black mane. The coarse hairs cut into his flesh, but he didn't care. That grip might be all that kept him on Joe Buck's back, and Joe Buck alone, of all the creatures on the Webber homestead, might be fast enough to save Miranda's life. Clyde begged his horse for greater speed. Joe Buck flattened his ears and stretched his neck, pushing into a hard gallop. Wind laden with grit whipped past Clyde's face, stinging his eyes; in the force of his flight, he could scarcely draw a breath. There was no hope of seeing the ground ahead. He could only pray Joe Buck wouldn't set a hoof into a prairie dog hole.

They crossed the pasture and broke through the far stand of brush, the last margin of thicket before the grassland gave way to cottonwoods and riverbank. Clyde turned his horse north, toward the confluence of the Nowood and Tensleep Creek. The mouth of the ravine lay just ahead, around a shallow bend and a clump of short, scrubby trees. Joe Buck's hooves pounded the narrow trail. To Clyde's right, the river was already on the rise, foaming and churning as it climbed the gravel banks. The water would soon spill over, scouring beyond the cottonwoods and the hedge all the way to the middle of the pasture.

Substance's grave lay just ahead. Clyde swallowed hard, fixing his eyes to the low mound as his horse galloped by. Very likely the grave would be washed away, and his father's remains scattered down the length of the river. But there was nothing to be done—not now, with a child's life at stake—perhaps not under any circumstances.

I should have thought better about the grave site, Clyde scolded himself. *It was too close to the river to begin with, and the river always floods, sooner or later. I'm sorry, Father.*

Substance's resting place was a blur as Clyde shot past, but the small, pale objects scattered over its weed-shrouded surface caught his attention, sending a jolt of superstitious dread up his spine. Were those animal bones? Who had placed them there? Nettie Mae must have visited the grave without Clyde's knowing.

But in the next moment, the grave and all thoughts of his father lay far behind Clyde. The mouth of the ravine yawned ahead. Under the flat blue shadow of the storm, the sandstone walls were forcefully red—red as the piercing of flesh. The stunted willows that grew up the canyon's sandy sides were all but overwhelmed. Only the tops of the tallest willows showed above the roiling surface of the water. Skeletal and dark, they thrashed in the cascade, bending and dipping with the force of the current. The flood had arrived in the full fury of its power.

Joe Buck sat back on his haunches, skidding to a halt, and Clyde fell heavily against the horse's muscular neck. Only his grip on Joe

Buck's mane saved him from crashing to the earth. Clyde pushed himself upright as Joe Buck squealed and tried to turn away. Relentless, Clyde kicked his horse onward and pulled the reins hard across his neck, struggling to keep Joe Buck from bolting.

"Miranda!" Clyde shouted. The roar of Tensleep Creek swallowed his voice.

The smooth, compacted sand of the riverbank was rapidly disappearing under a rising froth of red mud, flotsam, and small drowned animals. Clyde scanned the shore for footprints—and yes, there they were. One small set of prints, tiny boots, headed toward the canyon. The chop and rush of water consumed one footprint, then another, but a few still led on. Clyde hissed to Joe Buck, forcing him closer to the narrow ravine and the thick red churn that poured from its mouth.

Thunder fractured the sky, the shock of it stealing Clyde's breath, but as lightning flashed across his vision, it drove back just enough of the storm's darkness for him to see the small figure crouched on a flat boulder at the canyon's mouth. Miranda stared back at Clyde— huddled, hugging her knees to her chest, silent and paralyzed with fear.

The rising water had pushed a bare, gnarled branch onto the stone where she crouched. As Clyde blinked hard, trying to clear a searing violet echo of light from his eyes, he saw the branch shift and turn, ponderously slow. The flood was rising faster, and faster still. In moments it would sweep Miranda away.

"Climb higher," Clyde shouted to the girl.

But even as he spoke, he knew his words were wasted. The sandstone wall at Miranda's back was sheer and smooth. Not even a grown man could have pulled himself up that unfriendly face. The flat rock, Miranda's only refuge, was surrounded by leaping waves, the water red brown, silted by its own violence.

Clyde examined what remained of the riverbank. If he could find some route to the rock, no matter how perilous, he might—

Miranda screamed, a pathetically small and thin sound, like a featherless hatchling swept from its nest. A surge of water carried the girl and the gnarled branch off the rock into the river.

"No!" Clyde shouted. Then, as he wheeled Joe Buck around to race downstream, he bellowed even louder, the only advice he could think to give the girl. "Hold on!"

Grateful to leave the canyon's roar, Joe Buck galloped down the path. Every leaping stride threw up a spray of water, for the river had consumed the banks and was now encroaching upon the trail. Clyde gritted his teeth and kept his eye on Miranda. She did as Clyde had instructed; with both hands the girl clung to the twisted snag, holding her pale, frightened face just above the surface.

Joe Buck ran as swiftly as the flood, but Clyde knew his horse couldn't keep up the pace indefinitely. Unless he could devise some trick to snare Miranda and pull her to the shore—or unless God granted a miracle—he would watch as the flood carried her downstream, beyond Clyde's reach, beyond any hope for salvation. Still Clyde rode, urging his horse on, shouting encouragement to Miranda whenever he could draw a breath. They passed the broad clearing, footed with smooth, flat river stones, that marked the trail back to the homestead. The farm dwindled in their wake.

Beyond the homestead, the Nowood broadened, and though the water still rose, its surface ran more smoothly. Clyde narrowed his eyes at the grassland ahead, scanning for anything—a long branch, a length of discarded, long-forgotten rope—anything he might use to pull Miranda to safety. The girl's face was white as winter, her mouth clamped shut, her eyes huge and pleading behind the branch to which she still held fast.

The ever-broadening river flowed around a bend. A mass of branches and sagebrush had compacted near the middle of the Nowood—a jam, probably embedded in a bar of sand or gravel below the surface. Miranda's branch flowed past the mess of flotsam.

"No," Clyde pleaded—with God, with the river, with anything that might be listening. "Catch her. Please!"

Just as he feared the willow branch would avoid the jam, one end snagged. The branch held, kicking a spurt of water over its mass, obscuring Miranda from view.

That snag won't hold long. And if it does, she'll drown anyhow.

Clyde reined in his horse opposite Miranda, then guided Joe Buck farther upstream. He slid to the ground, splashing into the rising water, but his legs scarcely held him.

"Don't you go nowhere," he shouted to Joe Buck. He knew his voice was pleading, desperate, girlish and high. He didn't care. "Don't go nowhere, Joe, you hear me?"

Clyde staggered away from his horse, fighting against the current. The floodwaters battered his legs and sucked at his feet, trying to pull him down.

"Hang on, Miranda," he yelled again. "I'm coming for you!"

He hoped he'd gone far enough upstream; the current would carry him swiftly once he'd thrown himself in, and he mustn't pass the snag before he'd swum to the middle of the river. Clyde sucked in one desperate breath and threw himself belly first into the water. It was cold, bitterly cold, biting deep into his flesh till his joints ached, but he pulled and kicked toward the center of the river with all the strength he had. His hat left his head; Clyde caught one jarring sight of it as he came up for breath. The hat, brim up, rotated on the surface, then filled with water and slid below the red flood.

Went down easy as a fella swallows cream. Clyde's thoughts had gone strangely calm and observant—accepting of his fate. *It'll take me down just as easy.*

He kept pushing toward the center of the river, hoping to catch himself against the jam and fight, hand over hand, down its length toward Miranda. But he had misjudged the distance. The snag was sailing past him now, swift and mocking. Clyde kicked harder, harder still, and through the slap and churn of waves he saw the lightness of Miranda's dress floating on the surface. Clyde stretched out his hand, caught the fabric, and wrenched it toward him. A weight came along with it, dragging through the water. He rolled, pulling the weight closer to his chest, struggling against the grasping hands of the flood as those hands sought to take him and hold him under, hold him down till all the air and all the life left his body in one long, unheard scream.

His shin smashed into something hard, and Clyde nearly hollered with the pain. Then the tops of his flailing feet scraped against gravel. He could feel the hectic bump and tumble of smaller stones rolling around his boots. He scrabbled with his legs, pushed himself up in water waist deep, and hauled Miranda to the surface beside him.

Eyes squeezed shut, the girl choked and sputtered. A great gout of muddy red spurted up from her mouth and slapped back into the river. Clyde wanted to speak to her, to encourage her to breathe—demand that she live—but he was shaking so badly, it was all he could do to keep moving toward shallower water, racing the flood as it pressed the river's boundary back and back into the scrubland.

Clyde staggered on, falling to his knees now and then, gouging himself against unseen rocks and shards of broken wood. Finally, he came to a place where the water ran no more than ankle deep—for the moment, at any rate. Clyde sagged forward, holding himself up on hands and knees, and retched out water that tasted of blood and silt. Miranda floated on her back beside him, unconscious, rather blue around the mouth.

"God have mercy," Clyde muttered. He tried to rise, but his strength was gone. He crumpled to his knees again. He wouldn't let go of Miranda's dress. Whether she lived or died, he would bring her back home and lay the poor child at her mother's feet.

"Get up," Clyde said. His voice had gone hoarse with effort and desperation. "Get up. Get out of the water." The river was rising still;

he could feel it creeping up his thighs, pooling around his forearms. "Get up!"

The low vibration of Joe Buck's familiar whicker carried over the river's rush. Clyde raised his head, and there was his horse, only a few feet away, fetlock deep in the water, waiting for him. Joe Buck had followed him downstream.

"Good fella!" Clyde all but sobbed the words. "There's a good fella. Now wait, Joe, just wait there a minute . . ."

He mustered a last volley of strength and stood, his whole body quaking. He pulled Miranda along by a limp hand, dragging her first through the shallow water and then through the mud at the surging river's edge. Clyde drew a few deep breaths to fortify himself. Then he bent and lifted Miranda's small body. She was so much heavier than she ought to have been, little slip that she was. Clyde heaved her up to Joe Buck's back and slung her over the horse's withers, belly down. Then he tried in vain to mount, but he could manage no more than a weak hop.

Joe Buck seemed to understand. He moved away from the river, and Clyde clung to his mane, allowing the horse to take most of his weight. By the time Joe Buck had led Clyde some twenty paces away from the water's edge, Clyde's legs had firmed up just enough that he thought he could see his way onto the gelding's back. He took a few practice hops, then gathered his will and leaped as high as his exhausted legs would allow. Clyde put just enough of his chest over the horse's back that he could wriggle and kick and thrash his full weight up and over. When he was finally astride, he drooped over Miranda's body, panting and shuddering, his eyes blinded by tears.

"Go on home," Clyde croaked. "Joe, get us home." He didn't know the way—he had no idea how far the Nowood had carried them. If God was merciful, Joe Buck would puzzle it out.

Clyde didn't look up as his horse hustled away from the river. He clenched his fist in the back of Miranda's dress, concentrating on keeping her balanced over Joe Buck's withers, for if she fell to the ground,

Clyde wasn't sure he could lift her a second time. He prayed that the girl would wake. One sob after another tore at his chest, but Clyde refused to wail. That wasn't the sort of thing a proper man would do, he knew that much; and even here, in the blankness and solitude of the prairie, he was determined to be the right sort of man.

God, don't let her die, Clyde prayed. But God was somewhere far away, and His back was turned. He knew the prayer was futile even as he repeated it.

Joe Buck grunted, lifting his head in surprise. An instant later, Miranda's small body convulsed and heaved. She vomited water down the horse's shoulder, then coughed weakly and drew a long but ragged breath.

"Go on," Clyde called to his horse. "Get us home fast, old fella!"

Joe Buck broke into a jog. Clyde lifted Miranda as carefully as he could manage and sat her upright, cradling the girl against his chest. Her head lolled on her neck and she moaned, weak and frail, but she was conscious and breathing. The horse pushed through stands of grass, swerving to avoid sage thickets. Clyde's legs burned from the effort of keeping his seat. The gelding's neck had darkened from its usual gold to muddy brown. He was wet—hide soaked to the skin—and Clyde realized with a dull flush of surprise that the rains had reached the prairie. He couldn't feel the rain anymore—the river had chilled him too deeply; his skin was nerveless, stiff as stone—but he could hear falling water hissing in the grass all around him.

Through drifting blue-black columns of rain, Clyde spotted the small regular shapes of the farm. It lay half a mile or more away. He hugged Miranda tighter, murmuring close beside her ear. "We're almost home now, sweetheart. Don't you give up yet."

When he trotted up the cart lane toward the sod house, Joe Buck sent up a call to his herd. The horses whinnied back, their cries loud and sharp through the monotonous pounding of the rain. The calling horses brought Nettie Mae to the sitting-room window, then to the door. She left it hanging open behind her and flew down the steps toward Clyde.

"Lord have mercy," she exclaimed, reaching up for Miranda.

Clyde let his mother take the girl, and Miranda fell, limp and moaning, into Nettie Mae's arms.

"She was swept into the river," Clyde said.

"You were, too, by the looks of you."

She spoke with steady resolve, but nevertheless, Clyde could hear the anxiety in her voice. It hadn't been so very long since he'd been down in the grips of that terrible fever.

"I'll be just fine," he said. "Get Miranda inside and warm her up. I'll put Joe Buck away, then I'll come in, too."

The walk from the paddock to the house was a long and perilous march with no one to carry him, nothing on which to lean, and all the while he trembled, aware of the slash of rain around him and the dark weight of clouds hanging overhead. Lightning might strike at any moment. He was helpless and exposed, powerless before the rage of the storm.

When he staggered through the kitchen door, he found his mother kneeling before the hearth. Someone had spread two thick quilts on the floor, and there Miranda lay, stripped of her wet clothes, shivering violently, all color drained from her pale form. The girl was so small, so weak. White flesh sank into a hollow below her ribs. Her knees and elbows seemed too large for those delicate limbs. She was tiny and breakable, a figure carved from ice; when she coughed, Clyde held his breath, certain the spasms would shatter her frail body.

Cora lingered nearby, her back pressed against the wall, which was all that was holding her upright now. She had covered most of her face with her hands; only her eyes remained visible, dull and stricken, peering through her fingers with helpless dread. Beulah stood ready, another heavy blanket bundled against her chest, while Benjamin and

Charles appeared from the sitting room, their arms heaped with sticks of dry firewood.

"This is all the wood from the other hearth," Benjamin said.

Nettie Mae didn't look up from Miranda's body. She patted the girl's cheeks, none too gently—first one, then the other. "Good boys. Stack the wood there on the bricks. Benjamin, you put two big pieces on the fire. Do you know how to use the bellows?"

"Yes, ma'am."

"Get the fire blazing up good and hot, then. Your sister needs the warmth. Beulah, give me that blanket. Charles, you run upstairs and fetch me two pillows from one of the beds. I don't care whose bed; just bring me pillows. Then you and your brother will both go and change into dry clothes and dry your hair with towels, do you hear me? It won't do for you boys to fall sick, too; you must keep dry and warm."

The boys jumped to do as they were told, and Beulah helped Nettie Mae tuck the blanket around Miranda's body. Then they rolled her onto her side and held her there.

"What shall we do now?" Beulah asked. She was calm and curious, not shaken in the least by her sister's near drowning.

"We must tilt her body—so." Nettie Mae held one arm at a steep angle, elbow toward the ceiling, palm toward the floor. "That should cause any water left in her lungs to run back out again."

Beulah settled by her sister's feet, bent the girl's knees toward her chest, and propped her tiny hips on her lap. Charles appeared a moment later with the cushions, and Nettie Mae instructed Beulah in their arrangement. Soon Miranda's lower body was raised well off the floor. She coughed again, and this time it rattled with the sound of water. A trickle spilled from the corner of her mouth.

"Good. That's good." Tenderly, Nettie Mae petted Miranda's limp, wet hair. "Cough it all up, my girl. Go on." Without taking her eyes from the child's face, she said, "Clyde, you had better get warm and dry, too. You're no safer from fevers and chills than the little boys are. You ought to know that by now."

"Yes, ma'am."

He was grateful for the banister on the stair. Without it, he could never have climbed to the second floor, where he kept his pine trunk of clothing. Weak and exhausted as he was, Clyde had to haul himself up the staircase hand over hand, for his legs were shaking so badly, they were all but useless. In his former bedroom, he found the little fellows donning their woolen nightdresses and sniffing back tears.

"What's all this, now?"

"Clyde," Benjamin said, "we feel awful bad. It's our fault Miranda almost got drowned."

He laid a hand on each of their rain-soaked heads. "I don't know about that."

"I don't know either," Charles said, "but Ma and Nettie Mae—I mean, Mrs. Webber—they're gonna be real sore with us once they aren't so busy being worried about Miranda."

"We didn't know she followed us toward the river," Benjamin added. "If we'd seen her do it, we would have told her to go on home."

"I know, little fellas—I know."

"I wish Pa was here," Benjamin said solemnly. Little Charles could no longer hold back his tears, and he ground fists into his eyes, sobbing and choking.

Clyde took a bathing towel from a peg by the door and tossed it to Benjamin. "I know you miss your pa, but at least you got me, right? Dry off your heads, now. My mother was right; you shouldn't get sick yourselves. You won't be much help around the farm if you do."

Rain battered the roof and hissed against the window panes. When Charles had calmed himself—and dried off as well as he could—he returned the towel to Benjamin and said, "Was the river really flooded, Clyde?"

"It was flooded something awful."

He rummaged in his trunk and took out the good brown union suit his mother had knitted for him earlier that year. Then he peeled off his wet, clinging clothes and dried himself as best as he could with the used towel. He had bashed his leg badly on that rock in the river; a red gash had opened on his shin, already ringed by a purple bruise. Clyde dabbed at the wound with his towel, then shimmied into the union suit. The wool clung to his damp skin, and it took the last reserves of Clyde's strength to pull the thing on and work the buttons down the front.

"Will the flood come here? All the way to the house?" Charles stared out the window, but there was nothing to be seen, save for columns of silver—the terrible deluge blotting out all sight of the farm, the barn, and the animals' pens. "Will it be like Noah's time?"

"No, little fella. It won't be bad as that. Why, we've had rains like this before."

"I don't remember any so bad," Benjamin said, with all the wisdom and experience of an eight-year-old.

"Well, I do," Clyde said. "And I promise we won't need to build an ark. Now climb into bed, you two, and wrap up in your blankets."

"But it ain't evening yet! We ain't had any supper."

"And I bet you won't have any for a spell yet. We all got to help out with Miranda now, so you might have a long wait. But I'll try to bring you up a bite of bread and butter soon. How does that sound?"

"Can we have jam, too?" Charles asked, as he slid under the blankets.

"Maybe."

Benjamin followed his brother into the bed. He stared up at the steep-pitched ceiling for a moment, listening to the rain battering the shingles overhead. Softly, he said, "Clyde, will Miranda die?"

Clyde swallowed hard. A band of heat squeezed tight around his chest, and he found he couldn't speak. But he forced himself to smile, and the tightness relented a little. "My mother knows what to do. Don't you worry, little fellas."

He left the boys in their bed and made his slow, trembling way back downstairs. Miranda was still lying on her side, supported at that awkward angle by Beulah and the cushions. Nettie Mae rubbed the girl's back through her cocoon of blankets—slow, gentle circles, just as she had done for Clyde whenever he had struggled with childhood sickness. But he had never faced anything like this. The fever that had burned through him weeks ago hadn't been a patch on Miranda's plight. To be so small, so fragile, and to be tossed and battered by a flash flood . . . to have swallowed so much water, breathed it in . . .

Cora had sunk onto a chair. Her slender arms were wrapped tightly around her body and she was rocking forward and back, her eyes squeezed shut and her lips moving in silent, desperate prayer. Clyde caught the darting of his mother's eye, the look of exasperated anger she shot like an arrow in Cora's direction. He stepped between the two women and stood, arms folded, willing his mother to keep her tongue civil and cool.

"It's hardly proper," Nettie Mae said, "for you to be exhibiting yourself in your underthings, Clyde Webber. No, Beulah, don't turn around and look at him. Eyes forward."

Beulah kept her attention on Miranda, but although her back was turned to Clyde, he could still sense her mischievous smile, a giggle fighting to be free. The unexpected burst of humor was almost enough to make Clyde laugh aloud. But one glance at Miranda, still pale and shivering, stilled that impulse.

"This was the warmest thing I could think to wear," he said.

"You'd have been wiser to put trousers and a shirt over it."

"What can I do to help, Mother?"

Nettie Mae sighed—softly, so grudging an admission of weakness or frustration that no one but Clyde would have noticed. "I could wish for more firewood, but I won't send anyone out into that storm to fetch it."

"The little fellas are hungry," Clyde said. "Shall I bring them a bite?"

Cora stood—too suddenly, it seemed, for she gripped the back of her chair at once and swayed as if she might faint. A moment later, she regained her composure. "Thank you, Clyde, but I'll take something up for the boys. It's time I made myself useful."

Cora went to the pantry and emerged again with a plate full of sliced bread and pickled eggs. When she had vanished up the stairs, Clyde all but fell into the chair Cora had vacated. His legs were heavy with relief.

Nettie Mae narrowed her eyes. "Time she made herself useful, indeed."

"Mother, don't."

"That woman is perfectly helpless. She wouldn't know what to do for her own children if you gave her a book on the subject."

She would have said more, Clyde felt certain—but Miranda stirred in her swaddling of quilts.

"Ma?" The girl's voice was painfully hoarse.

Nettie Mae leaned over Miranda's back, stroking her cheek. "You're all right, precious one. Don't be afraid." She glanced up at Clyde and smiled. A smile on his mother's face was so rare and startling that Clyde leaned back—flinched, in truth—and the chair squealed. "The color has come back to her face. That's a good sign."

She rolled Miranda onto her back, then pulled the blankets apart just enough to expose the girl's chest. Nettie Mae pressed one ear against the child, but after a moment she lifted her head, scowling. "I can't hear her breathing. That cursed rain is too loud."

Miranda coughed, but it was a clean, honest sound. There was no wet crackle nor any bubbling rasp. "I want my ma," the girl said.

"You may go to her. I think the worst is over now. Or so I pray. Carry her upstairs, Beulah, and tuck her into bed. She may only get out of bed to use the chamber pot until I say otherwise, and even then, she must be wrapped up and kept warm. It's most important that she should take no chill. I'll start a good broth and bring her supper up soon. It won't take long to boil, with the fire blazing."

Beulah did as she was bidden, cradling her sister with all tenderness and dropping kisses on the little white brow. When the girls had gone, Nettie Mae stayed on the one remaining quilt. She stared vacantly into the fire.

Clyde pushed himself up from the chair, stifling a groan, for his legs and the muscles along his ribs stiffened in protest. He offered a hand and Nettie Mae took it, still watching the flames leap and bow before the gusts of wind that whistled down the chimney. Clyde pulled his mother to her feet.

"Will Miranda truly be well?"

"God alone can say. I might have some idea, if I could hear her breathing, but . . ." Nettie Mae closed her eyes. "How do you feel?"

"Tuckered out. I think I might sleep for a week, even with the rain pounding away. But I don't believe I'm feverish again."

Nettie Mae pressed her hand to Clyde's forehead. Her palm was cool, her fingers untrembling, yet still Clyde could sense her fear.

"You aren't feverish," she confirmed. "Not yet, anyhow. Thank the Lord for that."

"I saw to it that the little fellas dried off, just as you told them. They ought to be well, too."

"It's not the fever I'm afraid of, when it comes to Miranda. It's . . . it's . . ." Nettie Mae seemed unable to force the words out. Her voice had gone thick and she turned her face away, so Clyde couldn't see her weakness. Finally, she said, slow and deliberate, in defiance of her own terror, "Drowning."

"She can't drown now," Clyde said. "I pulled her out of the river. You're worn out, Mother; you aren't making sense."

The accustomed sternness returned as if it had never gone. "I know exactly what I speak of. You remember your sister Alta."

"Of course I remember Alta."

In the urgency of the storm and the fear of finding Miranda gone, Clyde hadn't thought of his dead sister at all. But now the memories came crowding back, forceful and hard, towering and cold as the Bighorns. He remembered his father pulling Alta from the creek. The small body dripping and limp. He remembered his mother sitting beside Alta's bed for days—never weeping, never speaking, never ceasing to work. Nettie Mae's hands hadn't stopped moving all those countless hours while the family had waited and prayed for Alta's recovery. But Alta hadn't recovered. Her breathing had only grown harsher, wetter, more strained and agonized with every weary, too-long moment.

"Alta died of fever," Clyde said softly.

"No. She drowned; I know it. She was on dry land for two days after falling into the creek, but still she drowned. Nothing will convince me otherwise; nothing ever has convinced me, through all these years. The water stayed in her chest. I know it, Clyde; I listened to her every breath. God help me, the sound of it has never left my memory. I've had no peace from that day to this."

"Mother . . ."

Clyde held out his arms, and Nettie Mae wilted into them. He held her tightly, swaying gently from side to side, unsure what else he could do to bring his mother comfort.

Nettie Mae mumbled against the wool of Clyde's union suit. "I tried to get the water out of her. I tried."

She wasn't speaking of Alta now. It was little Miranda she was thinking of—only Miranda, the child who needed her most this day, this hour.

"I know you tried, Mother. You did what you could."

Nettie Mae moaned, a wordless utterance of pain. Never in his life had Clyde heard that stoic woman make such a harrowing sound. Not even when Substance died—never. Never. The realization that Nettie Mae could be so affected, that she was not the bulwark Clyde had always thought her to be, struck him with visceral, instinctive fear. Not even the storm had frightened him so badly, not even the lightning. He clutched her more tightly still—not to succor her, now, but for his own sake. He was a little boy again, clinging to his mother in terror, trying to wring from her inexhaustible body all the strength and fortitude he lacked.

"Oh," she said, "did I do enough? Was it enough to save her life?" There was no mistaking the high, bent warp of Nettie Mae's voice. She was crying. Weeping against his chest.

"God have mercy." Nettie Mae still huddled in Clyde's arms. She spoke her prayer against his body, and Clyde felt too weak, too inadequate, to bear it. "God, spare that child's life. Do not take another precious baby from me, Lord. I cannot bear it, if You do. Save her, God, I beg You."

NETTIE MAE

When she heard the thunder, Nettie Mae knew something inside of her had broken, or would soon break. Not the way a stick breaks, or a bone, snapping into pieces that may be thrown in opposite directions, a permanent and emphatic separation. Rather, the break was a pot or a jug dropped to the floor. A heavy vessel, full, full to overflowing. Too heavy to be borne any longer, and it slips from weary arms, and when it cracks open, everything it had contained rushes out at once and drains away. That was the sound of the thunder: the shaking arms giving out, the weight plunging down, the bursting forth of everything Nettie Mae had held inside for too many years.

But when she heard the first distant notes of the lark, Nettie Mae knew the long night of the storm had passed. Morning would soon arrive. The rain had ceased hours ago, giving way to a still, windless night. The floodwaters had come no nearer than the far end of the pasture. The light of a full moon had broken intermittently through the clouds as they dispersed, and Nettie Mae had watched, from the height of her bedroom window, a long, slow gold-snake ripple of moonlight on water, out there in the grass where the sheep ought to graze, and the dark reflection of the cottonwoods had been like ink spilled or bleeding from one page to another. But the larks were rising now. The flood could come no nearer. The storm had expended its fury in the high granite spires of the Bighorns, and the sky moved in gentle peace.

Nettie Mae cast aside her lap blanket and tucked needle and thread into her sewing basket. She rose from the settee in the sitting room, where she had passed the night in a sleepless vigil, and padded to the kitchen. A heap of embers glowed on the hearth. Clyde had pulled his cot close to the fire, where he slept the determined, committed sleep of one who has tested and found the limits of human endurance.

She paused beside her son's bed. His chest rose and fell steadily beneath the apple-leaf quilt. She had stitched that quilt all the months she had carried Clyde inside her—her first child, her dearest hope—and had laid him upon the quilt as a baby, when he had been as round and fat and formless as all babies are. How strange to see him now, to truly see him, as if for the first time. He had become a man. When had it happened? There was no more boy about him. The defined set of his jaw, the thinness of his face, the shadow of coarse hair darkening his lip and chin. Even his expression—and even in sleep—was that of a grown man, thoughtful and concerned, a tilt of tension between the brows. Nettie Mae could see where the lines would form someday, the furrows above the bridge of his nose and the bird's feet at the corners of his eyes. They weren't there yet, but already she knew their placement. They wouldn't fall where Substance's lines had fallen. There was little of her husband in her son; Clyde's features were Nettie Mae's, and those of her father—what she could remember of him. She was grateful for that. Somehow it would seem unjust if God were to fashion Clyde too closely after Substance's pattern.

Clyde's chest had remained clear throughout the night, thank God, and the fever that had burdened him weeks ago showed no signs of returning. The knowledge that Clyde had come through this terrible night unharmed made Nettie Mae weak with gratitude. Her bones ached with longing for sleep. She thought of the settee, the lap blanket, and she wanted to curl up there in the light chill of the sitting room, in its blue-dawn silence, and finally rest. But she couldn't rest yet. She needed to know—needed to truly believe—that Miranda would survive, too.

Nettie Mae tucked the rag doll she had made that night under her arm. She stepped around Clyde's cot and ladled up a bit more of her shank-bone broth from the kettle above the coals. She carried the bowl upstairs. Every step was an effort, and her head grew lighter as she climbed, for her whole body was pleading for its rest. She paused beside the half-open door that had once been Clyde's. Cora's boys were sleeping peacefully, wrapped in one another's arms, their soft faces brushed and silvered by the first trace of morning light.

Nettie Mae crept to the other door, the crowded room shared by Cora and her two daughters. It wasn't the first time she had looked in on Miranda since putting her to bed. In fact, Nettie Mae had lost count of her trips up the stairs to watch the girl sleeping, to listen to her breath. As dawn came, the scene was much as it had been for hours. Cora was still asleep on her bed, sitting up against the headboard with her neck bent at a stiff, uneasy angle. Cora's left hand rested on Miranda's body, and the girl slept well at her mother's side. Beulah had sprawled across the trundle bed, half-covered by a dark blanket, with most of her bare, graceless legs exposed.

Nettie Mae edged closer to the bed. She could just isolate the sound of Miranda's breathing above the light snores of her sister. There was no rattle, no wet catch in the girl's throat, even lying on her back. That hadn't been the way with Alta.

She will live, Nettie Mae realized. *God has answered my prayer. Miranda will survive.*

Nettie Mae wouldn't wake the child from that healing sleep for the sake of more broth. Miranda had already taken enough broth throughout the night; any time she wakened and murmured in the darkness, Nettie Mae had come to her side and encouraged her to drink, even as Cora slept on. Instead, Nettie Mae drank down the bowl herself. It was salty and thick with fat, and had gone almost cold, but it braced her up at once. Her stomach ached for more, and Nettie Mae realized with dull surprise that she had eaten nothing since the previous noon. She had been too absorbed in caring for Miranda, too committed to doing what must be done.

For a moment, as Nettie Mae watched the three sleepers, she considered fetching a small cushion and propping it under Cora's head, folding it between her neck and shoulder. Cora would be stiff and in pain when she woke, without a cushion to support her. Instead, Nettie Mae slipped the new rag doll under the covers—carefully, so as not to wake Miranda—and tucked it in the girl's arms.

She eased herself back down the stairs and left the bowl standing on the drain board. Then she wrapped her thickest shawl around her shoulders and slipped quietly from the house.

The scent of morning rose up from every footstep: the clean smell of dew evaporating, of rain soaking into the earth. There was a richness and greenness to the scent—a clamor of gratitude from the scrublands, the rounded, peeled-wood smell of roots that have drunk their fill and leaves that hang fat and open on the stem, the heat of summer forgotten. Larks gamboled in a pearl-soft sky. It may as well have been spring, for all they sang, for all they madly dove and circled overhead.

Perhaps, Nettie Mae thought, *perhaps I am so weary that their singing only sounds louder to me than it ought.*

She found herself at the sheepfold and leaned her forearms on its stone edge. The flock looked up at her, subdued by the long, stormy night and the weight of their rain-soaked wool. Nettie Mae searched among the sheep for sight of the new lambs. Now and then as she'd tended Miranda, she had wondered whether the lambs could survive the violent downpour. But there they were, clustered with their mothers at the center of the flock. Every one was on its feet, every one suckling and butting the ewes' bags with their curly foreheads.

The sight should have gladdened Nettie Mae. She knew it ought to have lifted her heart. Instead, worn thin by her long night of fear and prayer, she felt herself harden again. The shock of almost losing Miranda had broken the vessel of her rage, and much of her hate had drained away. But she could repair the cracks. Time and life would give her sorrows enough to refill the vessel. That was the way of life. That was the way of time.

You answered my prayer for Miranda, God, she silently told the Creator. *But not for my own children. Didn't I pray just as sincerely over Alta? And Luther? Didn't I pray over Anna, whom You took from me when she was only three months old, and my baby boy, who lived two days? You didn't even leave him in my arms long enough for me to give him a name. You spared Cora's daughter. You even spared the lambs. Why will You never spare me?*

Cora. The mere thought of the woman was so choking, so bitter, that Nettie Mae spat into the mud. Cora had never lost anything of significance. Even her husband was still alive, protected in the confines of his cell. Fortune and God both seemed to smile endlessly on that helpless, vapid creature, while Nettie Mae had endured one sorrow after another, every day that she could recall, back to her earliest memory.

What have I done, God, to make you hate me so? Haven't I followed Your word? Yet You succor those who sin and punish the obedient.

The ram lifted his head and Nettie Mae met the animal's eye. They stood for a time and gazed at one another, the ram chewing his cud, Nettie Mae motionless even though her sleeves had soaked up the rainwater from the stones and now chafed around her wrists.

Her gaze drifted to the ram's horn—the smooth, confident arc of its curvature, the perfect proportion of the spiral. Dark against the creature's wool, the horn captured all of Nettie Mae's attention, and wrung out as she was by the tense, sleepless night, she couldn't force herself to look away. Between one beat of her heart and the next, she felt herself standing upon the horn, felt it grow to an unfathomable size, to the size of the world and all that lay beyond it. The ground beneath her was the dark spiral. The prairie was the arc of the curve. And in that brief moment, that flicker of awareness—bright and rapid as thought—she saw that all living things also stood upon the spiral, as she stood now, and moved along the curve as life directed them. At the point of the ram's horn was death, and all things flowed toward it. But the edge of the spiral, where horn sprouted from animal, forever remade itself—always new. From blood and air, from breath and bone, the horn generated and curled. The spiral grew wider every season, but death was always at its center.

Nettie Mae gasped. She lurched backward from the wall and lost sight of the ram. The earth was solid and flat beneath her feet, and away to the east, beyond the shoulder of the Bighorns, the sun had begun to rise. She could see it, forcefully red, its upper edge flattened and truncated by a dense shelf of cloud, the same storm that had wreaked such terror the night before now small and distant across the plain.

"Good morning, Mrs. Webber."

Nettie Mae started and spun to face Beulah. The girl had bundled up in her shawl and was carrying a steaming cup in both hands. She sipped from it as she came toward Nettie Mae, over the trampled grass of the yard, through the hens scratching and feasting on the new abundance of rain-fattened grubs.

"Coffee," Beulah said when she reached Nettie Mae's side. "I never liked it much when I was younger, but I find I've got a real taste for it now. Still, I don't drink it often, for my ma says it's better not to rely on drinks for your giddy-up-and-go. But last night wasn't especially restful, was it? I guessed I could use a little help with waking up this morning."

Nettie Mae didn't reply. She only narrowed her eyes at the girl. She had never seen a child of thirteen drinking coffee as if she had a right to it. It struck her as unnatural, and she thought, *Add that affront to all the rest of this odd creature's habits.*

241

"I had thought to make a cup for you," Beulah went on, "but I figured you need sleep right now, not pep. You didn't sleep a wink last night, did you?"

"No," Nettie Mae said reluctantly. "How did you know, anyhow?"

"It isn't your way to sleep when there's fretting to be done."

"A near drowning is nothing to be flippant about, girl. Not in any case, but particularly not when one's own small sister is fighting for her life."

"But Miranda isn't fighting for her life now. She's quite well. You saw how she looked this morning. You heard her breathing."

Nettie Mae pulled her shawl tighter against this tingling new chill. Beulah had lain soundly asleep when Nettie Mae had looked in on Miranda. How had the girl known she had been in the room at all, let alone that she had listened to Miranda's breath and found it steady?

She stepped back, distancing herself from Beulah's calm, smiling presence. She couldn't abide the girl, not now, weary and frayed as she was. Beulah's very health and pluck were as insults to Nettie Mae, a stinging slap across the face. Alta would be close to the girl's age now, if she had lived. If God had answered Nettie Mae's prayers and spared that child—her child.

But my daughter would never have been so unnatural. Eerie and wise, sipping coffee in the satiated, slow-moving dawn, with those unseasonable larks tumbling overhead.

"You ought to go inside and get some sleep," Beulah said. "Miranda will be fine—just fine. You did a powerful lot to save her, and we're all so grateful, but you must look after yourself, too, Mrs.—"

"Be quiet," Nettie Mae said. "It isn't your place to tell me what I ought or ought not do. Children should be seen, not heard."

Nettie Mae held her tongue for a moment, testing Beulah's obedience, waiting to learn whether the girl had understood the lesson. Beulah said nothing more, but Nettie Mae disliked her smile now more than ever before. It was too slow, too broad. It lingered in a manner that suggested mockery.

The kitchen door opened again. A fat bundle tottered out on stiff little legs—Miranda, wrapped up thickly in coats and shawls, so swaddled she could hardly move. The girl stood on the stoop, looking down at the steps in dismay. Then she called out plaintively, "Beulie."

Beulah turned and chuckled at the sight. She crossed the yard and helped Miranda negotiate the steps. The two girls walked hand in hand, slowly, accommodating Miranda's stilted pace—the best she could manage in the midst of her thick wool wrappings.

The girls moved toward the outhouse, but Nettie Mae hurried to intercept them. "I told your mother Miranda wasn't to come outside for any reason. Not until I said it was safe."

"You said she wasn't to go out unless she was bundled up. As you can see, my ma did a fine job with the bundling."

"She oughtn't to be outside at all. It's far too chilly."

"The rain has stopped," Beulah said languidly. "There's no danger. And I'll go with her to the outhouse, to see that she wraps up properly when she's finished. You needn't fret, Mrs. Webber. The danger has passed."

Nettie Mae was on the point of scolding Beulah again. But Miranda held up her free hand suddenly, revealing the doll Nettie Mae had spent the night sewing.

"Thank you for my dolly, Mrs. Webber. She's real pretty. You was awful kind to make her for me. I think you're a real nice lady."

"Oh." Surprise caught Nettie Mae by the throat—and a welling of reluctant sweetness, somewhere deep inside her chest. "I . . . I'm glad you like your doll, Miranda dear. Have you thought of a name for her?"

"No, not yet. What name do you like?"

Nettie Mae examined the rag doll in the child's small hand. The night had passed in a featureless blur of fear; she hardly recalled cutting the fabric or stitching the pieces together. Now the strange little poppet struck her with its uncanny resemblance to the daughter she had lost: the dark hair in two woolen braids, the large blue eyes, the rosy cheeks framing a small and hesitant smile. Nettie Mae had even dotted a few freckles onto the cloth where the doll's nose ought to be. It looked as much like Alta as any rag dolly could.

"I'm sure I don't know what you ought to call her," Nettie Mae said rather faintly. She dared not speak her dead child's name. "You'll think of something. Now run along to the outhouse, but be quick, my dear. You really shouldn't be out in this chill."

When the girls had gone, anger supplanted Nettie Mae's fear, and she was glad of it. Anger had ever been her fortress. Miranda did what was needed quickly, and soon enough the child was headed back toward the house. Beulah helped her up the steps again, but when her sister was safely inside, Beulah returned to the sheepfold and lingered near Nettie Mae, sipping her coffee, watching the world over the rim of the cup with that slow, persistent gaze.

"You had better go inside, too," Nettie Mae said, "or go where you please, but don't you haunt me. I've no use for you hanging about and chattering ever on. You never speak a lick of sense, anyhow. Leave me in peace, girl."

Beulah shrugged in a rather congenial manner. She began drifting away, angling toward the barn but never moving in haste. Heading toward some idleness, no doubt—not toward any honest work.

"And another thing," Nettie Mae called.

Beulah stopped, turned, cradling the cup in her hands, waiting for Nettie Mae to say whatever she would.

"You keep well away from Clyde, too. Do you hear me? Oh, the two of you must work at certain chores together, I know, for they can't be accomplished by one person alone." *Not without risking Clyde's health.* "But you are never to be alone with my son where I cannot see you. Never."

Beulah tilted her head, an expression of mild curiosity. "Why?"

"Like mother, like daughter." Nettie Mae forced each word out, grinding the words under the heel of her anger. "That's why. Am I understood?"

"Whatever you say, ma'am."

Beulah drifted toward the barn again, and Nettie Mae was left alone with her shivering weariness, with the subtle curve of the earth, long and slow beneath her feet.

8

At the Edge of the Spiral

I knew we weren't likely to see another storm as powerful as the one that had almost claimed Miranda's life—not till winter arrived. But the autumn winds blew as fiercely as they had in all the years before. With the harvest in, Clyde and I found ourselves with more time for leisure. Which was not to say either of us was exactly idle. Our fences could always stand a bit of fortification, so a few days after the thunderstorm, when we reckoned the river and Tensleep Creek had returned to their accustomed courses, we began making our daily treks to the canyon to cut willows. We took all the straightest saplings we could find, assured that plenty more would sprout from the sandy gorge when springtime came again, but with my family's livestock added to Clyde's—the cattle, the hogs, even our flock of fowl—there didn't seem to be enough willow to go around.

We've fences back at our homestead we might take apart, I told Clyde.

We were trudging side by side through the pasture, each with one last bundle of saplings on our backs. The grass had begun to right itself after the floodwaters had flattened stems and blades to the ground, but there were still drifts of red silt piled up around the roots of the sagebrush.

Clyde said, We might go over to your place, then, and see what we can find.

Your ma won't like it one bit.

Clyde looked at me with a crooked smile. He had lost his hat in the river, so he said, and he hadn't yet dug a replacement out of the trunks of his pa's old things, which he kept in the long shed. I wasn't used to seeing Clyde without a hat. His hair was so thick the wind couldn't even stir it.

He said, Have you been talking to my mother? I'm surprised she'll speak a word to you.

She don't speak one single word to me unless it's to scold me, I said. But I don't mind. I know she's only so hard and cold because she's afraid.

Afraid! Clyde said.

That word burst out of him sharp and loud, like the shot of a rifle. A covey of grouse broke from the pasture ahead, startled by his voice. As they lifted into the air, the birds' wings sounded like a fall of rocks rattling down the walls of a canyon.

Clyde said, My mother ain't scared of anything. She never has been in all her life. She's the bravest woman I ever knew.

I ain't said a thing about bravery, I told him. Your ma's as brave as a lion. You'll never hear me argue otherwise. But she is awful scared, too, Clyde. Can't you tell when you're around her? Don't you hear it in her voice?

What has Mother to be scared of?

I didn't answer Clyde. I thought I knew what Nettie Mae feared, but I couldn't be perfectly sure. Oh, she was frightened of death, as most people were. And as was true of most folks, religion gave Nettie Mae less reassurance on that subject the tighter she clung to its tenets, the deeper she delved into Scripture seeking knowledge of the great unknowable. But something else troubled Nettie Mae—the threat of a more immediate loss. I was at the center of it, somehow. Clyde and me, both at the point of Nettie Mae's short, dark spiral. Maybe she feared I would take Clyde away, leaving her stranded and lonesome as my own ma was lonesome, weak before the winds and the scouring floods of the prairie. That might have been true, for I was sure there was nothing a strong, self-reliant woman of Nettie Mae's sort could fear worse than weakness.

After a spell, I said, Your ma told me I ain't to be alone with you, even while doing our chores. She said we ain't to venture out of her line of sight.

Clyde laughed. We been going to the ravine for willow branches for days now.

I know, said I, but your ma's awful busy helping with Miranda, and pressing cider, too. I guess she's been too distracted to look out the window. When she finally does, and sees that we've gone off together, she'll be powerful sore.

You don't sound too worried, Clyde said.

Can't think why I should be. What's the worst she can do—strap me?

She wouldn't strap you, Clyde said. At least, I don't think she would. It was always my father who doled out the punishments, never my mother. But she might take to strapping just for your sake. She really don't like you much, I guess.

I wonder why she's taken such a bad shine to me, I said, and smiled to myself, for I knew exactly why. A spirit of mischief had entered into me. I wanted to see whether Clyde would come up with the reason himself, and if he did, whether it would make him stammer and flush.

But Clyde had nothing more to say on the subject of Nettie Mae, except to mutter, I'm the man of the house now, anyway, and man enough to make up my own mind about where I go and what I do. She can't go around scolding and ruling me forever.

We stacked our willow bundles in the barn and headed across the fields to the empty gray farmhouse, and neither Clyde nor I bothered to look back at the Webber place to learn whether Nettie Mae was watching. But by the time we reached my old home, a pleasant air of idleness had replaced our former spirit of industrious duty. Of course there was work to be done. When was there not? But we had no cause for urgency, with the crops safely stored and the animals housed and fed.

We sat for a spell on the porch steps, resting after the effort of scrambling through ankle-deep mud. The yard where I had played as a small child lay so still that every breezy shiver of grass stems seemed exaggerated. Too strong, too vibrant, each small movement as bold as if the world itself were quaking. It gave me a curious yet not unpleasant sense of living beyond time, existing just outside time's fragile and moveable borders. The steps on which we sat were mute with disuse. The house at our back—my home, the one I had known and loved best—seemed to hold in a great, painful chestful of memory, a breath it refused to exhale. Across the yard, abandoned to wind and scrub, and far over the pasture where Clyde's sheep grazed, the Webber house was bustling with life. Somewhere between my old home and my new lay the boundary of time. We had crossed it, and life at the sod house went on without us. Where Clyde and I sat, the hours hung suspended in the low autumn light.

When we had rested our tired legs, I got up and opened the door. The hinges squealed, which only made the silence within all the heavier. Clyde followed me, and for a long time we stood beside the cold hearth on my ma's rug of braided rags, feeling the present emptiness and the past joys and sorrows, all the simple acts of life those walls had contained. The crate with the president's china stood in the center of the kitchen. No one had bothered to nail the lid closed, and it set upon the crate just slightly askew, so a crack of dark shadow showed around its edge.

That made me remember the treasures I'd hidden all the months and years before.

Come along, I said to Clyde. I want to show you something.

I led him down the short passage to a small room, the one I had shared with Miranda. My bedstead was there, stripped of its sheets, with spiderwebs strung between the posts. The webs caught all the light that spilled in through one narrow window; they shone like silver threads and seemed to illuminate the whole space, casting back the gloom of disuse and welcoming Clyde and me to the heart of silence.

I got down on my knees and reached under the bed. Miranda's trundle used to be there, but Ma and I had moved it to the Webber place, so now I found it easier than it ever had been before to pry up the loose floor board and delve down into the cool black hollow below. I found my treasures by feel and brought them up, one at a time, for Clyde to examine.

As I set my things out one by one along the planks of the floor, I could feel Clyde's confusion. The stones and feathers and bits of wood I laid at his feet were ordinary things, I knew. I heard the words he didn't think it proper to say: Why would you show me such things, and why treat them as if they're jewels or gold? There's nothing worth saving here. But I went on pulling my treasures from the earth, and after a spell, he sat with his legs folded beneath him and looked at my collection in silence.

When I had taken the last rock from beneath the floor, I sat likewise with my back against the bed, watching Clyde over the spread of bright and beautiful things that lay between us. I picked up a crow's feather, blue black, and offered it to him. But when he reached for it, I rolled the quill between my thumb and finger, so the feather tilted in the light. Blue and violet and a deep, leafy green flashed across its surface, glorifying what had been mere blackness a moment before.

Clyde's hand paused in the air. He held still, and I rolled the feather again. His smile was slow, hesitant.

I like crows, I said. I know most folks curse them, for they'll pluck the seeds you plant right out of the soil and eat them all, if they can. And sometimes they'll eat chicks, if they can get at them while they're small. But crows are real bright, too. They have minds of their own.

Clyde looked up from the feather. The half smile had returned to his face—cautious, not quite sure whether his amusement was proper.

He said, Crows don't have minds. No animal does.

I said, You sure about that? I reckon that buckskin horse of yours has a real sharp mind, and a kindly way about him, too. Ain't you noticed?

Clyde was silent for a spell, watching the feather turn in my fingers. The colors shifted and danced. Then he said, real quiet and thoughtful, Joe Buck came back for me when I pulled Miranda from the river. We were washed far downstream. Joe was real scared by the flood and the rain, but he followed me instead of lighting out for home. He could have run off, if *he wanted to. If he hadn't come and found me, I might not have made it back to the farm. And Miranda surely wouldn't have lived.*

I said, I seen crows pick up sticks and snap all the little sharp snags off so the sticks are perfectly smooth and straight. Then they poke their sticks down into an anthill or a termite stump and pull up their supper. You ever seen another bird do such a thing?

No, ma'am, Clyde said with a little laugh. Never in my life. Birds ain't exactly the smartest of creatures, I guess.

Well, there you have it, I said. Crows ain't got no inclination to starve just 'cause somebody decided a proper bird ought to be dull and helpless. They've decided on their own what they'll be. Minds of their own, just like I told you. I can't help but admire them an awful lot, for the sake of that brightness—even if their brightness goes hard on a farmer when planting time comes.

I passed the feather to Clyde and allowed him to spin it for himself. He watched the colors shift from deepest purple to the blue of a summer sky reflected in water—dark and complete, the richest shade a blue could ever be. He would never again look at a crow and see only black. I felt certain of that.

I showed him the stones next, each in turn. One was shaped like an egg, and the light flowed soft and blurred around its curves, luminous, exactly in the manner of a real eggshell. Another was red, but it wasn't the same red of the limestone canyon or the ruts of the road that stretched clear to Paintrock. This was a shining poppy red, and where a flake of stone had broken away, it left an arching, pleated scar. I showed him another rock I'd found by the river. It was white flecked with black, smoothed by an endless flow of water. Pinpoint dots of some sparkling material shimmered when I rolled it in my palm. I showed him the tiny dimples in the surface, almost too fine to be seen.

You see, I said. Those dimples are the places where this stone has lost little bits of itself. Parts of it have fallen away. But they became something else, as soon as they left the stone. You know what they became, don't you?

Sand? Clyde said uncertainly.

Sand and riverbank. And mud and soil. And the soil falls apart, too, little by little, and what does it become?

Clyde stared at me, his brows pinched, and I understood that something I'd said had troubled him, though I couldn't think what it might be.

I answered my own question: The soil becomes all the plants that grow up out of it.

Clyde said, Soil only holds plants, like a bed for sleeping in. It doesn't become anything.

Well, I guess it does, I said. Haven't you ever sucked on a grass stem long enough to taste the dirt in it?

No, he said, laughing. How would I know what dirt tastes like, anyhow?

I didn't answer, for I thought it awful sad that Clyde had never thought to put a little earth in his mouth and learn the taste of his own land.

Look at this, I said.

I passed him a snail shell. It wasn't much bigger than the glass marbles my brothers played with, but it was ten times prettier.

I found it on the riverbank, I said. Isn't it the loveliest thing you ever seen?

Clyde shook his head, a small gesture, vague and unsettled. He said, It's just a snail shell.

But look at the colors.

Brown, he said.

You don't look very close. Maybe you need spectacles. Hold it up to the light. Really look, now, and tell me what you see.

Clyde held the snail shell up toward the window. He turned it slowly in his hand. Cast in the easy afternoon light, in the mirror light of the spider-webs, the shell seemed to glow from within. What had seemed brown at first careless glance revealed its layers of color. Oranges and reds, subdued like a shaded lantern, but no less warm for all that. Hues of gold and caramel lay one beside the other in delicate ridges, each ridge finer than a hair. One dark line and one pale, both lines carrying a hint of subtle green, wrapped from the shell's edge toward the fat bump on its side, the point where all line and color merged into one, at the terminus of the spiral. Clyde traced the dark line with his finger, around and around till it joined the pale line and the line gave way to uniform brownness.

I smiled. He saw the beauty in it now.

I said, Have a look here.

With the greatest care, I picked up a short stem of grass crowned by a dry, pale-golden seed head. I had snapped off the stem some months before, as spring had given way to summer, and I had taken care to keep one long, flat leaf attached to the stem. The whole arrangement had been green when I'd picked it and added it to my cache of pretty things. The green had long since faded, but I didn't mind. I hadn't taken it for its color.

Barley, Clyde said.

I passed the stem across, and Clyde held it up to the light, turning the dry stalk slowly. Light ran like honey along the filaments between the seeds.

It's nice, he said, as if he wanted to set some worry inside me to rest.

I said, You ain't looking close enough. You ain't seen what makes it so special.

I lifted the dry leaf with one finger, so Clyde could see its underside. There, fixed tightly to the lifeless matter, were a dozen new lives waiting to be born.

I said, I don't know what sort of insect put its eggs there, but ain't it the prettiest thing you ever seen?

The eggs were tiny, white as pearls, and rather longer than round. I couldn't help but feel the care and patience of the little mother who had trusted her eggs to the protection of that leaf. She had arranged her children in perfect Vs, nested one inside the other, and had coated them with some miraculous substance that had hardened around them, holding them fast to the leaf while they grew in their pale secrecy, securing their future against wind and rain and marauding birds.

I ran the tip of my finger gently over the eggs. Though they were impossibly small, I could feel every one.

Do you think they can sense me touching them? I asked Clyde. Maybe it frightens them. Maybe it gives them nightmares.

Clyde thrust the barley stem back at me. He brushed his hands together as if he wanted to clean them, as if I had soiled him for good.

No damn insect eggs can feel you, Beulah, he said. And no damn insect can have a nightmare, either.

Who are you to say so? You ain't an insect; you don't know.

Insects don't have minds. Neither do crows. You're making up stories, and it's all a lot of foolish talk.

I looked down at the barley stem and held my peace. It didn't hurt me, that Clyde said I was foolish, for I knew he was only speaking from fear. What hurt me was this: he had failed to notice the most beautiful thing of all about my barley stem. The eggs lay in exactly the same pattern as the barley seeds. Tight and close, all so perfectly aligned, every seed and every egg holding a new life, a dreaming life—waiting for its season.

I had thought Clyde could see, same as I saw. But he was still blinded to the truth.

He said, All this talk of animals with minds and critters having nightmares. My mother would call it blasphemy, if she was to hear it.

It ain't blasphemy, I said.

Clyde shot back at me: Nowhere in the Bible does it say that animals can think or feel.

Nowhere in the Bible does it say the sky is blue, neither, I said, but you can see it's so, just by looking up. You don't need the Bible to tell you.

Clyde's body gave a sort of twitch, an impatient jerk, and I thought of a horse when it wants to run away but knows it shouldn't. He hugged his knees up near his chest and sat and scowled for a minute, frowning down at the little things I'd spread before him as if I'd offered insults instead of beauty.

I didn't want Clyde sore with me, so I scooped up all my stones and feathers and the snail shell. I laid them back in the hollow beneath the floor and set the barley stem carefully atop the whole collection, in the stillness and dark where the eggs could go on dreaming till spring came again. Then I replaced the floor board and climbed to my feet, smiling.

All those lambs have done real well, I said. I was awful worried one or two might die in the storm, but they're hardy, ain't they?

They are, Clyde agreed, but rather sullenly. My father and I bred them for it—to survive the winter.

I offered my hand and pulled Clyde to his feet. With talk of such ordinary things as sheep and winter, some of his sourness seemed to dissipate. We left my old room and returned to the porch. There was a crisp, smoky scent to the air, a breath of cold coming down from the mountains. It wouldn't be long before the first snows arrived.

We stood for a while in amiable quiet. I could hear the ram's low, guttural calls far out over the pasture, and the answering bleats of his many wives. The sound seemed to relieve the last of Clyde's strain. With his good mood returning, I thought it best not to mention that snow was on its way.

Instead, I said, Just one more ewe left to drop her young, and then the fall lambing's through.

Clyde turned to me, surprised. There ain't any more young left to drop, he said.

There sure is. The ewe with the black legs, but no black on her face.

I know the one, Clyde said. But she didn't catch this year. She's young— she was just born last autumn. It's nothing strange for ewes to miss their first breeding. It happens all the time.

She didn't miss, I said. She's got a full belly. She'll be dropping soon. She may be birthing right now, for all I can tell.

He might justifiably have made some cutting remark, for he had been a shepherd for years longer than I had. But Clyde seemed determined to set his ill feelings aside. He suggested we go down to the pasture and look over the flock, so he could put his hands on the young sheep in question and prove to me, by virtue of his long experience, that I was mistaken. We forgot all notion of willows and fences, and walked across the field to where the flock was grazing along the margin of the recent flood.

I stood by for a good long spell, while Clyde counted his sheep, then counted again. He walked around the perimeter of the flock, which made the ram grunt and flinch and made the ewes and the new lambs lift their heads in alarm. But no matter how many times Clyde tallied his sheep, he still came up one short.

The black-legged ewe is the one that's missing, he finally admitted. She's nowhere to be seen.

The ram drew close to me, and I could feel his warm breath across my knuckles. I rested my hand on his dense crown of wool and felt the place where the horn arose from flesh, at the hard, broad edge of the spiral.

Of course the black-legged ewe is missing, I said to Clyde. She slipped away to be alone. Her time has come for birthing.

Clyde stared at me in silence. The look he gave me was slow and considering, but there was no doubt left in his eyes.

At last, he said, Come on back to the farm. There's a few things I need to fetch. Night is coming on, and we must go out and find that sheep, or the coyotes will find her first.

CLYDE

At the edge of the spiral, everything Clyde had once known to be true softened and blurred and shifted. There was no solidity anymore, no sense, no purpose. There was only the strange, disorienting motion of the pasture turning around him, circling him, the sheep's bodies drifting across his vision from right to left even though he knew the animals stood still.

Beulah grabbed him by the upper arm. Her grip was surprisingly firm, for a girl so slight. Clyde was always startled by her strength, every time he saw it displayed anew.

"You look dizzy," Beulah said.

Clyde stamped his feet to reassure himself that the world was real. It stopped lurching around him, and the pasture resumed its proper nature, flat and predictable, obedient to the laws of God and the stewardship of man.

"Spell come over me just now," he admitted. "But I'm all right."

"You ain't getting the fever again?"

She sounded as if she already knew the answer, and knowing that she knew made Clyde feel sick and spinning again. But he pushed the sensation away. He hadn't any time for weakness; one of his flock had gone missing. No good shepherd allowed his ewes to wander off, whether they were ready to lamb or not.

"I'm fine enough," Clyde said. "Come on; the sun will set in less than an hour. We got to find that ewe before dark, or likely we'll find nothing but her bones."

When they returned to the sod house, Cora was fixing supper in the kitchen while Miranda, recovered from her ordeal, played with her dolls at the table. The little girl's cheeks glowed with health and she was restless, as children of her age always are. But since the storm, Cora had insisted that Miranda remain within reach.

Clyde took his best lantern from the pantry and fitted a new candle inside.

"Beulah and I must go out to search for a lost sheep, Mrs. Bemis. If we're lucky, we won't be gone but half an hour. Will you keep a few bites warm for us in case we're kept away longer?"

Cora cast a nervous glance at the lantern. "Do you expect you'll be out after dark?"

"I don't expect it, ma'am, but I aim to be prepared."

Clyde retrieved his shotgun from its pegs, high above the kitchen door where the little fellows couldn't reach. Cora gasped.

"There's nothing to fear, Ma," Beulah said. "Clyde's only being cautious, ain't you? Anyway, the worst that'll come is that Nettie Mae will be sore when she learns we've gone off together. Where is Nettie Mae, anyhow?"

"In the root cellar," Cora said, "tidying up and packing in more straw where it's needed."

"Good," Clyde said. "We'll slip off, Beulah and me, before my mother can take notice. I know she doesn't like us to be out of her sight, but there's no helping it now—not with a ewe missing. A fella has to do what a fella has to do, given the circumstances."

"Be safe, then," Cora said. "And don't stay out late, or I'll worry."

Beulah took her pale-gray shawl from the back of a kitchen chair, kissed the top of Miranda's head, and followed Clyde out into the rose flush of evening. They held their tongues, stepping quickly till they were beyond the root cellar, from which Clyde could hear the rustle and bump of his mother working in near darkness. He dared say nothing till he and Beulah reached the long shed. Then he moved closer to the girl and murmured, "We ought to check all around the sheep pen and the barn first. Most often, ewes run to someplace familiar when their time comes. So if she is about to lamb, as you say, it's likely we'll find her there."

But a thorough search of pens and outbuildings produced no sign of the black-legged ewe. Clyde propped the barrel of his shotgun on one shoulder and sighed.

"The pasture next. We'll have to walk every inch of it. She could be lying down at the base of some scrub; we'll never see her unless we're right on top of her. We ought to spread out, six feet between us, and walk at the same pace, back and forth till we've covered the whole field."

Scouring the pasture left them empty handed, too, and by the time they reached the farthest corner, where the ground sloped up toward the foothills, purple dusk had settled over the prairie. The ram was already leading his band back toward the farm, and Clyde and Beulah followed, silent and pensive, and shut the flock safely in the fold.

Clyde turned in a slow circle, taking in the land that was his now, all the acres of his unasked-for dominion. His land; yet it hid secrets from its master. The land had a will of its own. The order and simplicity Clyde wanted—needed—meant nothing to the farm or the prairie. He would have cursed the ewe, but he didn't wish for Beulah to think less of him.

The root cellar door stood open by a crack. A candle was burning inside now, ruddy and weak, its small light easing out to touch the flat, dry gray of autumn grasses with tentative warmth.

"Mother's still in the cellar," Clyde whispered. "Come along now, quickly, before she pops out and catches us. She'll insist on going with me if she learns what we're up to, and she'll make you stay behind."

They returned to the pasture and took the river trail. Clyde paused at the tangled margin of the hedge, the interwoven mat of sumac and willow, a dense wall through which no grown sheep could venture. He looked back at the sod house. It seemed very small and far, diminished by the vastness of oncoming night. The sky wore a uniformity of featureless cloud from one horizon to another, faintly luminescent, lilac gray. There could be no hope for a moon tonight.

Someone had lit candles in the house. The two square windows of the first floor—kitchen, sitting room—looked like eyes wide open in the dusk. They stared across the tops of waving grasses, watching Clyde with an unblinking focus.

Side by side, Clyde and Beulah walked the path. Shoulder-high brush hid the Nowood from view, but Clyde could hear it, a sustained whisper, a sigh that went on and on. He thought the blood in his veins, or in any creature's veins, would sound the same way if he could make himself quiet enough to hear it. Twilight's purple sheen vanished from the world and everything reverted to a colorless state, dimmed by the oncoming night, gray fading into gray into deepest black. Clyde took his matchbox from his pocket and made Beulah hold the lantern while he lit the candle within.

"Keep an eye out for sheep dung on the trail," he said. "Or hoofprints."

"Not a lot of difference between a sheep's droppings and a deer's. Nor between their prints."

"Keep an eye out all the same. And I never sheared that ewe. If we're lucky, we might find some of her wool sticking to the brush."

Night pulled in around them. The world became a small circle of orange light, shifting and impermanent. Its boundary was the place where reality gave way to every possibility, every dark thing conjured up in dream or imagination. As they pressed along the river trail, the tall grasses hissed and shivered and came, blade by blade, into view. They were all the same ruddy shade, like candle flame, candlelight, a small light that couldn't hold the teeming darkness back for long. Clyde never heard the coyotes, the wolves, the shambling and hungry bears come down from the mountains. He didn't see them, nor did he see their signs. But he felt them—out there, waiting just beyond the light, melting ever backward into shadow. He felt worse things, too, creatures he had only known in stories and childhood terrors. The pale, ageless men who drank blood and slept in coffins. The men who could change their shape—wolves, but bigger than a wolf ought to be and clever enough to open doors with their long-thumbed paws. He thought of the tiny white eggs arranged along the secret side of a barley leaf. He remembered Beulah's finger running down the length of the leaf, and the sky above seemed to press down with all its eternal weight, and ripple and roll behind him. He shuddered.

Certainty came to Clyde all at once—a rising sensation in his stomach and a burning in the back of his throat, a hot rush of instinct that told him some living creature was just beyond the reach of his lantern, standing on the trail or just beside it. He stopped walking, and Beulah halted beside him.

"Something ahead," Clyde whispered. "Might be the ewe." He hoped it was.

"It's not." She sounded neither doubtful nor concerned.

"What, then?"

Beulah took the lantern from his cold hand. She made as if to lead the way, but Clyde caught her by the fringe of her shawl and made her stop.

"If it's not the sheep, then what is it? You can't just walk up on an animal in the darkness."

"Don't you know where we are, Clyde? Of course, I've been here a dozen times, but maybe you haven't. There's nothing to fear. Nothing here can hurt you, nor even get into your heart unless you allow it."

She moved, and Clyde moved with her, still clinging to her shawl like he must have clutched at Nettie Mae's apron strings once. The packed earth of the trail widened around them, broadening in the ruddy ring of their awareness. They had reached the clearing by the river—the place where Clyde had buried his father.

He cast his furtive eyes to the edge of the light, to the place where he knew Substance's grave should be. The flood had scoured the ground almost flat, but a tangle of willow and sage had fetched up against a slight rise—what remained of the burial mound. On that evening when he had ridden after Miranda, Clyde had seen pale stones and bits of wood arranged atop Substance's grave. He remembered the sight now, blurring past. He remembered that he had assumed Nettie Mae had been the one to visit—that his mother had left the stones as adornments or offerings. But Beulah's face turned down as they passed the grave. She seemed to peer into the tangle of scrub, searching for the pretty things she had laid out for Substance, looking to determine what the flood had carried away.

Once they had moved beyond the grave, Clyde released his hold on the shawl. The entrance to the canyon lay somewhere just ahead, not yet illuminated by the feeble light. A dry stick snapped in the darkness to their left, in the hedgerow that separated river from field. Clyde heard the two-beat rhythm of an animal trotting through the brush, a breath of foliage sliding over fur.

"Coyote," he whispered.

She nodded.

"Any sign of a sheep on the trail?"

Beulah shook her head.

"We ought to go back to the farm, probably."

"Not just yet. The ewe must be close by."

"How do you know? I ain't seen the least sign of her, and—"

"Look!"

Beulah lifted the lantern, and the ring of candlelight shivered and rolled and slid along the path till it caught the sandstone walls of the ravine. There was the flat rock on which Miranda had crouched days before. And at its base, hanging like a banner from the sharp projection of a willow branch, a pale twist of wool.

"She's in the canyon," Beulah said.

"Let's hope she hasn't gone too far up. It'll be rough going in the dark."

A few feet into the ravine, the well-defined path dwindled to a narrow track, the sort used only by the deer and pronghorns and the stone-gray wild sheep who descended from high places to water below. Clyde led the way, scrambling over lips of red rock, turning to offer Beulah his hand, which she rarely took. Whenever he ascended to a new ledge or a flat accumulation of chipped stone, spindled around its margins by the thin stems of saxifrage, Clyde paused and stared around him, desperate for any sign of the missing ewe. They followed the deer track till the river sounded small and weak below, but they found no further sign of the black-legged sheep.

"We can't go much farther," Clyde said. "The canyon is too steep for walking up ahead; we'd have to climb, and that ewe didn't climb, so unless she grew wings—"

"Hush."

Beulah held perfectly still. Clyde did likewise, so motionless and silent, his breath scarcely cooled his half-parted lips. Then he heard, from the deep shadows just behind and below the ledge on which he was standing, a soft grunt and the scrape of a hoof against dry soil.

Clyde and Beulah scrambled back down the ledge together and pushed their way through a screen of scrubby willows. The black-legged ewe lay on her side against the canyon wall; when the light fell upon her, she scrabbled with her forelegs and let out a pitiful moan. Then she subsided, her flanks rising and falling with her rapid, hopeless breath.

"By God," Clyde murmured. "We found her. But she's weak; something bad happened. Attacked?"

"Of course not. She hasn't yet recovered from the birth; that's all."

Beulah moved closer to the ewe—slowly, one step and pause, then another deliberate step. The girl's presence, and perhaps the light, seemed to have a calming effect. The ewe settled, raising no protest as

Beulah sank down on her heels and stroked the curve of the animal's forehead.

"There's blood on her hind end," Beulah said.

"Do you see any lambs?"

"No, but there's something dark here beside her. Dark and not moving." Still half-crouched, Beulah worked her slow way around the ewe's body. She bent her neck to peer down into the weeds. "It's the afterbirth."

"But no lambs. We got here too late, then; coyotes took the young."

Beulah straightened and seemed about to speak. But her eye fell on a flat, pale thing, motionless among the stunted clumps of willow.

"Clyde, look!"

She sounded breathless, and her face had darkened with a rising rush of feeling—of wonder. He moved carefully toward Beulah and the willows, though he still felt that roll of caution overhead, the weight of dark and unseen things watching him, touching him.

At Beulah's feet, bedded on a few dry curls of fallen leaves, lay a newborn lamb. Its body was thin, sodden, matted with blood and birth, pressed to the earth by its own weakness. It had rolled or crawled away from its mother, and the cord, shiny and wet as a bloated worm, snaked away from its belly through wiry grass. The lamb was small and motionless, but perfect in form from shoulders to tail. When Clyde looked at its neck, though—and what the neck carried—fear and revulsion rose so suddenly in his throat that he gagged. He barely kept himself from heaving into the weeds.

The lamb's face was cloven, deeply as a hoof. On either side of the monstrous divide, two perfectly formed muzzles worked feebly, the pink nostrils distending, the twin mouths opening in silent entreaty. Each side of the head bore a normal eye, and each eye blinked in the lantern light, first one, then the other. It was the third eye that struck cold horror into Clyde's chest. Dark and glittering in the seam of flesh, in the place where the two halves merged into one, the third eye stared at Clyde, far too small and unblinking, with an air of sickening patience.

"God have mercy." He backed away.

"I never seen the like." Beulah was rapturous, already in love.

"It's a monster."

Clyde turned his shotgun toward the creature, but Beulah pushed the muzzle aside.

"Don't you dare shoot that lamb, Clyde Webber. You're blessed by a miracle, something no one has seen before, and all you can think to do is kill it?"

"It won't live, Beulah. It can't! It'd be kinder to put it out of its misery."

"It ain't in any misery—not yet. The little thing only came into this world moments ago. Let it have its life, even if its life will be a short one."

"I . . . I can't take that thing back to the farm, and—"

"Then I'll take it. You see to the mother."

Clyde propped his shotgun against the willows. Gratefully, he turned away from the two-headed lamb. The ewe's eye rolled when she saw that Clyde had shifted his attention to her. She struggled again, bracing her forelegs against the stone, fighting to rise. But her hind end was weak, and she cried out in helpless pain, then fell heavily back to the ground.

I never was good at catching them.

Clyde remembered Substance grabbing for the wool, pulling at the animals without regard for their suffering. He remembered how the ewes had fought and twisted and screamed in their guttural panic when he, Clyde, had held them for shearing. The first shearing he'd done on his own, and hard work it had been. He had left the fold feeling sick and angry over the hurt he had caused, the nicked hides, the blood, the betrayal of animals who had trusted him, who had once thought him gentle and safe.

I can't go to her now, this ewe. She'll try to run. I'll never hold her. She'll fly into a panic and plunge right over the ledge and break her legs or her neck. I can't touch her. I can't.

From the black floor of the ravine there came a high-pitched yelp. Then another, answering from the river trail.

"Coyotes," Clyde said to Beulah. "We got to hurry, if we hope to get either one of them out of this place."

"Can the ewe walk?"

"I don't know."

Beulah had set the lantern on a flat-topped stone while she tended to the monster. By the twitching, fickle light of the shaded candle, Clyde strained to assess the ewe's condition. Blood had darkened her hindquarters, but it might only have been the blood of birth. He moved toward her again, and the ewe bleated, scrabbling toward the ledge.

"Damn." Clyde sank onto his heels. There was little time to lose; the coyotes were already slinking up the game trail, jaws gaping with hunger. Clyde might frighten them away with a blast from his gun, but then his shell would be spent. How would he and Beulah fare, going back through the darkness with a ewe—crippled and reeking of blood—and the terrible thing she had birthed? It was a long trek back to the farm. They might attract something far worse than coyotes—wolves, or a bear, or the pale drinkers of blood, or the thing that watched from the darkness at the edge of his father's grave.

He closed his eyes for a moment, breathed deeply, and fought to slow the wild flutter of his heart.

Improbably, for no reason he could discern, he thought of the snail shell Beulah had placed in his hand in the stillness and silver light of the abandoned bedroom. He remembered the feel of it, the smoothness, the dark line and the pale line curving around and around, merging into one. He had traced that path with his finger. He had seen more colors than brown—had seen that brown was, in the right light and carefully observed, golden and green and crimson layered one atop the other.

Clyde opened his eyes. He watched the ewe's face, the redness of pain at the corner of her eye, the tight smile of fear.

"You're hurting," Clyde said to the animal, softly. "I'm sorry you hurt, little mother. But I'll help you, if you'll lie still."

He crept toward the ewe. She moaned, but she didn't thrash or try to run.

"You know me," Clyde murmured. "You see me every day. I let you in and out of the pen." Closer. The ewe trembled and held still. "That's it; that's it, good girl. You know me now, don't you? I've come to help you. I'm your shepherd. That's what a shepherd does, isn't it? Cares for his sheep."

He moved again, but too close this time. The ewe tried to leap up in a sudden panic. She fell back, crying piteously, a high and agonized sound.

"Easy, easy. Of course you know me. We live on the same land. The pasture. It's yours, and mine, and we both know it, we both share it. Don't we? Don't we, little mother?"

The ewe turned her head. She stared at Clyde, a sharp, direct look that seemed to strike him hard, a blow to the forehead or to the center of his chest; he couldn't tell where the blow had fallen. But on the instant, a streak of pain ran from his groin up into his back, his belly. It was hot— scalding—and though he knew he wasn't bleeding, still he smelled the iron of his own blood and feared that it would all flow out of him, onto the rocks where little could grow, where it would all be wasted.

Clyde sucked in a deep, cold breath, a spasm of shock and wonder. The air tasted of the canyon, damp and red, the mineral closeness of the sandstone walls tingling on his tongue. He could taste a sweetness of grass, too, and the grass was familiar and good.

You see, he told the ewe silently. *We do know each other. And here I am to help you. There's nothing to fear. Nothing to fear. We are of the same place—the pasture, the land.*

Clyde crouched over the black-legged ewe now; she permitted his nearness, sagged back against the stone wall, and allowed him to run his hands down her heaving flanks. The wool of her back end was saturated with blood. He touched the birthing place and felt the ewe flinch, felt the disunion of warm flesh.

"She's torn," Clyde said to Beulah. "Little wonder, after birthing that thing. I don't think she can walk. I'll have to carry her."

Clyde spoke his quiet comforts to the ewe as he guided her to her feet, then crouched low to pull her up to his shoulders. She was young and small, weighing less than most of his flock; he could feel her disorientation, the swimming fear, as he straightened and bore her high above solid ground. With his left hand, he held the ewe's forelegs. With his right, he took the shotgun and snugged it under his arm, muzzle pointed out. Then he slipped the muzzle through the lantern's handle and lifted the light, too.

Beulah had wrapped the monstrous newborn in her shawl. The two joined heads were all that could be seen of the creature; Beulah cradled that sickening bundle against her chest, beaming down with soft-eyed tenderness as if it were her own child she held.

Clyde turned away from the sight. He shuddered in disgust. "Are you ready?"

"Yes. You got the light, so you lead the way. I'll follow."

As they picked their slow way down the game trail, the brush around them rattled and snapped—coyotes fleeing the light, retreating to the emptiness of the plain. Clyde's shoulders and right arm had already begun to ache by the time he found the river path, but he held the gun more tightly against his side and didn't pause to relieve his cramping muscles. The sooner he and Beulah were back at the farm, the better off they'd all be. He must convince the girl somehow that the two-headed lamb ought rightly to be killed. The thing would never grow, never thrive. God alone knew if it could even suckle. It might very well starve to death, unless it was spared.

Yet even as he mused over the lamb's inevitable fate, Clyde's senses sharpened. The river came to him as sound and smell. Brightness of water, crisp and compelling, making his mouth wet with the newness and power of the scent. He could smell, so it seemed, every leaf that hung over the bank and exhaled greenly in the air above the water— breathed out a green scent so that he could breathe it in. Murmur, rush, a chorus of voices, the voices of stones rolling and chattering, the countless cracks and pops of mineral breaking from mineral, of specks of sand departing from granite and leaving minute dimples behind. The sound of the river building its bank, endlessly renewing.

He had never felt the river so powerfully before. He had never known a world like this. It was as if he had multiplied himself, as if there were no longer one Clyde, but many. As if he had two minds, or more, with which to sense and think and feel.

The realization came to Clyde that he was experiencing whatever the two-headed lamb heard and smelled, just as he had felt its mother's pain for one brief moment, up in the ravine. That knowledge stunned him, and wiped all thought from his mind. He didn't wish to feel any sympathy with that deformed beast. The monster lamb was a thing that never should have been, a freak of nature, a revelation of God in His most creative and cruelest capacity. He refused to accept the lamb's awareness, refused to feel. This was not a thing Clyde could allow, this oneness with the weak—the feeblest, most inutile of all living things. Yet despite his resolve, tears came to Clyde's eyes. They blurred the circle of lantern light, obscuring the ground below him, where he placed one foot ahead of the other, step and step and step through the singing night all the way back to the order and safety of his home.

He looked back only once, just after they passed Substance's grave. In a halo of light, Beulah stood out against the darkness with vivid and fearful clarity. Her eyes were downcast, watching the two faces of the miracle she carried, heavy lidded with a kind of holy acceptance. And the lamb's four nostrils moved to catch the river air, breathing deeply of life while life still remained.

NETTIE MAE

At the edge of the spiral of her thoughts, her fears, Nettie Mae held herself aloof and still, hardened against the agony of unknowing. She was used to the pain, after all—or should have been, with so many years gone by. That rasp of doubt, the sting of injustice, had never left her heart since the first burial, the first child she had lost, the tiny grave among the roots of a willow tree somewhere in Wisconsin—the long flat nothingness of brown Wisconsin. She would never find that tree again, not if she searched for a hundred years. And now the bones of her baby—the boy who had lived not quite two days and was gone before she could give him a name—were laced about with willow roots, pushed apart and down into the long flat neverness below the earth.

Four children lost. Four children dead. And Clyde will be just as lost to me forever, if that witch of a girl ensnares him.

Nettie Mae hadn't spoken a word through supper—not that she was much given to idle chatter, especially during the solemnity of meals. She had hardly eaten a bite either; she had stared at Clyde's empty chair, his bowl unfilled in its customary place. And she had refused to look at Beulah's seat, also empty. The girl's absence was as stark as an accusation. She had defied Nettie Mae's command—her one command, her most emphatic wish. Beulah had spat on Nettie Mae's control, trampled her authority, and drawn Clyde off into the darkness of sin.

Sensing Nettie Mae's mood, Cora had kept the rest of her children silent at the table and had hurried them upstairs to bed as soon as they had eaten their fill.

Coming down the stairs, Cora had meekly offered to wash the dishes. At least she was timid, humbled now by the enormity of her sins—now that a man was dead. That was more than could be said for her daughter. Who must perish before Beulah saw the error of her ways and repented of her scandalous behavior? The mooning, the lazing, the chasing after Clyde when there was work to be done and better, holier things for a young man to think of than the convenient nearness of some city-bred hussy.

"I will wash," Nettie Mae had said shortly, and Cora had fled to her room.

When the washing was finished, Nettie Mae bundled herself in a long shawl and paced the rear yard, from kitchen steps to outhouse, from sheepfold to garden gate to root cellar, listening for any sound, any cries in the night, any sly note of Beulah's laughter that might tell her where the girl had gone to ground with Nettie Mae's son in tow. And after too long a spell—what might have been hours, with no moon or stars visible to gauge the passage of time—she spotted the glimmer of a lantern far across the dense black expanse of night. The lantern winked and dimmed as it passed behind the cottonwood trees. So they had gone to the riverside.

As you knew they would. As you knew they must, Nettie Mae told herself bitterly. *Like mother, like daughter.*

Nettie Mae had expected Clyde and Beulah to come directly back to the house, and she intended to confront them in the yard. As she watched the orb of light draw slowly nearer, she pictured the clash with no small amount of righteous satisfaction. Herself, looming up out of the darkness to challenge the sinners with their own foul deeds, cold and unforgiving as Judgment. But the lantern diverted, swinging wide of the usual route from pasture to house. In a few moments, the light vanished into the barn, and there it remained for far too long. No doubt Beulah, emboldened by the success of her deception and spurred on by the filthy glee of fornication, had pulled Clyde into the loft for another tumble in the hay.

Time crept by unmeasured. The darkness persisted. A few crickets still lived, defiant against the autumn cold, and note after faltering note, their desultory chirps from the denuded garden replaced Nettie Mae's anger with a helpless, trembling submission. The deed was over. Her son was ruined; he had tasted of sin and now he would thirst for it like a wretch in the desert lusting after any foul puddle he might find. That had ever been the manner of sin, since Eve first tasted of Eden's fruit.

By the time the lantern reappeared and came bobbing and swinging toward the house, Nettie Mae's wrath had abandoned her. What was the use of raging when the damage was already done? She felt withered and papery—dry—a husk stripped away from its kernel. She shivered, and told herself it was because of the cold.

By the time Clyde and Beulah passed the outhouse, Nettie Mae could see them, two silhouettes black within the private sphere of their light. They did not hold hands, nor did the foolish girl cling to his arm as girls think it charming to do. But neither was there distance between them—not exactly. They moved with natural ease in one another's presence. Something intimate had passed between them; Nettie Mae was sure of it. And now their voices came to her across the yard. Neither spoke loudly enough that Nettie Mae could discern their words—there was something low and cryptic about their speech, something furtive—but the tone carried a distinct note of familiarity, and it soured Nettie Mae's gut.

She stepped forward, invading the circle of their light. Clyde and Beulah both started, and the lantern swung violently in Clyde's hand. He cursed under his breath, stilling the lantern with his other hand.

"Mother! You frightened us. We—"

"I don't want to hear it. It's not a fit thing to speak of, in any case. I know. I *know* what you've been up to this night, both of you. You ought to be ashamed."

"Mother—"

"Hold your tongue, Clyde Webber." She rounded on Beulah. "What did I tell you? What did I say?"

The girl stared back at Nettie Mae unfazed. Despite the cold, Beulah held her shawl slung over one arm. The color rode high in her cheeks, and there was a glint of something in her eye—something Nettie Mae couldn't countenance, something unholy. Glee. Or bliss. An eerie, self-contained rapture.

"Well?" Nettie Mae snapped. "Answer me, girl."

"You said I wasn't ever to go off with Clyde alone, out of your sight."

"So you aren't as slow witted as you seem. You do remember. One must ask oneself, then, why you disobeyed me."

"We had to," Beulah said. "A sheep went missing."

Clyde nodded, but he kept his eyes on Beulah while he spoke. "The youngest ewe. I hadn't thought she'd caught at breeding time, but I guess she had after all. She ran off from the pasture and sought out a place for lambing. When Beulah and I penned the flock for the night, we saw that one was missing, but it was almost dark. We had to go out and find her before the coyotes and wolves did."

"A convenient excuse," Nettie Mae said, "and a rather paltry one. You don't expect me to believe it."

"It's true, Mother. I would never be false with you."

Something passed between Clyde and Beulah in that moment. A look—a silent exchange of understanding. Knowledge and agreement so unified of purpose that they had no need to speak. The familiarity between them, the bond, hurt Nettie Mae's heart more than the deception ever could have done.

"You're lying," she said at once. "Or you're keeping the whole truth from me, which is just as bad as lying. God counts it as much a sin, Clyde; don't be taken in by the Great Deceiver. It is your soul at stake."

Clyde drew a long breath, fortifying himself. Then he moved toward the house. "Mother, it has been a very long and difficult night. I need my rest."

Nettie Mae stepped in front of him. "I will not be disobeyed. I will not be mocked. I will be *heard*, Clyde Webber, in my own house."

"This is as much my house as yours." His words were gentle. "My farm, too, with Father gone. If I must make a decision for the sake of the livestock, then you must trust me, Mother. Land sakes, I'm almost seventeen years old, and managing this land on my own, more or less. When will you stop treating me as if I'm a helpless child?"

"Clyde never touched me, ma'am," Beulah said, "nor I him. I don't think I even took his hand when he offered to help me climb over the rocks. That is where we were obliged to go—all the way up into the ravine."

"The ravine!"

"Going after the missing ewe, ma'am. We tracked her all that way. It was her first time lambing, and she was frightened—wanted someplace quiet and protected, I guess. But that was all we did: Looked for the sheep, and found her. Brought her back. Her lamb, too."

Again, that knowing glance passed between them, and Nettie Mae felt the trembling certainty of prevarication. A thing left unsaid.

"You never went to the fold," she said. "I saw you. I watched you come all the way back from the river trail. You had no sheep with you."

"They're in the barn," Clyde said shortly. "I carried the ewe back on my shoulders; she was weak from the birth. Beulah carried the lamb. We bedded them down in the barn for the night, like I do with all the new lambs that come after dark. Predators, you know."

Nettie Mae squinted into the darkness, but she could see nothing of the barn, could see nothing beyond the circle of the lantern.

Everything outside that flickering sphere—the whole of the world, all God's Creation—might not exist anymore, for all Nettie Mae could perceive.

"I don't believe you. The fall lambers never drop their young so late in the season."

"This one did." Clyde moved again toward the house. "I hope there's a bite to eat. I'm powerful hungry, after all that walking and climbing up in the canyon."

Nettie Mae seized Clyde by the arm and he halted, staring back at her with his lips pressed tightly together. She could think of nothing more to say, no way to scold the truth from him, so she only watched his face, quivering with the need to win this fight, to keep her son a boy yet a while longer.

"Look, Mrs. Webber."

Beulah shook out her shawl, spreading it between her arms so it caught the lantern light. The pale-gray wool was smeared and stained with something brown as rust. It took Nettie Mae some moments to realize she was looking at blood, and plenty of it. An upward rush of heat made her cheeks burn, made her dizzy enough that she almost swayed where she stood. Then she calmed herself. It was entirely too much blood for a deflowering. Whatever the stains had come from, they hadn't come from the girl.

"What is that?" Nettie Mae said.

"I wrapped the lamb in my shawl, to keep it warm on the way to the barn. It's blood from the birthing. Clyde and I found the ewe just in time—she passed the afterbirth minutes before we arrived."

"There was a lot of blood," Clyde said. "A few minutes longer, and the coyotes would have gotten them both, mother and baby. I guess it was an ordeal for the poor ewe. That's why I've got her in the barn, and she's not to be disturbed." He drew another long breath. This time there was a tremor in it—fear or awe. "I don't know whether the ewe will survive. I've done what I can for her tonight, and I'll tend to her more in the morning, but everyone's to keep well clear till she's back to full health. I won't have her upset by too much commotion. Now that's my final word on the matter." He moved deliberately around Nettie Mae, starting for the house again. "Come inside, Mother. It's too cold to linger out here in the dark. Snow's coming soon."

Nettie Mae remained where she was, watching Clyde's back as he walked away. His shoulders were broadening. She must make some new shirts for him soon. They might be the last shirts she would ever sew for her son. All too soon, Clyde would find himself a wife, and it would be she who stitched and mended for him, not Nettie Mae.

The light dimmed around Nettie Mae as Clyde crossed the yard with his lantern. But just before the ring of light slipped away, leaving her to darkness, Nettie Mae looked back at the girl. Beulah had folded the shawl over her arm once more. She stroked the blood stain, rapt as a child petting a kitten. And over the broken notes of the autumn's last crickets, Nettie Mae heard the girl humming, low beneath her breath. The song sounded like a lullaby.

CORA

Cora wavered at the edge of a spiral of dreams. Deeper, down where the ease of sleep lured, she could sense Ernest waiting for her, beckoning. He was kneeling in the mud, as he often did in Cora's dreams—in the gray drift and half mist she remembered, sometimes, upon waking. Kneeling in the mud, reaching up to take her hand, asking *Will you be my wife? For you are the prettiest girl I've ever seen, lovelier than a rose.* Ernest was always young when Cora dreamed of him, young and glad of her company, glowing like a candle in the darkness, bright with love for her. She wanted to go to Ernest and drop to her knees beside him, and never mind the mud on her dress. It was a borrowed dress anyway, lent by the president so she would look fine at the spring ball, as fine as all the other girls. What did a little mud matter when Ernest was there to hold her and stroke her hair?

Cora longed to surrender to the thick, slow exhaustion that never left her now, not since Ernest had fired his rifle and the fragile world had shattered in her hands. Weariness dragged her always toward sleep, and in sleep she found a refuge of dreams. Dreams always tasted sweeter than this life of toil and isolation, even when the dreams were bitter.

But that night, something restrained Cora, tethering her just beyond the comfort of real sleep. She rolled onto her side and tried to open her eyes, tried to learn what lone, white-glaring anxiety was holding her where she was, neither sleeping nor waking. The boys were safe in their shared bed; she had tucked them in and kissed their brows and heard their murmured prayers. Miranda was warm on her trundle bed. Even mired somewhere on the slow, dragging margin of her dreams, Cora was sharply aware of her youngest daughter's breathing—smooth and unbroken, recovered from the ordeal of the flood.

I should write to Ernest and tell him what happened to our daughter. Tell him we almost lost Miranda. I almost lost her, in my carelessness.

Cora could imagine herself taking up her pen, confessing her inadequacy—as a mother, and as a wife. She could all but feel the rapid dash of her hand across paper and smell the half-dried ink. The words she might write, if she were honest and courageous, filled her head—a yawning dark awareness that had opened wide in place of sleep.

Our child nearly died because of my weakness, because I couldn't lead myself from the wilderness of my own thoughts. Because I was preoccupied and afraid. And that is also why I betrayed you, my husband. I cannot ask you to forgive me—not for what I have destroyed, nor for what I would have destroyed. I cannot ask forgiveness.

She might convince herself to write those words, but they would remain sealed in the blank sterility of a folio, girded by wax, and unread in the darkness. Slipped into her apron pocket along with the first letter, the one she had already written but had not sent, detailing her intent to return to Saint Louis. Cora did intend to tell Ernest of her plans. Of course. But if she sent the letter now, would he read it? Or would he hold the folio to a candle flame, unopened? Any word she might send—imploring Ernest to keep his spirits through the long years of his captivity, begging for his pardon, confessing her sins—seemed far more likely to end as smoke than to reach her husband's heart. What right did she have now to pen his name, let alone call him husband?

Hinges creaked as someone opened the door—slowly, as quietly as they could manage. The sound, though small, pulled Cora from her miserable stupor into wakefulness. She half sat up, propped on an elbow; the mattress crepitated faintly in the darkness, the dry stuff inside shifting and speaking. No candle burned.

"Who is it?" Cora whispered.

Beulah didn't reply, but Cora knew her daughter from the rhythm of her steps. The careless ease, the light tread even now, far beyond day's end. Cora listened as Beulah shut the door and found her pine chest by feel. The lid of the chest opened, and a scent of lavender lifted into the confined space, hung for a moment, and vanished. There came a sustained rustle of clothing being removed and a nightdress donned. Then Cora shifted, held back the bedding while Beulah climbed over the trundle bed and lay down at her mother's side.

"I asked you not to stay out so terribly late," Cora whispered.

"I'm sorry, Ma. We couldn't help it, Clyde and me."

"And I."

Beulah paid no heed to the correction, as was her custom. She kept her voice low, so as not to wake Miranda, but Cora could sense the girl's excitement. Even Beulah's whisper carried a tremor of awe, and the mattress quivered faintly with her tension. "We tracked the missing sheep all the way up into the canyon. And we found her."

"That's very well. Now you must get some sleep. And the next time I ask you to heed the time, you must heed it, Beulah."

A pause. The sound of swallowing, then a sharp inhalation, as if Beulah were considering whether she ought to say something more.

"What is it?" Cora whispered. "Tell me."

Beulah answered so quietly, Cora scarcely heard her, though she was lying by her daughter's side. "Something miraculous was born tonight, Ma. Something never seen before."

"Whatever do you mean?"

"Nettie Mae can't learn of it, though. She mustn't know. Clyde didn't want to tell her. She met us in the yard as we came over from the barn, and she was sore, but Clyde didn't tell her what happened—what we saw. At least, he didn't tell Nettie Mae the whole truth. Clyde doesn't want his mother to know."

"Tell me, then." Cora's patience was fraying. Ernest was waiting for her in the shelter of dreams—a husband who still loved her, a man whom Cora had not yet betrayed. "What is the whole truth? And then you must go to sleep; it is far too late for chatter."

Beulah waited a moment longer. Cora could sense a current of wild joy traveling through her daughter; the girl was savoring the moment, strumming a tight string of waiting. The world would be a different place once she spoke, once she revealed her secret, and Beulah was reveling in her moment of power.

Clyde has kissed her, Cora thought, *or held her hand, and she thinks herself in love. That's all this is; girlish tomfoolery. She will learn soon enough that kisses mean nothing. But let her find what little joy she may while her innocence still lasts.*

"The runaway ewe," Beulah said, "gave birth up in the canyon. And the lamb has two heads."

Cora lurched up in bed, stripping the blankets from Beulah's body as she went. Beulah laughed softly and pulled one corner of the quilt back up to her shoulder.

Cora pressed a hand to her mouth; it was all she could do to hold back a shout of disgust and fear. "Oh! How horrible!"

"Ma, how can you say such a thing? That lamb is a wonder! Nothing of the sort has ever been seen. At least, not as far as I ever heard."

The night was biting, sharp as ice. Even Cora's legs trembled, though they were still covered by the quilts. Dread racked her, and she longed for a candle or a lamp—anything to light the room, to drive back the fell creatures that now seemed to leer at her from the unseen, unseeable corners.

"Lay yourself down, Ma," Beulah whispered. "You'll wake Miranda with all that tossing and rustling."

Cora lay back, pulling the blankets up to her chin. Her heart pounded; she could feel every beat of her pulse heating her cheeks, hear the blood roaring in her ears. What did this mean—what could it mean—an unnatural thing born among them, a horror sent to this farm, this family?

It is a Judgment. A rebuke from God; a warning.

Worse things were certain to follow, the nature of which Cora could only imagine, only dread. And she was helpless against the darkness yet to come. Helpless to protect her children—she had always been helpless, battered by fate, powerless to raise a hand in defense. Even if she had known how to defend herself, she had no strength against the evils of this world.

Beulah sighed happily as she settled on her pillow. Perhaps the girl really was as witless as Nettie Mae seemed to believe. What cause had Beulah to rejoice in such a monstrosity as a two-headed lamb? The girl was either stupid or tainted by evil.

No. I cannot believe such things about my child—my firstborn. She doesn't understand; that's all. She doesn't see God's hand at work, and she is still too innocent to read a warning from the Almighty.

"The poor creature," Cora said, quiet and fearful. "Surely it cannot live."

"It won't; I'm sure of it." Why was there such warmth in the girl's voice, such love?

"It would be a mercy to kill it, then. Why didn't Clyde kill the thing?"

"He wanted to," Beulah said. "At first. He doesn't want to now."

Cora lay in silence and the roaring abated in her ears. At length, she said, "Why doesn't he want to end the lamb's suffering? What is the point in allowing it to live?"

"Well, it *is* alive. I guess that's the point."

Cora turned her face on the pillow, staring through the close blackness of the room. She could just make out Beulah's profile, a faint, deep gray barely visible in the dark. The family killed animals all the time—hens, pigs, sheep. Deer and elk, when they could. How else did one survive, but to take the lives of the living? And wasn't that the power God had granted to man—dominion over all the earth, over everything that goes upon the earth? Beulah herself had slaughtered fowl for the pot more times than Cora could count. She had helped with the culling of the spring lambs. Why this sudden tenderness for an animal that, above all others, deserved to die?

Beulah whispered, "There's no point in killing a thing that's already so close to death. Let the lamb have its life while it may." Then she rolled onto her side and slipped easily into sleep.

Cora stared up at a black void where the ceiling ought to be. The ease with which Beulah had read her thoughts shouldn't have frightened Cora. After all, Beulah had displayed such uncanny abilities from a tender age. She had always been observant, insightful, and confident in her judgments, unafraid to name whatever she saw, whatever those slow, hooded eyes fell upon and knew. But tonight, Cora's transparency only made her feel more vulnerable. There was little hope for sleep now; Cora wanted nothing to do with dreams. She felt certain she wouldn't find Ernest kneeling in the mud, but a monster: a sheep with two heads, its jaws slavering with hunger, its many eyes red and fiery as embers.

Little wonder Clyde said nothing to Nettie Mae. She would have killed that abomination at once.

But Nettie Mae wouldn't have flinched at the sight of the beast. Cora knew that much was true. Nettie Mae was bitter and hard, but she was also a sensible woman, as fearless as Cora was not.

I should tell her. First thing in the morning, I'll take Nettie Mae aside and tell her what has happened, what God has sent to this place. I'll tell Nettie Mae, and she will end the creature's cursed life.

And then, with a pang of misgiving, Cora knew she would say nothing. Nettie Mae would only take it for meddling—Cora begging around behind Clyde's back, and Clyde was the man of the house now, the head of the farm. Clyde himself wouldn't take kindly to Cora's interference, and she couldn't risk making an enemy of the only strong, able-bodied man to be found for twenty miles in any direction. Miranda owed her life to Clyde; Cora owed all the world to him, for saving her daughter from the flood. In any case, Cora had already inflicted enough damage upon the Webber family. There was no sense in setting Nettie Mae and Clyde at cross purposes.

I must do it myself, then. Clyde has shut the thing up in the barn, I suppose. I must go out and kill it myself. Then Nettie Mae need never know.

She tried to imagine it—tried to make it real, this picture of herself as a woman capable and determined. A fearless woman. She would wait until she was certain Beulah was sleeping deeply. Then she would creep from her bed and down the stairs, out into the night. She would cross the cold, black expanse of the farm. Cora felt it—the barn door dry beneath her hand, the weight of it as she pushed it inward. The smell of hay and animals, a sinister sound of movement in the dark. The monstrous creature waiting for her, waiting and knowing, alert, seeing everything Cora could never see.

And then she tried to imagine what it might look like, the two-headed lamb. She forced herself to confront the thought, the idea, to strip away all its terror and power until only the simple fact of it remained: animal flesh, blood and bone, a thing that could be killed. But she saw, in her flinching vision, two sinewy necks that curved like serpents, two mouths fanged like the jaws of a wolf. Horns curling from the two vile heads, sharp and inescapable as Judgment.

Cora gasped, then breathed deeply again, stifling a sob of terror. The lamb would live on for as long as God saw fit to visit His curse upon the farm. Cora couldn't end its life. She had never killed a sheep—had killed nothing larger than a bird, and whenever she did it, the act always left her sick with remorse, trembling from the blood and commotion.

If I am not strong enough to destroy a cursed thing, nor even to ease the suffering of a doomed and deformed creature, how can I be strong enough to take my children away from this place?

Beyond the vast, cold nothingness of the prairie, there was a place of refuge. But Saint Louis was so far away that Cora couldn't see its beacon. Night hung too heavily around her. The days were growing shorter, the lightless hours longer. And the Judgment of God, His terrible omen, was out there, waiting, in the dark.

9

ALL OF THE WORLD

The flood hadn't done for Substance Webber's bones. I could still feel him, rancorous and intact, lingering somewhere just above or below the earth. The waters had flattened the burial mound and scattered all the nice things I'd brought to appease his spirit, and the big river stones I'd placed with care around the perimeter of Substance's grave had been pushed out of place, rolled far long the red-sand shore. But Substance remained just where Clyde had planted him.

Hullo, Mr. Webber, I said as I lifted the nearest stone and dropped it back into position.

It was the morning after the miracle, the first and last day our two-headed lamb would ever see. I felt eager to get back to the barn and watch over the creature, and come to know it while I still could. But the night before, while Clyde and I were searching the river trail, I had seen the disarray of Substance's resting place. My conscience wouldn't leave me in peace till I'd tidied up his grave.

I said to Substance, I see you're still here, despite the storm's best efforts.

Substance bore me no more affection than he'd borne anybody else. He made no answer, and I went on working, toting the biggest stones I could find from the riverside to the frank, red flatness where he lay.

When the grave was properly marked again, I sat down for a spell to catch my breath. I could feel Substance all around me. He had spread some, in the time since his death—expanded, loosened the rigid strictures of himself. He no longer cleaved to a narrow column of strength, the shape he reckoned was the proper shape for a man. Instead, he flowed and reached through the air and soil, and pushed himself out and drew himself in like the flank of some great creature breathing. But he was still himself. There was no mistaking Substance, if ever you found yourself in his presence—living or dead.

I sat for a few minutes in silence till my heart slowed. Then I said, Mr. Webber, why are you still here, anyhow? This is no kind of existence, drifting up above this single patch of ground like a rain cloud. Or are you under the ground with your bones? I can't rightly tell.

He didn't answer, but that was out of spite. I knew he'd heard me. Substance was often hungry for my talk, as I was the only person who ever came to visit.

I said, I know you're there and I can tell when you hear me. I can feel it. You ain't never been good at hiding your thoughts. I'm sorry to be the one to tell you this, Mr. Webber, for I know it was always important to you, to keep everything hidden but your anger and your strength.

After I said that, Substance made no more pretense of hiding. Like a whiplash, his anger licked out at me; it stung right in the center of my chest. And though I never heard any words when Substance spoke, I felt his meaning, true and clear, as was the usual way between us.

Get away, you rotten girl. I've got no use for you.

I said, Seems you've got a powerful lot of use for me.

I never minded saucing at a spirit, for I knew no spirit could harm me.

I said, I'm the only one who comes to tend your grave, after all, and you are so hell bent on hanging around here, when you know—I've told you a hundred times—that you don't have to stay.

I asked him, Why are you so dreadful sore at me, anyway? Why don't you tell me and have it all out?

Substance answered in the only way he could. I saw Clyde in my mind's eye—or, I ought to say, I felt Clyde. Though I knew he was back at the barn, tending to the black-legged ewe and her glorious lamb, I caught the sense of him as clearly as if he'd been seated there beside me. The quiet, thoughtful nature; the earnest longing to do good; and the ever-present fear that he never would know what good really meant, that he wouldn't recognize right when he saw it and never could tell it from wrong—those things belonged to Clyde as much as did his tall, strong body or the voice that got a little deeper every day, or the hair so thick even the wind couldn't move it. It startled me, to realize Substance had understood Clyde's nature all along, almost from the cradle. I hadn't thought a man like Substance capable of seeing way down deep into any person's spirit. But he saw Clyde, all right. He just didn't heed what he found in his son.

You're making Clyde too soft, Substance told me—the welling disgust in my stomach, my mouth bending into a frown. I felt an urge to push Clyde hard, just to get him away from me; and maybe I would have pushed him then, if he'd been near me in truth.

Substance said, You're making my son soft when he ought to be strong.

Mr. Webber, I told him, I haven't made your son anything. He has made himself.

I made him, Substance insisted. He is mine. I set him on the path to manhood but you—you diverted him. Why won't you leave me this one small peace, you miserable girl? Why won't you let me rest knowing that my son is a man?

I stood up and brushed sand from the back of my skirt. I said, Clyde is a man, and a damn fine one at that. I'm sorry you ain't got sense enough to see it.

A great, hard pulse of anger came up from below the earth. There was a time, in the days just after his death, when Substance would have tried to make himself whole again. He would have pulled and pulled at the world, would have sucked at the liveliness that flows through all things—not only the things that live, the birds and deer who left their tracks in the hard red river-damp sand, but the things that never lived, too: the stone walls of the canyon, the direction of the water's flow, a sudden brush of wind. He would have pulled and taken, and he might have shaped just enough of himself to stand there before me, towering in his rage. But Substance had begun to accept the fact of his death, a little and a little. A pinch more acceptance every day. He was reconciled to his condition, and so he remained as he was, spread but whole, mute before my merciless honesty.

I said, You don't have to stay this way, Mr. Webber. There don't seem much point to staying, far as I can see. What good does it do you, being a shade? You could be anything else you pleased. You could be everything. All you need to do is spread yourself a little farther. Loosen yourself a little more.

Still, Substance kept his peace. He subsided back into the earth. There he remained, coiled and secretive, a rattlesnake sleeping off the winter.

I turned toward the trail, but something small and white and sharp caught my attention. It hung in the sage a few feet away from the grave. I stepped closer, bending low to the earth, and there was the old crow's skull that had once decorated the burial mound. The floodwaters had swept it away, of course, but a twig of sagebrush had pierced the great round socket of its eye. The skull hung at an angle, its dark bill pointing toward the river.

I plucked the crow's skull out of the sage and returned to Substance's resting place.

Clyde is a good man, I told him.

I pressed the skull down into flat red sand. Then I left before Substance could answer.

The barn was all gray shadow inside and the hush of animals breathing. Clyde never looked up when I came in through the southern door. He remained crouched beside the low gate of the farthest stall, huddled as if in the grip of some vast and slow-moving, inevitable misery. When I reached him and stood looking down at the black-legged ewe and her lamb, Clyde spoke to me quietly.

It's weak. I can't get it to suckle. I don't think it has eaten all night through.

The lamb lay folded peacefully in the deep straw, each face looking in a different direction, the two good eyes blinking in a slow, resigned way, and the third eye—the shared eye—staring out between the two halves of its understanding with a bright, piercing curiosity. The ewe had pressed herself against the wall. She didn't tremble; her flanks did not stir with rapid, fearful breaths. The ewe was calm, but she knew what I knew. There was no point in trying.

Clyde said, The ewe won't stand still for suckling. I tried to convince her, but she walks away. Doesn't kick out or try to run—only walks. I might try another ewe. The fall lambers are still in milk.

If the little thing's own mother won't stand still for it, I said, the others surely won't. Is she still bleeding?

No, Clyde said. She's healed up, far as I can tell—or she will heal.

That's good, then. You ought to send her back to the flock.

He shook his head, slowly, never taking his eyes off the lamb. He said, Not while her baby's still living.

The two dark eyes blinked; the two heads nodded on a single neck. The lamb was dry now and soft, the crimp of its hide begging to be touched. But it moved almost not at all. It only stared and nodded, accepting what was to come.

It won't be long now, I said to Clyde, gently.

He kept his silence for a long time, watching the creature where it lay. Then he said, It don't seem right, that I can't make it live.

Just last night you were all for shooting it.

I know, he said. Maybe I still ought to shoot it. Now, for sure—now that it's getting weaker. Now that I know it won't drink, or can't drink.

I said, What made you change your mind?

Clyde didn't answer, except to shrug. There was a studied placidity to his face, a fixed hardness, a deadweight mask he had to struggle to hold. I could discern nothing else by looking at him. I wished in that moment that I could speak to Clyde as I spoke to his father—as Substance talked to me—with the simple ease of understanding, each thought and emotion passing from one to the other because there was no barrier anymore, no flesh to stop it.

He said again, It don't seem right.

And then: All it knows of the world—all it ever can know—is the inside of this barn. That's an awful small world, I guess. Small and dark with walls all around you.

I said, It ain't dark outside. The sun is shining. It's a lovely day.

But my mother—

I went to the east-side door, opened it, and let in the sweet rain-scented air and the silver autumn light. I could see Nettie Mae far across the yard, her thin strong arm working the handle of the pump. Faintly, I could hear the whine and clack of the mechanism, its metallic rhythm, a small, cupped-hand splash of water in the pail. But the sounds came across the open ground laggardly, and Nettie Mae in her black dress and black shawl seemed to move and work beyond the borders of our reality, the world I shared with Clyde. Presently, she stopped pumping and hefted the water pail, and she set off back toward the house. The last few echoes of the pump handle sounded in the stillness. Then the farm was silent again.

When Nettie Mae had gone, I said, Your mother's inside the house.

Clyde remained where he was, hugging his knees, looking up at me with a lost, hopeless expression. The light from outside, from the threshold where I stood, fell upon him as if it meant to, as if it had sought him out. Clyde in the band of silver was as vivid as new-dyed cloth. Folded up that way, uncertain, waiting for me to make whatever choice must be made, he put me in mind of an egg just beginning to hatch, with the chick inside afraid of the crack in its shell, too stunned to shrink away from the light that had pierced a familiar darkness.

It's cold out, I said. Proper cold. There's snow on the way; maybe soon. Wrap up the lamb in your coat.

Clyde rose from the straw-covered ground with the slowness of aching joints. How long had he been crouching there, I wondered, watching the newborn? He removed his coat, then took from the gatepost the hat he'd found in his father's chest. The hat settled easily on his brow. Then he stepped over the stall gate, moving carefully, murmuring to the ewe as he went. He bent low, and I heard the straw rustling. When he straightened, both heads of the lamb peered out from the bundle of Clyde's coat, and the bundle was cradled in his arms.

We left the shadows of the barn together. Outside, the air was crisp and biting, promising snow. When I breathed in, I could feel the cold tingling on my tongue and along the roof of my mouth. A clump of vetch weed, limp and dry, had lain all morning in the barn's shadow, untouched by the cloud-muted sun. Stems and brown leaves wore a pale picotee of frost.

Clyde whispered, What should I do now?

You know what to do, I told him. You don't need to ask me.

He walked a few feet with the lamb, out into the pasture where its family grazed in the distance. It would never run among those grasses, never skip and play as its siblings played. Clyde stopped where the grass grew knee high. He stood with his back to me, and I could see his warm breath rising in regular plumes. For a long time, he only stood with his neck craned back so he could look up at the mountains, their ancient sides steep and hard, bluing and graying into layers of cloud. The flock called at the sight of their shepherd, low bleats rolling across the winter-ready ground. Clyde turned in a circle. He moved slowly—slowly, giving the lamb all the time he could, every precious second to see what lay beyond the walls of the barn, what beauty could be found in daylight. As Clyde turned, as he carried the lamb around to face the endless sweep of the prairie, the two heads lifted from within the bundle, and all three eyes opened wide in wonder. The lamb saw all of the world.

CLYDE

All the world. That was what he showed the two-headed creature, the soft, almost weightless thing that lay so trusting in his arms. It was, at the very least, everything Clyde knew of the world. The long spread of land that had belonged to his father and now belonged to him. He had learned the boundaries as a child and learned them so well that he felt them now by instinct; no need for fences along the perimeter of his farm. The flock, alive and ripe with the promise of life yet to come—the ewes who always bore twins, those who lambed in the spring and those who lambed in autumn. After they had gone, their daughters would go on bearing. And there stood the sod-brick house, gray and austere. Within its furtive walls dwelt every person who gave his life purpose, all those who needed him. Without his mother, Cora, and the children, his days would have no shape nor his labor meaning.

Beyond the borders of the land that was his lay the wilderness that was its own. The upthrust stone, the shoulders of the Bighorns, reddish gray where they stood near to the homestead and blue where they stood far—bluer, dissipating veils of blue lost against an indistinct horizon. The pale gold of autumn grass like the rough hide of an animal, wind-riffled down the mountain's flank. The low trough where the river ran, a score mark in wet clay—dark, shadow-and-green, redolent of moving water, of soil that never went dry. And the infinite sweep of the prairie, yellow shaded with folds of violet until, a hundred miles away or more, the whole plain was swallowed by color and consumed, taken up by the lower edge of a sagging purple sky.

Slowly, slowly, Clyde turned in place, presenting everything to the creature he held. First sight, last sight, the only and sweetest sight of the world and all that lived upon it.

The lamb was so light it almost wasn't there. Thin, more bones than flesh in Clyde's arms; he could feel the shape of its bladed scapula and the knobs of its joints even through the swaddling coat. But it was warm. And he could feel its breath, the steady rise and fall of its pliant ribs. It shifted, turning its neck so both faces could see, and the baby fleece of one head brushed against Clyde's cheek. Soft. Just like any lamb born on the farm. Just like, and nothing like. Nothing seen before.

When he had completed the circle, Clyde found himself facing Beulah. She stood wrapped in her gray shawl, unconcerned by the blood that still darkened its fabric and fringe. Wind—the never-ceasing prairie wind—lifted her hair and toyed with it and tangled it, but she made no move to tie it back. It spread around her shoulders. The sparrow color reminded him of the bird that had flown into the long shed that summer when he had been busy within, repairing the handle of his scythe. Startled by the sudden confinement, the bird had flapped high among the dark rafters, but when it passed across the open door, time seemed to pause in its course. For a fraction of a second, Clyde had seen its wings spread against the glare of sunlight, and the moment suspended and wrote itself into his memory. Every feather limned in gold, every feather distinct, the dark veins of each shaft incised into light. The wings were like two human hands thrown up in terror. When the bird lighted in a corner, its breast a rapid pulse, the small head darting to stare, Clyde had eased his hat down carefully over the soft brown body and trapped the bird inside. He had set it free in the sunlight, but he couldn't remember what it looked like flying away.

Beulah's quiet eyes, those eyes that saw everything, were fixed now on the lamb. Clyde heard the words she didn't say. He knew the words were true.

It won't live much longer. The time is coming soon.

He should have shot the lamb the night before. That was true, too; he ought to have done the proper thing, the manly thing. Clyde couldn't tell, couldn't imagine, why he hadn't gone through with it. But the night before, after he and Beulah had bedded down the ewe and her offspring in the stall, he had lain awake on his cot listening to the hearth fire. At first, every snap of cinder and spark had been distinct, but as sleep settled into him, the crackling fire had blurred and blended to a low and steady music. It was one sound, one song, as the wind across the prairie was one endless breath, a body that never stopped sighing. It put Clyde in mind of the dream—the fever dream, and the certainty of oneness that had come to him then—all separate and distinct sounds merging into one endless hum.

Clyde had killed animals before. Of course. How else could you survive? But every life he had taken before, he had taken in its season. You do not cut the cornstalk while the tassel is still damp and white. The two-headed lamb must live a short life, Beulah had been right about that, but it seemed a terrible injustice to deprive it of whatever time remained in this small and vivid season.

Worse, the more Clyde had handled the creature—trying to make it stand, stand and nurse—the greater grew his affection for the strange, ugly thing. He would never enjoy a bond with this animal like he had with Joe Buck. It was impossible—with any sheep, perhaps, for the nature of sheep was different from the nature of horses or dogs or people. But he admired the lamb's persistence, the singularity of its goal. The creature was weak, but it never gave up. It wanted to live. And Clyde had gone into the darkness to save its life. He was the lamb's savior; he couldn't also be its executioner—not without trying to provide what was due, what the very fact of its birth had promised.

As the morning wore on, however, and the lamb remained unfed, Clyde came to understand that hope was futile. He had almost felt relieved when Beulah returned to the barn, back from her private sojourn. She could always see a situation clearly for what it was, without any sentimental foolishness clouding her judgment. Beulah would know what was best; she would tell Clyde, *This is what you must do, and next this, and you mustn't worry over whether it's right or wrong.* She never fretted over such things herself. She seemed to make every decision with the calm composure, the ready confidence, of a person who stood beyond the reach of fear. Perhaps, Clyde thought, the girl had never really learned what fear was. After all, Beulah hadn't been raised under the thumb—under the fist—of Substance Webber. Perhaps without the need to question what a raging father might think of her every choice and thought, without the need to wonder what such a father might do if she made a mistake, the seed of fear had never taken root inside her.

Beulah raised her eyes from the two-headed lamb. She smiled at Clyde, and though the smile warmed him, it was also a throb of agony. There was something sad in Beulah's expression. She had resigned herself to the inevitable.

"I think he liked it," the girl said, "seeing."

"I hope so."

Clyde's cheeks burned with shame. His father would mock him, if he could hear such talk. *Sheep don't like or dislike. They only live—act—do what their bodies instruct. They cannot think, cannot feel.*

"Now," Beulah said, "we ought to bring him back to his mother."

The black-legged ewe bleated and moved toward them when they returned to the stillness of the barn. Clyde stepped over the stall gate and tucked the lamb into the straw, rested his hand on its flank, and felt the gentle breaths coming and going. The ewe nuzzled her offspring, then settled in the straw close by.

"It doesn't seem to be suffering," Clyde said. "Only falling asleep." Deeper and deeper into sleep.

"This is best," Beulah agreed. "Let it go when the time comes, right here, next to its mother."

This is best. To drift into a comfortable dream. Not to end in a sudden burst of noise and passion and blood, the way Substance had ended—the way he'd ended all things.

Beulah extended a hand and Clyde went to her, climbing back over the gate, brushing straw from his trousers. He shook out his coat and put it on. It smelled faintly warm, faintly sweet, like the precious thing it had enfolded. Beulah put her arm around Clyde's shoulders and led him away from the stall and outside, into the wind and the persistent smoky purple of low-hanging cloud.

"Work to be done," Clyde said shortly.

"Yep." After a pause, Beulah added, "I'll go back to the old house and bring more wood for the fences."

Clyde nodded but couldn't look at Beulah, couldn't speak. After a moment, the girl slipped away, and Clyde busied himself in the long shed, cleaning and sorting his tools just for the mercy of distraction.

As he worked in the dim half light, his vision blurred now and then, and he was obliged to blink away a sudden rush of tears or blot them on the edge of his sleeve. It was the cold that did it—stung his sleep-deprived eyes till they watered. Just the cold. Snow was coming, sure enough. He could smell it plainly: the unmistakable sharpness of ice, the mellow, woodsmoke aroma of cold rolling down from the granite heights. The first snow of autumn—early, as all things were this year. The first snowfall wouldn't last more than a day or two, Clyde felt sure; the ground hadn't yet begun to freeze. But this was the promise of a long winter ahead.

He coiled a length of wire and set it aside, then added a heavy tin rattling with nails. He and Beulah would need those things for their fences. With a harsh winter well on its way, they'd have little time to fortify their pens and gates, making fast against the six-foot drifts that would accumulate beside every structure for miles around.

He found his sturdiest mallet and added it to the growing collection of fence-mending supplies. Then he had to stop and blink again till the mist dissipated from his sight.

Why did it pain him so, the lamb's coming death? The loss of an animal to disease, to deformity, was no great shock to a farming man. But he had touched the ewe, up there in the canyon. He had put his hands upon the black-legged ewe and she had allowed it without fear, almost as if she had understood that Clyde had come to help her. He had felt, for one startling flash of a moment—a lightning strike, a candle flaring in the darkness—just what the ewe had felt, her fear and pain, her desperate hope. In that moment, he had found the animal to be as living and feeling as he was. And now, knowing the black-legged ewe for what she was, Clyde couldn't help but imagine her grief, too. She had hoped, as all mothers hope, for a healthy babe. Something twisted had come in its place, but the two-headed lamb was still hers—her child. And it could not live. It would die, leaving the ewe empty again, bereft of the purpose she had carried all the months of her pregnancy.

And the strange, frightening wonder of the lamb itself. Was it truly one animal with two heads, or had twin lambs grown so closely together that their flesh had merged? Clyde heard again the long hum, the chorus of life singing in its ceaseless harmony. The voice and the purpose of every creature—every tree by the river, every blade of grass and twist of sage, every person who walked the land—expanded beyond the borders of flesh and self. He let his arms hang limp at his sides; he allowed the tears to come, to fall as they would. He loved the monster, the miracle that lay dying in the barn. He knew he shouldn't, but he could mute his aching heart as easily as he could lift his hand to the sky and halt winter's advance.

The first snowflakes fell just after noon. Large and wet, fat with the marginal warmth of fall's remainder, they drifted down like feathers spilled from a ripped-open tick. The sky subsided from violet to flat gray. Clyde's flock gathered at the edge of the pasture, massing together, made nervous by the change. He heard a new tension in their guttural calls. They wanted to linger near the safety of the fold. Through a haze of snowfall, he could see Beulah approaching from the Bemis house, carrying a fat bundle of staves across her shoulders.

Clyde leaned against a corner of the long shed, hands deep in the flannel-lined pockets of his coat, and watched Beulah make her way across the open field. At a distance, she seemed less of a girl. Her skinniness and her coltish lack of grace were transformed by the field or by the snowfall or by the persistent ache in Clyde's chest to the lean, upright, capable strength of a woman. Her dark dress and the gathered staves, black with damp, showed starkly among a blurred, featureless gray of snowfall. For a moment, Clyde wished he could erase the edges of himself as easily as the lamb had done—the two lambs with one body—and learn all the secrets Beulah knew, the clear-eyed sight, the placid acceptance in the place where fear should have been.

The horses whinnied, high and sharp, a cry of panic. Clyde turned toward the paddock in time to see a low brown shadow bolt away from the fence into the brush. Joe Buck led the small herd in a gallop around the pen; cold air misted with the horses' harsh breaths, the indignant huffs of animals offended.

Clyde ran toward the paddock, shouting and waving his hat, but the coyote had already vanished. Cursing under his breath, he hurried instead to meet Beulah.

"Well, here's the snow, right on time," the girl said cheerily.

"Animals are restless." Clyde took the staves from her shoulders, slung them across his own. "I spotted a coyote near the horses."

Beulah rolled her neck to work the stiffness from her muscles. "It didn't harm the horses any, did it?"

"No." Coyotes were too small to inflict any real damage on the larger stock. "But if it's coming in so close, it'll be after the sheep next. It could take down the new lambs, for certain. Maybe some of the older sheep, too."

"Let's get the flock into their pen, then," Beulah said. "We can feed them on hay till tomorrow."

The sheep went eagerly to the fold. It was the work of a few minutes to guide the flock through the gate and settle them in with a few armfuls of hay. Clyde and Beulah tended to the cattle and horses next. By the time they'd finished settling all the stock in their pens, the snow had accumulated ankle deep, but the snowfall had ceased, leaving the world huddled and still, drawn in upon itself. The cloudbank hung so low Clyde thought he might reach up and touch it. The afternoon was stifled by cloud, gray and subdued as dusk.

"Hungry?" Beulah asked.

Clyde nodded.

"I ain't had a bite since breakfast. Let's get inside and see whether my ma can scare us up something to eat."

Cora provided bread with apple preserves and cut each of them a good thick slice of smoked ham, which Clyde and Beulah ate cold. Clyde hadn't realized how famished he was. Not only the day's work but also the day's grief had drained him of strength and will. He sat at the kitchen table, chin propped on a fist, chewing slowly and staring through the bubbled glass window at a world gone white and silent. The fresh coat of snow had rounded and softened the yard, rippling over clumps of grass and weeds. The land looked like nothing so much as the fleece of a newborn lamb—and thinking of the one that lay dozing and fading in the shelter of the barn, Clyde's throat tightened all over again. He had to rub his eyes in a show of weariness to make an excuse for the tears.

Benjamin and Charles came into the kitchen to petition their mother for an extra slice of bread.

"Look," Charles said, pointing toward the window. "Is that a wolf?"

Benjamin rushed to the glass and pressed his nose against it. "Where? I can't see anything."

"Over by the sheepfold."

"There it is!"

Clyde lurched up from the table. His thighs bumped the edge so hard the table rocked; Beulah grabbed her cup of water to keep it from overturning.

"Show me," Clyde said to the boys.

He spotted the coyote at once, sly and low, dodging around a corner of the fold. "Damn," he muttered, and the little fellows looked up at him, wide eyed with shock or admiration.

"It can't get into the pen," Beulah said. She remained at the table, picking at the crust of her bread. "The boards on the gate are too close together, and I guess the walls are too high and smooth for it to climb."

"I don't like it lurking around."

"It can't harm anyone or anything. Not with the sheep off the pasture."

Clyde reached above the kitchen door and took down his rifle, and the boys gasped with delight.

"Clyde, don't," Beulah said.

"I won't have that damned coyote harassing my stock."

From the drain board where she worked, Cora emitted a soft and hesitant "Oh . . ." She didn't dare scold Clyde for his language, but he knew she had no liking for rough words, especially not where her children could hear.

He shrugged uncomfortably in Cora's direction—an apology of sorts—and stepped outside. The boys tried to follow.

"No, you little fellas stay in here where it's warm."

"We want to see you shoot the wolf!"

"It ain't a wolf," Beulah said, "it's a coyote, and it's of no harm to anybody."

Clyde rounded on her, furious that she couldn't see what danger the predator posed. She, of all people, who usually saw clear as day, even with her eyes shut.

"Shush, Beulah," Clyde said—nearly shouted. "Can't you shush?"

He closed the door firmly behind him.

Clyde moved out into the snow. It crunched with every step, and he would have cursed the sound if cursing wouldn't have rendered him all the more conspicuous. The sheep had caught the coyote's scent, even if they couldn't see the beast that circled their pen, menacing them from beyond the stone walls. Clyde could hear the restless rhythm of his flock, the thin, high bleating of the ewes and the basso grunts of the ram. The horses, too, were pacing nervously in their paddock. Even the milk cows crowded along their fence, heads raised, ears flicking toward the coyote.

Clyde couldn't see the creature from where he was standing. It had slunk to the opposite side of the fold, but the flock's sounds of distress went on unabated. Clyde slipped behind the outhouse and crouched low amid a leafless tangle of lilac branches. From there, he could just make out the gate of the sheepfold and the pen's farthest corner. He raised his rifle and sighted toward the corner, waiting for the coyote to show itself beyond the stone wall. But the animal was too clever for him; Clyde's legs began to cramp and at last he abandoned his cover, circling wide around the fold, eyes on the pen, hungry for any sign of the hunter.

The cattle shied away as Clyde neared their enclosure, made anxious by the rage that burned around him like a brushfire. The heavy rumble of their hooves gave him the sound cover he needed, and he quickened his pace, jogging in a wide arc toward the far side of the fold.

There, at last, he spotted the coyote. Brown and lean, it was half-crouched beside the stone wall, looking up as if judging the distance to the top. It thought to leap up and over, Clyde saw—and it was big enough that it might make the jump. He raised the rifle to his shoulder, but the coyote bolted at the sudden movement. The animal flew back into the cover of sage and snow just as Clyde's gun kicked hard. The roar of the shot stifled all sound—but with cold horror, Clyde watched a gout of wet, dark earth and a geyser of snow erupt from the mounded roof of the root cellar.

He lowered his gun, numb with shock at his own foolhardiness. A moment later, the kitchen door flew open and Nettie Mae stormed out into the yard. Clyde's ears rang and hummed from the shot, but there was nothing wrong with his eyes. He could see his mother's mouth working on a furious tirade. Little by little, the whine in his ears diminished and he could make out her scolding.

". . . never seen such a careless stunt in all my life! You could have killed someone! Get over here at once, you fool of a boy!"

Clyde's feet dragged, but he went to face his mother.

"What in the Lord's name did you mean by that?" Nettie Mae said. "Shooting toward the house? What if your aim had been worse? You could have shot right through a window. You could have done for anybody inside."

Her face was all hard angles, tight with anger and fear. Clyde hung back, reluctant to come too close to Nettie Mae; she looked as if she might twist an ear.

"I'm sorry," he muttered.

"I should say you are sorry. Give me that gun."

"Mother—"

"You heard me."

"I'm not a child anymore; I'm the man of the house."

"Then you can damned well act like it!"

Clyde hesitated. He could see shadows on the other side of the kitchen window, the little fellows pressed close to the pane. Watching. Clyde didn't wish to set a poor example for the boys. He handed the rifle over to Nettie Mae.

She tucked it under her arm, brisk and scornful, then headed back toward the kitchen door. But a few paces away, Nettie Mae stopped and whirled again to face her son. Her small, hard eyes raked him from head to foot, and Clyde felt himself wither under the authority of her stare.

"I have always hoped," she said quietly, "always prayed, Clyde, that you would turn out better."

"Better?" He could manage scarcely more than a whisper.

"Than your father. He was hot headed. Vengeful. You know that well; you aren't a little child anymore. You understand who your father was . . . what he was. I had hoped you would be different, but this—this reckless, dangerous behavior . . ."

She said nothing more, but pinned Clyde with a stare. He clenched his fists inside his trouser pockets where Nettie Mae couldn't see, willing himself not to writhe with the discomfort of guilt. Finally, Nettie Mae strode back to the house, taking the rifle with her.

Clyde lingered in the yard, too ashamed of his own foolishness to go back inside. Anger at his mother sat heavy and sour in his stomach. Nettie Mae had humiliated him—treating him like a child there in front of everyone, everyone who made up Clyde's world. Worst of all, he couldn't help but feel his mother had been right to scold him. He had acted rashly, and for no good reason.

If I don't protect those who depend on me, what good am I to anyone? One wide shot, and he could have killed his mother. Or the little fellows, or Cora or Miranda. He could have killed Beulah.

He drifted back to the long shed and leaned against an outer wall, hat pulled low over his eyes. The gunshot had sent the sheep into a panic, but they were settling now. Clyde could hear the ram calling to his ewes, leading them back to the hay. The ram's low, gruff voice put Clyde in mind of his mother—Nettie Mae unmanning him with a stare, stripping him in an instant of all the esteem that had been his since Substance's death.

It ain't right for a woman to take away a man's authority.

Clyde had heard his father mutter those very words more times than he could count. That particular declaration had always sickened Clyde, for it had never preceded anything good. Yet now he couldn't seem to banish his father's voice from his mind. A black pit of rancor opened inside him. Moment by moment, it gaped ever wider. Soon he could feel a vapor of outrage rising from the pit, stinging the back of his throat.

After some long while, Clyde heard the kitchen door open and shut again. He lifted his head just enough to peer past the brim of his hat. Evening was fast approaching. The light hung low and sideways, slanting down to the earth through a threadbare patch of cloud. The colors lay warm across the snow—soft, pale orange like the skin of an apricot, the yellow of goldenrod but wan and diluted by cold. The hour of sunset had almost come. And it wasn't Nettie Mae who had left the kitchen this time, but Beulah. She was still clothed in that dark dress, wrapped in the bloody shawl.

Clyde hoped for a moment she would divert from her course. Go to the outhouse, or to the sheep pen to check on the animals. But she headed directly for the long shed, her thin arms wrapped around her body, hands tucked away beneath the shawl's swinging fringe.

Clyde pulled his hat down even farther. If Beulah read his reluctance to speak, she ignored it.

"Ma's about to start fixing supper."

Clyde grunted.

"She's doing it early, on account of the snow and how dark the day is. Says there's no point in waiting, since soon there won't be light enough to work by."

Clyde made no response.

"Won't you come back inside? It's so much warmer by the fire."

"I don't mind the cold."

"I know you're sore over what your ma said to you, but—"

"How do you know what she said to me?" Had the whole damned house heard—witnessed his humiliation? "Listen, Beulah," Clyde added before she could make her excuses, "I ain't no use to anybody if I can't protect this farm. That's all I was trying to do."

"I know," she said. "Now come back inside and get ready for supper."

"Not just yet." He kicked one foot, then the other, sending crystals of snow flying into the air. They fell back to earth, snow against snow, with a dry, crackling sound.

Turning away, Beulah sighed. When Clyde was certain he was alone again, he marched to the paddock and slipped between the rails of its fence. The horses had already trampled most of the snow; tracks of red-brown mud circled the pen, crossing the paddock at angles. He stood in the fading light, hands in his coat pockets, till the horses left their hay and came toward him. Joe Buck was the first to reach him. The gelding stood blowing softly with welcome, and Clyde leaned gratefully against the broad yellow shoulder.

Joe Buck's hide was warm, sweet with the odors of hay and dirt and a horse's sweat, the rich earthy scent that had always been a sanctuary to Clyde. He hid his face against Joe Buck's withers and breathed in deeply. With every inhalation, he tried to push away the shame that still veiled his thoughts. And each time he exhaled, Clyde sought to rid himself of his father's presence. He could feel Substance hanging all around, dominating the cold sky as if watching, unblinking, from above.

It ain't right for a woman to take away a man's authority. And if I can't protect what's mine—if I can't control what's mine—then what good am I to anybody?

The horses milled and Clyde stood, one hand wrapped in a lock of Joe Buck's mane, wrestling with his father's shade. The peace of the horses' presence, the unity of the herd, soothed some of his anger and instilled a welcome distance between Clyde and his shame—or the better part of it. He had little inkling of time's passage, and he wanted none. The break in the clouds closed overhead; the soft golden tones of the hour before sunset gave way to purple dusk. He could hear the doors of kitchen and outhouse squealing on their hinges, banging in the silence of a world gone still beneath its first layer of snow. Hunger crept in around the edge of his awareness. Ought he to go inside and apologize? That would be best, he reasoned—apologize to his mother for his careless behavior, to the little fellows for doing what no sensible man should have done. For cursing, too. Apologize to Cora for making her hold his supper.

He straightened and released his hold on Joe Buck's mane. The gelding had been dozing; Joe Buck lifted his head in surprise when Clyde picked himself up off his withers. He had cocked one hind foot in rest, too.

Clyde patted his horse on the neck. "All's well, old fella. I'll just head inside and smooth things over."

But the weight hadn't eased in Clyde's stomach. As he stepped out of the paddock, he could still hear his father's voice.

A real man has no need to smooth things over. What does the anger of a woman matter?

Clyde didn't know where Substance's voice had come from, what memory had woken in his head or his heart. But he could feel his father's presence as clearly as he seemed to hear the words. Substance was nowhere, unseen—and yet he was everywhere, towering and immovable, a force like the mountains against which even the most powerful storm must break.

I'll be my own man, Clyde answered.

But Substance seemed to feel Clyde's uncertainty, his trembling self-doubt. And Clyde remembered his father's broken, mirthless laugh.

There's only one way to be a man, Substance said. *And if you aren't a man, then you're nothing.*

Clyde shoved his fists deep into his coat pockets and trudged through the snow, shoulders hunched against the memory or the presence of his father. But just before he reached the house, he caught some small motion from the corner of his eye. The movement was distant, not obtrusive, but unusual enough that it brought him up short, even captured in the periphery of his sight. He stared toward the barn, wide eyed, waiting for the thing to move again.

A fitful breeze stirred from the river, swinging one of the barn doors on its hinges. It was the door that had captured his attention. Open. Someone had left the barn door open.

Clyde abandoned all thought of apologies and ran for the barn. Well before he reached it, he heard the black-legged ewe bleating in desperation, crying from the confines of her stall. The interior was dark as pitch; without a lantern, shadows surrounded him at once, and he was obliged to stand blinking for several agonized moments till his eyes adjusted. Then he made his way down the aisle to the stall where he had spent the morning crouched in straw, trying in vain to teach the two-headed lamb how to suckle.

Clyde stared down at the bedding, searching it frantically with his eyes and then with his hands while the ewe paced and moaned around him. The lamb was gone. Vanished entirely.

That damned beast. It must have been the coyote.

He sprang back over the stall gate and ran to the open door. Prairie and yard alike were cast in the same monotonous blue of encroaching night. With everything all of a color, there seemed no distance anymore, as if the faraway southern horizon stood near as the mountains at his back. With all the world compressed, pressing in upon him, Clyde felt smaller and weaker than he had at any time since his childhood. But he wasn't a boy—not anymore. And he would do what needed doing.

He searched the snow around the barn door—and yes, there were the expected tracks. The narrow paw prints, each with four sharply defined claws like bullet holes shot into the snow. The coyote had come to the door and then run away again when its foul deed was done. Clyde could see the tracks of its flight, spread wide as the animal picked up speed—toward the orchard.

"Damn you!" Clyde shouted into the night.

He didn't bother going to his mother; he wouldn't beg for the return of his rifle. Besides, if he had to argue with Nettie Mae, the thief would only run farther, and would surely live to come raiding another day. Clyde didn't need his rifle. There were other ways to deal with vermin who raided your stock. Any shepherd worth his salt knew that much.

He sprinted to the horse shed and grabbed Joe Buck's saddle and blanket from their wooden stand. He tore the bridle from its peg, threw it over his shoulder, and then whistled sharp and loud for his horse. Joe Buck came to the fence at once; the gelding's ears twisted this way and that as Clyde tacked him up, quick as he could manage in the dying light. Clyde's lariat hung from the saddle horn, coiled and patient as a snake.

Clyde swung up into the saddle as soon as he had Joe Buck clear of the gate. The gelding hadn't been ridden in some days, and he was eager for the work, tossing his head and wringing his tail. Clyde urged him into a trot. The snow was wet and mucky beneath its shallow crust. He didn't dare push his horse faster—not till he had clean sight of the coyote.

As Clyde sped across the yard, he caught sight of the boys' faces pressed against the kitchen window. A heartbeat later, the door flew open. Joe Buck threw his head high and let out a growl of surprise, but it was only Beulah, flying down the steps into the snow, shouting, "Clyde! What are you doing? Come back!"

He didn't draw rein, but urged Joe Buck on. As Clyde rounded the other side of the house and struck out toward the orchard, he heard his mother, too, calling his name with a rising note of desperation.

A pool of thin blue light still lingered on the far horizon. The clouds were too dense to admit either moon or stars; that sickly western glow, rapidly fading, was all the light Clyde had. He scanned the snow to either side as Joe Buck's trot ate up the ground. The coyote's tracks were just visible, divots of bluer gray in a gray-blue flatness, a cold illusion. Clyde slowed his horse to a walk. He followed the tracks as they wove between the apple trees—the leafless trees, skeletal and black, sentinels of a barren world.

Something low and dark slipped from one tree to another. Clyde drew rein and Joe Buck stopped, blowing with excitement, ears pricked toward the movement. Clyde squinted, though it didn't make a difference in his sight—not as dim as this moonless twilight was. But he did catch a quick flash of paw and brushy tail as the raider slunk toward the rutted road and the open plain beyond.

Not this time. You won't get away from me. Clyde never took his eyes off the coyote, and his right hand moved with the assurance of long practice. The lariat was in his hand, uncoiling against his thigh, the running knot snicking down into the snow. He set his heels to Joe Buck's ribs and the horse leaped forward, churning white dust with his hooves.

The coyote bolted from hiding, a lean shadow streaking for the safety of the brush. Hunger had made it quick and clever, but Joe Buck was an experienced stock horse and dauntless in the bargain. The gelding covered the distance in a few thunderous heartbeats. Clyde whipped up his lariat, spun the rope above his head—once, twice, building the momentum he needed for a good, long throw. He could feel it, when the moment was right, when the weight of the knot swung just so and whistled beside his ear. He threw the lariat and sat deep in his saddle, pulling his horse to a skidding stop—and it was only then, with Joe Buck already backing, already sensing the tension of the rope, that Clyde thought, *No lamb in the coyote's mouth.*

The rope had flown true. Clyde was young, but he was a good stockman—maybe one of the best within a day's ride of Paintrock. Even in the moonless dusk, he found his mark. The rope snapped tight in his hand; the knot around his saddle horn creaked, a lonely and ominous sound amid the crunch of Joe Buck's hooves. Out there in the blue-dark shadows, the coyote's body jerked into the air, fell heavily to the ground, thrashed and scrabbled in the snow.

"Clyde!" A shout from the house, the front yard. It was Beulah. "Stop, Clyde! Stop it!"

And his mother. "What are you doing? You must stop, this instant!"

Clyde roared in response. "Get back, damn it!" A quick glance over his shoulder showed they hadn't gone farther than the front stoop. What did women know of predators, of protection? This was his land to defend, his flock—

Your rifle. She had no right to take it from you. That was Substance's voice. He was back, spilling his words like oil, like pitch, into Clyde's head. *No right to humiliate you. To strip you of your strength. This is your land, your farm, your family. Take it. Claim it all, like a man.*

Clyde jerked the rope hard and hauled at his reins; Joe Buck backed all the faster, dragging the coyote through the snow. The animal twisted and flipped, trying in vain to rise and run. Relentless in his rage, shamed by his helplessness—by the damned softness he felt for that disgusting monster, that freak of a lamb—Clyde held the rope taut. Joe Buck still backed toward the house; Clyde kept his eye steadily on the creature fighting for breath at the end of his rope. The coyote's paws were twitching now, its tail lashing in helpless fear. Its body left a long track through the snow, a straight line running from orchard to yard, but still it moved, still it fought for its life.

He set his jaw hard, clenching his teeth till they ached. Why wasn't this animal consenting to die, as the culled sheep had done for Beulah?

"In God's name, stop!" Nettie Mae's voice was so high, so piercing, that for a moment Clyde didn't recognize it. He had never heard his mother scream before—not once. "Please! Clyde!"

Still he dragged the coyote, his heart pounding loudly in his ears. It had stopped thrashing by the time Clyde passed the stoop. The body was long, thin, and so flat and motionless it scarcely showed above the snow.

Clyde eased up on the reins. Joe Buck stopped backing and swayed for a moment on his hooves. The horse shivered under Clyde's body, tense from his rider's rage.

The lariat slackened, but the coyote didn't move. Clyde stared past its diminished form, following the furrow of its path through the snow.

A black line that seemed to stretch for miles—forever, to the very end of the world.

Clyde heard a sniffle from the steps. Then a whimper. He turned in the saddle and saw Benjamin standing with both hands over his mouth, and Charles hiding his face in Beulah's skirt so no one would see him crying. Nettie Mae had drawn the corner of her shawl up as if to shield behind it, but she was staring over its edge at Clyde. Even in the darkness, Clyde could see how pale his mother had gone. He had never seen her so frightened before, not even when Substance had been at his brutal worst.

Clyde drew a ragged breath. He forced himself to look at Beulah. The dreamy, heavy-eyed expression had fled. Her eyes were alight with terrible agony, her mouth wide open in a silent cry.

The reins slid from his nerveless fingers. His feet dropped from the stirrups, but for a long moment he could do nothing—nothing but sit atop his shuddering horse, staring blankly into the night.

No lamb in the coyote's mouth.

By God, what have I done? What have I made myself this night?

He slid heavily from the saddle and staggered toward the animal's body. The lips had pulled back in a permanent snarl, the mask of its last futile struggle. The dark fur around its mouth was silvered with frost or age. The coyote's eyes were half-closed, the teeth very white in the darkness. One of the long canines was chipped at the end, broken flat. For some reason, Clyde couldn't tear his dull, stricken gaze from that broken tooth—the tooth and the fleshy fold of tongue behind it. There was no blood on the coyote's muzzle. Whatever had taken the lamb, it hadn't been this creature.

"Oh, God." Clyde fell to his knees beside the dark furrow and the limp, dead thing that had made it. He bent over the animal, pressing his face against its hide. The body was still as warm as life. Each rib stood out distinctly against his cheek, and he breathed in the animal smell, the musk and sage, the dryness of fur mingled with a sharp, wintery bite of ice.

"I'm sorry." Clyde stroked the pelt. The fur was soft—silky as risen dough beneath its coarse guard hairs. "I'm sorry, I'm sorry. Please—" *Please what? Forgive me?*

He wept openly now, tears burning on his cold face, nose running faster than he could sniff it away.

Substance's words crept in around a flat expanse of regret. *What kind of man cries? And worse—where anyone can see?*

Clyde was finished with his father. What had Substance ever given him but pain? What had Substance given anyone but suffering? *It was you who did this, you who made me do it. I have no use for you; this world isn't yours anymore. Go lie in your grave where you belong. Leave me be—leave me be.*

The sound of footsteps over the snow broke through Clyde's misery. He straightened on his knees, every muscle tight and trembling. He didn't dare look around. Whether it was his mother who came toward him or Beulah or Cora or her children—whoever approached would see him now; there was no chance to hide. They would know Clyde for a weak and helpless thing. His remorse would redouble. Having fallen into the pit, there could be no escape from his shame.

"Clyde . . ." It was Beulah's voice, warped and thickened with sorrow.

She knelt beside him, so close their shoulders touched. Clyde shrank back from the contact. He didn't deserve her nearness or her comfort. She spoke his name again, but Clyde couldn't look at her. Even in the darkness, he would see rebuke in her eyes—and disbelief, and fear. He couldn't bear it. He knew it was his duty to bear it, to face this brutal thing he had done, and accept what he had become. Strangling was a terrible death. The coyote had done nothing to Clyde or his stock.

"Take the rope off its neck," Beulah said.

Obediently, he plunged his fingers into the thick fur. His hands shook so badly he could scarcely grasp the knot, but he worked it loose and pulled the lariat over the coyote's ears. The rope slithered over snow as Joe Buck moved away.

Beulah sighed, a breath of sorrow so deep and long it seemed all the world mourned with her. She ran her hands down the coyote's pelt, slowly, from muzzle to thin shoulder, over the curve of its ribs, the long flank stretched against whiteness. Even the tail, down to its pale tip. She learned the flesh and fur, the shape and angle of the bones. And she wept all the while—quietly, not wailing as some women do, or as little children do. But the hard, choking sobs were worse than any cries. They shook her body like blows, each one. Clyde might as well have beaten her with his fists.

"Beulah, I'm sorry. I—"

She silenced him with a touch—took his nearest wrist in one hand, then reached across his body and took the other. She raised his hands from his lap, moving them toward the coyote.

Clyde resisted.

"Yes," Beulah said. "You must."

He heard the command in her words, but even if she hadn't compelled him, still Clyde would have obeyed. For he heard something more than command: knowing. *You must. You must.* He believed her. If there was any escape from himself—any hope to evade the shadow of his father—it lay in this girl's understanding. Clyde surrendered, and Beulah guided his hands to the lifeless animal before him.

Sick with shame and self-loathing, Clyde made himself do what Beulah had done. He rested his fingers on the coyote's muzzle. The lips had slackened in death; they moved freely over the jaw, and he could feel the teeth like pebbles in the riverbed—pebbles when you went wading, smooth beneath your feet, firm among flowing silt. He traced the bridge of the animal's nose, around the eye, open, for the coyote had seen its death coming. The ears were stiff and strong like a horse's ears, the ruff at the coyote's neck soft beneath his palms. When he reached the animal's ribs, Clyde paused. The stillness rebuked him. This body should have stirred with breath. Breath and life were the coyote's by right, but Clyde had stolen them both away. He had cut the stalk before its season. He hung his head and wept as Beulah had done, racked by the impact of a sorrow he could never control.

"More," Beulah said.

Clyde didn't open his eyes; he couldn't bear the sight of what he had done. But his hands moved again at Beulah's command, touching the legs that had run their last, the back that would no longer bend in flight, the tail that had thrashed in final defiance against the evil Clyde had wrought.

When he had finished, Clyde sat back on his heels, shuddering for his breath.

Gently, Beulah said, "Why did you do this?"

"The lamb." Clyde choked, coughed, and wiped his nose on the sleeve of his coat. "I went to the barn, but the lamb was gone. I saw the coyote's tracks in the snow."

"Oh, Clyde," Beulah whispered. "The lamb died all on its own. Its time had come. I heard the ewe crying after supper, and I went to the barn. I found our lamb there in the stall, where we had left it."

Clyde nodded.

"I took the lamb," Beulah said. "I wrapped it in some jute I found in the barn. Then I went back to the house to find you, but by then you were already on your horse."

"Beulah." He hated the way her name came tearing from his throat. He sounded like a child lost in the forest, crying for its mother. But when she wrapped her arms around him, Clyde knew at least that Beulah didn't hate him. "What should we do now?" Clyde's face was pressed against her shoulder. Beulah smelled of the lavender and cedar Nettie Mae sprinkled in the blanket chests. And more, too. Sage and rain, and warm red earth, like the coyote's hide.

"We should bury them," Beulah decided. "Both."

She climbed to her feet, and after a moment, Clyde did the same. Tentatively, he looked toward the house. His mother had vanished; so had Joe Buck. But Cora remained, an arm around each of her sons.

"Your ma caught your horse and took him back to the paddock," Beulah said. "I guess she'll unsaddle him and turn him loose."

"Where ought we to make the graves?"

"By the creek, I think. Easier to dig where it's sandy, and the ground will freeze last near moving water."

Beulah lifted the coyote as if it weighed no more than the lamb. Its head and tail sagged from her arms, yearning toward the earth. "You go and get the lamb. Meet me at the river trail."

Clyde couldn't stand the sight of the trench in the snow, the long track attesting to his own unreasoning violence. He went the other way around the house, stumbling through the darkness. He passed the paddock—the horses had gathered against the cold, one mass of living shadow—and heard Joe Buck whicker from the midst of the herd. A moment later, the shed door opened, and a sudden flare of lantern light made Clyde throw up an arm to shield his eyes.

"Clyde. Where are you going?" It was his mother's voice.

Blinking, he lowered his arm. "To the river. Beulah and I will bury the coyote. And . . . and a lamb that died, too."

"Bury them? Why? Better to drag them out to the brush and let the varmints take them."

Clyde lowered his eyes, wondering what excuse he could give. Finally, he said, "Because it's the right thing to do."

He waited for his mother's castigation. She moved toward him, and the ring of her light glided across the snow till it surrounded Clyde, too. Nettie Mae said nothing. She only laid a hand on Clyde's cheek. When he looked into her eyes, he found them brimming with tears.

"I've feared for you," Nettie Mae said softly. "All these years. You don't know how I've feared."

Before he could ask what she meant, Nettie Mae turned away, and in her usual brusque manner said, "You'll need a light, if the job is to be done tonight."

"I'll go back to the house with you. Then I can take your lantern."

"No. I'll hold the lantern and come along with you. That way, you and Beulah can see what you're about."

Clyde stood for a moment, numb with surprise. Nettie Mae offered him a smile. It made her seem shy, almost girlish.

"I—I must go to the barn first," Clyde said, "and fetch something Beulah left there."

"Very well, then. Off we go."

As they crossed the farm, there was nothing to be heard but the steady tread of their feet through the snow and the restlessness of the wind. Neither spoke. Clyde sensed in his mother a peculiar release, an easing of some habitual strain, and a vision returned to him—the lariat slipping over the coyote's ears. The knot buried deep in warm fur, loosening under his hand.

In the barn, Clyde found the still, small bundle on the shelf where Beulah had laid it. Coarse jute cloth shrouded the lamb's body. He didn't unwrap the covering, for fear of what his mother might think. He scooped it against his chest and turned at once to go. The body inside had stiffened; it seemed heavier than the lamb had been in life. He took his spade from its hook and led Nettie Mae toward the river trail.

Beulah was waiting for them beside a stand of leafless brush. The coyote still hung in her arms, just as it had before, limp and piteous in defeat. She nodded to Nettie Mae, who returned the silent acknowledgment. Then Beulah stepped out onto the trail and led the way to the place where the creek met the river.

Beulah didn't go as far as Substance's grave, and Clyde was grateful for that mercy. The girl stopped at a flat expanse of undisturbed snow, nodding once to Clyde. He laid the lamb's body at the foot of a nearby sapling and bent to his work. No one uttered a word as wet earth came up and mounded dark upon the snow. Nettie Mae held the lantern high, watching with somber poise. When Clyde had dug the first grave—more than a foot deep, long enough to hold the slain coyote—Beulah stepped to the edge of the pit and lowered the body into the earth.

She looked up at Clyde, unspeaking, and he came to her side and helped her arrange the slack limbs and straighten the coyote's head. The animal looked as if it lay in peaceful sleep.

Clyde stood and took up his spade once more. But Beulah stopped him. "Wait. Bring the lamb, too."

"In the same grave?"

"Yes."

Clyde hesitated, casting an anxious glance at his mother. But Nettie Mae seemed cognizant of nothing except Beulah. She was watching the girl's face with an expression somewhere between fascination and fear.

Clyde lifted the wrapped bundle and bore it to the graveside. He peered at his mother once more—then, swallowing his worry, he unwound the cloth from the animal's body. Nettie Mae gasped when the two-headed creature emerged from its shroud into the light of her lantern. Beulah gave no sign that she had heard. The girl tucked the lamb between the coyote's forelegs. The two creatures lay chest to chest. Both heads of the lamb—that brief-burning miracle—nestled below the coyote's jaw.

"Is there anything you want to say before we cover them?" Beulah asked softly.

Clyde stared down into the grave. It struck him that this humble processional, this ceremony, amounted to far more respect than Substance had been given on the occasion of his burial. He reached down into the pit, felt cold air lace through his fingers. He stroked the coyote's pelt one last time.

"Forgive me, please," Clyde whispered, "for I never will forgive myself."

When he withdrew his hand from the grave, Beulah took it in her own. And where the warmth of her skin met his, there was no barrier between them, no notion of self to keep them apart. One sound, one song, one breath he exhaled and Beulah breathed in.

NETTIE MAE

Nettie Mae would have given all the world to prevent her son from becoming like his father, if only the world had been hers to give. Not one coin would she have kept for herself, not one speck. Diamonds, gold, the great power of influence, even love meant nothing to Nettie Mae when set against her son. Her last remaining child. But she had never held the world and had no riches to spare. Prayer and hope were the only paltry treasures at her disposal—small and fragile things, levers inadequate to shift a man's fate.

By the first of November, winter had come in earnest: true winter, white and silent with snowfalls spanning days at a stretch. Drifts piled against the house, reaching to the windowsills; wind heaped the snow halfway to the eaves of the barn. The stone walls of the sheepfold turned to white hillocks, which Clyde dug away every morning, wary of the countless wild things that still menaced his flock. The livestock moved in despondent lines along stinking, mud-dark avenues beaten through the snow by weary hooves. Every day, Clyde turned the animals out to their pastures, but it was hard work browsing through heavy snow, and the stock never ventured far from the barn's weak blue shadow. Hay was their only real sustenance now, bland as the porridge and dried beans upon which the residents of the sod house would depend before spring came again.

Nettie Mae worked at her spinning wheel, squinting through the day's white glare toward the fold where Clyde was pounding sharp stakes into the earth. He had cut the stakes from scrap wood recovered from the Bemis farm and had whittled their ends to wicked points. The stakes angled outward from the stone wall, a deterrent against the wolves, coyotes, and mountain lions who would inevitably come prowling around the farm once the real hardship of midwinter set in.

When Clyde had first begun the work some two days before, the sight of that bristling palisade had filled Nettie Mae with disquiet. Since the death of the coyote, she didn't like to think of Clyde and predators together, her only remaining child facing the hungry, sharp-fanged beasts of an unfeeling world. Her son—the first babe she had cradled at her breast—a predator himself, potent with rage, capable of swift and merciless brutality.

From the moment she had seen him in pursuit of the coyote, Nettie Mae had known that sixteen years of prayer and pleading had been in vain. Clyde had become, between one moment and the next, exactly what his father had been. Vengeful. Unconstrained. A man not governed by sense or will, but by the darkest passions of a veiled heart.

As she had stood transfixed on the stoop, watching her son kill that creature—slowly, cruelly, without the quick mercy of a clean shot—Nettie Mae had thought, *Perhaps no boy can grow to manhood in Substance's shadow without becoming Substance himself. Without the infection of violence and hate, without the love of power.* Fear had gripped her so tightly that night that Nettie Mae had felt herself paralyzed, scarcely strong enough to draw a breath. She had known in that instant— known—that Clyde was beyond all hope, even beyond the reach of prayer. He would become the very thing Nettie Mae had sworn her beloved child never could be.

That night, the night of the first snow, Nettie Mae had faced her darkest hour. But the girl had changed it all. Beulah had taken Clyde in her arms and remade him—Nettie Mae could find no other word for the transformation she had witnessed. Remade. Shaped into a new, more hopeful form by Beulah's strange and miraculous hands.

A gust of wind picked up, strewing ice crystals against the window. They crackled and chimed, the sound almost swallowed by the chatter of Cora's children. The boys had sprawled belly down on a blanket in front of the sitting-room fire, taking turns reading aloud from Nettie Mae's Bible. Word by staggered word, syllable by syllable, they read out the story of Daniel in the lion's den, a halting tale impeded by mispronunciations and storms of laughter.

Miranda occupied herself on the sofa with her two rag dolls—the one she had always had and the new one Nettie Mae had sewn for her. She watched the girl surreptitiously over the edge of her spinning wheel. Nettie Mae still feared for the girl, though the incident of the flood lay weeks in the past. She found herself checking on little Miranda ten times a day or more, searching her face for the flush of fever, finding any excuse to draw near and listen to the sound of her breath.

Miranda looked up from her dolls and met Nettie Mae's eye—the girl seemed to know whenever Nettie Mae cast the briefest glance in her direction. Miranda grinned and raised the rag dolls to her face as if to hide behind them, as if to start a game of peep-bo. Nettie Mae couldn't help but smile in response. A treacherous warmth flooded her heart whenever she found herself in Miranda's presence or whenever she thought about the child, which was far too often for her liking. There was no sense in developing a fondness for the girl, nor for Benjamin, nor Charles. None of Cora's brood could replace the precious babies Nettie Mae had lost. Yet she couldn't save herself from that fatal foolishness, a growing affection for the Bemis offspring. That was the nature of children, Nettie Mae supposed—they instilled a rising hope in even the hardest of hearts. Children were a persistent reminder that life went ever onward, that a future lay ahead, for them if not for you. Perhaps Nettie Mae needed that remembrance now, when everything else had been taken from her.

She let the wheel slow and released the soft white roving to hang unspun. Then she covered her eyes with her hands and opened them like shutters, peeking across the room at Miranda. The girl laughed—a high, pure music. Contented, she returned to her dolls.

Miranda only likes me because I gave her that poppet, Nettie Mae thought, taking up her spinning again. But what did the reason matter? At least someone in the sod house felt warmly toward Nettie Mae.

Cora was still at work in the kitchen. Nettie Mae could hear her at the drain board, washing out the crocks that had contained the last of the potted meat. How quickly such luxuries vanished in the winter, and all the faster with three small children to feed—to placate during the long hours of confinement.

Cora and Nettie Mae maintained their custom of avoiding one another as far as they were able, with the exception of breakfast and supper. But all the same, Nettie Mae felt Cora's presence like a burr in her stocking. Every step along the kitchen floor, every clink of a spoon against pottery, sent a jolt of resentment along Nettie Mae's nerves. She had long been accustomed to tranquility in her house—more or less, when Substance had been in a fair mood—and winter had always been, for Nettie Mae, a time of rest and recreation, a time to spin and make, to watch the snow fall while the soft click of her knitting needles accompanied her inmost thoughts. This year, the house felt hectic and close. Winter would last far too long.

Beulah was perched on the brick hearth, her cheeks flushed from the heat of the fire, struggling to piece a quilt patch out of a few torn scraps of old fabric. Nettie Mae allowed the spinning wheel to stop once more. She watched the girl fold her scraps this way and that, pinching corners, pressing the needle longwise between her lips as she frowned in concentration. Beulah hadn't sewn much before; that was plain, just by watching her clumsy technique. But the fabric was part of the problem. It looked far too worn, almost threadbare, and had the faded appearance of old shirting. She had torn up some of her father's disused clothes, Nettie Mae realized, and was trying to make something useful of the scraps.

Nettie Mae hesitated, wondering whether it was really safe to speak with the girl. She never could stand in that child's presence without a subtle thrill of trepidation. She hadn't forgotten how Beulah had laughed that day in the kitchen, with Clyde scarcely free from the grip of fever—that day when Nettie Mae had told Beulah the meaning of necromancy. But for all her strange ways, the girl had never done Nettie Mae any harm. In fact, she had mended the sudden break in Clyde— God alone knew how—and restored the precious hope Nettie Mae had thought dashed for good.

Nettie Mae tucked her fleece against the wheel's mother-of-all and rose from the spinning stool. She stepped over the boys' legs and climbed the stairs to her room, where she found her little basket of neatly folded cloth scraps, all arranged by color. Then she returned to the sitting room and stood a few feet away from the frowning girl.

Nettie Mae cleared her throat; Beulah looked up and took the needle from between her lips.

"I couldn't help but notice," Nettie Mae said, "that you seem to be struggling with your work."

Beulah smiled. Lazy eyed and slow, as ever. "My ma has tried to teach me how to sew, but I guess I got no talent for it."

"Nonsense. Sewing doesn't require talent, only practice and concentration."

"I do well enough with embroidery when I'm pushed to it," Beulah said, "but stitching into cloth isn't the same as stitching two pieces of cloth together. You're an awful good hand with a needle and thread, ma'am. Miranda loves her new dolly. I'd be grateful if you'd teach me what you know."

Nettie Mae cleared her throat again, shifting from one foot to the other. Then she forced herself to sit on the bricks at Beulah's side. She kept a healthy distance between herself and the girl, leaning over to assess the attempted quilt patch.

"The biggest problem I can see," Nettie Mae said, "is that your stitches are uneven. See here? You started out with proper, short stitches, but as you worked along the patch, they grew longer and looser. That alters the tension of the fabric and creates these puckers. You ought to discipline yourself to make the same stitch length each and every time. Haven't you ever worked a sampler?"

"No, ma'am. I never saw much use in a sampler, even for embroidery."

"The purpose of a sampler is to *learn*. To practice."

Beulah twisted her mouth, an expression of deep and complicated thought. "How does a body make a sampler, anyway?"

"You must begin simply and keep the work small. Perhaps you ought to stitch a little blanket for Miranda's dolls. That would be a proper sampler for a girl of your age."

And she thought, *If either of my girls had survived to your age, I'd have taught them so well that they'd already be sewing their bridal trousseaux. This is what comes of a feckless, city-bred woman—Cora's sort.*

Nettie Mae kept her less charitable thoughts to herself. She said, "That fabric you're using is the other half of your trouble. It's too thin for good sewing; it won't hold its shape. Better use it for rags, or to stuff another doll for your sister." She lifted the scrap basket to her lap and opened the double-hinged lid. "These are bits and pieces I've saved from old quilting work. You may use anything you like from this basket."

Beulah's eyes widened. She ran a finger down one row of neatly sorted fabric. "It's all so pretty. Look, this piece has flowers. And this one has tiny birds! It's awful generous of you, ma'am."

Nettie Mae took a paper folio from the lining of the basket and spread it open on the brick hearth. It revealed dozens of stiff card cutouts, diamonds and perfect squares, yellowed with age, punctured by old needle holes. How long had it been since she'd purchased that card

and snipped out the shapes? Wisconsin. The first year of her marriage—
or the second?

"What's this?" Beulah asked.

"Piecing paper. I'll show you how to use it once you've learned to
sew an even stitch. You cut out your fabric just a bit larger than the
paper shape, then fold the edges of the cloth over and baste it to the
paper. You do know how to baste, don't you?"

"More or less."

"Then you lay two pieces atop one another, right sides facing, and
stitch their edges together. When you've finished, you'll have a lovely
quilt block with all its corners perfectly aligned."

Laughing, the girl looked up. "Isn't that cheating?"

Nettie Mae didn't want to smile, but a marginal curve fought its
way to her lips. "More or less."

Nettie Mae helped Beulah sort through the scrap basket and choose
a few likely pieces for her sampler. Then she showed her how to thread
a needle properly and set the girl to work making fine, even stitches.
The boys had, by that time, jumped up and begun to act out the Bible
story. They took turns playing the lion, roaring as loudly as they dared
in Nettie Mae's presence.

The noise gave Nettie Mae enough cover that her bravery was
inflamed. If she had thought anyone other than Beulah could have
overheard her words, she never would have spoken.

"What you did for Clyde," she said softly. Then stopped. Would
the girl understand what Nettie Mae meant? Nettie Mae hardly knew
herself what she intended to say.

She swallowed, fighting back a rising current of anxiety. How *had*
Beulah healed the break in Clyde's spirit? She recalled with vivid, trembling clarity that day when Clyde had tossed, incoherent, in the grip of
his fever. And later, Beulah—unconcerned, sweeping out the kitchen
as if nothing in the world had ever been wrong, as if there had been no

chance Clyde might have died. *I'm a sorceress, ain't I?* That's what the child had said. The impertinent, blasphemous child.

Maybe that comment had been no impertinence, after all. What else could explain the ease with which Beulah unpicked Substance's stitches, erasing the shadow of the man from his son's heart? Perhaps it had been no coincidence that Beulah had done her work over an open grave, with two dead beasts—one of them malformed, twisted like a demon—laid at her feet.

Nettie Mae's ears throbbed with the sudden pressure of her pulse. Her throat went tight with a terrible certainty, a conviction that it was blasphemy merely to sit beside the girl, to acknowledge her. Even so, she owed much to Beulah, and more than she could ever hope to repay. It was Beulah—not sixteen years of prayer—who had delivered Clyde from his fate. For the sake of her last living child, Nettie Mae would do anything. She would even suffer a witch to sit quilting by her fire.

Nettie Mae tried again. "What you did for Clyde, that night . . . with the coyote."

Beulah looked up from her stitches, patient and waiting.

"Thank you. For . . . helping him."

The girl shrugged, slicking an end of thread between tongue and front teeth. "I didn't do much."

Nettie Mae paid no heed to the girl's demurral. "I will admit that at first I thought it blind foolishness to hold a funeral for a coyote." She wouldn't mention the abomination, the two-headed freak. "But the affair seems to have comforted Clyde. He's a different boy now—a different man."

"I rather think Clyde's the same fellow he always has been, ma'am. I hope you don't think it sauce for me to say so."

"No," Nettie Mae said vaguely, watching snow strike the window pane. "No, he has changed, and for the better. He has settled, I suppose one might say. Something uncertain in him has found its footing. I'm grateful to you, Beulah. Grateful."

The girl returned to her stitching. Progress was painfully slow, but she seemed determined to do the job well this time. Her stitches showed white and even against the dark plaid fabric she had chosen.

"I can't really tell you," Nettie Mae said, laughing lightly at the force of her emotions, "exactly what Clyde means to me. He was the first of my children, and he is also the last."

Beulah didn't look up from her work, but the cup of her silence held something warm and companionable, patient and inviting.

"I've had five babies, you know. But the Lord saw fit to take them all—except Clyde."

Now Beulah did raise her head. Her eyes had lost their habitual sleepy heaviness. They shone with sympathy, wide and clear sighted. That strange color. Pale yellow brown, more like an animal's eyes than a proper girl's.

"I'm sorry," Beulah said. "That's just terrible, Mrs. Webber. It's an awful sad thing, for a mother to lose even one child."

Nettie Mae huffed out one short laugh. She couldn't help it. Beulah had spoken as if she really knew, as if she had felt that pain herself. It was too absurd. If the girl wasn't mocking her, then she was dull witted for certain and sure.

"I shouldn't have spoken of this," Nettie Mae said. "It's no fit story with which to trouble a young girl."

"But I ain't troubled in the least." She resumed her stitching. "I don't mind if people tell me this and that—even if they tell me all the things that weigh heaviest on their hearts."

Nettie Mae opened her mouth as if to speak again. The words were there on her tongue, eager to spill. Her throat burned with the need to tell this girl everything. Every sorrow, every lost hope. To speak and be heard—to be understood—after years of silence was a temptation bordering on compulsion. Then Nettie Mae remembered the girl in her kitchen earlier that fall, laughing at the word of God. She closed her mouth and laced her fingers together in her lap. What wicked power did this child have, to conjure such dangerous complacency?

Nettie Mae scolded herself. *Don't be a fool. She is Cora's daughter, tainted by sin; you know that much already. She may be something far worse, for all you can tell. Don't be so quick to reveal your weakness to one who may be an enemy.*

An enemy of Nettie Mae. An enemy of God.

Beulah seemed to understand that Nettie Mae had silenced herself, and not without effort. She smiled lightly, plying her needle. "You needn't fret, Mrs. Webber. And you needn't worry about Clyde the way you do—him growing into a man, I mean, and all that comes along with it. Marrying and having children of his own someday. You won't be left out of the good that's yet to come."

"What do you mean?" Nettie Mae said sharply. She intended to add, *I don't fret over such foolish things.* But she couldn't make herself say those words. The lie wouldn't come.

"You will have a family again someday." Beulah never looked up from her sewing. She spoke as easily as she did to the little children—all the authority and confidence one might claim in reassuring Charles or Miranda that the sun would rise the next morning. "I've seen it. I know."

Nettie Mae's words didn't stick any longer. They burst out so roughly that the boys faltered in their play, casting wary glances toward the hearth. "You've seen it? What foolish talk is this?"

"It's no foolish talk, ma'am, if you'll forgive me for arguing. It's only the truth."

"And where have you seen it? How do you know?"

She feared the answer, recoiled from the possibility with a knot of dread in her middle. Feared the answer and hungered for it. She wanted it to be true. So powerful was her longing for a family that she knew she would believe whatever the girl told her in that moment—accept Beulah's words like the utterance of a prophet. Panic burned inside her chest, for it was a sin to heed the speech of evildoers. But even as she warned herself away from sin, Nettie Mae succumbed to the stillness that settled like a snowfall in her mind: the peace of acceptance, the quiet of surrender, a welcome blankness muting all fear.

If it's a sin to listen to this strange child and wish her words might be true, then I am a sinner, and God in His mercy will forgive me.

What hope could she otherwise claim? In the bleak and colorless grip of winter, to what guiding staff might she hold? Did she not, after all, believe in redemption? Clyde had been granted a second chance beside that animal's grave. Surely it wasn't too much to ask, that grace might afford Nettie Mae an opportunity to right her wrongs, too.

And if I were given that chance, O God—to start over, to make myself anew, to set aside the bitterness that has poisoned me all these years—I would not be ungrateful.

She watched Beulah's hands as the girl sewed. Browned and roughened by her work outdoors, they were nevertheless slender and moved with a latent, naive grace. The skin was yet unmarred by the marks of age—sun spots, scars—and the tendons didn't rise distinct from bone and flesh as they did on the backs of Nettie Mae's hands. The image of Clyde's fingers twined with Beulah's returned to Nettie Mae. The memory was distinct, sharp: The lantern light stark and golden on their skin. Two hands clasped as if God had made them that way, fitted together, and all around, everywhere, the dark of night. Darkness masking the rest of the world, swallowing the world in all directions. Nothing remained of reality save for Clyde and Beulah, joined.

No. This girl is not for him. She cannot be.

Clyde would have a wife someday, when he had truly grown into a man. Nettie Mae knew there was no staving off the inevitable. He would marry when the time was right; it wasn't right now. But when he did begin courting, it would be with good girls, proper girls from town—not this strange, slow-blinking, sun-browned daughter of a trollop, who might or might not meddle in witchery and other corruptions, for all Nettie Mae could tell.

Nettie Mae turned her attention to the window again. Snow had gathered along the bottom of the sill, an inch deep, maybe more, and was still climbing up the edges of the panes. A long, dark winter with little hope for peace. She breathed deeply till her nerves were somewhat soothed. Then she swallowed hard, summoning her accustomed bluntness.

"You mustn't be alone with Clyde. Ever. I said I'm grateful to you for helping my son as you did, and I am. But make no mistake, Beulah. My rule still stands. I won't have you ruining Clyde's future."

The girl looked up from her patchwork, but she only smiled with a tolerant air.

Nettie Mae's stomach twisted. She could abide Beulah's uncanny self-possession no longer—not for today, at any rate. She left the girl to her sewing and took herself to the kitchen, even though Cora was skulking there.

Cora had just begun to mix a cornbread batter for the midday meal. She looked up with a hopeful half smile as Nettie Mae passed the kitchen table. But Nettie Mae never slowed. She took her heavy winter shawl from its hook, wrapped it quickly around her shoulders, and left the house.

The cold struck her hard as the kitchen door closed behind her. The skin of her cheeks tightened, and her eyes filled with stinging tears. Nettie Mae blinked until the tears had gone. Every breath burned in her throat and rose again in a thick plume, white against a white sky. Through a fog of falling snow, she could make out Clyde's dark form, bundled in wool, and the hard line of the sheepfold wall, the stones black with moisture. Sheep called now and then, their voices made thick and small by the deadening silence of winter.

Nettie Mae tucked her hands into the protection of her shawl and watched her son at work. He bent with his spade, his back strong and level, and flung a load of snow toward the great heap he'd already built several feet from the corner of the fold. Then another spadeful, and another. Clyde was tireless, determined, just as a man ought to be. From a distance, and with Clyde half-veiled by snowfall—edges gone blurry, features obscured—Nettie Mae could find no trace of the boy she had cherished and raised. Were it not for the fact that she had watched Clyde take up his shovel that very morning beside the kitchen steps, Nettie Mae might have mistaken the man at the sheepfold for a stranger. Fate and Ernest Bemis had robbed Clyde of his remaining youth. Now he was a man before his time, and all too soon he would yearn for a man's life. It was no use trying to hold him, nor trying to hold him back. Nettie Mae could see that clearly enough; the truth was plain as the damp stone wall running hard through an indistinct whiteness.

The kitchen door opened and closed, and even that sound was muffled by the snow, though Nettie Mae was standing only a few paces away. She turned and saw Cora coming gingerly down the steps, and looked away again with a tight scowl.

Nettie Mae hoped the woman would proceed to the outhouse and leave her in peace, but Cora stopped beside Nettie Mae, albeit with the customary distance between them.

"My goodness, but it's a cold day." The forced pluck in Cora's voice set Nettie Mae's teeth on edge. Her witless chirping rang like a bell through the quietude. "And to think, winter has only just begun."

"Yes, to think," Nettie Mae answered dryly.

"Nettie Mae, I . . ." Cora edged one step closer, timid and shrinking. "I have hoped for a chance to speak to you in confidence, without the children about. I hate to think how they would clamor, if they knew. And Beulah—she would try to convince me to change my mind. Tell me, please, when do you think one might be able to ride to Paintrock? This snowfall hasn't let up for days, and—"

"I'm sure I can't say when the snow will end. Nor can I tell when the next one will come." Nettie Mae added under her breath, "I'm no witch, to conjure such knowledge."

"There have been winter days when Ernest was able to ride to town. Well—he could make it to Paintrock in one day, and return the next, with daylight hours being so short. But not until later in the winter, when enough sleighs had gone by that the snow on the road had been packed down flat."

Nettie Mae didn't answer. She kept her arms folded tightly beneath her shawl, staring into the blowing white, waiting for Cora to tire of this idle chatter and return to her work.

"Or perhaps you have a sleigh," Cora said. "We never had one, though Ernest was saving up to buy one. We'd hoped to have a small sleigh of our own by the time the snow fell this year, but it wasn't meant to be."

"I haven't got a sleigh."

On the rare occasions when some dreadful winter emergency had required a trip to Paintrock, Substance had strapped his lacquered wooden skis to his boots and covered the twenty miles in that fashion. Nettie Mae had no intention of disclosing the skis' existence; Cora would only send Clyde off on some flippant errand without regard for his safety. And Clyde, eager to prove his manliness and worth, would go at once, without pausing to ask whether the trip was truly necessary. Unless one of the children fell dangerously ill, Nettie Mae would keep her son at home.

"Then I suppose I must wait until the road is packed down," Cora said. "The matter *can* wait, I suppose, but this promises to be such a dreadfully long winter, and I'm . . . well, I'm eager to be off."

"Off?" Nettie Mae looked at the woman sharply.

"Yes. You see, I've decided not to stay. Here, I mean." Cora swept one arm in a wide arc, indicating the snowbound farm and the distant Bemis homestead—the foothills beyond, too, and the ghostly presence of the Bighorns, more felt than seen through a shifting white mist. "I've decided I must return to Saint Louis as soon as can be managed."

"Have you?" Nettie Mae's brows lifted in surprise.

Cora's departure would resolve the worst of Nettie Mae's troubles. She would no longer be forced to work alongside the woman who had destroyed her family and her life. And Cora would take Beulah with her—back to the city, far from Clyde's reach.

Cautiously, Nettie Mae said, "But it must be a costly endeavor, to travel from here to Saint Louis. How will you manage the expense?"

"The president's china. I've thought it all out. I'll sell the china set in Paintrock—surely one of those wealthy ranchers up north would like to buy it for his wife—and I'll use the money for travel expenses. We can hire a wagon to take us to Carbon, and from Carbon, we can take the train to Saint Louis."

"Have you any family in Saint Louis?"

"Not any longer," Cora admitted. "But if I can get my asking price, I should have enough money left over to board somewhere for a few months until I can find work."

"Work?" Nettie Mae didn't try to stifle a derisive grunt. "What work can you do?"

"Why, you've seen for yourself how well I can work when necessity demands." Cora sounded rather wounded. "I might take up as a cook in a fine household. Or I may find work as a seamstress."

"Might. May. These aren't certainties, Cora."

Even as she spoke, Nettie Mae scolded her own foolishness. *Don't spoil this, you witless woman. You could be rid of her by the spring thaw. What does it matter to you whether she finds suitable work or starves?* If Cora Bemis ended in a Saint Louis gutter, some noble Christian charity would take in her younger children and see that they were raised in kindly homes. There might be little hope for Beulah, old as she was, except to take up as a maid or something worse. But Beulah's fate was none of Nettie Mae's affair, either. Let God do with the girl whatever He liked.

"And your husband?" Nettie Mae went on, against her own better judgment. "What of him? He's to be set free in under two years."

"Yes," Cora said, turning her face away, lowering her eyes in shame. "About Ernest. I've written a letter for him. The letter explains everything— what I mean to do, where I mean to go. I've told him in the letter that I can't go on this way." Her voice broke, but she pressed doggedly on. "I never took to life on the prairie, as Ernest hoped I would, and living here without him is far more than I can bear. I told him he may come and find me and the children, when he is free . . . if he still wants me after . . ."

Wisely, she trailed off into silence. The sheep called intermittently, husky and low. The space between Cora and Nettie Mae, the distance they kept, felt dense with the weight of mistrust, and Nettie Mae resisted the urge to shift her feet, to flinch from the discomfort of her long, steadfast hatred.

After a pause, Cora resumed. "Anyhow, I will send the letter along with whomever can ride to town, once the road is passable. He can deliver the letter to Ernest at the jail."

"He. So you expect Clyde to go traipsing off on this errand." Not that Nettie Mae had harbored the least doubt of Cora's intentions. But it did give her satisfaction, to pin Cora to the wall with her own words. "Well, Clyde can't be spared. In case you haven't noticed, he's the only person who does the bulk of the outdoor work now that the snows have come. Unless there's some dire emergency—and I pray every day that God will spare us such suffering—Clyde will stay right here."

"It doesn't have to be Clyde," Cora said timidly. "A rider may come here from Paintrock, and—"

"For what purpose?"

"Who can say? A delivery."

"In the dead of winter?"

"Stranger things have happened."

"Not here. Not in November."

"The sheriff rode down from Paintrock, after . . ."

Again, Cora stumbled into stillness. Nettie Mae narrowed her eyes at the woman, taking in the flush of her fine, pretty face with no small amount of satisfaction. More than winter's chill had brought the color to Cora's cheeks. It was shame that made her blush. Well-deserved shame.

"Your plan is a foolish one," Nettie Mae said. "It's time you faced the truth, Cora Bemis. No one in Paintrock will believe that the china truly came from Ulysses Grant, and without the president's name attached to it, you'll never get enough money to see you all the way to Saint Louis. If they do believe the china came from the president, then they'll see it for what it is—what you would see yourself, if you were an honest woman. A payoff. A bribe meant to buy your silence."

Trembling, Cora pulled the edges of her shawl tightly around her shoulders. Even in the cold air, the rosy glow faded from her cheeks, replaced by the pallor of shock.

Cora's air of breakable delicacy only fed Nettie Mae's resentment as tinder feeds a fire. "I speak the truth, and the sooner you accept the facts, the better off you'll be. If President Grant truly did send that china set to you, he didn't mean it as a kindly gesture. He meant for it to stop your mouth. Oh, don't look so startled, Cora. Surely you can understand. Now that the general has ascended to the White House, the Grant family won't have it whispered about that one of their number got a bastard daughter on some licentious girl. Yes, Clyde told me everything. I know all about your birth. And I've sense enough to see that President Grant intends to keep the tale from spreading any farther and sullying his family's good name."

Cora stared at Nettie Mae for a long moment, mouth working in speechless dismay. Finally, the woman croaked, "Well, I . . . I . . ." Then she turned on her heel and stalked back toward the house.

Snow lifted on a sudden gust of wind, spiraling around Nettie Mae's skirt. She stamped her cold feet to bring feeling back to her toes and tried to smile with grim satisfaction, but the smile slid at once from her face. Had she not begged the Lord, just minutes before, for a chance at redemption—an opportunity to cast bitterness from her heart and make good on a new start, a new life?

But there is no mending the damage between Cora and me, Nettie Mae told herself. *Why should I be kind to a woman who dealt me so grave an insult? What sense is there in forgiving an adulteress—in forgiving the death of my husband?*

Nettie Mae summoned memories of Substance: his broad, imposing body, the loudness of his voice, the irrefutable authority of his command. If she had hoped to find comfort in recalling her dead husband, that hope proved to be in vain. For what she remembered most clearly was not the man's steady work, nor his capability as a provider—not the early days of their marriage, when Nettie Mae still had reason to hope, with the fruitless optimism of a callow girl, for the bliss of wedded life. What she recalled most vividly was Substance's fist. How tightly he could clench it, how the dry skin of his knuckles would crack with the pressure and go white with strain. How those stone-hard knuckles could split a lip or bruise a cheek or an eye and how the color would linger for weeks, purple fading to brown fading to yellow.

The past held no warmth for Nettie Mae. The present was cold, winter bitter, but she took comfort in the persistence of snowfall. Snow reshaped the world. It suppressed memory, drawing everything that mattered here and now into a tight and immediate circle. Far beyond the fields, obscured by a shroud of white, the snow was mounding over a riverside grave, softening the curve of the soil, pressing memory down beneath the mute silence of the season.

CORA

All of the world had surrendered to winter. Whenever Cora paused beside one of the sod house's windows and stared out, she saw nothing but the endlessness of white. White fields piled so high with snow that no rounded heaps remained to mark the fences or the boundary posts of the Webber farm. White flat nothingness where the road should have been. And beyond—where once lay the parched pale gold of prairie, the monotony broken by a mercy of violet shadows—only a featureless expanse of snow remained, unvaried, losing itself in the white void that had replaced the horizon.

Cora had never liked to face the winter, to confront its vast sameness, the dreadful long reach of its stillness and power. Winter had always made her feel lonely and small, even in the city. On the prairie she had gained a whole new understanding of what it meant to be isolated and insignificant. And this winter was worse than any Cora could remember. The snows had come so early and had persisted for weeks, until the first-story windows of the sod-brick house were half-buried and Clyde was obliged to shovel away the dense, wet plague every two or three days, lest the house grow too dark and confined. Hemmed in by bleak cold, Cora would have preferred to distract herself by sewing or baking bread or playing with the children, always with her back to the snow-muffled world. But if she didn't watch, she wouldn't see—wouldn't know when fortune smiled on her at last and the chance came to send her letter to the Paintrock jail and a messenger to town bearing word of the treasure Cora intended to sell.

And so Cora stopped beside every window whenever the rounds of her chores carried her near a frosted square of glass. There she would watch for signs of a break in the snowfall, a stretch of clear days to come, a sleigh creeping slowly down the buried track of the road. A sign—any small sign God cared to send that Cora wouldn't remain imprisoned forever in this dim house with its cold, hard-eyed mistress. A sign that she might soon put the prairie at her back and turn her face toward the beacon of the city. When necessity took Cora outdoors, she would stand for as long as she could bear the cold, gazing toward the road, with one hand raised to shield her eyes against the glare. Hope made every breath shallow in her chest. But the road to Paintrock remained untraveled, the snows deep and impassable.

Weeks dragged by, and though the snowfall did slacken and finally cease altogether—though the cloud cover lifted, revealing a sky of sharp, brittle blue, hanging high and alien above a painfully brilliant plain—still no sleigh appeared to cut across the drifts where the road ought to be. There was no use trying to ride the twenty miles to Paintrock as long as the route was buried. Cora knew that much, yet not a day passed but she looked down from her bedroom window to the horses in their paddock, shaggy and huddled against the cold, and wondered how far she could expect to ride before daylight faded. It had been years since Cora had ridden a horse; she had never been good at it. But she would gladly have gone to Paintrock herself—no need to ask Clyde for the favor—if she'd thought she could survive the journey.

In the weeks since Nettie Mae had so cruelly taunted her about the president's china, Cora had steadfastly refused to believe what the mistress of the sod house had said. Even in winter, there was no lack of work to be done, and as long as Cora kept her hands and thoughts occupied with mending or baking, she could convince herself that President Grant's gift had been kindly intended. But when night fell—when Cora had washed the children's faces and heard their prayers and tucked them into their beds, when she lay abed herself, with Beulah already sighing in the sleep that came so easily to the young—Cora found herself haunted by a suspicion that every word Nettie Mae had spoken was the truth. Why indeed would a man so important, so perpetually busy, go to the trouble of locating one woman in the untamed wilderness of Wyoming Territory? Why trouble with the expense of the china itself, to say nothing of its shipment? President Grant gained nothing by extending his kindness to a stranger, a woman whom he would never meet. But silencing the evidence of a family scandal—surely that would be an end to justify both the effort and the cost.

Late at night, her hands and eyes aching from hours of sewing, Cora would lie with her quilts pulled up to her chin, weeping in silent despair, willing herself not to sob lest the bed shake and wake her daughters. She had hoped her relation to the president, now a proven fact, might secure a place for her and her children among Saint Louis society. Or if not a place among society, then at least some small measure of security: dependable work, a decent home, enough friendships that she would no longer suffer in isolation. Cora hadn't even realized she had built her hopes upon that foundation—not until Nettie Mae shattered it with the hammer of her unrelenting bitterness.

But there was no sense in denying the truth, now that the truth was plain. Cora could only scold herself for the foolish nature of her hope. Hadn't her dear old grandfather already tried to secure some place for Cora amid the finer families of the city? Hadn't he devoted his life, his every breath, to building a proper future for the cast-off girl—orphaned by one parent, unwanted by the other? If Grandfather could make nothing of Cora's connection to the Grants, then Cora herself could expect to do no better.

November gave way to December, each day weakening, the low-riding sun casting a feebler light. If there had ever been a chance that Cora might ride all the way to Paintrock, it died a little more as the days yielded to ever-longer, ever-colder nights. Yet still she paused beside every window, staring and praying. Still she watched the place where the road ought to be. And still she slipped one work-chapped hand into the pocket of her apron, checking for the letter she had written to Ernest on that dreadful day of the flood. The letter had taken up permanent residence in Cora's pocket. If any chance came to send the folio north to Paintrock, she was determined not to miss it.

On the day when a traveler did appear, Cora was so worn down by the futility of her long vigil that at first she could only stare down from her bedroom window, dull and stupid with surprise, gaping at the small figure as it crossed a wilderness of snow. The sun was preparing to set, and a wash of fleeting color lay warm and low across the winter plain. Cora pressed a hand to her lips, then blinked hard to clear her weary eyes, but this was neither vision nor dream. There was in fact a man gliding toward the Webber farm on a pair of long, shining skis. A huge black animal loped in the man's wake. Cora gasped, afraid it was a wolf, afraid the man had no inkling of its presence. But then she noted the round, blunt head, the waving tail. It was no wolf, but a large black dog. Broad paws carried it effortlessly across the snowpack.

Cora hurried from the room and caught Beulah's eye as she carried a pitcher of warm water upstairs for the night's washing.

"What is it, Ma?"

"Someone's coming. At least, someone is headed toward the farm. I don't know whether he intends to stop, but—"

Cora didn't finish her thought. She brushed past Beulah and all but ran down the stairs, determined to be waiting outside to meet the man if he turned up the lane toward the Webber farm. If he didn't, Cora would wade all the way out to the road and plead with him to speak to her, beg him to carry a message back to Paintrock. This might be the only chance God provided all the long winter through.

Benjamin and Charles were seated at the kitchen table, picking bread crumbs off their plates and licking smears of apple-peel jelly from the corners of their mouths. Benjamin started up with interest when Cora took her shawl from its hook and turned back toward the sitting room.

"Where are you going, Ma?"

"To the outhouse."

"No, you're not. You always take the kitchen door when you go to the outhouse; everyone does."

Charles sprang from his chair. "Take us with you!"

"Yes," Benjamin pleaded, "we're dreadful bored."

"It's almost time for bed. If you're bored, go upstairs and wash your faces and clean your teeth. Beulah has the water ready."

"We don't want to clean our teeth!"

"Do as I say."

The boys did not do as Cora said. They hurried into their coats and were on her heels before she could shut the front door behind her. By that time, the man on the skis had drawn abreast of the sod-brick house. He paused, resting on his poles, a featureless silhouette in the fading light. The black dog circled him, sniffing the ground, lifting its head now and then to bark with excitement.

"A dog!" Charles exclaimed. "Bully!"

"Is it the sheriff?" Benjamin asked. "Does he have news about Pa?"

"Of course not," Cora said, with no idea whether she spoke the truth. "Run along inside now, both of you."

From the second story there came a whine of damp-swollen wood against wood—a sash. Cora looked up and found Beulah's face at the open window.

"Close that window at once," Cora said. "You'll let in the cold."

"Who's coming, Ma?"

"You heard me, Beulah. Close the window."

Beulah obeyed, but moments later the front door opened, and Nettie Mae appeared with Miranda in her arms. The girl was wrapped in a quilt. She rubbed one eye, murmuring a sleepy complaint.

"I thought I heard a dog barking," Nettie Mae said. When she noticed the two figures at the end of the lane—man and dog—she added faintly, "Oh."

"I don't know who it is, or why he's come," Cora said. As she spoke, the man turned toward the house. With a flick of his poles, he began skiing up the featureless track that was the farm lane, in gentler seasons.

"Clyde!" Nettie Mae's shout was high pitched, laced with fear. "Stranger coming."

Sensing Nettie Mae's concern, the boys each seized a fistful of Cora's skirt. Miranda whimpered and hid her face against Nettie Mae's high collar. Clyde emerged from the house with his shotgun tucked under one arm and Beulah at his side.

"Who is it?" Clyde asked his mother.

Nettie Mae only shook her head.

By that time, the stranger had covered considerable ground. Though dusk was settling in, Cora could make out the man's features, for he had nearly reached the house. He was young—a few years older than Clyde—with a dark mustache and a broad grin. Evidently, he was glad to have found the Webber farm, whether it was his intended destination or merely a convenient stop along the way.

"Hullo," the stranger called.

"Wait right there, fella," Clyde answered, stepping forward so the man could see his gun.

"No need for that, Clyde Webber. Don't you recognize me?"

"Your face looks familiar, but I can't place you."

"Wilbur Christianson. We met in town a time or two before, though I confess it has been more than a year since we last set outside the general store winking at the girls."

Nettie Mae shot Clyde a furious stare. The young man's cheeks flushed, but he ignored his mother's ire.

"Wilbur—I'll be! I never knew you with that dandy new mustache." Clyde strode out into the snow, extending his hand to shake. The black dog trotted out to defend its master, growling deep in its chest.

"Come back, Mike." Wilbur put two fingers into his mouth and whistled, and the dog returned to his side. "Don't fret none over Mike. He's a good dog; just tetchy about new people till I tell him it's all right. I brought him along to keep the wolves away."

"Did you come all the way from Paintrock?"

"Yep." Wilbur eased a bulging pack from his shoulders and lowered it to the snow. "Set off just before dawn this morning. I'm right tuckered out, I don't mind telling you. Twenty miles on skis in one day. Reckon I'll still be aching by the time summer rolls around, and I still got to make it back to town."

"Tomorrow," Clyde said. "You'll stay the night here—you and Mike both."

Wilbur touched the brim of his hat. "Obliged. Truth is, if you hadn't asked me to stay, I would have insisted on it. I ain't fool enough to ski back to Paintrock in the dark. If I didn't lose my way, the wolves would get me for sure, even with Mike at my side."

Cora untangled the boys' hands from her skirt and hurried down the steps. "So you came to this farm on purpose, Mr. Christianson."

He touched his hat again. "Yes, ma'am. I guess you must be Mrs. Bemis."

"I am." The words came out as little more than a whisper. Cora's throat had gone dry.

"You're just who I come to find." Wilbur lifted his foot from the snow and tapped his pack with the edge of a ski. "Mr. Bemis sent me all this way with gifts for you and the children. For everyone, in fact." He looked up at the stoop and nodded. "Mrs. Webber. Awful sorry to hear about your husband's passing."

"For Heaven's sake," Nettie Mae said. Impatience—and no small measure of relief—had replaced her fear. "Come inside where it's warm, if you aim to do so much talking. I suppose I must bring that great wet dog of yours inside, too. I can't leave any creature out in this snow without proper shelter."

Inside, Cora took Wilbur Christianson's coat and several layers of scarves and sweaters. She laid them out before the sitting-room fire to dry while Nettie Mae assembled a hasty supper for the man and his dog. Both tucked in with obvious enthusiasm. The children lingered around the kitchen fire, eyeing the dog and Wilbur with equal curiosity.

When he had eaten his fill, Wilbur leaned back in his chair and patted his stomach. "That was a fine supper, Mrs. Webber. I'm obliged."

"You've come a long way in dreadful cold. I hope you had sense enough to bring some food in that pack of yours."

"I did, though stale biscuits and hard cheese don't make for good eating."

"Are you a peddler?" Benjamin asked.

Wilbur chuckled. "Laws, no, young man. I'm just an ordinary fella from Paintrock. But two years back, your daddy helped my daddy pay the doctor's bill when my mother fell sick. I guess I owe your family a lot, and that's why I've come." Cora had taken the chair opposite Wilbur; he offered her a nod, deferential and sympathetic. "When Mr. Bemis put word out that he needed some goods carried down here to your farm, I knew I was the man for the job."

"But to come all this way on skis," Cora said. "It would have been a thing more easily done by sleigh."

"That's as may be. But now I've had a chance to repay the kindness your husband showed to my family. I don't regret taking the journey, even if it was a long one."

Cora lowered her eyes. Her cheeks and forehead burned with the force of her blush. "I don't deserve the kindness you've shown me, Mr. Christianson."

Wilbur slapped his thigh. "Drag that pack over here, Clyde, if you're strong enough to lift it. Mr. Bemis may be shut up in jail, but he sure hasn't been idle."

Wilbur pulled a small folio from his pack and handed it to Beulah. She opened it, moved closer to the firelight, and read.

"Christmas is coming soon. I couldn't let the happy day go by without seeing that you all got a little something special. I miss all my children terrible, every day, and long to see your sweet faces again. I pray that God will keep you safe from harm till I return to you. I have many regrets but my eyes is turned to the days to come instead of the days that is passed. Remember to be good and helpful and obedient always. Your loving pa."

The children clamored around Beulah, laughing and exclaiming in wonder. Cora kept her gaze fixed resolutely on the tabletop. She could feel Nettie Mae watching—that accusatory stare like a needle digging into flesh.

When the ruckus had died back, Wilbur reached into his pack again. He produced a cloth bag that rattled when he shook it. Then he passed the bag to Charles. "What do you think's in there, little man? Open it and see!"

Charles loosened the drawstring and peered inside. "Soldiers!" He pulled one from the bag and held it up for all to see. The toy was no longer than Cora's finger, newly carved, the wood still pale. She recognized her husband's hand in the work—the fine detail and careful proportions. A hard lump formed in her throat.

"There must be ten or more," Benjamin said, looking into the bag. "We'll have a jolly time playing with these!"

"There's more," Wilbur said. He took another cloth-wrapped bundle from his pack and passed it over to Benjamin.

The cloth came away in no time, revealing three prancing wooden horses, each with a rider complete with military uniform. The boys gasped. They turned desperate, pleading eyes toward Cora.

"Run along to the sitting room and play," she said. "But you must go up to bed soon."

Miranda was clinging to Beulah's hand, staring at Wilbur and his pack with wide, solemn eyes.

"Well now, little lady," the visitor said, "your pa told me you like dollies. Is that so?"

Miranda nodded. She looked rather pale and frightened, but the fascination of the pack was too great to resist.

Wilbur extracted her gift: a miniature crib on rockers, its sides carved with vines and flowers. It was just the right size to hold the girl's rag dolls.

As Miranda carried her treasure off to play, Cora dabbed her eyes with a kerchief. "You're so kind, Mr. Christianson. You've brought so much joy to this house when it is sorely needed."

"Well, Mrs. Bemis, I guess I've got more joy left to spread."

He reached into his pack again. A set of wooden spoons came out, newly carved as the toys were, tied together by a length of twine. Cora leaned toward him, but Wilbur extended the spoons toward Nettie Mae.

"For the generous Mrs. Webber," he said. "Mr. Bemis instructed me to tell you that he knows nothing can atone for what he done. But you are a kindhearted and respectable woman, and he didn't like that you should go without something nice for Christmas."

Nettie Mae stood with her arms folded, frowning down at the spoons. Her lips pressed together tightly, and for a moment Cora feared she would burst out with some vile curse. Then her chin quivered with emotion, quickly suppressed. Nettie Mae accepted the gift, murmuring, "Thank you."

"This here is for Clyde."

Wilbur held up a small round box, turning it so the firelight gleamed over the intricate pattern of bone inlay decorating its lid and curved sides. Clyde took the box and held it for a moment in his open hand. In diameter, it was the size of his palm, and not quite two inches high.

"It's beautifully made," Clyde said. "I had no idea Mr. Bemis was such a talented woodworker."

Ernest knows, Cora realized. *He has worked out—assumed—that Nettie Mae and I have joined together in order to survive the winter. Does he have any idea how difficult it is? How I suffer under the yoke of her hatred—and how she must suffer from my constant presence, the reminder of all she has lost?*

I have no one to blame but myself. Nettie Mae has no one to blame but me. If I suffer, it is just. I have brought this pain down on my family and on the Webbers. On everyone I care for.

Nettie Mae turned away abruptly. She laid her spoons on the drain board, then excused herself to see to the children, for the boys had begun to squabble over their soldiers.

"And I've something for Miss Beulah," Wilbur said. "That must be you, young lady."

Grinning with anticipation, Beulah stepped forward, stretching out her hands before Wilbur had even reached back into his pack. He withdrew another carved wooden box, but this one was large and sturdy, more than a foot long and a good eight inches deep. The lid and sides were carved with a checkerboard pattern, stained with walnut ink. The initials *B. B.* adorned the lid in intricate script.

Beulah examined her gift in silent awe, running a forefinger along the dark depressions of the checkerboard. She lifted its tight-fitting lid and peered inside, then bent over the box to smell the resinous perfume of freshly carved wood.

"Your pa said to tell you that he knows you're a big girl now, and not much for playthings. He hopes you'll put the things you treasure most inside this box."

"Oh, thank you, Mr. Christianson. If you see my pa again, will you tell him I think it's just about perfect?"

"That I will, miss. I promise."

Beulah glanced at Cora, twisting her mouth in that thoughtful way she had. To Wilbur, she said, "Did my pa send along anything else for you to deliver?"

"There is one gift more." Wilbur drew the final offering from his pack and slid it across the table toward Cora. It was yet another box, smaller than Beulah's and not so fancifully carved.

Cora's heart leaped with sudden, painful force. She hadn't realized until that moment how much she had desired some small present from Ernest's hand. His letter had mentioned only the children; she had already resolved herself to being forgotten, discarded—and deservedly so. Yet Ernest had not forgotten her. Nor had he cast her aside. These gifts, these treasures Ernest had made with his own hands, carving away one curl of wood at a time, were his offerings of peace. Cora pictured her husband with startling clarity, seated on the edge of a hard cot that would be his only furnishing in a bare and cheerless cell. Shaping with infinite care these small yet beautiful things, thinking all the while of the family he had left and the family he had destroyed. Cora could see him—those familiar hands running over smooth wood, the frown he always wore when he was concentrating on an especially worthy task, the shavings of pine and oak scattered at his feet, one thin twist of fragrant wood fallen across the toe of his old, worn-out boot.

The family he left. The family he destroyed.

But haven't we made a kind of family, Nettie Mae and I, from the ruin of what we once were? They had fashioned themselves as one carves a stick of wood—shaping themselves from the rough, the useless, into something functional, if not good.

Cora scolded her own dangerous musings to silence. Nettie Mae wouldn't be pleased to hear such a sentiment spoken aloud. Cora blushed again. *I mustn't make her life harder than it is, more difficult to bear. God knows, I've done enough already.*

Cora took the box between trembling fingertips and pulled it closer. The sides were plain, though joined with tight, sturdy dovetails. The lid bore only a single flower—a prairie aster with a wide, dark-stained eye and six long petals. But when she opened the box, Cora's hand flew up to cover her mouth. Tears came so suddenly to her eyes that she hadn't a chance to blink them away. They spilled down her cheeks, running hot between her fingers.

Into the floor of the little wooden box, Ernest had cut two simple hearts, intertwined.

~

Early next morning, when dawn was still a dream—a half-formed idea of light, rosy and low on the pale horizon—Wilbur strapped his skis to his boots, hefted his much-lightened pack, and whistled to his dog. The children gathered on the stoop to wave good-bye, yawning and knuckling their eyes.

"Be safe," Cora said as the young man touched his hat in farewell. "And thank you for all you've done."

She wanted to say more. She ought to have said more. *I've a set of fine china, come straight from the White House, and I want to find a buyer. Put the word out, won't you, among the ranchers and their wives?* But she bit her lip to silence herself, and watched the young man glide across the snow to the place where the road should have been.

She slipped her hand into the pocket of her apron and worried at a corner of the folio, bending and folding it over the side of her finger until the paper was soft and creased like the vein of a leaf.

There would be time enough to send the letter to Ernest. If indeed she was still set on leaving for the city after all. Cora thought of the hearts intertwined inside the box. No one could see that delicate carving until the lid was lifted, but she knew the hearts were there.

10

WE'VE FINISHED HERE

There are some seeds that refuse to grow until they've been tempered.

You can lick clean the most perfect apple seed, shiny and fat, and tuck it in the soil on a perfect spring day. You may tamp the soil down till it's snug as a moth in a cocoon, and bathe your seed daily with sweet water from the well. You may whisper to your apple seed and sing it private hymns. And the sun will shine down, warm and coaxing, all the clear, blue months till autumn comes. But the sprout will not emerge. The seed sleeps on, patient in its dark sanctum, and maybe you'll forget where you planted it. Maybe you'll forget one day to carry the water and sing your songs, and the earth that surrounds your seed will crack and go dry; the worms and grubs and beetles will delve deeper into the soil and deeper still, abandoning the hope-less sterility near the surface, abandoning your seed.

It's only next spring that you'll remember, when you look down at the place where there should be only bare, wet ground, and instead you find twin leaves unfurling, long and slender, eager for the sun.

It's winter that raises the apple from the earth. The bitter cold, the ice like knives, the crystals of ice underground that cut into the hard coat and breach the soft, pale place inside where root and stem and leaf are one. The apple won't be coddled. Until it knows true suffering, the seed won't sprout at all. The tree will never live.

There are seeds that will not open till they've been cracked by fire, till the mother plants that gave them birth are burned away to ash. Others refuse to grow unless a bird has swallowed them down, or a mouse or a coyote, till they've found their way through a churning dark labyrinth, the body of another being. I have seen the tracks of cattle and buffalo through acres of mud, the land scoured and lifeless in the wake of floodwaters. But wherever the animals have stepped, their hoofprints burst with green—islands of new growth in a barren world, brought to life by the pressure, the crush of weight from above.

I will not lie and tell you that the winter passed with ease. We suffered, all of us—the children from confinement, and Clyde from uncertainty. It fell to me to watch and deflect, to guide the little ones away from Nettie Mae's temper, to guide my ma toward patience and acceptance of her place in the world. The watching made me tired, for it seemed I never could shut my eyes, even while I slept, and so it was a kind of suffering, though I did the work gladly.

But none of us struggled more than my ma and Nettie Mae.

The gifts my pa sent at Christmastime seemed to resign them both to their fates—for the winter still to pass, if not for the months that waited beyond the thaw. But though they tried to maintain a tenuous accord, I could see how both women fought against their respective natures for the sake of a fleeting, fragile peace.

My ma worked harder than I had ever seen her do. She was first to rise from bed every day and last to rest at night. Whichever of Nettie Mae's burdens Ma could take upon herself, she bore without complaint, and without Nettie Mae needing to ask. Stoking the fire, cooking the morning porridge, baking the daily bread. What meager laundry was done in the dead of winter, my ma washed and dried herself. She scoured the floors and washed up after supper; she trudged the hard-packed, slippery path to the outhouse and emptied every chamber pot, every morning. Any task my ma could take was one fewer for Nettie Mae, and so Ma worked till her fine hands cracked from the hardship and the cold, and the red-raw splits in her dry, callused skin made her wince with pain.

Nettie Mae was left to tend the children—a duty she preferred—and to teach my brothers their lessons. When she bundled up the boys and let them outside to play, or to help Clyde tend the animals, she retreated to her spinning wheel and turned the last of the autumn fleece into countless bobbins of smooth, perfect thread.

But though spinning seemed to bring Nettie Mae some comfort, and though her duties were light compared to Ma's, still I saw the pain that afflicted her. You couldn't miss it, if you stood long enough in Nettie Mae's presence. Whatever my ma did, no matter how mundane the work— kneading dough, carrying dry wood from the barn, scrubbing the kitchen floor on her knees—Nettie Mae would watch with a stricken, far-off, desolate expression. Sometimes I'd look up from my patchwork sampler to find Nettie Mae silent and staring, the treadle of her wheel gone still. I would follow the path of her eyes and there would be my mother, sweeping the ashes from the hearth, her sleeves pushed up to reveal the skin of her forearms, white and smooth as marble. You couldn't help but notice how gracefully she moved, even when her back cramped from weariness, even when her face was smudged with soot. Sometimes Nettie Mae passed by the kitchen, pretending not to look, but I would catch the sideways dart of her eyes, and I, too, could see how the downward angle of Ma's face brought out the delicacy of her small nose and the thick dark fringe of her lashes—how the candlelight by which she worked in the deepest part of winter never made her coloring sallow but golden as a locket, and the natural curls of her hair were like filigree.

I think Nettie Mae suffered worst of us all.

Many people who've met me think me a fool, and I can't say I blame them, for I speak little and don't fret much, even when others are beside themselves with worry. But I am not witless. I knew Nettie Mae harbored a powerful dislike for me. If my ma and I were the sum total of Bemises left behind when my pa went off to jail, no force on earth or in Heaven above could have induced her to extend her charity. What she did—what great sacrifices she made—she did for the sake of my brothers and Miranda. She loved little children. She ached every day for those she had lost, the trail of tiny graves she had left behind as she and Substance Webber had moved west. It was only for the sake of the boys and my little sister that Nettie Mae choked back her hatred, tolerating my ma's presence and mine. It was Nettie Mae's determination to maintain our precarious harmony—even in the face of her daily agony, the constant reminder that Cora was a prettier, lovelier, more desirable woman than she herself could ever hope to be—that kept our queer, ragtag family together.

For that was what we had become, by the time the spring thaw finally arrived: a family. We didn't love one another—at least, Nettie Mae and my ma didn't love one another—but we had grown close in the confinement of the sod-brick house, as close as natural-born family. We had each learned to rely on the strengths of those around us. The little ones knew to run to Nettie Mae for the things only she could provide—firmness, decision, certainty enough to guide them through their days. All of us depended on my ma for feeding and the maintenance of our routines, the slow-moving clock by which winter kept its monotonous time. Clyde was our protection—and, as the man of the house, the one who made whatever decisions Ma and Nettie Mae couldn't agree to with mutual interest. Ma and Nettie Mae certainly didn't delight in one another's company, but they had learned to pull together for a greater good. By winter's end, most of their sharper angles had worn away. Each had come to tolerate the other's weaknesses and habits, and perhaps that was the best any of us could hope for, given our circumstances.

I can well recall the moment when I knew we had come through the grimmest of our troubles. I had just crawled into bed—still shivering, for the blankets hadn't warmed yet—and I was watching Ma as she bent over the basin. She rubbed a sliver of cracked, soot-darkened soap against her washcloth, then worked it over her forehead and nose, clearing away the grime of another day's labor. Just as she bent to splash clean water on her *face, something outside our bedroom window gave a short, wet crack. A moment later, we heard the soft sound of impact from the ground below.*

Ma looked around, water dripping from her pointed chin. The water caught the glow of our single candle and looked like golden beads or drops of honey.

Ice is melting, I said. Icicles breaking off the eaves.

Ma stood up straight, and in that moment—just for that brief, sighing moment—the weight of winter lifted from her shoulders. She said, The thaw has come. Thank God. Not a moment too soon.

The thaw had come, sure enough—weeks later than it usually began. But once the world determined that spring must come in, the season progressed with as much speed and determination as the winter had shown. Next morning, when I went out to scratch the cows between their soft, mournful eyes and feed them their breakfast of faded hay, the snow felt loose, sliding beneath my feet. The sun had lost its weak, white outer ring of light; it shone with a new energy, so near and warm it felt like a thing remade. By day's end, the drifts had begun to recede from the side of the barn. They left dark undulations in their wake, wet impressions against the wood like ripples on the surface of a running river.

In the days that followed, as I went about my work, I could feel life rising, stretching, waking from its months of slumber. The trails we had worn through the deep snow melted away first. Compacted footing, dirty with the leavings of our animals, thinned and formed fragile, icy crusts that broke under my boots, revealing the chestnut red of clean, wet mud below. The paths broadened as drifts melted, opening wide their windows to bare and ready earth, till only the great heaps of snow Clyde had shoveled away from the sheepfold and the walls of the house remained. The yard and fields greened with tender new shoots. Under the apple trees, where the naked branches cast a net of shade across the ground and patches of snow hung on, the slim, dark spears of turkey peas and yellow bells protruded through the ice. The spring-lambing ewes grew fat and restless, complaining of their swelling udders, rubbing against the gate, longing for the freedom of the open fields.

I felt the emergence within myself, too, more forceful and definite than any other spring I could remember. Change was coming for me—for all of us, perhaps—a shift like the turning of the seasons, wise and inevitable, a change to remake a world we'd only thought we knew. I was unafraid; I welcomed the rolling of the wheel. But whether my ma and Nettie Mae were prepared, I surely couldn't say. If they could open their hands and release the old guide ropes to which they had always clung—anger and timidity, lonesomeness and fear, judgment and the fear of being judged—they would free their spirits to seek and find a new way of being, new eyes through which to see.

By late March, the garden was cleared of winter's debris, its fences had been repaired, and the hens and pigs had turned the soil. The first weeks of planting had begun. Clyde and I rummaged through the barn shelves till we found the seeds we had saved for a new year of sowing. We carried our jars across the farm—the wakened, restive farm—and the seeds made music to accompany our steps. The rattle of peas, yellow and wrinkled, and the chatter of spinach and beet seeds sounded like rain against a roof.

The restriction of cold and snow, the long slumber of our land, had kept us separated, Clyde and me. But though we had scarcely worked together since the first snowfall, we fell back into our pattern of trust, our quiet cooperation, as if the winter had never been. Side by side, we walked the garden rows, pressing our planting sticks into wet red ground, weaving trellises for the peas out of thin new twigs of willow. And then it was time for the task I loved best, the one I looked forward to all year round: committing the seeds to the soil.

Clyde tipped a jar and filled his palm with peas, then went to the head of his row and began dropping them, one by one, into the planting holes.

What are you doing? I said.

He looked up, curving one side of his mouth in that funny way he had—the way that said, *You're cracked as an old eggshell, but I like you all the same.*

Aloud, he said, *I'm planting peas. What does it look like?*

You're doing it wrong.

No, I ain't. If there's some way to plant seeds other than putting them in the ground and covering them up, I'd sure like to know it.

I laughed and left my row, joining him where he stood.

My pa showed me, I said. *You'll grow a bigger harvest if you plant enough for everyone.*

That's what I aim to do, Clyde said. *Enough for you and me and the little fellas, and Miranda, and—*

No, I said, *that's not what I mean.*

I held out my cupped hand. Clyde poured the remainder of his peas into my palm.

You must plant enough for everyone. Everyone who comes to feed from our garden. And you must let all the creatures take what they will—within the bounds of reason, of course—and if you've planted enough seeds, then you'll have plenty left untouched for the rest of us to eat. My pa showed me how to do it right when I was just a little girl.

All right, Clyde said, stepping back, hands on his hips. *Then show me, if you're so smart.*

There's a rhyme you say as you tuck the seeds in, to be sure you plant enough.

I stooped and let four peas fall from my fingers into the soil, reciting the rhyme as I did it: *One for the blackbird, one for the crow, one for the cutworm, and one to grow.*

Then I straightened and returned half the peas to Clyde.

That's mad, he said. *If four shoots come up out of one hole, they'll only crowd each other and die off.*

Not if the cutworms and the birds eat some of the shoots first. They'll eat their fill, and then move on.

You're crazy if you think we ought to feed a lot of crows and grubs.

Well, why shouldn't we?

Because they're . . .

Clyde stopped. He looked away, past the fence and the field to the river trail, to the bank where the coyote lay buried. He had almost said, *Because they're only animals.* That wasn't the sort of thing Clyde said anymore.

When he looked at me again, he shrugged, but I could see the flush fading from his cheeks. He said, *Because we got to feed our own. Let the other critters worry about their hides and their bellies; we got enough work to do around here.*

Are the birds so different from us?

He laughed. I ain't never seen you flying. Then his eyes slid down the garden row, away from me, for he couldn't bear to look at me just then. Quietly, so quiet I don't think he meant for me to hear, he said, *Though it wouldn't surprise me much if I did see you fly.*

I said, *My ma reminds me of a bird, you know. A blackbird. They love society; they never go anywhere but in a flock.*

Yes, Clyde said, *a great big hungry flock that'll strip a garden bare.*

All the more reason to plan for their visits, and plant some extra peas. I sure don't like the idea of running outside waving my bonnet whenever I see a flock of blackbirds coming.

Clyde jabbed his planting stick into the ground and leaned on it one handed, as if it was a walking cane. *All right,* he said, *if Cora's a blackbird, then what sort of bird is my mother?*

She ain't a bird at all. She's the cutworm, I guess. Gnawing and gnawing, never satisfied. She'll eat up anything you put in front of her, and it'll stick in her gullet and make her all the angrier, and then she'll go on gnawing all the more.

The smile slid from his face. He said, *My mother's got plenty of reason to be angry, and you know it.*

I know, I said. *The only wonder is that she's not any crosser. I've never seen a woman endure so much. What strength of character she has, that life hasn't broken her, and hasn't made her harder than she is. She's a right tender spirit, when she's with the little children. I don't dislike your ma, Clyde. In fact, I admire her.*

That seemed to placate him. He took up his stick again and shook the seeds in his hand. We'd best get back to work. There's plenty more to be done once we've finished here.

Clyde moved along the row in his usual brisk way, reaching down to drop the peas into the waiting soil. But each time he bent, I saw four small golden seeds fall from his fingers before he tamped the earth flat with the toe of his boot. And now and again I saw his lips move, silently reciting the words I had given him.

CORA

We've finished here. Cora took one last look at the sod-brick house as the children ran ahead, skipping and tumbling through the sage toward the Bemis farmhouse—their house, their home. *Finished, and thank God; I can be the mistress of my own life again, free from Nettie Mae's ceaseless anger.*

The little gray house was musty from months of disuse, but Cora set to work at once, tidying, sweeping, directing the children in new chores. When she grew weary of the work, she sent the children back to the sod house to gather up their toys. Then she took a rag from her apron pocket and flicked away the cobwebs that had gathered along the spindle back of her rocker. She pulled the chair across the floor to the sitting-room window that looked south, across the sage-dotted pasture to the Webber farm. There she sat, swathed in silence, save for the minute echo of wood dragged over wood, more vibration than sound. She could feel the stillness, dense and palpable against her skin, and she didn't know whether the sensation was a relief or a new sort of anxiety.

She hadn't set foot inside her own home for nigh on half a year. Reality was difficult to credit. The gray farmhouse no longer felt like her home at all, yet she must make it a home again, must resurrect the place from its sudden, untimely demise. Shrouded in dust and cobwebs, muted and begrimed by long disuse, the house was a grave-yard of memory. Here the ghosts of Cora's past walked their restless circuits, footsteps scarcely heard below the beating of her heart. When the spring wind moaned across the chimney and stirred the black ash in the hearth, Cora heard the cries of those she had wronged—long wails eloquent with pain.

A haunted place, and yet she had escaped to it gladly. The thaw was complete; Easter would soon be here. The waist-high snows had vanished from the fields, and the swollen river kept up its throaty roar. Cora had waited for this day—the day when she could escape the sod-brick house with its noise and cramp and the endless clutter of the children. A day when she could seek the refuge of peace, sink down in its forgiving depths and release some of the strain she had been carrying all those months under Nettie Mae's eye. Her home, deserted, was a sad and colorless place. But the quiet was so welcome that Cora never minded the ghosts.

Cora lifted the lid from her carved box—she had carried it with her across the fields—and traced with a finger the shape of the two hearts carved inside.

Imagine me, Ernest, relieved to find myself alone.

Merely thinking of his name, his face, his hands that had fashioned the box, brought tears to Cora's eyes. She made no attempt to hold them back, no attempt to wipe them away. In her own house, her own abandoned nothingness of a home, there was no one to see them fall. They traced hot lines down the sides of her nose, and salt stung the corners of her lips.

Was his jail cell cold? she wondered. Had the sheriff given Ernest enough blankets and warm woolen garments to see him through the winter in comfort—as much comfort as a man could expect in prison? Cora was gripped by a nightmare vision of her husband, pale and shaken, his hair long and tangled, eyes wide and unfocused with the strain of long imprisonment, the slow, monotonous torment of being held so long in a cage. Thin as a desiccated corpse. And Ernest still had time yet to serve—a year and a half more.

He'll never survive. And I will not survive. There's another winter to come before Ernest is set free. I'll spend it under Nettie Mae's roof and thumb again, unless I leave this place. Leave it all behind.

There was no need to travel all the long way back to Saint Louis. Cora saw that now. She traced the interlocked hearts again. Another tear fell. Surely the box was a sign that she had been forgiven—or would be forgiven, someday. Cora need only get herself and the children as far as Paintrock. There she could live off the sale of the president's china— and the charity of the church, if need be—until Ernest had served his time. If indeed he had forgiven Cora, or might be convinced to forgive, then he might take comfort in her proximity. She could visit him at the jail. Bring the children to visit. Surely that would cheer him. Surely it would stave off the nightmare, the madness Cora felt certain must be creeping up upon him, day by day, reaching out its clawed hands to rip away his sanity and his gentleness, and everything else that had made Ernest a good and decent man.

If he does take me back, and I end up with a broken man for a husband, then it will be no more than I deserve.

Crows called, loud and harsh, from the untended garden. Cora looked up from the box. Through the rippled window pane she could see her daughter coming across the field. Beulah had grown over the winter; she was taller now, and more womanish. Cora could see it in the subtle flare of her hips, just visible through the windblown silhouette of her skirt, and in the way the calico had begun to strain across her chest. Beulah still tied on a pinafore every morning. The one she wore now was soiled from her work in the garden; the earthy red stains looked garish against the soft mauve of her ruffle-collar dress.

I will make for her several new dresses, as soon as we settle in Paintrock, Cora decided. *And she must put away the pinafores. It's time.*

The decision flooded Cora with sorrow, for the first of her babies would never be a baby again. Her eldest was a child no longer; time had flown on its heartless and rapid wings. But this was a sadness more easily borne than the rest.

Paintrock was a far cry from Saint Louis, in every conceivable manner. It was hardly the sort of place where a young lady could expect to find good prospects for marriage. Certainly, there would be no hope for Beulah that she might rise appreciably above her present lot. In that small town she might hope to wed a farmer, or a rancher at best. But at least in Paintrock, Beulah could expect to meet some suitable young men and plan for a proper woman's future.

The sooner we've left this desolate ruin behind us, the better.

Beulah climbed the porch steps at her usual unhurried pace.

I must teach her to step lively, if she's to have any hope of catching a young man's eye. And I shall teach her how to dance. Surely Paintrock has dances. Where else might young people meet?

The door squealed open and remained open. Beulah would let in the flies, but what did it matter now?

"Are you here, Ma?"

"Yes, dear. I'm in the sitting room."

The girl entered and leaned against the wall. Somewhere between the field and the porch, Beulah had untied her braid. Now her hair fell across one shoulder, limp and plain, the braid still half-formed, loosening its weave.

"I must teach you how to fix your hair," Cora said briskly.

"Why? What's the matter with braids?"

"Nothing, if you're a farm girl."

Beulah grinned. The spring sun had already dotted a few freckles on her cheeks and the bridge of her nose.

"You must wear your bonnet in the sun, too, Beulah."

"I do, most days. I don't like to get burned."

"It's not only sunburn of which you must beware. You ought to take more care with your complexion. Freckles aren't fashionable."

The girl looked around the empty farmhouse for a moment, then raised her brows. "Who's to mind what's fashionable and what's not?"

"The boys up at Paintrock—that's who."

Beulah fixed Cora with a long, searching look. Then she said, slowly and with ponderous gravity, "Are we going to Paintrock anytime soon?"

Cora sighed and closed the lid of her box. There was no sense in trying to conceal her plans from Beulah. There never was any sense in trying to hide any truth from that girl. Cora stood. The rocker swung gently behind her, rumbling against the floor boards. "Yes," she admitted. "I've made up my mind. We will all go to Paintrock just as soon as the ground has dried enough that we may take a full wagon on the road. I've thought it all out. Clyde will drive us, for his wagon is much larger than ours. It should be able to hold almost everything we will wish to bring. I shall pay Clyde for the service as soon as I've found a buyer."

Cora didn't say what she intended to sell; there was no need. Beulah looked over her shoulder into the kitchen where the china crate stood. When she turned again to stare at Cora, her brow was furrowed in disbelief.

"You can't mean to sell the president's dishes."

"Indeed, I do mean to sell them, and I shall."

It was clear the girl was struggling to hold back a laugh. "To who?"

"To *whom*." Cora didn't wait for Beulah to respond; the girl seldom paid any heed to grammatical corrections. "I don't yet know to whom I will sell the dishes. But I am determined to find a buyer all the same."

"Whatever for, Ma? Spring is here. Me and Clyde have begun the planting. Sorry; Clyde and I. We've made it through the winter; better days are ahead. We don't need the money."

"This isn't about money." The words were very nearly a shout, high and strained. Cora pressed her lips together, fighting for control. When she trusted herself to speak coolly, she said, "Money has very little to do with my decision; though of course we will require some money if we are to survive in town. We must find a house to rent, and without a farm, we must buy our food, so there is some necessity."

Beulah straightened abruptly—lurched away from the wall. "Ma, you're talking of moving to Paintrock, not just visiting."

Cora tucked her carved box under one arm. "Indeed, I am speaking of moving to town. Why should we not live closer to your father, where we may visit him if the sheriff permits?"

"Because we have everything we need to live right here, on our farm."

"This isn't *our* farm, Beulah. Don't you see? Without your father, we cannot work our own land. We are obliged to the Webbers for their charity—slaves to them. Or so it seems to me."

"Come now, Ma. We ain't exactly living like slaves."

Something bitter stung the back of Cora's throat. She laughed. "Aren't we? Well, perhaps you haven't felt like a slave these past six months, but I have. It's no life to lead, and I've no inclination to keep Nettie Mae's house for her any longer. Not now that winter has passed and the way to town is clear."

"We'll move back here, to our own house, and wake the farm. Make it grow again."

"Who—you and me? And which of us will tend the children while we break our backs in the fields?"

"Clyde will help us, just like he did last fall."

"Don't you see?" Anguish wrung Cora's chest. The words came out strangled, as small as she felt herself to be. "I can't live here any longer. I cannot abide this place. The memories of what I once had . . . the certainty of what I've lost, what I ruined. Destroyed with my own hands, my careless, selfish hands. And that, out there." Cora pointed at the still-open door, the pale-blue light spilling across the threshold.

"The prairie?" Beulah sounded as if she couldn't be made to understand—as if no mind could wrap itself around the crux of Cora's despair.

She all but wailed her answer. "The loneliness. The isolation. For mercy's sake, girl, how can you stand it? It's nothing, *nothing*—and it goes on and on forever! I need other people around me. Grown men and women. Women who don't hate me and wish me dead in my grave. I want society, Beulah. Visitors and friends and church services on Sunday. Not this dead, lifeless plain where nothing lives but what grows between my fences. And not that terrible distance, the emptiness stretching clear out to the horizon. And beyond the horizon, too. God knows for how many miles that desolation continues."

"Ma," Beulah said softly, "the prairie isn't empty. Nor is it desolate."

"Oh, isn't it?" Cora's answering laugh was so short and bitter, she put herself in mind of Nettie Mae. "I don't see any other farms, but for the Webbers'. I never see chimney smoke rising from the plain at sunset. It is empty, Beulah. As empty as my heart."

Beulah came to her then, and eased the carved box from Cora's arms. She set it carefully on the stone hearth and took Cora by her hand.

"Come along, Ma. I want to show you something."

Cora remained rooted to the spot, though Beulah tugged her toward the door.

"What do you want to show me?"

"What's out there," Beulah said. "What's really out there, out in the world, and all around you."

Cora thought of the long horizon, its hard, straight edge unrelieved by any sign of human habitation. And the wind that blew without ceasing, the endless motion of the grass—waves—mesmerizing the eye, sickening the stomach. The whole world one color, and that the color of the void. "I already know what's out there. I don't need to see it."

But Beulah pulled her hand again, and Cora's feet moved as if under a spell. She stepped across the threshold. Prairie swept out from the porch steps. Six months, and it was already seeking to reclaim the Bemis farm. And the farm was already surrendering: pale-green spears of grass thrusting up between the cracks of the steps, low sagebrush buttercup creeping inward from the garden's edge, overtaking the ground that should have been weeded and planted. Anger flashed in Cora's breast. She thought, *After all the years we've spent working this land, shouldn't it have fought against the wilderness?* One autumn, one winter, a few scant weeks of spring, and the prairie was already reclaiming what had once belonged to the Bemis family, everything for which Ernest had so tirelessly worked.

Beulah led her down the steps into the garden—what remained of the garden.

"You say the prairie is empty and lifeless, Ma, but that's not true."

A patch of spring beauties had come up where the first row of carrots ought to have begun. Beulah stooped and picked a stem. She held it up for Cora to examine. Two flowers had already opened; the petals were as white as sun-bleached cotton, veined in vibrant pink. Beulah rolled the stem between her fingers; the blossoms and their fleshy leaves rotated slowly. Cora thought of the stars in the night sky, how she had read in a book once that they turned, too, wheeling high above the earth.

When she was young—when her marriage was new and unblemished—on the first night after Ernest had staked his claim on forty untamed acres on the bank of the river, Cora had crept from the wagon box in the dark of night. Ernest never stirred; he slept on in a nest of blankets, with Beulah and little Benjamin, a swaddled infant, safe beside him. Cora had walked as far as she'd dared from the wagon, not more than a few yards. The river glinted between the cottonwoods, for the night had been cloudless, the sky thick with stars. Magnified by moonlight, every detail of the trees had stood in sharp relief against the night. The full moon hung like a lone jewel against black velvet.

Cora had sunk down in the grass. It crepitated around her, under the hem and circumference of her nightdress. Blades and seeds pricked at her skin through the fabric. Believing then—in her youth and naivete—that she could come to love this place, Cora had lain back and looked up into the sky. And she had told herself, *I'm far from the city here, as far as I can get. Far from all the things that once distracted me. Now at last, I will be able to see the stars turning.* But they hadn't turned. The stars had remained as fixed and distant as they ever were in Saint Louis. There were more stars to be seen on the prairie—many more. So many, Cora had felt as if the stars had weight and substance, felt she could breathe them in. But if they moved, she never saw.

Now, though, as the stem of flowers turned in her daughter's fingers, the ground seemed to shift under Cora's feet. Addled, she swayed and clutched Beulah's shoulder for balance, and recalled all at once—a memory so vivid, so present she could smell the dry paper and feel the pages whispering under her fingertips—that the book had said it was the earth that turned, not the stars. If the stars seemed to move, it was only an illusion, and the world never ceased spinning.

Cora shut her eyes, swallowing again and again until the wave of nausea dissipated.

"I don't understand you," she said to Beulah, her eyes still closed.

"Of course you understand me. You're my mother."

"I don't understand why you can't see it—the emptiness. Why you don't feel it, too. It must be because you never knew the city. You were so young when we left Saint Louis, so small."

But that wasn't the reason, and Cora knew it. She remembered Beulah, no taller than her knee, brushing a tuft of grass across her lips.

Beulah answered softly, "I don't understand why you can't see what I see, Ma. But I wish you would open your eyes."

Cora squeezed them shut, more tightly still.

"I wish," Beulah said, "you could feel it. All the life around you. You miss society—I know you do. You miss the dances and the supper parties and just saying hullo to a stranger as you walk down the street. You miss the streets, the carriages, the buildings and smokestacks, the church bells ringing—"

"How did you know that?" At last, Cora opened her eyes, but only to fix her daughter with a stern look.

Beulah only smiled. "I remember the church bells, too. You might not believe me, for I know I was awful small when we left Saint Louis, but I do remember. The sound was soft and pretty. It made me feel calm."

"Yes. Calm." Placid and protected, shielded from despair.

"But, Ma, society is all around you. There ain't a powerful lot of women or men out here, I admit, but we have our horses and our cows, our chickens. And the wild birds, too—all the wild things. The prairie dogs, the jackrabbits, the deer and antelope. The wolves and coyotes, even if they are a danger now and then."

Cora folded her arms tightly—like Nettie Mae, she thought—and began striding back toward the Webber house. Beulah stuck to her side like a bedstraw seed.

"There's more life and more society besides just animals," the girl insisted. "The plants will speak to you, if you let them. And the river and the hills and the canyon. The mountains, too."

Cora cast her daughter a withering glance. "It's lucky for you we aren't in the city, for I'd send you to the hospital if we were. Such talk—imagine!"

Beulah grinned. "Lucky for sure."

"It saddens me, Beulah—truly saddens me—that you've come to think of grass and canyons and prairie dogs as good company."

"But they are good company."

"I've failed you as a mother. All the more reason to move to Paintrock. You need the company of people your age—other girls, and nice boys from good families, with whom you might make a match someday."

"If you move me to Paintrock, I'll run off. I'll go back to the prairie."

She said it with such conviction that Cora stopped dead in the field. The girl spoke the truth. Cora couldn't prevent her mouth falling open as she stared at Beulah—who went on smiling with such perfect serenity, they might have been discussing what to fix for supper. Cora seldom struck any of her children, but she raised her hand now, poised to slap the girl's cheek. Beulah stepped back, beyond Cora's reach. If Cora wished to strike her now, she would have to chase her through the field. She lowered her hand to her side.

"This is a dreadful lonely place for you, Ma, but it ain't so for me." The girl's words were soft, each one deliberate, chosen with patient care. "This is where I belong. You could belong here, too, if you'd only allow yourself to *see*."

"There is nothing to see but grass. And that ugly flatness."

"If you would listen—"

"I've listened to you endlessly, Beulah Bemis, but I will listen no more to your foolish prattling."

"I don't mean listen to me. Listen to the world speaking. It's speaking to you, Ma. It wants you to hear."

"I've no intention of listening." Where had this acerbic streak come from, she wondered. Six long months in Nettie Mae's company.

"If you did listen, you might be comforted by what you heard. Any rate, there's some weeks to go before the road will lose its mud. We can't take a wagon all the way to Paintrock till then. If you listen now, what the prairie tells you might be of some comfort. It might sustain you all those weeks, till you can finally leave. If you decide to leave after all."

Cora narrowed her eyes. She seemed to feel again the prick of sharp seeds through linen. She hadn't gone more than a few yards from the wagon that night. Any farther, and she would have lost herself to the prairie.

She said, "If I agree to listen, will you then leave me in peace? I've work to do back at Nettie Mae's house—more packing up and cleaning before we can return here to our home. Time isn't running any slower."

"I'll leave you in peace," Beulah promised.

"Very well, then."

Cora heaved a sigh, crossed her arms once more below her breasts, and stared down at the grass around her feet. A soft breeze stirred. Stems and leaves, eagerly green, hissed as they rubbed together. From the distant cottonwoods a flycatcher called, a sound like a baby's rattle.

"What do you hear?" Beulah asked.

"Wind," Cora said shortly. "Birds. That's all, child—no society." No company, no relief from years of isolation.

Beulah laughed. "You got to listen harder than that."

"Work," Cora said. "I've no more time to play games."

Beulah took her hand again. Perhaps it was only because Cora had longed so desperately for company since Ernest had gone, and the girl was growing fast now, almost a woman. Whatever the reason might have been, Beulah's touch stilled Cora, rooting her to her place. She stared at her daughter, wordless and waiting.

"Close your eyes."

Against her better judgment, Cora shut her eyes.

"Now," Beulah whispered, "listen to the world."

At first there was little that Cora hadn't heard already. The grass rustled around her hem. The flycatcher went on buzzing in the cottonwoods, indolent and droning. Cora waited, but the sounds never changed. She was on the verge of opening her eyes and scolding Beulah again when a strong gust of wind came down from the foothills. It pressed Cora's body, rocking her back on her heels, so she clutched Beulah's hand more tightly. The wind smelled of cool damp heights, of snow still clinging to the shadowy places, of cracks running deep through granite. The grass at Cora's feet hissed louder, and louder still. And all at once, with Beulah's fingers laced between her own, Cora heard not one uniform sibilance but the minute and individual striking of each blade of grass against its neighbor. She was aware—suddenly, a precarious lurch of perception—that every stalk and stem of grass was a life, an individual. And they were myriad, numerous, so countless they made the word "countless" a mockery of human understanding.

That teeming expanse of living things, reaching greedily out from the foothills to an eternity Cora couldn't comprehend. Alive, alive. Next she heard the click and clatter of sagebrush rubbing branch against knotted branch, adding its voice to the cacophony. And she thought of the sage branches, arms twisted by wind and weather, the small leaves gray and thin enough to survive the heat of summer. *We've a story to tell,* the sagebrush whispered. *Each one of us, bent and buckled, the kinks and crevices of our bodies, the broken places speaking of all that we have seen.* There was a new kind of murmuring somewhere near Cora's feet, a susurration running counter to the song of the prairie grass. Her eyes remained closed, yet somehow she could *see* the sound; knowledge of that intrusive whisper came to her as an image of the letter *S*, the letter undulating, tunneling through grass, slipping over sun-warmed earth. A snake, Cora knew. A snake was moving nearby. She would have taken fright if her eyes had been open—if she had seen its movement with her eyes. But the creature was slipping away, unhurried. It meant her no ill. The call of the flycatcher doubled, multiplied; rattling filled Cora's head. And now she could hear—could feel—five of the birds. Then six, then seven. Their voices were layered one atop another, but in her stillness, she picked them apart, peeled back the sounds like the layers of an onion. Some of the birds sang from the cottonwoods, yes. But one was perched somewhere near the Webber barn, and one among the sage on the slope at Cora's back. She picked more birdcalls out of the silence—the chorus that had once seemed to her like silence. Shrike. Vireo. The low, nasal scolding of a jay, far off and echoing, so Cora knew it must be high in the foothills, calling among the cracked red boulders. Birds she couldn't identify: a high, repetitive chitter and a mellow, liquid coo. She heard the sheep bleating and the buzz of the flies that beset them, heard the knife-edged slice of horses' tails whisking through air. *It cannot be,* she told herself. *I'm acres from the paddock, acres from the farm.* She heard the boys laughing and playing in the shade of the Webber house. And Nettie Mae speaking—not her words, but the tone of her voice, its harsh, demanding note.

A heavy throb kicked at her chest, deep inside, for something was missing from the chorus—a critical note. Ernest should have been singing with the others; the land strained to hear his voice, but he was silent, muted by distance, cut off by Cora's blundering.

This is my husband's place as much as my daughter's, Cora realized. He belonged there, like the birds and the sage and the snake slipping easily through the coolness of shadow. *If I leave the farm—even if I only go as far as Paintrock—I will lose Ernest for good, in the end.*

Cora opened her eyes and pulled her hand out of Beulah's grip.

The girl gazed at her expectantly, pale brows lifted.

"I heard nothing," Cora said. "Nothing but wind and birds."

Beulah's answering smile was slow and knowing. Cora clenched her fist, for she ached again to slap the girl. Beulah could sense the lie in her voice; Cora knew it. That lazy smile, distressing in its self-assurance, said everything the girl would not say.

Is this how she lives her life? Always so dreadfully aware?

Cora could no longer meet her daughter's eye. She turned away, pressing a hand to her forehead as if she expected to find herself burning with fever. The grass still sang around her, clamoring from all sides. She could hear the jay, far off and faint though it was.

Everything alive—all of it, the flat green monotony she had once thought so lifeless and unfeeling. The sky was a clear gentian blue, no stars visible by which to chart her movement, but Cora could have sworn in that moment she could feel the earth turning, rolling as slowly as a sleeper in a dream. All of it living, all—and life itself, the fact of it, its commonality, so vast and certain it made religion, even God Himself, small by comparison.

In such a large and living world, such a conscious and speaking world, Cora knew she would drown or suffocate before she could find her way back. To society. To the place where mankind was distinct, set properly apart, the way God had intended and ordained.

Society or your husband, the sagebrush murmured. *You cannot have both. Ernest is ours; we will not let him go.*

Cora knew it was madness to answer. She couldn't stop herself. *I need my husband. I will die without him; my children will die. I am not strong enough to weather this life on my own. I haven't the heart, haven't the courage. Ernest knows what's best to be done, how to be strong and survive. I cannot live without him—not here.*

Nevertheless, the grasses hissed, *he is ours. We will hold him here, as our roots hold the soil. And if you take your daughter away, we will call her back to us. We will call, and she will come.*

Cora curled her fists in the pocket of her apron. To Beulah she said, "We will go to Paintrock as soon as the roads are fit to travel. And, God willing, we will leave for Saint Louis the moment your father is free. If not Saint Louis, then some other city. Carbon—I don't care which city. But we are leaving, Beulah, and that is my final word."

"If we go," Beulah said, "we must leave Clyde and Nettie Mae behind."

Cora turned and strode through the murmuring grass, trying to ignore the chorus of its voices. "All for the best. If you think I'll shed a tear over parting ways with the Webbers, then you're—"

Cora stopped. She had very nearly said, *Then you're even madder than I thought you to be.*

Beulah scuttled after her mother, reaching for her arm, but Cora pulled away. "How will the Webbers work their land, without me to help?"

"It's none of my concern—not anymore."

"Ma, how can you say such a thing, after all their charity?"

"I don't care, Beulah. I'll soon be done with Nettie Mae, and glad enough for it. I've weathered her temper and her evil looks all winter long, but no more. Let her hire some boys from Paintrock if she needs the help. Or let her sell the place and move away; it's all one to me. Whatever happens to Nettie Mae, I am content to leave it in God's hands. She will be none of my concern the moment I set foot in Paintrock."

Beulah fell silent, and Cora marched on through the brush. With every stride, anxiety wrapped itself more tightly around her heart until her chest felt hot, fit to burst.

Why this fear? she asked herself, more cross than curious. *What have I to fear, now that I've made up my mind?*

Then she slowed, stopped, and gazed around the prairie with a chill of new understanding.

Something had changed. The sound was no longer the same—the murmur, the calling of the flycatchers. There was a new sound now, rushing, intense. Dangerous. Cora stared at the Webber house, straining to hear, struggling to understand.

"Ma?" Beulah paused at Cora's side. "What's the matter?"

The flycatcher on the barn roof had gone silent—flown. Horses milled in the paddock, whickering with alarm. The children were still playing in the slanted blue shadow of the sod-brick house, and Nettie Mae was busy in the yard, pinning laundry to a line. A peaceful, ordinary scene, welcome in the springtime sun. Yet something had gone wrong.

Then Cora understood—she saw. Smoke was rising from the chimney, but it was too dense, too dark, rising much too fast.

She seized Beulah by the wrist and ran.

NETTIE MAE

We've finished here, and none too soon. My home will be my own again.

Spring's emergence had cheered Nettie Mae considerably. Even the dampness of the boys' shirts felt warm and welcoming as she lifted them from her basket and pinned them to the line. The winter past had been the hardest Nettie Mae had ever known; she prayed God would never again see fit to send such a trial. But now, with the afternoon sun angling over the horse shed, falling gently upon her cheek, she felt some part of her old self give way, caving at the center like the hard crust of a melting snowdrift. The thaw had released her from winter confinement, and now something vital swelled inside, something saturated by the runoff and nurtured by the sun. The sensation rather put her in mind of her pregnancies, though of course she wasn't with child now. No, this tentative, fragile newness was something entirely her own—of her, belonging to no one else. The hard, unyielding shell that had surrounded her spirit for so many years had softened and eased. Furled roots and stem tested their confines, probing into hopeful space. What readied itself to grow inside Nettie Mae would be something new, if not better.

The boys giggled over their wooden soldiers where they lay sprawled in the newly green grass, the grass cropped by contented sheep. Nettie Mae smiled as she listened to that simple music; her eyes misted, quite against her will, and she ducked her face to scrub the tears against one shoulder. How long had it been since she had indulged in something so sweet? She snapped the wrinkles out of Charles's best blue shirt and secured it to the line. One of Miranda's little dresses came up next from the basket, all ruffles and yellow flowers. Nettie Mae pinned the frock to the line, then lingered over the pleats, arranging them carefully even though the wind would soon blow them loose.

She told me I would have a family again—that girl. That strange, slow-talking girl.

Caution surged within. Nettie Mae swallowed her hope, setting pragmatic sense in its place.

You're getting old, Nettie Mae; don't be a fool. Don't set your heart on what can never be.

She resumed hanging the wash, determined to think only of the task at hand. But she couldn't help gazing up to the barn and to the pasture beyond. Numerous and thriving, the sheep herd grazed between clumps of sage. The sow in her pen was already growing fat with a new litter of piglets. The hayfield looked like a great square of green chenille, soft and inviting in its garb of new growth. The land was ripe with promise. Surely it wasn't beyond the realm of good sense to believe that some man—a good man, better than Substance had been—might agree to wed Nettie Mae for the farm alone.

In the next moment, Nettie Mae shook her head at the futility of the dream. The land was Clyde's now. It had to be his alone. He was young, with hope for a good life ahead. Nettie Mae would never strip her last remaining child of his inheritance.

Where would you find a man, anyhow? Who would come courting all this way, even if he knew you were here . . . and what man would choose you, of all the women in this world?

She bit her lip and hung three more shirts in rapid succession. The dream was a foolish one; Nettie Mae could see that now. Such disappointments were the least one could expect when one listened to witches—or whatever that Beulah girl was. Now that starvation was no longer an imminent threat, Nettie Mae would send the whole Bemis clan packing, back to their own house and land, where they belonged. She would miss Miranda. The little boys, too, but—

"Nettie Mae!" The shout carried high and hard across the fields.

She parted two damp shirts with her hands, staring toward the pasture. The spectacle of Cora and her daughter in full, panicked flight struck her mute with shock. She hadn't seen either of them run since that dreadful day of the flood. The sight struck her as bizarre, now—Cora had always seemed too delicate for such wild displays of haste and Beulah far too careless and lazy. Yet there they both were, tearing over the field hand in hand, each carrying their skirts so high that their petticoats flashed blinding white in the sun.

"What in God's good Creation—"

Beulah was screeching, over and over, though Nettie Mae could make no sense of the noise. Had the girl blundered into a hornets' nest or been bitten by a rattler? But if she had suffered snakebite, why in the Lord's name was she running?

Then Nettie Mae realized the girl wasn't merely screaming. She was shouting a word.

"Fire!"

Slowly—numb and distant with terror—Nettie Mae turned to face her home. But no flames licked behind the windows; she could make out no signs of smoldering, no threads of smoke wending their way between the bricks of gray sod. But the cry came again, piercing through the drowsy lull of afternoon.

"Fire! Fire, Nettie Mae!"

The boys glanced up from their play, looking to Nettie Mae for reassurance. From somewhere near the lilacs, she could hear Miranda whining in wordless apprehension.

Nettie Mae turned to stare at the barn, but it, too, stood sound, as did the long shed and the horses' shelters. She shook her head vaguely at Cora and Beulah, but still they came on, both shouting now, both screaming with urgent fear.

Then something shifted, the breeze or Nettie Mae's clouded senses, and she caught the smell of smoke. Thick, hot, appallingly present—she gasped and tasted the sting of it on her tongue. Nettie Mae darted a quick, knowing glance up to the roof of the house, to the chimney. How long had it been since anyone had brushed the chimney out? A winter's worth of creosote had coated the insides of the narrow brick passage. More than that; a year's worth, for hadn't Substance cleaned it the previous spring?

God have mercy!

Nettie Mae had seen a chimney fire once, when she was a very young girl. It had been at the home of her family's nearest neighbor, and though the fire in the hearth was quickly extinguished, the flames had found their way up into the roof beams and spread outward from the chimney bricks, smoldering where no one could see. Two nights later, when the neighbors had thought the worst long past—while they were sleeping soundly in their beds—the roof had caught ablaze, ignited by some secret ember that had burned its way out from the chimney into the rafters or the attic.

Never would Nettie Mae forget the sight of that farmhouse burning across the cold Wisconsin night. Her father, who seldom slept well, had noticed the ruddy glow when he'd risen to pace the sitting room, as was his late-night custom. He had roused his own family first, then ridden his fastest horse bareback over the snowy fields—no time to waste with a saddle—and thrown open the neighbors' door, shouting to wake them. By dawn, the house had burned to the ground. Everyone had come out on their own two feet or carried in men's arms. But not every life had been spared. Susanna, the youngest child—a girl of Nettie Mae's age, and her dearest playmate—had never wakened at all. Susanna's room had been nearest the source of the flames. She had choked to death on the smoke, still lying in her bed, before anyone had known of the peril.

The pounding of feet wrenched Nettie Mae back to the present. She glanced over her shoulder in time to see Cora and Beulah rounding the long shed. They had let go of one another's hands and now flew with their skirts raised well above their knees; never in her life had Nettie Mae seen women run so swiftly. At the edge of the pasture, Clyde had thrown down his sickle and was running, too, but he wouldn't reach the house for some time yet.

Clyde doesn't know how to put out a chimney fire anyhow, Nettie Mae thought dully. Then, with a long, paralyzing chill, *Neither do I.*

She looked around the yard with dim perplexity. Why did her wits move so slowly now, when she needed them most? Miranda was half-crouched under the green-budded lilac trees, her dolls forgotten in the grass. Nettie Mae held out one hand, a summoning gesture, and Miranda tottered at once toward her. She turned to the boys, calling, "Come here at once, Benjamin, Charles. At once, do you hear?" At least her voice was smooth and controlled, if her thoughts were not.

By the time Cora and Beulah reached her, Nettie Mae had gathered the children against her skirt. They clung to her, wide eyed and frightened, whimpering at the commotion.

"Chimney fire," Cora panted. Her body had pitched forward at the waist; she braced her hands against her thighs as if to hold herself more or less upright while she heaved for breath. Her face was near as red as a peeled beet, all her fine chestnut curls in disarray.

Nettie Mae stared at Cora. Her mouth had gone dry. She could feel the color draining from her cheeks, feel herself going cold with panic and indecision. The face of her long-dead playmate emerged from memory with sudden, vicious clarity. She remembered how Susanna had looked lying in her coffin—pale and small, her pretty golden braids dulled by the soot. "I . . . I don't know what to do."

Cora's eyes locked with Nettie Mae's and hardened. The woman drew one long, steadying breath. Then she straightened deliberately—unwilted. "We must put the fire out. Now," she said. "Or it will spread."

"I know." Nettie Mae's voice rose to a frantic wail. It wasn't the sort of sound she was accustomed to making. Ringing in her own ears, the cry only frightened her all the more. "I know, I know!" She clutched the children closer about her legs. *At least they are all alive.* It was the only clear thought she had, and it repeated itself in a maniacal rhythm. *All alive. They are all alive.*

Cora took Nettie Mae by the shoulder; the woman's thumb pressed hard against her collarbone, digging into the sensitive flesh just below. Cora had never touched her before, except by cringing accident, and Nettie Mae hadn't suspected the woman could harbor such strength in her hands. She spoke, low and commanding. "Get hold of your wits, Nettie Mae, and follow me. Benjamin, Charles, Miranda—you will all remain with Beulah. Keep them away from the house, Beulah. Take them to the barn and make them stay put. When you meet Clyde, send him to me with his tallest ladder."

Beulah shepherded the children toward the barn; Nettie Mae felt their small hands tearing reluctantly from her skirt. Then Cora hooked her arm through Nettie Mae's and hauled her toward the house.

"I'll . . . I'll pump water," Nettie Mae said.

"Water won't do much good. It will take far too long to pump enough from the well and carry it inside. By then, the fire will have spread, if it hasn't already. Dry soil would do the trick, but there isn't any dry soil now. It would make a dreadful mess, anyhow."

Cora marched up the back steps and threw open the door. Smoke hung in a thick, brown haze along the ceiling. Flames leaped and billowed in the hearth; the heat battered Nettie Mae's face, filling the kitchen with sinister orange light.

"The fire hasn't spread beyond the hearth yet," Cora shouted above the roar. "But how far up the chimney it has gone, I cannot tell. Salt," she added briskly. "Salt will do. Come and help me lift that big sack of preserving salt in the pantry."

Together they skirted the hearth and made their way to the narrow confines of the pantry. Nettie Mae seized a corner of the salt bag and leaned all her weight against the burden. It slid only a few inches along the pantry floor. Cora squeezed in beside her. Sweat was already beading on her smooth, perfect brow. Cora's fingers dug into the sack; Nettie Mae saw one of her nails bend back at a sickening angle, but Cora neither complained nor released her grip.

"Now," Cora said. "Pull!"

They dragged the salt sack foot by agonizing foot out of the pantry, into the kitchen. Cora maneuvered it ever closer to the hearth. Heat assailed them like the whiplashes of Hell, but Cora never flinched. She backed away from the fire just long enough to retrieve a deep mixing bowl from its place above the drain board. Then she dipped up a load of salt and threw it onto the fire.

Nettie Mae had expected a hiss, as when water flashes to steam, but the fire merely crackled and popped. For one terrible moment, she feared the salt would have no effect. But a billow of smoke gushed from the hearth, and when it cleared, Nettie Mae could see that the worst of the flames had been smothered under a great heap of white. Cora threw another bowlful of salt; only a few small flames licked up the sides of the chimney.

Cora dropped to her knees before the hearth, tossing handfuls of salt at any burning patch of creosote she could reach. The smoke thinned to a gentle stream, but the smell of it still hung thickly in the hot confines of the kitchen. Nettie Mae reeled back, pressing a hand to her mouth, resisting the urge to vomit. She didn't know whether the foul sensation arose from the noxious, biting smoke, or from sheer, devastating relief.

"Open the sashes." Cora's face was shaded by soot, streaked here and there where sweat had run down temple and forehead. But she remained where she was, throwing out handfuls of salt now and then, leaning into that dreadful pocket of hellish heat to peer up into the chimney.

Nettie Mae did as she was told, propping the sashes of both kitchen windows wide open. She removed her apron and waved it at the ceiling, chasing smoke from the kitchen as best she could.

"Mother!" Clyde shouted from the yard. "Mother, where are you?"

Nettie Mae staggered to the open door and leaned heavily against its frame. She drank fresh air in great, shuddering gasps. Clyde had dropped a long ladder in the yard; Nettie Mae could see twin tracks through grass and mud where he had dragged it, all the way from the long shed to the stoop. He leaped up the steps two at a time and crushed Nettie Mae in his arms.

"Thank God," Clyde said. "Thank God you're all right."

She pushed away from his embrace. "Chimney fire. We've put out the flames in the hearth, but there may be more in the chimney itself. There must be more."

Cora appeared at her elbow. "Is that ladder long enough to get you up onto the roof, Clyde? Good. Set it up and climb."

"We must get water up to him," Nettie Mae said, "now that the immediate danger has passed. How shall we do it?"

"Rope," Cora answered. "Where will I find rope?"

Clyde jumped down from the steps and lifted his ladder, swinging it ponderously toward the sod wall. He spoke over his shoulder as he worked. "In the long shed, on a shelf below the table. The length with a stripe of red in the fibers is good and long. It should reach all the way up to the rooftop."

"Start pumping water now," Cora said to Nettie Mae. Then she hurried toward the shed.

Under Cora's direction, Clyde knotted one end of the rope around the handle of a pail, then carried the rope to the rooftop. Nettie Mae shuttled water from pump to ladder, dumping each bucketful into Clyde's tin pail. The pail ascended slowly to the roof. Each time Clyde emptied his pail down the mouth of the chimney, a pillar of ash and steam erupted, darkening the sky—and every time, Nettie Mae feared for her son, terrified he would breathe in that devilish cloud and lose his senses, stumble and fall from the roof. She lost count of how many circuits she made between well pump and ladder, and of how many frantic prayers she muttered while the pump handle rose and fell, as fast as her aching arms could manage. By the time no more steam rose from the chimney, Nettie Mae was weak with exhaustion, and Clyde's face and hands were blackened from his work. The sun rested low in the western sky; white moths had begun to gather above a patch of blooming phlox in the half-trampled yard.

"We've done all we can now," Cora said, dabbing sweat from her brow with a corner of her apron. "You had better climb down, Clyde. Go slowly. You're tired, and apt to put a hand or a foot wrong."

When his feet were back on blessed, solid ground, Cora sent Clyde to the barn to fetch Beulah and the children. Nettie Mae leaned against the sod wall. She tipped her head back till it met the wall, too. Her body shook so forcefully from the long exertion she couldn't trust herself to stand upright. The yard was empty save for the two of them—Cora and Nettie Mae.

The fear that had supported her, holding her upright and determined all those hours of desperate work, vanished in a blink. A dreadful trembling weakness flooded in. Nettie Mae covered her face with her hands, and felt the grime of frantic labor beneath her palms. *You will not weep,* she told herself sternly. Never would she forgive herself such a display—a show of weakness in front of Cora Bemis, the woman she was supposed to despise. *There's no sense in weeping, anyhow. The house is saved, or so we may now reasonably hope, and no one has been harmed. Pull yourself together; you aren't some soft, city-bred pet.*

"Are you well, Nettie Mae?"

Nettie Mae forced herself to stand upright. She did not quite meet Cora's eye. "Quite well, thank you. Only . . . tired."

Cora moved toward the steps. "I suppose I ought to begin cleaning up that salt. There's no sense in lighting another fire until the chimney has been brushed clean—it would only catch alight again. But it's late, and the children will be hungry. I suppose we can have bread with apple preserves and cold smoked lamb for supper. Then we can wash this soot away and go to bed. I'll be grateful for sleep, after such a trial."

Nettie Mae caught Cora by the arm before she even realized she had reached for the woman. Cora halted with one foot on the step, staring at Nettie Mae, astonished by the contact. Her face was so pale, she might have been frightened.

"We can't sleep in this house," Nettie Mae insisted. "Not tonight. Not for two nights at least."

"Why ever not?"

"This isn't the first chimney fire I've witnessed. Not in my own home, thank God—but all the same, I've seen this before. The danger is only halfway past now. If any embers have remained high up in the chimney, the heat may spread. The fire may rekindle and set the rafters alight on the second floor. The roof could blaze up before we know it—before we had a chance to escape."

Warily, Cora looked up at the eaves. "Are you certain?"

"Quite certain. If you hadn't your own house nearby, I would insist we all sleep in the barn until the danger had passed. As it is, let us move the children to your place. I will remain here, if you prefer—but the children must be kept out of harm's way."

"Don't be foolish," Cora said at once. "You will stay with us, too. You are welcome in my home, Nettie Mae. After all, it's really the least I can do; you welcomed me and mine for six months."

I never welcomed you. Guilt curdled Nettie Mae's stomach. *With good enough reason, perhaps—but still, I never welcomed you. And you bore my anger with a patience I didn't deserve.*

"Very well," Nettie Mae said quietly. "We should gather up the things we'll need. How many beds remain at your farm?"

"The boys' bed, and Beulah's. It's a shame the hour is so late now, but tomorrow Beulah and I can take the bed from our room upstairs and carry it back to my house. The thaw is over, and the planting is done—here on your land, at least. It's time we returned to our house, with thanks to you and Clyde for your generosity."

Together, they trekked across the pasture to the Bemis farm, and even the children were laden with blankets, bags of warm clothing, and baskets filled with bread and jars of preserves. By the time they reached the little gray house, dusk had dropped its fine purple veil across the land. Cora assigned Clyde to the small room that had once belonged to the boys. Benjamin and Charles complained bitterly when their mother told them they would not be permitted to sleep on the floor near Clyde.

"He's a grown man," Cora said. "Let him have a little dignity." She turned to Nettie Mae. "You must take Beulah's old bed. I am sure it wants airing, after half a year, but we haven't found the time. I hope you'll forgive any unpleasant odors. I shall sleep on the sofa—Benjamin, take a cloth and clear away the cobwebs, will you?—and we will make a good, soft nest with all these blankets, here on the sitting-room floor for the children. Beulah, lay a fire in the hearth. No one has burned a stick in this house for six months, so we needn't worry about this chimney catching alight. When you've started the fire, you can fill all of our ewers with water for washing up."

When the beds were ready and the fire laid, driving back the chill of a spring night, Cora spooned sweet apple preserves over thick slices of bread and shared around the cold, meager supper. Clyde ate his portion quickly, then scrubbed the last of the soot from his face and lit his lantern.

"I'd like to stay near the sheep for a couple of hours," he said. "The spring lambers are close to bearing now."

Nettie Mae rested her hand on his shoulder. "Don't stay out too late."

She followed Clyde to the Bemises' front porch, then stood wrapped in her shawl, holding tightly to her own body. Nettie Mae watched as her son disappeared into darkness—his fine, strong, confident form giving way to silhouette, the shadow made stark and unfamiliar by the lantern light surrounding him. He was as broad shouldered and tall as a man ought to be.

I've no child of my own any longer. I've a son—and one who has grown to manhood, thank God for that mercy. But no child left for me to hold.

Clyde's light diminished as he crossed the pasture, an orb of ruddy glow bobbing and wavering in the darkness, growing smaller and more distant with each passing heartbeat. She tore her eyes away from her son and found the sod-brick house. Her home—hers alone now, with Substance gone, with Clyde walking off into manhood's shadowed landscape. He would want a family of his own soon enough, and God alone could say where his future would take him then. But Nettie Mae's house still stood. She could make out its high, stoic walls in the faint starlight. She watched the roofline for signs of fire, but no sparks arose; no plume of smoke obscured the stars. The night held itself calm and still.

She had been spared. God had delivered blow after blow, battering Nettie Mae's spirit, testing her faith for years—all the long years of her life. But now, this once, the Lord had withheld His power. He had granted Nettie Mae mercy instead of pain.

A great surge of gratitude rose within, so sudden and strong she couldn't keep the tears from her eyes. That thankful glow settled high in her chest, suffusing Nettie Mae with a comfortable sense of satisfaction. She heard Cora's voice inside the house—speaking to the children, chiding them toward their beds—and the sound warmed Nettie Mae. A flush prickled her cheeks; her throat felt tight. For a moment, she thought it was the old feeling, the habitual rancor that had marked her every moment in Cora's presence. But no—this was a new sensation, unfamiliar but not unwelcome.

The door opened with a shy, tentative sound, then closed just as softly. Nettie Mae didn't look over her shoulder to learn who had joined her on the porch. There was no need; she already knew. Cora's steps drew nearer, as near as the woman dared, then stopped some feet away.

Nettie Mae drew in a long breath and held it while she prayed—for what, she didn't quite know. Patience? Atonement? Then she sighed, and with deliberate humility, turned to face Cora.

Cora's eyes flicked away at once. She twisted her hands inside the pocket of her apron; Nettie Mae could see Cora's fingers writhing through the blue-check fabric, agitated, a nest of snakes roused from hibernation. But Cora's carefully lowered face bore no evidence of her turmoil. She hid, as always, behind a mask of cringing delicacy.

"You're a far tougher soul than you make yourself out to be," Nettie Mae said. "You oughtn't to look so afraid. Timidity doesn't suit you, after all."

Cora looked up from the faded wood planking. She didn't shift from foot to foot, as once had been her way. She met Nettie Mae's eye with steady confidence. In the apron pocket, Cora's hands unclenched, and her slender shoulders eased all their tension.

"How did you know what to do?" Nettie Mae asked. "About the fire, I mean."

"Oh." Cora gave a gentle laugh, as if sparing a house from burning were all in a day's work. "I saw two or three such fires when I was a young woman in Saint Louis. I was just a girl, really. I must admit, I found myself surprised at how quickly the knowledge came back to me after so many years. But I remembered watching some neighbors contending with a chimney fire, one especially miserable winter. Firefighters came to the scene and instructed all the men in how to extinguish the flames. My grandfather helped. He thought it splendid, to work side by side with those strapping young firefighters. He chattered about it for days afterward, telling me everything he had learned. I never imagined I would ever use that knowledge myself, but thank God I learned enough to be of some use. Or, I ought rightfully to say, thank God my grandfather learned." She gazed out over the dark fields, pulling her shawl close around her slender frame. "Grandfather died the following autumn. That winter was the last one I spent with him—our last Christmas together. By the time he died, I had already agreed to marry Ernest. Grandfather wasn't pleased by my decision. We quarreled about it often. He had worked so hard to advance me, you see, to give me a better life. He wanted more for me than . . ."

Cora lifted a hand, gesturing at the sleeping prairie—its long black desolation, the unstirred void. By chance, she had reached just beyond the porch eaves. Thin starlight struck her palm, silver against pale skin. The delicate illumination only seemed to stress the emptiness of Cora's hand. The nothingness she held.

Cora glanced at Nettie Mae again, shrugging one shoulder reflexively, a twitch of discomfort. "I'm sorry," she said. "You've no interest in hearing my talk."

"It's all right," Nettie Mae said at once. "I don't mind." In fact, she found the woman's voice melodious, comforting. All winter through, she had thought Cora weak and stupid, worthy only of ridicule and scorn. Yet who had kept her head, faced down the fire—and who had lost her wits to fear?

I never saw your true measure, Cora. Not until today. You are as strong and capable as I. Perhaps even stronger.

That strange flush of warmth returned to Nettie Mae. She wondered at it, pressing a hand to her stomach where it stirred. What was that odd sensation, so foreign and yet so sweet?

Sisterly. That was the word that came to Nettie Mae, whispered on a half-heard breath.

She stepped closer to Cora. One step, another, closer than she had ever come before. Her scalp tingled, and her cheeks burned as they had done before the fire in her hearth. *What in the Lord's name are you doing?* Nettie Mae asked herself. But she could think of no answer.

Nettie Mae reached out and caught Cora by her shoulders. She pulled the woman roughly into her arms. Cora stiffened with surprise, but Nettie Mae pressed her all the more tightly against her bosom.

"Thank you." Awkward, faltering words, stumbling down the length of her tongue. "Thank you, Cora. You saved my home. Or I think you've saved it; another day or two, and we'll know for certain."

Cora disentangled herself from Nettie Mae's arms. Even in anemic starlight, Nettie Mae could see Cora's flush of bewilderment.

"Why—I didn't do a thing."

"Don't play at bashfulness." Nettie Mae found it something of a relief to slip back into her accustomed, harsher ways. "It was I who did nothing. I hadn't the first idea what to do, how to put out that fire so quickly. Nor would Clyde have known. Without you, I doubt my house would still be standing tonight. Everything I own would be a pile of ashes, but for you."

Cora stared down at her hem. Her mouth opened as if she might speak. Then she closed it again. Those fine, slender hands—perfect, despite their months of hard work, their grace undiminished by chapping and callus alike—slipped once more into the apron pocket.

"It's true," Nettie Mae insisted. "You may be too humble to accept my praise, but I'm not so proud that I don't know when praise is due. That is to say, I'm not so proud any longer. I was, once. I treated you dreadfully, Cora, and for far too long. My life has been—"

Nettie Mae's voice broke. For a moment, she found she couldn't speak. Words had left both her head and her heart, torn suddenly away and held beyond her desperate reach, beyond her strength to retrieve. She recalled with a shudder the times—more times than she could count—when Substance, at a loss for words to describe his lonesomeness and grief, had beaten her so badly that the breath had left her body. In those terrible moments when her ears rang with panic and she writhed on the ground, willing herself to inhale, nothing mattered but the next breath, not even the blows that continued to fall on her back, her legs, her half-covered face. The world seemed to close like a pen around her, like the tight chute into which Substance herded the cattle he would kill, one by one. All the world drawn in close, all the world throbbing in her chest, the airless void. That was how Nettie Mae felt in that moment, facing Cora directly as she had never done before, fighting against fear and shame for words that refused to come.

Patiently, Cora waited. The fists she had bunched within her pocket relaxed again; the apron went flat and smooth.

"My life has been hard," Nettie Mae managed at last. "I'm a woman who has lost much—practically everything I've ever held dear. Losing Substance, too, made me . . . more bitter than I ought to have been."

"No." Cora reached out as if she might take Nettie Mae by the arm, might offer some comfort. Her hand fell back to her side. "No; you were no crosser than I expected, Nettie Mae, and a good deal more patient and forgiving than I had any right to expect. What I did to you—to Clyde—to everyone." She faced the night once more, watching Clyde's lantern as it drifted among the distant pens. At length, Cora said, "What I did was unforgivable. I have never forgiven myself, and I expect forgiveness from no one else—least of all you."

"Perhaps what you did with Substance was wrong, but still I wouldn't have felt so hard, I think, if I hadn't already lost so much." Nettie Mae paused and swallowed, attempting to ease the knot in her throat. It only grew larger. She couldn't have said whether that stricture was born of sorrow or of the wild, sisterly affection that had flourished so suddenly in her heart. Of gratitude and gain. Tentatively, she said, "Clyde wasn't my only child, you know. I had five babies, altogether. But only Clyde has lived so long."

This time, Cora didn't restrain herself. She clutched Nettie Mae just above the elbow, and again Nettie Mae was startled by the strength of her grip. "I never knew. Oh, Nettie Mae, how dreadful."

Nettie Mae tossed her head, as if they were discussing something inconsequential—the price of cloth by the yard or when to cull the chickens. "It's behind me now. All behind me."

"No; it never can be. No mother could lose even one child and forget. To lose four . . ."

Cora released her hold on Nettie Mae's arm, but she didn't move away. The two women stood side by side now, close as they had never been in their months of mutual toil.

"Such losses are a wound not even time may heal," Cora said softly, "though I will pray every night of my life that God will grant you relief."

"Thank you. To be remembered in your prayers is a kindness I feel I don't deserve."

Cora clutched both of Nettie Mae's hands. "It's I who doesn't deserve your kindness. Even rescuing your home isn't enough to repay you for the winter, let alone to wash away the stain on my soul. What's one home saved, when I've destroyed so much with my selfishness? God have mercy on me—I never meant to hurt you, nor Ernest, nor the children. I was lonely, that's all. Lonely and craving conversation, hungry for the company of someone new. My life had grown so monotonous and small. I acted without thinking. But still, I make no excuse. I did what I did—I'll never deny it—and now I shall pay the price in shame and regret all the days of my life."

Nettie Mae could think of no reply. She squeezed Cora's hands, and wasn't certain whether she meant the small gesture as conciliation or comfort.

"You may stay under my roof as long as you wish." Cora spoke quickly now, animated by some sudden burst of energy, as if she had come all at once to a decision long pondered. "Until you're entirely sure your house is safe—longer, if you please. I intend to take the children up to Paintrock instead of Saint Louis. We'll settle in town. I intend to leave as soon as the road is fit for a heavy wagon."

The sweet unfolding in Nettie Mae's chest withered. She could feel the petals dropping. "Paintrock? Why?"

"We'll be closer to Ernest until his sentence is finished. I must apologize to him—make him forgive me, if I can. If I can't, then I shall live apart from him. But it's time we left. There's no life for me here on the prairie, out in the open wilds. And Beulah—I've her future to consider. I can't say what Ernest will choose to do, but if God has any mercy upon my unworthy soul, then Ernest will remain with me in town. If he doesn't decide to come back to this farm—without me, for I certainly will not return—then you and Clyde must have it."

"That's . . . quite generous," Nettie Mae said. And yet she couldn't feel any pleasure at the offer. She would miss Cora terribly if she pulled up stakes and moved away. Bitter as the winter had been, still Nettie Mae had found some affection for her neighbor. And the bond that united them now—of shared hardships overcome—held them more tightly together than mere friends. "But you can't simply leave, Cora. You can't just give away this farm. The decision must come from your husband, in the end."

"It will. I assure you." Cora's fingers tightened until Nettie Mae almost winced. "It will; I'll convince Ernest. I'll prove to him it's right. After all you've done for me and my children, nothing else seems just."

Nothing seems just but that you should go on living here. We have had our time as enemies. That season has passed. Now let us live in a new day. Let us come together as sisters. Nettie Mae couldn't force herself to speak those words. The pressure in her throat was too much to bear.

Cora's shoulders heaved as she drew a long, deep breath. She squeezed her eyes shut for a moment, then burst out, "I know I ought to move to town, and yet I'm afraid. Isn't that just like me? Frightened to go, frightened to stay. I'm dreadfully worried that Ernest will choose the farm over me, if I do go. Oh, Nettie Mae, I wish I had your strength and resolve!"

Bewildered, Nettie Mae shook her head. "You are strong, Cora. The way you took it all in hand, today with the fire . . . I wish you could see yourself through my eyes. The way I see you now. But I won't push you to up and leave, if you're hoping I'll make the decision for you. The truth is, I should be sorry to lose you as my neighbor. And as my friend."

"You . . . you consider me a friend?"

"How not?" Nettie Mae laughed, and the burst of humor cooled her a little, like water on a fevered brow. "You saved my home, after all."

"It would ease some of my fears," Cora said, "if I could believe I had a friend—some society."

Nettie Mae offered a wry smile. "We hardly make a society, you and I."

"But we might come to be true friends someday, close as sisters, with time."

"I would like that," Nettie Mae said quietly. "I believe I would like it very much indeed."

The lantern moved out in the darkness—Clyde making his round of the pens. Nettie Mae watched the distant orb of light for a moment, a pensive air dampening her mood. At length, she said, "But if you remain, Cora, we must be clear about our children."

"Clyde and Beulah?"

"Yes. It is for the best if they don't associate more than is strictly necessary. Clyde can't afford to be distracted now. He's trying to become a man—growing into the man he ought to be. But he isn't, just yet. God alone can say whether Clyde and Beulah will marry someday. Until the Lord makes His will known, you and I must do what our husbands cannot. I must guide a young man onto a righteous path, and you must guide your daughter."

"I see."

Nettie Mae took Cora's arm, fearful that her insistence on Clyde's safety might smother this fragile, precious thing—the tentative new friendship blossoming between them. "Please understand. I mean you no ill, and I don't wish to see Beulah hurt by the same mistakes you made."

"I don't want to see my daughter hurt, either. Oh, Nettie Mae, I can't ask you to forgive me for what I did—taking Substance away from you. But the truth is, I never cared for him. He never meant a thing to me, nor I to him; I know it's true. I'm quite sure that makes it all the more terrible . . . what I did. I dallied with your husband for no good reason, but there was never any love between us. I wanted you to know that. I wanted to tell you before I leave for Paintrock. If I leave for Paintrock."

Nettie Mae gazed out toward the steady spot of light. It no longer moved; Clyde had set his lantern on the wall of the sheepfold, perhaps, and was now keeping the long watch of hours. Minding the land—his land. She imagined her son leaning on the stone wall, quiet and self-assured. She could almost hear the rustle of animals in the night, the soft puff of breath as the herd ram drew near and smelled Clyde—not Substance—strong and vigilant in the dark. Satisfied, the ram would slip back among his ewes, and none of the animals would bleat or shiver.

"To tell you the truth," Nettie Mae said, "I didn't much care for Substance, either."

CLYDE

We've finished here. I've finished. Time to move on, to leave the past behind. My future is waiting.

Those were Clyde's first, cryptic thoughts on waking late next morning. For long moments, he lay disoriented in an unfamiliar bed, breathing in a faint scent of mildew from the unturned mattress, groggy and still half-asleep. He listened to his mother's voice. Nettie Mae was speaking to someone. Another voice answered now and then, soft and melodious, clearly belonging to a woman. But to whom?

His thoughts strayed to Beulah and he slipped into a dream of her, but in the dream all he could see was her hand running along the fringed tops of grasses. A crow called—in the dream, or in the waking world? He clawed his way up to real wakefulness, listening for the crow to call again, but the field outside the small window lay silent, lit by a gentle sun that had already climbed well toward its apex.

Nettie Mae spoke again. Clyde couldn't make out her words, but the tone caught his attention, sharpening his focus. She sounded happy. She laughed, a sound Clyde had rarely heard unless the laugh was bitter. A moment later, he realized the other voice must belong to Cora.

And this is Cora's house. That's why the bed is unfamiliar.

He rolled carefully to the edge of the bed, for his body was stiff from hours of toiling on the roof, and his chest still burned from the hot smoke he had inhaled. The future might indeed be waiting just ahead, but Clyde felt like an old man, aching and hesitant. The little fellows' bed wasn't long enough to accommodate his body; he'd been obliged to lie corner to corner, and his back and shoulders had worked themselves into further knots while he slept. Clyde stretched carefully in a slant of sunlight, then dressed and went out to the kitchen, hoping his pained hobble wasn't too readily apparent.

In the kitchen, Clyde witnessed a wonder: Nettie Mae and Cora were working together over new bread, sleeves rolled above their elbows, each pressing and rolling a ball of dough side by side at Cora's long table. A dusting of flour hung around them, silver and shimmering in the morning light. They chattered like town girls as they worked, like two old friends. They smiled—Nettie Mae *smiled* at Cora. Clyde halted on the kitchen threshold and stared, disoriented, half-convinced he was still dreaming, or that exhaustion had rotted his mind.

Nettie Mae noticed her son and turned that startling smile on him. A streak of flour lay along her jaw, which only made her seem younger, more improbably girlish.

"You're awake," she said. "We thought it best to let you sleep as long as you would. What a day we all had yesterday! Have you rested well?"

Clyde rubbed the back of his aching neck, hoping it seemed a casual gesture. "Fairly well, thanks. What time is it? How long did I sleep? The work—"

"Is all in hand," Nettie Mae said. "Don't fret about that. You were out so late tending the sheep; you needed a good long rest, Clyde."

"Beulah has gone over to milk the cows," Cora said, "and the children are out playing in the garden, though I told them to gather the eggs and feed the hens. We've fed the little ones already, but let me fix you a good breakfast. No bread and butter for you; after all that happened yesterday, you need a proper meal."

Clyde sat gratefully at the far end of the table, where the flour hadn't yet found its way. Cora left her dough to rise in a cloth-covered bowl, then busied herself with eggs and an iron skillet, which she positioned over a bed of carefully raked coals.

Nettie Mae resumed her kneading. "Did any lambs come last night?"

Clyde didn't answer right away; her air of contentment was so foreign to him, it startled the words and sense right out of his mind. "Not yet," he said at length, "but soon."

"Any trouble with varmints so far this spring?"

"No more than usual."

"That's comforting news. After such a long winter, I half expected we'd find ourselves surrounded by starving wolves."

The eggs began to crackle on the skillet. The pork fat in which Cora was frying them filled the kitchen with a salty, compelling scent, and his stomach grumbled loud enough for the women to hear.

Cora spooned the last of a hearty porridge from the kettle and set the bowl in front of Clyde. "The eggs will be ready soon, but it sounds as if you can't wait." She placed a crock of preserves on the table, too. "Strawberry. I found a few jars of good preserves in the pantry. We neglected to bring them over to your place, so they've survived the winter. Don't let the children know, or the preserves will be gone in a wink."

Clyde spooned a generous helping of strawberries over his porridge and tucked in. The preserves were so sweet that for a moment he could scarcely draw a breath. The sweetness cheered him enough to drive back some of his aches. Refreshed, he sat up straighter in his chair and watched his mother's hands working over the dough. There could be no doubt that something had lightened within her. Nettie Mae had never been derelict in duty, but neither had she worked with such pluck. Cora, too, had changed overnight. Much of her timid nature had fallen away. She moved about the kitchen with an air of authority, a straight-backed confidence that looked as foreign on Cora Bemis as cheer did on Nettie Mae. Perhaps Cora's altered demeanor was merely a matter of living under her own roof again.

She scraped the eggs from her skillet and handed the steaming plate to Clyde. Weakened as he was from the previous day's exertions, Clyde's body craved the hearty food so desperately that he had to remind himself to use his fork and to take the eggs one bite at a time. The richness of the yolks almost made him giddy.

When he had finished eating, he eased back in his chair. "When do you expect Beulah will be back with the milk?"

Clyde had done his best to sound casual, but he didn't miss the quick flick of his mother's eye, a searching consideration so brief, only Clyde could have noticed—he who had known Nettie Mae for sixteen years. *Ah,* he thought, *so Mother hasn't entirely abandoned her accustomed ways.*

"She likely won't come back any time soon," Cora said. "You know how she is—dreamy, always allowing herself to be distracted by something."

Clyde cleared his throat, stacked his dishes, and rose without any great show of haste. "Well, anyhow, I'll head over to our place and see to the sheep. Check the house, too, for any new signs of burning."

Nettie Mae spoke up at once. Her old note of sternness had returned. "You mind your work and leave Beulah to hers."

Clyde took his mother's meaning. He couldn't say what this strange new truce between the women might signify, but Nettie Mae hadn't relented. She still expected Clyde to obey her command and keep well away from Beulah.

He struck out across the pasture. The season flourished all around him, sending up that which was fresh and green in vertical bursts, a clamor of renewal striving toward an open sky. Clyde's pain relented as he walked, as his young body loosened. He was as eager as the growing field—rising, reaching for what was his, leaving the darkness of winter behind. As he drew near his own land, he noticed some boards blown askew down the side of a horse shelter, and old shingles rattling on the roof of the long shed. He must make repairs—and he would begin right away, that very afternoon, if no lambs were born. Perhaps he would build another shed this year, and a second coop for his mother's hens. His right hand tightened in a fist, longing for a hammer or a saw, ready for industrious energy after months of subdued survival.

Clyde found no sign of Beulah near the cow pen, but the cows seemed content, relaxing in the sun, cropping new growth that spilled from the edges of their paddock into the muddy enclosure. The milking was finished; otherwise, the cattle never would have been so quiet. Clyde opened the gate and the cows crowded through, jogging toward the pasture, swinging their ropy tails. When they had gone, Clyde gazed around hopefully, searching for Beulah. But she was nowhere to be seen.

At the horse corral, the herd pushed to greet him, each animal seeking his touch, his approval. When he had patted and praised them all, Clyde held Joe Buck around the neck, breathing in the familiar scent of his hide.

"We ought to go for a ride soon, old Joe. No reason; just for the fun of it." He fairly itched to get up into the foothills, to look down from their height at a fresh world waking. Joe Buck whickered in agreement.

No farm lacked for work, so Clyde didn't fritter away his time at the corral. He headed for the sod house, intent on inspecting the rafters for signs of fire, but before he reached the kitchen steps, the door of the root cellar swung open. He stifled a shout, but surprise quickly turned to a warm rush of pleasure. There Beulah stood in the doorway, blinking at him, half smiling, her brightness framed by the dark inside the cellar, so she seemed to exist in sharp clarity, the most compelling figure in a world made imperatively new.

"There you are," Clyde said. "I was looking for you."

"I put the milk pails in the cellar to keep them cool. I figured you could hitch up your float and we could drive them back to my ma's house. That'd be faster and easier than carrying them all that long way."

397

"Mother won't like it much, to see us driving together." He pressed his lips together for a moment, then blurted, against his better judgment, "I don't much care what she likes, though."

"Of course you care. She's your ma."

Clyde's face turned hot. He couldn't quite make himself look at Beulah—not directly. "But she won't be the only woman in my life forever."

Beulah made no reply. She only pushed the cellar door with her toe so it swung outward, then slowly returned to her. Clyde could feel the girl waiting, patient as ever, for him to say something more. He didn't know what to say, though, couldn't even tell what he'd meant in the first place. She pushed the door again; its iron hinges creaked as it swung.

If I knew what words I ought to say, I doubt I've got courage enough to speak them. And he didn't know what he wanted to tell Beulah, anyhow—what pounded so urgently inside his chest, flapping like a trapped bird. He had no name for the feeling. It was springtime itself, a great green flush of wild newness, an awareness of the sky. She was the prairie, and the prairie was his home. If he said those words, she wouldn't understand—not even Beulah would understand.

The girl seemed to realize Clyde had no wits to break his own silence. She left the cellar, shut its door, and moved toward him with an air of setting about her business—getting to work. Beulah pulled something small and dry from the pocket of her pinafore and held it up in those slender, sun-freckled fingers.

"See what happened," she said. "I checked this morning, when your ma got up and left my old room. Look!"

She pushed the thing she held into Clyde's hand. It was the barley head with its single long parchment leaf—the dried scrap to which the insect eggs had been affixed in their row of perfect chevrons. Gently, Clyde turned the barley leaf over and examined its underside. The ivory eggs were gone—shattered, opened to release whatever strange new life had slumbered within. Only their imprints remained, a delicate interlocking pattern of ovals set into the pale hardened stuff that had held them to the leaf.

"It's pretty," he said. "I mean, the pattern the eggs left behind. Like a picture woven into cloth."

All at once, and for no good reason Clyde could name, something thick and hot surged in his chest. The sensation so overwhelmed him that it almost brought tears to his eyes. He blinked hard, thrusting the leaf back into Beulah's hand, and turned away. He stood that way, unable to face her, but with hands braced on hips as if nothing had moved him at all. It had felt good to be moved, though, to have noticed a small, subtle beauty. Like the pain he'd had on waking, the ache was not unpleasant—a tightness of muscle that comes after hard labor, and heralds not weakness but a greater strength to come.

Clyde had always seen his farm as a necessity, the center of an unadorned life that sustained him and his mother but gave little more than what he put into it. The land had always been, in Clyde's reckoning, a simple machine—functional, but lacking in elegance or beauty. Never before had it struck him as something lovely; but now, with the pattern of life imprinted in his mind, woven into awareness, he saw not the spiritless machine but the intricacy of its workings. Sun and soil and leaf and root, animal and stone, bone, human strength, human weakness, all moved together, worked together, dictating one great pattern of dependence. Each creature and plant, every person, fitted into its place. The perfection of the weave sped his pulse; his ears roared with awe. He was pressed down into the mystery that held them all, pressed like a track in river mud. And like red mud, like the richness of damp soil, the substance into which Clyde was pushed flowed and fitted around him, held him precisely in his place, sited him in the great and intricate order.

Maybe, Clyde thought, there was no need to tell Beulah how he felt about her, after all. Maybe she already understood. Did she not feel, as Clyde felt now, the way they had fallen into this natural, perfect state—the way their two small lives fit together, just so, interlocked like the insect eggs or like the seeds at the head of the barley stem? Beulah saw. She knew. Clyde was certain of it; Beulah saw everything.

"I'll hitch up the float," he said, "and drive the milk across myself. You stay here and watch the ewes. When I get back, you can tell me which ones you think are ready to lamb."

Beulah nodded. Then she turned her face up toward the sun and stood for a moment, eyes closed, accepting the warmth of the season like a kiss on her brow. She held the barley sprig up to the sky. Her fingers opened and wind took the barley, the ever-present wind. The dry scrap tumbled out into the prairie, gone from sight in the blink of an eye, lost among all that was green and new. Then she turned away without another word, without a glance at Clyde, and left him to see to his work.

11

The Frogs Began to Sing

I can't rightly say that I have a favorite season, for each brings unique beauty and each bears a lesson for the human heart, for anyone who cares to watch the turning of the seasons closely. But spring has always held a special magic in my estimation, and that spring, when I was just on the verge of my fourteenth year, seemed brighter and more brilliant than most. After our long and arduous winter, the warmth of a strengthening sun felt as close to a blessing as anything I'd ever known. The pasture was rich with the smell of growing things, a warm, rounded spice of scent that blew in from beyond the hedge—the damp of the river, the coolness of its run, the fragrant shade beneath the cottonwood trees that trapped and held the day's hours so their memory lingered there till long after sunset. Insect life wakened and filled the air with glittering light as the sun refracted from countless veined wings. Every night, when I brought the milk cows in from the pasture, the frogs chorused up and down the length of Tensleep Creek, so the violet dusk rattled with song.

Substance had been long buried by the time spring arrived. The memory of his rule was fading from our land, from all whom his fist had struck. The lambs were born in their due course, and the flock was culled once more. This time, Clyde made the cull himself. I sat on the stone wall, warming my back in the sun, and watched as he made his way among the sheep. They never followed Clyde with the same ease they showed me; there ain't many people can claim my knack with animals. But Clyde handled every sheep with gentle care. He looked into the broad dark gaze of each member of his flock—eye to eye, life to life—and saw in them all the wonder and ecstasy of living. He hadn't my sense for knowing where a creature stood on the great, unseen spiral—how near or far death might be. Clyde only knew that his sheep felt, in their particular way, the same hopes and fears and loves and agonies that stirred in his own heart. And so he touched them with respect, and asked for their forgiveness, with no care for what his father might think if his father could see. And when he led them to the killing pen—those lambs who would die so that we might live—I saw the morning light fall bright and golden on his tears.

I came into my womanhood that spring. I was neither surprised nor dismayed when the change came upon me. During rare moments of quiet that winter, while I worked at my patchwork samplers or stirred porridge over the fire, I had felt girlhood receding, yielding to a new identity that was my own and yet unknown to me, a welcome stranger. When the change came, I found myself looking at Clyde through new eyes. He had always been my workmate, a strong back on which I could depend, and I had found some inkling before of a greater fascination, a curiosity about our differences and a certainty of the ways we were the same. Now, though, I noticed him much more—his keenness to do right, his patience and determination. I saw all the small ways he made me smile or laugh, and when we couldn't work side by side, I felt as if half the joy had drained from the world. I longed to be near him again—scrambled for any excuse—just so I could watch him smile or see the way the muscles tensed in his arms when he dug post holes or brushed his horse's coat.

My family had returned to our little gray farmhouse by the time April arrived with its blustery days and frost-hard nights. But though we no longer lived under one roof, Clyde and I still spent as much time in one another's company as we could contrive. Now each of us saw the whole of the land—that is to say, all the land our two families owned—as ours, belonging to us both. We shared responsibility for the animals and the fields. With great pride in our strength and our hard-earned knowledge, we toiled side by side, paying no heed to the boundary posts, for all that was mine belonged to Clyde, and all that was his became mine. More often than not, we worked in contented silence. There was seldom any cause to speak. Even without words, we could feel—in the tireless bending of our backs, in the rhythm of our days—the satisfaction of knowing that we could manage so much land between us.

Both farms seemed to respond eagerly to our collective stewardship. Substance's time had come to a close; all eras must end. I knew it, and Substance knew it, too, for he seldom spoke to me anymore when I carried my treasures to his grave. Our parents' hold over the earth was weakening, their grip falling loose. A new world unfolded around us, welcoming our youth, our quiet and subtle power—ushering us to our rightful place as the stewards of our land. Though the ground was still afflicted by frost, and only the hardiest peas and springtime greens could yet grow, still I sensed a readiness in the earth. The soil was waking, like the frogs from their secretive burrows. Soon the land would open wide its green throat and sing.

Nettie Mae was still rather cagey that spring, if truth be told. I think she didn't know what to make of her own confusion, and not knowing made her feel cross. She was glad to see her home returned to her, but she missed the children, too. She made it a point to come calling every few days, bringing my ma a loaf of bread when she had baked one too many, or giving the boys and Miranda sweet molasses cookies. She and my ma would stand on the porch and chat for a few minutes till Nettie Mae grew flustered by her own conflicted heart and went away again. She kept to herself for days at a stretch, but sooner or later she came calling again, and I began to wonder if she ever would allow herself to be entirely friendly with my mother—real friends, without reservation. I supposed it must take an awful long time to let go of one's old habits.

At least I could be certain that a peace had fallen between them, my ma and Nettie Mae, a truce unimpeded by anger. If either woman still felt *bitterness or shame, she kept her feelings hidden. I couldn't swear that Nettie Mae especially liked my ma—nor, come to that, could I be certain my ma actually liked Nettie Mae. But they had come to an understanding, struck a balance that kept their two families working in harmony with the land.*

Together with my brothers, Clyde and I reclaimed the garden outside the gray farmhouse and planted it well with cold-season crops. It was difficult work, for Nettie Mae's edict still stood, and we were never trusted far beyond her sight. The only days when Clyde and I could work that garden together were on Nettie Mae's wash days. As we planted and tended the peas, Clyde and I could feel her hard eyes upon us, even across the great distance of the pasture. Now and then I would straighten in my row and gaze down the length of the greening, sun-struck pasture. There I would see Nettie Mae, as still as carved marble beside her lines of flapping white sheets. She stared back at me, forever alert and watching.

Try as she might, though, Nettie Mae couldn't watch us all the time. Now and then, Clyde and I took our chances and slipped away together for a few minutes when we thought we wouldn't be missed. We came to learn one another's routines and set off alone from our separate houses at sunrise or at dusk, only to feign surprise at finding one another at the far edge of the pasture or along the river trail. Some evenings, after we'd finished our chores but before we heard the twin ringing of our two homes' supper bells, we roved up the slope of the foothills. From that vantage we looked down on the thing we had made together: one great expanse of thriving beauty with no boundary to cleave it. And sometimes, in the soft purple stillness, with bats flitting and wheeling among the lilacs—with the scent of opening flowers sweetening the air—Clyde would hold my hand.

That was the way April passed; before I knew it, spring had almost gone. But the tail end of the season held something more for me, one last bright spot of color in the most brilliant of all my springtimes.

On the first night of May, just as I shut my bedroom door to make myself ready for bed, I paused and held my breath, for I heard a powerful voice calling—a voice I didn't understand. I shut my eyes in the dim

---

confines of my room and tried to listen with greater care, but all I could hear was a thrum and a murmur, a quiet, compelling summons whose purpose I couldn't discern.

I waited till my ma was occupied with dressing the little ones for bed. Then I slipped out of my room and through the quiet house, moving on my toes so no one would hear me go. I followed the voice outside, down from the sheltered porch into the thriving garden, out into a vibrant, welcoming night. An unexpected light threw itself sideways across the fields, slanting, hard and sharp as ice even though the night was mild—the first night of the year that held any claim to warmth. That stark light seemed to make every blade of grass and every leaf of sage stand out clearly, numberless individuals among the teeming multitude.

I made my way through the rows of knee-high crops to the garden fence, where I leaned, gazing toward the river. A great silvery moon, full and white, hung low behind the cottonwoods. It was fat as the bud of a flower. The sight awed me to perfect stillness, and I smiled as I stared—an open-mouthed grin with dazed eyes, like the milk-drunk smile of a baby worshipping its mother. I had never seen the moon come so close before, had never seen it so large, so present. The cottonwoods were black sentinels arrayed before the moon's greatness; it shone so brightly between the trunks that the light seemed to bleed around the trees, softening their edges like dye running from patterned cloth.

I was drawn to that moon; it called me. I didn't think to tell my mother where I was going; I just went, stumbling out the garden gate and through the brush, faster with every step, never taking my eyes off that impossibly grand sight. The spectacle was so rare, it seemed like fairy magic—like the old Welsh tales Nettie Mae had told the children in winter, while they were gathered around the hearth. I didn't dare lower my eyes for a second, for I convinced myself that if I looked down to find my path, or if I even blinked, the moon and its intoxicating light would vanish, and I would never see such beauty again.

I wanted to see the moon over the river, to watch its reflection stirring and breaking and forming again in the endless flow of the current. I thought, *That will be a kind of magic, too; something rare enough that I'll remember the moment and think of it all my life.* So I headed toward the river trail—more or less, drifting as I was with my face turned up toward the sky. But by the time I reached the edge of the pasture, I found another magic entirely.

Hullo, Beulah.

Clyde stole my attention from the moon; he was likely the only force that could have done it. It seemed he had heard that strange voice calling, too, for though he knew it was rude not to look a lady in the eye when you made conversation, still he was half turned away, transfixed by the grand presence that hung so low in our night sky.

You came out to see it, too, I said. *You want to get as close as you can.*

Staring through the cottonwoods, Clyde nodded. He said, *I know it's foolish to go running out into the night, for you can't get no closer to the moon as long as you're still bound to the earth. But somehow it didn't seem like it was enough, just to see it from my bedroom window. A sight like this demands a fella's full attention.*

I'm headed to the river, I said. *I want to see the moonlight on the water.*

He said, *That sounds real nice.* Then he swallowed hard and glanced at me, then looked away again just as quickly. In a wary kind of voice, he added, *I guess moonlight on water can't be no prettier than moonlight on your hair, though.*

I smiled at him. Then I laughed. Clyde didn't laugh back; didn't even grin. He wasn't teasing, wasn't making any sort of joke. A fearfully sober expression came over him, and for one moment—suspended forever in my thoughts, a memory I've carried all these years—I saw his face isolated by moonlight. A slight frown, an expression of grateful suffering as he bore the singular pain of love.

Then Clyde stepped closer to me, and closer still.

When he kissed me, all the frogs on the riverbank began to sing.

NETTIE MAE

The frogs had begun to sing, but Clyde still hadn't returned to the house. Nettie Mae set aside her sewing, checked to be certain her candle was secure in its holder, and went to the back steps. The evening felt flushed, tinted by a promise of summer warmth to come, and cicadas called in eager chorus from the pasture. The lilacs by the outhouse had clamored into bloom. The air was heady with their fragrance, and bats darted among great drooping bracts of purple flowers, chasing after insects that had been drawn to the sweet scent. But the yard was empty and the paddock still. Clyde was nowhere to be seen.

He's a grown man now, she told herself, *or close enough to it.*

There was no real cause for alarm. She knew Clyde was strong enough now to protect himself from wild beasts and sensible enough to avoid danger. Yet he was still her son. She couldn't help dwelling on the dangers of night—the animals that might come down from the foothills and mountains, still hungry after that impossible winter. Wolves, mountain lions, bears wakened from hibernation. True, the bears would have rolled from their mysterious slumber weeks ago; their hunger would have abated by now. But her arms still trembled with the need to hold her child close, to shield Clyde from whatever might try to take him away.

Nettie Mae scolded her fears to silence, willing herself to proceed with rational calm. She eyed the outhouse carefully, but the diamonds cut high into the shack's wall were black—no flicker of lantern light within. The horses were settled in their pen, not pacing and whinnying as they did in the presence of wild animals. Nor did the sheep complain in their fold. Wherever Clyde had disappeared to, he had gone of his own accord—not taken by some marauding beast come down from the untamed mountains. That, at least, was some relief.

The night sky hung in a peaceful wash of violet dark, burnished by a huge, low-riding moon—one of the largest and most forcefully present Nettie Mae had ever seen. She had always enjoyed moonlight, but tonight, somehow the moon made her feel ill at ease. It was no longer the familiar white body that kept predictably to its velvet courses. Now it seemed a force unto itself, a startling new presence, a thing Nettie Mae couldn't choose to ignore.

Huddling into her shawl, her shoulders hunched under the moon's all-seeing eye, she circled the house in search of any sign of her son. A hundred potential terrors ran unchecked through her head, though she could name none of her fears. They trailed in her wake, faceless and formless, but no less menacing for that. She considered taking a lantern and crossing the field to Cora's house. Certainly, there was no need on a night so brightly lit, but the idea of holding her own light—illumination within her control—struck Nettie Mae as a comfort.

As she returned to the rear yard and climbed the kitchen steps again, Nettie Mae glanced toward the pasture once more. Clyde was clearly visible, cutting across the field toward the river trail. Nettie Mae sighed and closed her eyes for a moment, releasing that dizzy sensation of unease. The barn had merely blocked him from Nettie Mae's view a few minutes before. He was well beyond the barn now, striding through knee-deep grass, intent on some errand of his own.

Nettie Mae's relief was to be short lived. Comfort shifted at once to a wave of cold anxiety. Beulah appeared at that moment, too. The girl was walking from the direction of the Bemis house—thank God for that, for at least she hadn't been with Clyde. But from her distance and the vantage of the porch steps, Nettie Mae could see that their paths would intersect. There was no doubt the two would soon meet. By design? Had they plotted together to slip away in defiance of Nettie Mae's command? Beulah moved with her face turned up toward the sky; it was a wonder the girl hadn't tripped and fallen, for she paid more heed to the moon than to where she set her feet.

Nettie Mae swallowed hard and stared, willing Beulah to turn aside, demanding in her heart that Clyde ignore the girl and let her continue on her reckless way. But the wish was for naught. Beulah stopped near the edge of the pasture, as did Clyde, exactly where Nettie Mae had predicted their paths would cross. They were speaking, Nettie Mae realized—and standing much too close together for her liking.

Flaunting my only request. Disregarding my authority.

Her stomach twisted as she watched them together. They didn't touch, yet still there was something horribly intimate about the encounter, something irrevocable. Even across the field, Nettie Mae could read the longing in their frozen postures—a tension, a giddy wavering, as if they tipped toward some precipice—still and uncertain, anxious, yet with all the fateful momentum of a seedling rising from the soil. The sight flooded Nettie Mae with a sick dread she couldn't restrain.

I must shout, Nettie Mae thought frantically. *Tell them to stop. Demand that Clyde come home.* The next moment, she discarded the idea. There was no use shouting, no sense in raging. Clyde and the girl had grown so familiar that they would only sneak away again, endlessly defying the rules, until sin caught up with them at last.

She might go to them, Nettie Mae reasoned—cross the fields as silently as a shadow and startle them into better obedience by emerging suddenly from the purple night to bluster over their behavior. But no, they would see her coming long before she reached them. That fae child Beulah would only melt away into the moonlit grass, to work her enchantments another night.

As Nettie Mae stood transfixed by indecision—made helpless by the current of time—Clyde stepped closer to the girl. Then he bent his neck. Their lips met.

Nettie Mae clutched at her throat, uncertain whether she tried to hold back a cry of despair or whether she tried to summon one from wordless shock. Her legs quivered; she sagged against the kitchen door, staring wide eyed and weak till the kiss ended and the girl moved away.

Clyde and Beulah parted company; the boy turned his back on the moon and drifted toward the house at a slow, thoughtful pace, hands deep in the pockets of his trousers. Nettie Mae slipped into the kitchen, cognizant of nothing save a diffuse gratitude that at least Clyde was returning to his own bed, not following that girl through the moonlight toward an irrevocable tryst. There was still time to save him from ruin, but only if she acted quickly.

Nettie Mae didn't wait up for Clyde. Her anger at seeing her authority betrayed would only cause her to go cold and sarcastic, and no good would come from such a confrontation. There was little she could say to Clyde, anyhow; she put no faith in her voice, which felt small and weak, a timid thing cringing inside her chest. Instead, she took her candle and climbed the stairs to her room. She dressed for bed, and by the time she had washed her face and hands, she heard the kitchen door open, heard Clyde's boots pacing near the sitting-room hearth. She stood beside her window for a long time, listening to her son, who walked the floor below. Nettie Mae watched the moon rise ponderously over the cottonwoods, bright and vast and knowing.

∾

At breakfast, Clyde ate heartily, but Nettie Mae only picked at her food. She would not speak of the vision that had haunted her all the long night through: the scene she had witnessed at the pasture's edge. When Clyde left to tend his sheep, Nettie Mae lingered near the kitchen window, waiting until her son was well occupied in the fold. Then she crossed the field to the Bemis farm.

Best to have this business done and over with before Clyde even notices I've gone.

That cursed, unnatural moon loomed in her thoughts, coloring with a sinister light the memory of Clyde and Beulah together. As she pressed toward the neighboring land, resolve to end this trouble once and for all warred with an unexpected weight that dragged at her heart, making every step leaden and reluctant. Nettie Mae knew what she must do now—the course she must insist upon, if Clyde's future and happiness were to be preserved. Yet there was no relish in the work. How strange, to realize she had come to enjoy Cora's company, and she would miss the woman when she had gone. Yet since the night of the chimney fire, when Nettie Mae had confessed her deepest wounds to Cora and found unconditional sympathy—even the love of sisterhood—she had come to understand how dearly she had missed true fellowship and what its lack had cost her. Bitterly did Nettie Mae regret what must come next. She even mourned. But she didn't fear the loss of a friend as sorely as she feared the ruination of Clyde's future.

All too soon, Nettie Mae reached the Bemis property. She passed the garden, which was beginning to thrive as the days and nights warmed. She could hear the children playing back behind the house, and she sighed, grateful the little ones hadn't seen her coming. If they had, they would have run to her with greetings, eager to show the little treasures they'd found—smooth stones and bits of wood that seemed to have faces in the grain. Nettie Mae would miss the children most of all. They had brought unexpected joy to her life and shown her just how bleak and colorless her days had been before they had come to dwell beneath her roof.

Slowly, reluctantly, Nettie Mae ascended the porch steps. The door swung open before she could knock; Cora must have heard her coming.

She greeted Nettie Mae with a smile and a damp towel in one hand; she tossed the towel casually over her shoulder as she held the door wide.

"How good it is to see you this morning," Cora said. "Come in."

Nettie Mae smiled rather tremulously, following Cora to her kitchen. She sat at the table and accepted a cup of chicory-root tea. Cora sank down in the chair opposite with a cup of her own, already sighing in contentment, eager for whatever convivial chatter she thought Nettie Mae had brought along.

Nettie Mae turned the cup on its saucer, not certain how or where to begin. The cup and saucer were ordinary—simple white ironstone without any adornment. "Not the president's china?"

Cora flinched, and Nettie Mae was assailed by instantaneous guilt. She had tried to keep her voice neutral. Still, it was little wonder that mention of the china elicited a painful wince. The last time they had spoken of the president's extravagant gift, Nettie Mae had insisted no one would believe Cora about its provenance.

Cora recovered herself smoothly. "No; I've kept those dishes crated up all this time."

"Are you still planning to sell them?" Nettie Mae looked up from her tea. She held Cora's eye. "Still planning to move to Paintrock?"

The significance of Nettie Mae's tone wasn't lost on Cora. She blushed and looked away. With one forefinger and an absent air, she traced the cracks of the wooden tabletop. At length, Cora answered. "I suppose the road is dry enough now that we may make the trip to town."

"Yes. I intend to send Clyde with the wagon soon. I've plenty of spinning to sell, and I must replenish my pantry after such a long winter. If . . ." Nettie Mae faltered. She swallowed hard, struggling to steady her nerves. "If you really do intend to move to Paintrock, it's better done sooner than later."

Cora sat in silence for a time. The rosiness of welcome had faded from her cheeks, leaving only a pallor behind. Nettie Mae sipped her tea purely for the distraction, for the excuse not to meet Cora's eye. She tasted nothing of the chicory, its earthy spice. She tasted nothing but ashes.

Cora sighed again, but this time it was deep and sad. "It is best to go, I suppose. I still don't know whether Ernest will take me back as his wife, or whether he will come back here to the farm without me. I thought if I stayed here, I might have greater hope of atoning for what I've done and rejoining him again. I thought if I could strengthen myself—make myself into the kind of woman who can care for a farm, care for her husband's land . . ."

Cora's hands disappeared from the tabletop. Into the apron pocket, Nettie Mae assumed. By now, she had come to know all the woman's little gestures and habits—the concessions Cora made to uncertainty or fear. And how not? Friendship bred familiarity. Sisters could read one another like open books.

"I had hoped," Cora went on, "with affairs easier between we two . . . And Beulah and Clyde have started the garden so splendidly—"

"About them." Nettie Mae cleared her throat and straightened abruptly. The old rigidity had returned to her, the stiff armor of resolve. "It's because of Beulah and Clyde that I think you ought to go, Cora. You must go. I won't have Clyde's life endangered by his lust for your daughter." Heat rose suddenly in Nettie Mae's chest, a fire of much-needed outrage. And fear, too—far greater than the outrage. It was all she could do to keep the venom from her voice. "I saw them, Cora. Your daughter and my son. Kissing. Last night."

"Oh." Cora covered her mouth with a delicate hand.

"I devoutly hope that you have already spoken to your daughter about . . . the things a woman must know. If you haven't, now is the time. It may even be too late, for all I can tell, though I pray there is still time. I know only one thing for certain: Clyde and Beulah may no longer remain together. They mustn't work as they have done, side by side, always in one another's company. It isn't proper behavior, anyhow, for a girl to toil on the farm as Beulah has done all these months: mending fences, culling the sheep, goodness knows what else. I grant you, it couldn't be helped, our circumstances being what they were—the loss of our men, and that loss coming upon us all so suddenly. But we have gathered our wits now. We are back on stable ground. It's time for both our families to return to propriety, as much as we are able. That's why—" Nettie Mae hesitated, for the words caught in her throat. She had to force them from her tongue. "That's why I believe your plan to move to Paintrock is a sound one. The sooner you set about that business, the better for us all."

"But next winter," Cora said. "How will you manage, with only yourself and Clyde to do the work?"

"We've the summer and fall ahead of us yet—plenty of time to plan. I'll take a young man from town. Maybe two, if one can be convinced to sleep on a cot in the kitchen. That Wilbur Christianson had a likely look, and Clyde seems to enjoy his company. Yes, I think that will be just what Clyde needs: friends of his own age, respectable men who can be his chums until . . ." She broke off, rotating the cup on its saucer. "Until he's old enough to go courting."

He was old enough now, she knew. There was no sense denying what she had seen. It was Nettie Mae who felt unready, she who resisted the change. Perhaps she would never be able to accept losing her son, no matter when the separation came, no matter what thief stole him away—a woman or God Himself. Either way, she would lose him.

One year longer, Nettie Mae prayed, stiff and miserable in her chair, refusing to look her friend in the eye. *One more year as a mother, before my last child leaves me for a family of his own.*

Cora spoke tentatively, breaking into Nettie Mae's thoughts. "Do you really think I ought to leave? Is it truly for the best?"

Irritation flared up in Nettie Mae's stomach—at the woman's weakness, her inability to *decide,* for God's sake, to be mistress of her own life. Where was the calm air of command Cora had exhibited the night of the fire? Why did she hem and haw now, all but pleading for Nettie Mae to make the choice on her behalf? Oh, Cora Bemis belonged in a town, surely enough—in a city. She hadn't the strength for this life. She needed a man to guide her, to dictate every moment, every thought.

"I really do think you ought to move," Nettie Mae said, wondering where she found the self-control to maintain a pleasant tone.

"I suppose it's for the best, then." Cora rose from her chair, as slowly as a crone, as if Nettie Mae's words had the power to wither.

Nettie Mae also pushed herself up. Her knees trembled. For a long moment, the two women faced one another in the Bemis kitchen, still and silent among the sunbeams that danced with bright flecks of dust—an absurdly cheerful sight. The children laughed outside.

"It has been the greatest surprise of my life," Cora ventured, "to find companionship in you. Dare I call it friendship?"

Nettie Mae kept her eyes on the tabletop and the cup of chicory tea—gone cold. "I never expected to find a friend in you, either."

"I still feel as if I don't deserve the kindness you showed me all those long months of winter, the kindness you show me still."

Perplexed, frustrated by her own feelings—by her inability to name them, let alone express them—Nettie Mae turned her back on Cora and headed for the door. She paused at the threshold just long enough to say, "I'll speak to Clyde this evening, and learn when he can take the wagon north." Then she crossed the yard briskly, before the children could call out.

The walk back to her own home felt longer than it ever had before. Every step dragged through dew-damp grass; the sagebrush caught at Nettie Mae's skirt with clawed fingers and held her, slowing her down. The land felt desolate, though it was spring and new growth flourished everywhere she looked. Never in her life had she felt so isolated, so small, and the prospect of a lonely year to come—and all the many years after, without company of any kind—stretched out before her, all the way to the flat and distant horizon.

This is right, this is proper, the decision I have made. I would do anything for Clyde's sake, even cut off my own hand.

Cora may have proved a friend of sorts, but she was still a woman shadowed by shame, a woman whose morals were loose enough to mire her in sin. Her daughter was cut from the same cloth. Wasn't it always the case, that children followed in the footsteps of their parents? What came before would always come again.

Though the spring day was warm and sweet with the taste of nectar, Nettie Mae remembered the bite of frost, the first snow of autumn. She remembered the dark furrow dragged through the snow, the coyote's tail lashing as it struggled at the end of Clyde's rope. She wrapped her arms tightly around her body, but Nettie Mae couldn't stop herself from shuddering.

CORA

The frogs still chorused on the riverbank by the time Cora found herself in the garden, among the green and growing things, half-blinded by the bright morning sun.

She had hardly known what to do with herself after Nettie Mae left. For at least an hour, she drifted about the house, restlessly taking up one task after another, then abandoning her work again—the mending, the wash, dusting more cobwebs from the corners of the ceiling. She had wandered out into the garden with a vague intention of pulling up weeds from among the newly sprouted onions, but now she stood as if stunned, staring dully at the plants around her feet, listening to the distant frogs.

So Beulah had been kissing Clyde. God send that the girl had done nothing more.

Cora could have cursed herself; she ought to have known this was coming, should have suspected it once Beulah and Clyde had begun working so closely side by side. She had no reason to disbelieve Nettie Mae's accusation; Clyde and Beulah did spend far too much time in one another's company—more time even than courting couples spent. And Beulah was growing up; there was no delaying the inevitable.

Cora bent, slow and clumsy with surprise. She pulled up a handful of weeds and cast them aside. Then she straightened and sighed, uncertain what to do next, what she ought to say to Beulah—if anything at all.

Beulah had lived on the farm nearly all her years. Surely the girl understood the workings of life, how lambs and calves and babies were created. What a woman needed to know, as Nettie Mae had so delicately said, was not the mechanics of the physical act, but rather the implications. The importance of reputation—of maintaining chastity so that no one may ever accuse you of wrongdoing, so you will never be tempted to do wrong.

My daughter cannot understand the importance of reputation out here, so far away from the world. She needs the town—needs an ordinary life. Nettie Mae was correct about that.

Nettie Mae was usually correct, about everything.

Cora could only wish God had endowed her with the strength and resolve he had given to Nettie Mae. What she wouldn't have given for a fraction of her neighbor's self-confidence, the power that allowed Nettie Mae to live in isolation, without fear or sadness. Even before Cora had dwelt beneath the Webber roof, she had admired her neighbor's ability to meet each day with the same fearless mien. True, Cora hadn't known Nettie Mae well before the disaster, the fateful—and fatal—business with Substance. In all the years past, her conversations with Nettie Mae had been cordial but brief. A visit to the Webber farm to trade a few wheels of cheese for a good hank of yarn or a jaunt across the pasture to borrow a little sugar until the next trip up to town. But even in the smallest of interactions, Nettie Mae had seemed an edifice like the mountains above, constant and unshakable, never succumbing to any hardship—not even time.

Time had caught up with Cora. And with her girl.

We must go with Clyde when he drives to Paintrock, Cora decided, *and there we will remain. And if Ernest would rather have the farm than me—well, so be it. I must think of Beulah now, not my own heart. The girl still has hope for a future and a good reputation, so long as her mother doesn't spoil it. When we reach the town, we'll take up at the church—or in some charitable woman's home—until we've sold the dishes and can rent a place of our own.*

Cora wouldn't allow herself to consider what might happen if there were no homes to let in Paintrock. It had been well over a year since she had visited the town herself. Her recollection of its more populated streets was vague at best, and kept merging with memories of Saint Louis—the cobble streets, the flat sidewalks that always kept one's boots and hem dry in a rainstorm. Most of all, the homes, the families everywhere. Hundreds of homes—thousands. She would have had no trouble finding a suitable home to rent in Saint Louis. She could only pray that Paintrock would afford some likely shelter, and hope her decision was a sound one.

Cora abandoned the garden, as she had abandoned countless other tasks that morning. She returned to her kitchen and stepped into the pantry. There stood the sealed crate, at the rear of the narrow space, below the shelves that held the remainder of last autumn's preserves. She approached the crate slowly, frowning with what might have been caution, and laid a hand on its lid. Even after deciding to remain on the farm and keep good company with Nettie Mae, Cora hadn't unpacked her china. The crate had remained untouched, nailed securely shut. Perhaps God had whispered in her ear that she must leave, no matter what her heart now desired—leave for the sake of her children, and for Nettie Mae's sake.

Yet this newfound certainty that she must leave Nettie Mae behind, just when a delicate and lovely peace had grown between them, filled Cora with heartrending regret. Their friendship was still new, tentative, but she had sensed the possibility of a greater bond, a greater love to come. Something small and fragile had unfurled in the space between them, nurtured by the laughter and camaraderie they had shared in the days since the chimney fire. For eight years, Cora had hungered for society. Now that she had found it, she didn't wish to leave the familiar gray farmhouse after all. Paintrock might be home to hundreds of people, but they were all strangers to Cora. And Nettie Mae was . . . if not a friend, then at least a trusted neighbor.

Restless, Cora left the pantry and the waiting crate. She paced the kitchen, then her cramped sitting room, and found herself at the window, staring over the pasture toward the sod house. That house had once seemed distant and cold, as had Nettie Mae herself. Now it was the rock of Cora's life, her only bulwark against isolation.

If I were as brave as Nettie Mae, I could do this without fear.

But Cora was not brave. She wouldn't delude herself with pretense. She was what God had made her, nothing more. If the Creator had granted her a small portion of Nettie Mae's courage, then Cora would never have fallen prey to her own lonely heart. She would have sent Substance packing when he approached her with his shocking proposition. Ernest wouldn't have landed in the jail, with his soul forever burdened by the sin of murder.

If she were courageous, Cora wouldn't have made a ruin of so many lives.

Cora twitched away from the window and the sight of Nettie Mae's home, ready to pace again. But her toe caught the wicker of her sewing basket and she paused. Now there was a task to which she could apply herself on this dismal day. If she must be parted from her neighbor, then she would give Nettie Mae some small gift by which to remember . . . what? Their friendship?

You presume too much, Cora told herself, *in thinking Nettie Mae will wish to remember you at all.*

Yet despite that bitter thought, Cora sank into her rocker and sorted through the basket. She still had a few cards of fine silk thread, which she had bought years ago upon leaving Saint Louis. Cora had intended to save those lovely threads and embroider the finest, laciest delights for Beulah's trousseau. Crisp white kerchiefs, a ladylike chemise. Time had gotten away from her, though, and now here Beulah was, already stepping into womanhood, already taking notice of young men. *All the things I ought to have done but failed to do. The changes I should have noticed. But my eyes were closed.*

Tucked among her quilting scraps, Cora found the linen kerchief she had hemmed and folded carefully, then forgotten for goodness knew how long. She spread it across her knee, trying to smooth away the creases with her hand. Then she stretched the linen on a small wooden hoop and sorted through the silk threads, choosing only the best and brightest.

Cora rocked gently as she worked, allowing her hands to move as they would, laying in the first stitches of an unplanned motif. As needle slipped into linen and the glistening silk hissed softly through the fabric, Cora wandered through the desolate landscape of her thoughts. Amid fear of the changes that must soon come, she dwelt most often in the cramped stone confines of regret. She would have missed Nettie Mae just as much, Cora realized, even if they hadn't come to build this tentative friendship. They had shared too much not to feel something for one another. Old hatred notwithstanding, how could two women live as they had—cooperating, surviving together, beating back the terrors of isolation and darkness—without mourning their separation?

The needle jabbed Cora just beyond the rim of her thimble. She started at the pain, surprised by her carelessness—but then, she had sunk so deeply into her thoughts. She dropped the thimble into her lap and sucked her finger until no more drops of blood welled. Only then, blinking back tears, did she think to study the design she had worked into her linen square. She traced with one finger the shining silk outline of two flowers. Spring beauties, their petals veined in pink, opening atop a single stem.

CLYDE

The frogs began to sing as Clyde left the pasture behind and entered the flourishing sanctuary of the river trail. The sun had set moments before, and a long, slow-lingering golden light still stretched across the prairie, hanging among the green bristling fringes of the grass. The evening was mild, still free from the flies and mosquitoes that would all too soon make their vexing appearance and hinder a fellow as he walked. The river smelled richly of leaves and new growth, but though he breathed in the intoxicating scent deeply, it was done by habit alone. Evening's beauty couldn't reach Clyde, couldn't pierce the palisade of his thoughts. A thick, hot anger had walled him in—anger and a sinking desperation that had made him feel entirely powerless.

His mother had told him over supper, just as she rose to begin the washing up, that Cora Bemis intended to leave for Paintrock. Clyde was to drive them, and Nettie Mae would hear no argument. The matter was settled; the family would soon be gone.

Beulah would be gone.

He tried to imagine the journey, tried to prepare himself for what must come. The long road to Paintrock in a crowded, rocking wagon— all the family's possessions packed in, the children squabbling and fussing. Twenty miles of a slow, agonizing drive, no time alone to bid farewell to the girl he had come to . . . what—to love?

Maybe. Maybe it was so. He might love Beulah, Clyde supposed, and if he did, it was all the more tragic that he would have no time to bid her a proper farewell. It seemed likely he might never see her again.

Clyde had tried to argue with his mother. "What about next winter? How will we run the farm on our own?"

"The decision has been made," Nettie Mae told him. "There's no point protesting, Clyde. The Bemises are moving away, and that is that."

What cruel twist of fate was this, he wondered—to take away the girl on whom he had come to depend? His trusted partner about the farm, his only companion. The girl he had come to admire so very much, too.

Clyde wouldn't allow himself to think beyond admiration, to acknowledge that small, persistent thrill of warmth inside his chest. What use to think on it now?

Twenty miles off—might as well be twenty thousand miles.

Clyde would be lucky if he caught sight of Beulah once a month, on his routine trips to Paintrock to fetch the post or buy sugar and coffee at the general store. He tried to picture Beulah outside that very store, giggling at the window with new friends, dressed in the stylish mode of a town girl. He tried to imagine her entering the baking contest at the church, lifting a little raspberry tart in a delicate, pale hand and saying, *One would think a gentleman would remember the girl he danced with at the spring jubilee.*

The image didn't fit. The very thought of Beulah as a town girl was so absurd, Clyde might have laughed aloud, if he hadn't been too angry for laughter. He could more easily picture a pronghorn or a hawk in a fancy dress than Beulah—batting her eyes, simpering and perfumed and curled. No life suited the girl but this one, here at the edge of the wilderness, the boundary of the world. Beulah was part of this land, just as the land was part of her—intrinsic, inseparable. How would she survive in Paintrock?

And how could Clyde ever hope to get by without Beulah? The dull promise of lonely days yawned before him—an endless monotony of work unrelieved by the girl's conversation, her strange and beautiful observations, the simple comfort of her silent presence.

I don't want this life without her. The realization came to Clyde with a thump in his chest, an impact, a dull pain. He knew it was a true thought. But what was he to do? Abandon the farm—his animals? Abandon his mother? He couldn't possibly. Neither he nor Nettie Mae had any other means of living. Cora had come from a big city, Clyde knew; she understood how to get along in a place like Paintrock. Clyde and his mother would be lost there, obliged to throw themselves on the mercy of the church. Such weakness would break his mother's spirit. *I don't much like the thought of it myself.*

As the dense undergrowth of the river trail wrapped around him, some of Clyde's anger eased. Serenity had become a balm—once Beulah had shown him how to find it. He made his way to the bank and stood at the chattering, murmuring edge of the Nowood, watching the bats come down from their roosts. They flitted over the water, dark and agile, turning on the wing. The remnants of the day faded, replaced by the gentle blue half light that sweeps in just before dusk and lingers but a few rare minutes. Above the river, bands of thin cloud arched across the sky. The clouds glowed with an echo of sunset, pink and luminous, and the choir of frogs sang loudly up in the damp, green canyon. The sounds quieted Clyde's racing thoughts—the chanting of frogs, the Nowood's endless flow, even the minute cries of the bats, only the nearest of which he could hear. But the river didn't carry off his pain.

When the pink light had faded from the clouds, he left the bank and returned to the trail, and soon came upon the grave. Not his father's grave, but the one he and Beulah had made together. Spring runoff or animals had disturbed it since Clyde's last visit many weeks before. He looked around in dismay. Something had unearthed the coyote's bones, scattering them across the flat red sand. It made his heart pound, to see the creature again—this time stark and white and permanently cold. Most of what the coyote had once been was gone now, forever. The animal had come up out of the earth as if to accuse its killer.

Here on the farm, the bones seemed to say, *only you hold yourself to account. You are your father's son. This is a lonely place, and you will become what loneliness made of Substance—the hardness, the hate. That's the way of the world, the way of parents and children.*

I ain't a child any longer, Clyde said to the coyote's spirit, to his father's, to his own. *I'm no longer a boy. I will make my own world and build my own future.*

But even as he answered, Clyde suspected he had no real power to alter the path of his fate.

He gathered all the bones he could find, dropping the smallest into his pockets as he picked his way among brush and stone. Then he laid the bones out on the sand. They lay mute but sharp against the gray, dusky ground. Clyde set the ribs and pelvis and leg bones where he thought they ought to go, but he couldn't reassemble the coyote's body. Too many parts had washed away or had been carried off by scavengers. Still he worked, jaw clenched, determined. Scapula and long, graceful leg bones, the small white vertebrae like fragments of a broken crock.

Clyde would have laid out the two-headed lamb, too, but he found no trace, not a single bone. The miraculous creature had vanished from the world—so thoroughly gone Clyde wondered whether it had truly existed, or whether he and Beulah had dreamed it up together.

It can't have disappeared entirely. There must be some remains, something left for me to see.

He picked his way back down to the stony riverbed and searched among the rocks, but still he found nothing.

As Clyde returned to the grave site, however, something round and dark caught his eye, just below his feet. He halted just in time to avoid treading on the thing and took a hesitant step backward. He bent to examine the object, squinting against the oncoming night. It was the coyote's skull, and the circle of darkness that had snared Clyde's attention was an eye socket, staring back at him from among the rocks.

Clyde had to pull hard to lift the skull, for sand had accumulated around the bare bone. Dust had gathered in the seams of the bone, blushing what had once been white to canyon red. He turned the skull over in his hands. Sand and fragments of leaves ran out of the hollow braincase, pattering as they fell back to earth.

He looked down at the skull where it rested in his hands. The teeth, still sharp; the one broken flat, just as he remembered. The void where the eyes should have been, the dark hollows that still seemed to see and know. He shrank from the memory of the animal's death, yet he knew he had no right to absolve himself of that pain, the pain he had caused—so Clyde shut his eyes and remembered. He watched the scene play out on the ruthless stage of memory. He felt again the sickening rage, felt it rise and crest to overcome him. He felt satisfaction at his own brute force. And underneath the satisfaction, fear—of being weak, being alone. The need to prove, as his father had proved, that he was a man, merciless, undisputed.

When the vision had passed, Clyde stood for a moment, trembling, alone with the bats and the river. The frogs had fallen silent, stilled for a moment by the passage of some unknown creature. Clyde left the bank and carried the skull back to the other bones—the scatter of white, the body diminished. But he couldn't bring himself to set the skull in its proper place. Instead, he sent out one final apology to the coyote's spirit, then returned to the trail, delving deeper into the rank, dusky heart of the cottonwoods.

The sight of his father's grave never failed to strike Clyde with a jolt of dread or satisfaction. He never could name the emotion. He had visited only rarely since his father's death, yet the grave was ever present, a thing Clyde always felt—the absence of his father, the absence in himself, a void once occupied by Substance. The void that remained in Clyde longed to fill itself with the same dark water, the force that had filled his father. He could feel its hunger, its ravenous nature—an emptiness that couldn't be sated.

Thaw had scattered many of the artifacts Beulah had brought to the grave. Clyde didn't spare the time to hunt for those small, bright things, as he had searched for the coyote's bones. Instead, he carried the skull to the head of his father's grave. He set it atop what remained of the mound, the almost imperceptible rise—all that was left to mark the place where the man had fallen. Clyde pressed the skull down till its long teeth sank into red soil.

I ain't what you tried to make me, Clyde said to his father's shade. He didn't know whether Substance heard, whether Substance tried to listen. *I won't be you. I'll make myself into a different man, a better husband and father—good and useful and kind.*

For he would be those things; Clyde knew it. Husband and father. The time was coming, the change of his seasons. Whatever his mother might wish, however she may long to delay the inevitable, Clyde felt his future open before him like the certainty of dawn or the coming of the autumn lambs. The pattern of his life was set now. The threads had woven themselves around him, bright and intricate in the nimble fingers of time.

I've chosen, Clyde told Substance and Nettie Mae. *It's my choice to make, for this ain't your world anymore. The world has passed to me—and to Beulah. We'll make of it what we choose.*

"Clyde?"

He turned, flushing with surprise. Beulah was moving down the trail at her usual pace, the unhurried amble, the drift of a dream. Where she went, the evening didn't seem as dark, as if she pushed back the coming night with her simple, natural radiance. She was carrying flowers in both hands. She had gathered them in exuberance, Clyde could see—a tangle of color even twilight couldn't dull. All the blossoms that filled the springtime pasture, plucked without regard for order or symmetry. Spring beauties and buttercups, yellow bells, even the leggy, dark stems of saxifrage with their dull, dry stars for flowers. She must have picked them while she walked through the dusk, taking every stem that slanted or trembled across her path. Pink yarrow blushed in the half darkness; bindweed and buttercups trailed over her wrists. Angelica from the Bemis garden held up a spray of flat umbels, its tight buds yet to open. She had even collected the humblest flowers, those that were little more than weeds—pale spikes of henbit, circlets of fleabane, orange poppies, the tiny warm flames of geranium. They burst from her hands as if they still grew, as if she were the force that gave them life.

Beulah tucked her bouquet beside the coyote's skull. When she straightened, Clyde could see tears standing in her eyes. "Ma says we're to go to Paintrock after all."

"I know."

"I don't want to go, but I guess there ain't much I can do to convince her we should stay. I tried already. I tried to show her what a good place this is, how lively it is. But she won't have it any other way."

"It is a good place," Clyde said. "I always knew that, but I never saw it so clearly . . . before you and I grew close."

Beulah looked down at the grave. One of the tears broke and ran down her cheek. Clyde had never seen her weeping before, except on the night of the coyote.

"It won't be the same," he said, "living here without you."

"You'll still have the land. I hope that's some comfort. Our land and everything in it." Beulah sighed and turned to gaze north, though she couldn't see a thing from where she stood—nothing but the undergrowth. "You'll have the land, but up in Paintrock, I'll have . . . who knows what?"

"Paintrock ain't so terrible." Even as he spoke, Clyde grieved, for he knew what it would cost Beulah to be separated from the land that was herself.

"I don't want to go, Clyde. I don't want to part with this place. Or with you."

He took her hand. He could feel the faint stickiness of sap from the flowers. She smelled of yarrow, pungent, green, and sharp. They said nothing more, for it had become their custom to feel rather than speak—to sense the mood and direction of the other, to trust as the creatures of the prairie trusted to their instincts. Wordless, hand in hand, they mourned.

The clouds had moved on. Dusk muted the earth, but in the purple sky the first few stars glittered, distant and pale. A few late birds called from the cottonwoods, high in their murmuring roost. Clyde whistled—a sage thrasher's call. The river sighed between its banks; the wind moved lazily, stirring the leaves. Then, from the mouth of the canyon, a thrasher responded, high and shrill.

Beulah looked up into Clyde's face. The tears had dried on her cheeks. "I'll marry you someday."

Clyde laughed—a choking, bitter sound, for what chance had they now of marrying? "I never asked you."

"You will someday," Beulah said. "So I'm telling you now: my answer is yes."

12

A Long Way Down

Nettie Mae and my ma worked faster than I'd ever believed possible. They chose the date when they would send Clyde north to Paintrock, driving the wagon laden with all the possessions my ma wished to keep, and everything she hoped she might be able to sell. The wagon would carry us, too—the Bemises in exile, casting ourselves to the wind, praying we would land safely and take root in friendly soil. I had only three days left on my beloved land.

Ma made good use of her time. She busied herself with sorting and packing, and kept the children occupied with tasks that excited them— pounding nails into the corners of wooden crates, gathering their toys and favorite belongings. Ma worked with an energy and focus I hadn't seen in her since the winter, when she had toiled for redemption under Nettie Mae's eye.

I went on tending to the animals and crops, for though a great, heavy sadness had settled in my heart at the prospect of leaving this land—my land—still I couldn't believe it would truly come to pass. A world in which I was separated from the prairie was not a world I recognized. I didn't always see change coming before it struck, before it washed over those less observant like the sudden wall of a flash flood. But this shift in my fate seemed too big, too important, for me to have missed. So I tended the living things that were under my care and watched the passing of the days, sunrise and sunset, each afternoon warming with the golden approach of summer.

Clyde and I didn't stop meeting in secret. Knowing we might never see one another again—and if we did, it would only be in passing, on the streets of Paintrock—we slipped away every chance we got. He didn't try to kiss me again. I would have liked for him to do it, but he seemed too sad now for kissing; Clyde was as melancholy as a story that has reached its end. Instead, we walked beside the river or climbed up into the ravine to visit the place where we had found our two-headed lamb. There we laid flowers and bright stones polished by the creek, and sat in silence, hand in hand, thinking over all we had found in one another, and all we seemed poised to lose.

It don't seem right, Clyde said. He moved the flowers this way and that on the lamb's stone, rearranging them, then replacing them in their original position.

I said, I know. It positively ain't right. There's nothing right about it.

He said, Mother's worried sick that I'll court you, but what does a fella do when he turns seventeen?

She wants you to wait till you're eighteen, I guess.

He said, Mother can't keep me a boy forever.

I didn't say anything to that. I knew Nettie Mae had no real opposition to Clyde courting—at seventeen or any time thereafter. If he had chosen any other girl to court, she might have felt a trifle sad, just because her boy was growing up. But she would have accepted the inevitable, and she would have done it with good grace. No—I knew it was me she didn't like. I was the cause of Nettie Mae's endless vexation. She never had grown accustomed to my ways, my sense of the world. She had tried her level best to make peace with me over the winter, when she had given me her cloth scraps and taught me how to stitch. But Nettie Mae hadn't shed that lingering sense of mistrust. Her quiet, simmering fear of all that I was.

Clyde rose suddenly from the rock and dusted off his britches. He said, We should go for a ride. Whenever I'm troubled, Joe Buck makes me feel *better. That horse has a knack, I guess. And I'd like to go up into the hills, up high where I can see our two farms.*

He wanted to look down on the whole of us—see the unity we had made before his mother's whim tore it all asunder.

I agreed, though I hadn't ridden in a terrible long time, and that had been on Meg, the gentle gray mare who had never come back from Paintrock.

I said, Tiger is a spirited horse, and I ain't ridden him without my pa in the saddle behind me.

Clyde said, Tiger's a fine horse. I've ridden him a few times this spring—I guessed your pa would rather I rode him and kept him in shape than let him get too fat in the corral. He's got a bit of ginger, but he listens real good. He'll take care of you.

When we returned to our land, we found that Nettie Mae had gone across the pasture to help my ma with the packing.

The sooner your ma can be rid of me, the better, I said to Clyde. She's even willing to pack up our things for us, if it means she'll no longer need to trouble her mind over me.

Clyde said, Never mind that. It's a fine, sunny day. Let's enjoy the time we have left.

He sent me around to the front of the sod-brick house, where Nettie Mae wouldn't see me if she looked out from my family's porch. He saddled Joe Buck and Tiger himself, then led them around to the apple orchard. I met him there, in the dappled shade of the trees, among the last white blossoms hanging ragged from the branches. Clyde legged me up into the saddle, and Tiger danced and pawed at the ground and flexed his neck, but when I pulled on the reins and told him sharply to settle, he listened.

I hadn't set a horse's back in well over a year. The feeling was strange to me now: the shifting weight, the swaying motion, my towering height above the earth. But I liked the feeling of understanding that flowed between Tiger and me. He was a fine horse, as Clyde had said; he knew his business, his place in the world, and tried to do right by the people who tended to his *needs. But he could also taste the bright, rich air of springtime's end. It made him eager to run. And, I'm afraid, he knew me for a girl—one of the smallest and weakest of humans. He settled when I told him sternly enough, but he stamped his hoof and snorted, and seemed to sauce me, saying, I'll settle if I must, but you just mind the truth, miss: I could be off like a shot and you couldn't do much about it, except hold on and pray.*

Clyde swung up into Joe Buck's saddle with all his usual confidence and grace. He understood horses about as well as I understood the prairie, and it always pleased me to watch him ride—to see Clyde in his element, sure of his worth. He took the lead, riding out through the orchard, making for the cottonwoods well south of the river trail so no one would see us from the little gray farmhouse and catch us in our mischief. I was glad to ride behind, for it gave me more opportunity to watch Clyde doing what he did best: becoming as one with his horse, merging with the buckskin gelding, reacting to every sight and sound in perfect union, so there seemed no difference between man and animal—no difference that mattered. I stared at Clyde with a kind of desperate hunger, willing myself to memorize every movement, every second that passed. The way the shadows of the cottonwoods fell in long blue bars across his shoulders, the way he lifted a hand to steady his hat when a hard wind threatened to blow it away. If Nettie Mae had her druthers after all, and we were sent off to Paintrock the following day, I intended to carry these memories of Clyde with me, and keep them close all the years of my life.

We rode along the river, peaceful and cool, with no need for either of us to speak. The cottonwoods shielded us from Nettie Mae's view as we made our way up the slope toward the foothills. Where the trail yielded to a narrow deer track—the rocky path we'd taken up into the ravine, searching for the black-legged ewe—Clyde turned west and led the way along the hill's open face. A strong yellow sun beat down on our shoulders; I could feel its warmth through the cloth of my bonnet and under my arms, my calico dress dampened with sweat. The summer was making ready to take its rightful place in the turning of the year.

From the vantage of the foothills, we could see the two farms spread below us, small but distinct. The tracks of our routines—our daily lives— were beaten deep into the earth. We had made a permanent mark upon the land, but if a stranger were to look down from where we rode, he would never have known where one farm ended and the other began. The months we had lived since Substance's death had consumed all our boundaries. We had made of our two worlds one shared and thriving reality.

Hard to believe your house will soon be empty, Clyde said.

I didn't answer, for I still couldn't countenance Nettie Mae's plan.

Clyde said, Come on; there's something up here I been meaning to show you.

He reined his horse away from the view.

I followed Clyde along the slope and into a depression, those long tracks of shady green that branch like veins up the faces of foothills. The ground there was stony, as it was everywhere, and dotted with sage. But in the lee of a great red boulder, down in the lowest and dampest part of the depression, a tree rested sideways along the earth. It wasn't a terribly large tree, but it was old—I could tell by the bark, fissured and gray, and by the gnarled curves of its branches. The trunk had long since fallen, succumbed to lightning or wind. The tree should have died long ago, for its roots had torn free of the shallow, rocky soil and now hung suspended near the boulder, sun dried and tortured by the weather. But as I rode closer, I could see that a few slender roots had remained in their rightful place. New branches were reaching out along the earth, twisting and twining, splitting their rough bark to expose the soft, living wood underneath. The branches that survived held aloft their banners of fresh green leaves. And now, in the final days of spring, the ends of those branches were jeweled with late flowers. The still air at the heart of the gully held their delicate perfume.

A tree may fall, but if even one root remains in the soil, it will live.

Clyde said, I found it a couple years back. It's a pear tree, of all things. Lord knows how it got up here. Some rider must have spat a pear seed from his saddle years ago, and it sprouted. I've ridden up here at the end of every summer and eaten so many pears I'm fit to bust. You never tasted anything so sweet.

I saw Clyde in that way I had, my special sense of knowing—saw him as a younger boy, riding alone to this place. I watched him slide out of his saddle and step up onto the felled trunk, reach up among the vertical new branches, the life ongoing, and pick the green fruit till his hat overflowed with it, till he couldn't hold any more. I saw him bite into the flesh, but the fruit wasn't ripe after all. He had come early that year, and the pears were still tannic, almost bitter. He licked the bitten surface, the grainy white flesh, and considered the taste of the fruit. Though the pears hadn't been sweet that summer, still he ate them all.

I said, Wish there were pears on the branches now. I don't think I ever tasted a pear, but I'd like to.

They're delicious, Clyde said. Then he added, Well—they're delicious if you get them when they're ripe.

I didn't look at him then, but I said, I know.

Clyde didn't ask me how I knew. He held his tongue and accepted my words. He was remembering, just then—the taste, the solitude, the way the underripe fruit had left a funny feeling in his mouth, a tightness and tang.

Impulsively, I swung down from my saddle—sore from the long ride— and handed the reins to Clyde. Then I climbed up onto the sideways trunk, just where Clyde had stood years before to gather his pears, and I sat down among the rustle of leaves and blossoms. The prairie stretched out below the foothills—below the two of us, Clyde and me—far off into a living eternity. I knew even if the next morning saw me taken off to Paintrock, I would still be part of this land, as it was part of me. I whispered to the tree, I wish I'd found you before today. I might never see you again. And then I looked at Clyde, who was looking steadily back at me, unblinking, and I thought, You'll still be part of me, too. There's no separating us now, no matter what tomorrow brings. My roots are forever in your soil.

After a spell, Clyde said, I'm awful tempted to join you there, in the shade. But to look at the sun, my mother'll start fixing supper soon. We should go home.

Not together, I said, or your ma will be sore.

No, I guess not. I'll go back first and distract her—keep her mind fixed on me. That way she won't see you putting Tiger back in the corral. Be sure you brush him down real good, or he'll get saddle sores the next time he's ridden.

All right, I said. I know the way back. You go on home; I'll follow in half an hour or so.

And I thought, I'll always know the way back home. If I do find myself holed up in Paintrock tomorrow, what of it? Someday I'll be old enough to strike out on my own. I'll find my way back to this place. If fate is kind to me, then Clyde will still be here, and he'll still be looking out for me.

I stepped down from the tree and used the boulder to get myself back up into Tiger's saddle. Clyde urged Joe Buck to step a little closer. Then he reached across the space between us and took my hand. The earth seemed a long way down; we rode high atop the world, high above everything, just for that afternoon.

CLYDE

It was a long way down from the foothills to the river trail, but Clyde had taken the route countless times before. He made good time, choosing the easiest route along the great rocky slope almost by feel, and returned to the sod-brick house while the yard was still empty.

As Clyde stripped the saddle and blanket from Joe Buck's sweat-darkened back, Nettie Mae appeared between the barn and the long shed, returning from the Bemis farm at a leisurely pace. Clyde watched her approach over Joe Buck's withers. Guilt and wariness warred inside him. Nettie Mae moved with pronounced ease, a swinging gait Clyde had seldom seen her use, as if the stitches of her soul had come unpicked—as if everything that had once been bound so tightly within had loosened. But the nearer she came, the better Clyde could make out her face. It wore a pinched, thoughtful expression, at odds with her buoyant step. Something about the day's work had troubled her.

Nettie Mae caught his eye; Clyde nodded a greeting, working over Joe Buck with a hog's-hair brush, hoping he looked too busy for conversation. But Nettie Mae diverted from her course and approached the horse's far shoulder. She lingered there in silence, stroking the yellow hide.

"Work go well over at the Bemis place?" Clyde asked, hoping he sounded nonchalant.

Nettie Mae's only answer was to frown more deeply. She went on petting the horse as if she hadn't heard Clyde at all.

Clyde had seldom seen his mother so distracted. The phenomenon would have made him uneasy even if he didn't feel the sting of urgency, a need to hustle her into the house before Beulah could return to the corral.

He finished grooming his horse as quickly as he dared, then said, "Guess I better put him back with the rest of the herd now."

Clyde avoided glancing toward the river as he led Joe Buck to the gate. All the while, his stomach churned with anxiety. What would he do—what would he say to his mother—if Beulah showed herself among the cottonwoods just then, astride her horse, waving all the guilt she and Clyde bore together like a flag overhead? Come to that, what could he say if his mother noticed that Tiger was missing from the paddock?

But when he returned to Nettie Mae, Clyde found her still sunk in her distraction, wearing that far-off expression of vague distress.

"Just about everything is packed up now," she said. "Everything they mean to take with them to Paintrock."

Clyde nodded again.

"You'll set off tomorrow morning, won't you?"

"If that's what you want."

Nettie Mae sighed, pressing two fingers to the bridge of her nose. The skin there went white; she was pressing hard, trying to do away with some lingering tension. "It's for the best. I must believe that. Yes—the time has come for Cora to move on."

Clyde risked one more surreptitious glance toward the cottonwoods. The dark line of the trees remained undisturbed. "Come inside, Mother." He put his arm around her shoulders, guiding her gently toward the house. "You wore yourself out. Lie down on the sofa and let me fix you a cup of something. Do we have any coffee left? No? Tea, then. Or chicory root if there ain't no tea."

Nettie Mae took a few dragging steps toward the kitchen door, but she stopped again. She turned and stared over her shoulder, looking back at the Bemis home. The moment stretched and lingered. Clyde could feel the heaviness of her spirit.

He wanted to say, *You know this ain't right. It ain't what either of you want—not you nor Cora Bemis. And all this because you think you can keep me a boy forever. Let me go, Mother. Let me grow up; let me become the man I was meant to be.*

But he couldn't make himself speak those words, couldn't force himself to confront his mother. He guessed he wasn't much of a man yet, if he couldn't speak his mind when it mattered most.

Clyde pushed gently on Nettie Mae's back, urging her to move. Time was running short. Beulah might appear at any moment, and if Nettie Mae caught wind of how Clyde had defied her, she would be so sore that she might force him to haul out the wagon and load it up that very minute. He almost laughed with reckless tension when she moved again. He hustled her up the steps into the kitchen and shut the door, shivering with relief.

Nettie Mae drifted into the sitting room. Clyde heard the springs creak within the sofa as she lay down, just as he had suggested. Alone in the kitchen, he set about brewing a cup of hyssop tea. He dropped a healthy pinch of the dried candy-scented leaves into a cup and stood in despondent silence, watching the steam rise much too slowly from the teakettle spout, a thin white curl of insubstantial nothingness. Even the house around him seemed unreal, unimportant, though it had been the center of his world almost as far back as he could remember. The only image that seemed solid and bright to him now was the memory of Beulah in the pear tree, illuminated by patterned sunlight, haloed by a gathering of blossoms that had formed, by chance, an arch above her tawny head.

Nettie Mae had said, on the morning when she'd told Clyde that the Bemises must go north, that she intended to hire a fellow or two, to help him work the land. The company of other young men was enticing, but Clyde missed Beulah already. He tried to imagine going through his routines with Wilbur or one of the other boys from town. Shearing, lambing, culling the flock. Planting peas in the damp bite of spring. But the scenes he tested were as formless as the steam. They fell apart before they could make any sense, and Clyde knew the only way this world would ever be real to him—the only way his land would remain whole and living—was if Beulah worked at his side.

Clyde carried the hyssop tea to his mother. She sat up to take the cup, but didn't drink. Instead, she blew on the steam—a long, slow exhalation—and watched it dissipate before her.

"We'll see them again." Nettie Mae sounded as if she was trying to convince herself, not Clyde. "When we go to town. We may visit, may call on the family, and—"

She cut off abruptly, turning toward the window, her dark brows raised in a curious arch. Hoofbeats pounded outside—a horse running fast. A bolt cold as ice struck Clyde in his chest; before he could move, Nettie Mae lurched to her feet and hurried to the window. Clyde could only scuttle in her wake. They reached the glass in time to see Tiger streak through the orchard, galloping toward the corral. His saddle was empty.

"Beulah!" Clyde flew to the front door out into the yard before he could think.

He pelted after the big bay horse, every breath already a fire in his throat. Tiger circled the paddock, throwing up dust. The empty stirrups beat his ribs with the rhythm of his stride, urging him on to greater speed. The reins had been knotted and remained at his withers, thank God, for in such a state, the horse could have stepped on a trail of leather and flipped himself end over end, breaking his own neck.

Clyde seized hold of his wits with brutal force. He must stop Tiger from bolting, first and most importantly. If Tiger sent the other horses into a panic, they might crash through the fence or try to jump it. They could break their legs. Worse, they might run wild across the two farms, endangering Nettie Mae, Cora, and the children.

Clyde spread his arms wide and stepped into the horse's path. Tiger wheeled on his haunches, crying out in a harsh, growling voice. The big bay tried to circle the paddock in the other direction, but again Clyde moved calmly to interrupt his flight. He spoke all the while, gently and low, moving with deliberate ease, and finally diverted Tiger from another mad dash. Clyde stepped closer, pushing the horse back toward his companions. Joe Buck whickered, calmed by Clyde's presence, and when Tiger heard the voice of his herdmate, he stopped at last, twitching and blowing.

Clyde stepped up smartly and seized a rein, a heartbeat before Nettie Mae appeared at his shoulder.

"Land sakes," she cried, "what is the meaning of this? Who saddled this horse and set it loose?"

There was no hiding the truth now. Clyde turned to face his mother and met her eye with a grim and silent confession.

"You said her name." Nettie Mae spoke quietly, tense with anger. "Back there in the house. You said that girl's name."

"She's hurt, Mother. Fallen off, or—"

"You disobeyed me."

"This isn't the time for arguing. Beulah's out there somewhere, hurt or worse." Clyde swung up into Tiger's saddle. Nettie Mae looked very small, staring up at him, up to his great height. "I got to go and find her. You get back over to the Bemis place and tell Cora what's happened."

"What should I tell her—that her daughter and my son went riding together like a couple of . . ." She trailed off, her face reddening, then added, "You deceived me. Both of you."

"You can be angry at me all you please, later." He wheeled Tiger around, holding the horse in firm control with his knees. He could feel

Tiger's muscles bunching, the animal's power taut as a great steel spring. Why hadn't he put Beulah on Joe Buck? He should have ridden Tiger himself. "For now, get across the field and tell Cora what's happened. She needs to know!"

Clyde didn't wait for another argument. He set Tiger's head toward the river and let the bay run.

Tiger was faster than Joe Buck. He could have been a racer up in Paintrock on festival days. Under other circumstances, Clyde would have exhilarated in the feel of that speed, the smooth control of the horse's body, the tireless stride, the muscle and hot breath and thunder of heavy bones. But now all he could think about was Beulah. Where had she fallen? Perhaps she had broken a leg or an arm. God send that something worse hadn't happened. He cursed himself again and again for having left her alone with such an animal. Whatever her strange power over nature might be, she was still a girl, not strong enough to control a creature of Tiger's size and strength.

I was afraid to face my mother with Beulah at my side. It was a coward's plan—and all my fault.

If Beulah had been seriously hurt, Clyde knew he would taste bitter regret for the remainder of his days.

With every stride the horse took, he became more hopelessly convinced that Beulah was crippled or dead. He didn't know which would be the greater shame to bear, for her liveliness, her free movement through the world, was the best part of her. The pasture that had always brought him such peace, the black line of the cottonwoods looming nearer with every stride, the cold parapets of the Bighorns above—the whole world seemed to close in around him, menacing and dark, as he raced back toward the foothills in search of the girl he loved, praying it wasn't too late to save her.

CORA

*It's a long way down from Paintrock to this farm. I don't suppose I'll have
many opportunities to return and visit—to see Nettie Mae.*

Cora packed the last of her linens in a sturdy basket and tied its
woven lid shut with a bit of twine. Then she sat back on her heels, staring dully at the basket, unwilling to lift her eyes from its tight-woven
sides to see the emptiness of her home.

*Tomorrow morning we'll say good-bye—perhaps forever. And perhaps
Nettie Mae will be glad of it.*

Benjamin called plaintively from the porch. "We're hungry, Ma.
When can we have our supper?"

"You oughtn't call me 'Ma,' Benjamin. You'll be a town boy tomorrow, and proper boys in town say 'Mother,' not 'Ma.'"

Cora rose from the floor and went to the kitchen, but its emptiness
was no easier to bear. Nettie Mae had helped her pack up almost every
dish and spoon and pot, leaving only a few implements with which to
feed her children. Cora had been nervous, at first, when Nettie Mae
had appeared to assist with the packing. She had assumed Nettie Mae
had only offered to help so she would see Cora's back all the sooner,
but in fact her neighbor had seemed rather melancholy over the affair.
Melancholy—but firm of mind, as ever. Once she came to a decision,
Nettie Mae always saw it through, no matter the cost.

How bittersweet, Cora mused as she assembled a simple meal, *that I was granted a few hours of fellowship with Nettie Mae.* Now at last they had truly worked side by side, cooperating as friends. If only the winter could have passed so pleasantly.

She filled the tin plates, the only dishes that remained unpacked, and set them on the table, then called the children inside. They came eagerly, but Benjamin paused as he pulled out his chair.

"Will Nettie Mae eat with us tonight?"

"Heavens, no," Cora said.

"Why is she coming here, then?"

"She's coming fast, too," Charles added. "Just about running. I guess she must be real hungry."

"What's all this, now?" Cora reached into her apron pocket and found the kerchief she had embroidered, her parting gift to Nettie Mae. It was tucked behind the letter she had never sent to Ernest. There was no need for that letter now; tomorrow she would go to Ernest herself, first thing upon arriving in Paintrock, and tell him of her plans. She would look him in the eye through the bars of his cell, and learn whether he had truly forgiven her—if he ever could. But she would give Nettie Mae the kerchief next morning at dawn, when Clyde drove them north to town.

The front door banged open. Cora jumped, biting back a shriek of surprise. Miranda began to cry at the table, her mouth full of bread and jam.

"Hush," Cora said, more sharply than she'd intended. "It's only Nettie Mae."

Nettie Mae spoke up at once. "There's been some sort of accident." Baffled, she shook her head. "Beulah has fallen from a horse."

Cora gasped. The floor seemed to sway beneath her; she couldn't trust her footing. "A horse? Why was she riding?" Then the true horror of what Nettie Mae had said struck Cora with its full weight. She clutched the back of Benjamin's chair as her legs went weak beneath her. Nettie Mae wouldn't have come all this way—flushed and panting, no less—unless the situation were dire. "Where is Beulah? Is she badly hurt?"

Nettie Mae glanced at the children. Then she took Cora's hand and pressed it hard between her own. Her skin was cool, despite her haste and fluster. "Be brave, Cora. We don't know where she is. The horse ran back to the corral, lathered and with an empty saddle. Clyde has gone out to find her."

"Oh, God!"

A shudder racked Cora's body; she crouched, easing herself toward the floor, for now she knew she couldn't remain standing. Her head swam; a strange, high keening rang in her ears. Nausea rose in her gut and she remembered, with a dark rush of certainty, the conversation she'd had with Nettie Mae the night of the fire. Nettie Mae had told Cora how she had lost one child after another. And Cora—stupidly, uselessly—had said, *That's a wound that can never heal.*

The hard planks of the floor bit into her knees, though Nettie Mae was still clutching her hand. She prayed aloud, begging God for mercy, begging for Him to spare her child, but God felt more distant than He ever had before. The only nearness was the prairie and the wild things that dwelt upon it. The prairie, and Nettie Mae—whose fingers had gone colder, even as her grip on Cora's hand tightened.

"God save her," Cora wailed. "Have mercy! I have no strength to help my child. I am weak, God—weak—and no fit mother."

"Get up, Cora," Nettie Mae snapped. "I said get up, this instant."

"I can't. I cannot stand."

"You can, and you will. On your feet. Move! There's no reason for either of us to remain here; we can do no good as we are. We'll go and look for Beulah, too—you and I."

"I . . . I can't." Cora struggled up onto quivering legs, though she never knew how she managed. "The children. Someone must watch over them."

The children were weeping now—Cora knew they were frightened, but she had no more strength to comfort them than she had to save Beulah from her fate. Benjamin had gathered Charles and Miranda to him; the boy stood with his arms wrapped tightly around his brother and sister, but his eyes pleaded with Cora for guidance.

Nettie Mae eyed the children for a moment. Then she left Cora swaying on her feet and knelt before the little ones. "Listen to me now, all of you. Beulah will be well, but she needs our help. Your mother and I must go and help her, for we are big enough to carry her if need be. Do you understand?"

The children sniffled, nodding in despondent silence.

"We will come back. I promise you that. We won't leave you alone for good. We would never do that to you—not your mother nor I."

The children nodded again.

Nettie Mae placed a hand gently on Benjamin's round cheek. Through her tears, Cora could see how the woman's thumb traced down the side of his face, as loving as only a mother can be. "Benjamin, you're old enough now to be the man of the house . . . for a little while, at least. I need you to do something for me. It's an important job—very important. Are you fit for the task?"

Benjamin scrubbed away his tears with his sleeve. Then he nodded solemnly.

"Good. You must keep Charles and Miranda here in the house. No matter what may come, keep them inside. And you mustn't light any candles or oil lamps, and you mustn't try to light a fire in the hearth, even if your mother and I are out late helping Beulah. If you get cold, what should you do?"

"Get under our blankets," Benjamin said.

"That's my boy—my smart, good boy." Nettie Mae kissed Benjamin on the forehead. Then she stood, beaming down at the children as if she hadn't a care in the world. But when she turned back to face Cora, the smile fled at once, replaced by a darkly sober expression. "Come along, Cora."

Numb with fear, Cora allowed Nettie Mae to take her by the arm. Together they stepped out into the low light of sunset, but despite the evening's pleasant warmth, Cora shivered.

NETTIE MAE

It seemed an absurdly long way down the porch steps and across the Bemis garden, but Nettie Mae placed one foot doggedly in front of another, dragging Cora along at her side. She marched the woman out into the pasture that lay between their two farms, but once there, Nettie Mae's resolve faltered. She had no idea where to go, what she ought to do next. She and Cora huddled close together, gazing around at a world that seemed suddenly too large, too unfeeling—and far too clever for Nettie Mae to contend with. Never in her life had she felt so small and helpless. The two farms and the prairie beyond, the mountain range high above them—everything had taken on a sinister quality, calculating, indifferent to human fears. Never, in all the long years of her habitation, had the land Nettie Mae thought of as her home, however impersonal and functional that home might be, seemed so predatory and wild.

Pressed close, shoulder to shoulder, the two women turned in a slow circle, staring helplessly into the vast, breathing body of nature. A thousand pairs of eyes seemed to stare back from between every grass stem, from the heights of the mountains—but no eye blinked, and none warmed with sympathy.

Nettie Mae took a few faltering steps toward her own house, but paused, then retreated again to Cora's side. In their desperation, the two women had moved in one another's orbits. Now Nettie Mae found her back pressed against Cora's. She could feel Cora trembling, or perhaps it was her own fear she felt reflected in her neighbor's flesh. For now—since touching Benjamin's face, since kissing the boy's warm head—Nettie Mae knew with a wrenching certainty that she could not lose Beulah. Whoever, whatever, that strange girl might be, she had become the critical force in Nettie Mae's life, the wind that filled the sail of her fate. It was Beulah, after all, who had remade Clyde with her strange, unholy power. Beulah had delivered Clyde from the shadow of his father. With stabbing clarity, she understood that if Beulah died, so, too, would the girl's prediction—the promise she had given that Nettie Mae would have a new family, children to love again, a life begun anew. If death claimed the girl before her time, all of Nettie Mae's fragile hopes would wither on the vine.

Nettie Mae said, "Where might she have ridden to?"

"I don't know," Cora answered faintly.

"Think. You must think clearly now. Where does Beulah like to spend her idle time?"

"I truly don't know—I never knew. Beulah has always kept to herself, gone her own way. And I've always been too frightened to follow her or join her out here in the wilds."

"This land is too big for us to search without some plan. And the grass is tall; she might have fallen anywhere. If she's lying somewhere, we won't find her unless—"

A ragged sob burst from Cora's chest. Nettie Mae turned and found the woman covering her face with both hands. She was on the verge of rebuking Cora, insisting that she focus her will and make herself useful. But before Nettie Mae could speak, Cora stilled herself. She trembled— then the trembling ceased. Cora seemed to brace herself, willing herself to perfect calm. With eyes still covered by her hands, she lifted her face.

"Cora, what in the Lord's name are you—"

Cora hushed her, quickly, with the confidence of one who expects to be obeyed, exactly as she might have done with little Miranda. For a few shuddering heartbeats, Cora held herself motionless—that delicate face tipped up toward the sky, wreathed all about by an air of concentration. Nettie Mae realized Cora was listening, and most intently.

After a long moment, Cora's hands left her face. Those brilliant blue eyes opened. No more tears shone along the lashes. Nettie Mae could still read Cora's fear, for the woman was pale, and her eyes wide and staring. But she had gathered her wits—composed herself.

Cora pointed toward the cottonwoods. "There."

"She's out there?" Nettie Mae said eagerly. "By the river—are you sure?"

"I don't know; I can't possibly be certain." Cora's voice was tinged by panic, yet she maintained her grip on sense. "But there are birds scolding up in the trees—crows calling. Can't you hear them? Crows don't normally call that way, do they? Not at this hour."

Nettie Mae stared toward the trees. She could hear the birds, all right, a raucous chorus with a distinct note of . . . what? Effrontery. Offense at having been disturbed. "I can't swear that crows never call that way. They might do it every evening, for all I can tell."

"No," Cora said, "this is different. I'm sure of it. I've never heard them like this before—angry and . . . and excited. Something has upset them, or drawn their interest. It could be Beulah. Come; we must find out."

Nettie Mae nodded, but she didn't set out toward the cottonwoods. Not just yet. For Cora was right: there was a difference to the calls, something novel, out of the ordinary. She had no great desire to disturb the roost of those black carrion eaters. Fear surged in her breast. The crows; harsh screams leaped at her across the field, the birds number-less and angry, their wildness all too near. *How absurd,* she told herself, *to be frightened of a crow.* But she was frightened of the birds, of the openness of the field, of her own small, frail body—how breakable it was, like Beulah's.

"I haven't gone to the river often," Nettie Mae said. "I don't know how to get there."

Cora looked at her steadily for a moment. Then she said, "I know the way."

They crossed the pasture together. As they drew nearer to the cottonwoods, a great flock of birds rose from the trees, circling madly, hectic as a cyclone. The crows shouted their displeasure, and a few dark feathers plummeted into the undergrowth. Nettie Mae shrank from the tumult, but Cora took her hand and led her on, faster along a narrow trail, then faster still. The trail's margins were rank, overgrown with plants, with brambles that clawed at Nettie Mae's skirt and scored the backs of her hands.

The river came into view, flat and silver between the trunks of trees. The smell of the place overwhelmed her senses. Water and minerals— water and earth—and the warmth of the day dissipating, fading. The sky wore a low band of orange; a white, waning moon hung just above the trees. The sun would shortly set. If they didn't find the girl quickly, they would have to contend with darkness and predators, too.

Cora hesitated only a moment, staring up at the roiling cloud of birds. Then she pressed on, breaking through a stand of brush into a small clearing strewn with river stones. The birds wheeled overhead; the sound of them drove back everything else—wits and thought and even, finally, fear—so that only bare senses remained. Nettie Mae noticed a low mound, scarcely risen above the earth. It was covered in creeping plants, a mat of weeds. Red earth showed among thin vines. A white stone, little bigger than her fist, stood at the mound's far end. No, not a stone. It was the skull of some animal. That stark reminder of death sent a jolt of awareness through Nettie Mae's body, and all at once, she realized what she must be looking at: her husband's grave. The place where Clyde had buried Substance. Nettie Mae gasped and stepped back, but in the same moment, Cora leaped forward with a wordless cry and ran across the clearing.

Nettie Mae blinked hard, struggling to sort her thoughts through the cacophony overhead. Then she saw what had drawn Cora's attention: a slender wrist and pale hand extending beyond the low hillock of the grave. They had found Beulah—lying on her back among the green things, one arm thrown up over her head—all but hidden by the weeds.

The girl is only mooning about, dreaming, the way she always does. Even as she thought it, Nettie Mae knew it wasn't so. Beulah was lying much too still, unresponsive to the clamor of the crows.

Nettie Mae followed Cora over the hard-packed sand. Both women dropped to their knees beside the girl's motionless body. Cora called Beulah's name, over and over, but the girl lay as if sleeping. Nettie Mae noted the shallow rise and fall of Beulah's chest. That was one small mercy, at least: the girl was still breathing.

"Come now," Nettie Mae said firmly. "Wake up." She patted Beulah's cheeks—first one, then the other, each strike falling a little harder than the last. But the girl's eyes never opened.

"We must carry her back to the house," Cora said.

"My house is nearer. If she's badly hurt, even a few minutes' time could make all the difference."

Cora swallowed hard, staring down at her daughter. "How will we move her?"

"We must try not to shift her neck or her back too much. If we do, it could make her injuries worse."

"But how? How can it be done?" Cora looked up to the wheeling birds, as if she might find a solution to this grim dilemma among frantic wings and wild cries. She began to weep. "I don't know how to help her! God save us!"

Nettie Mae gathered Cora in her arms. "Come now. Crying won't pull us out of the brine. Let us put our heads together; we can think of a plan. Look, there are branches downed among the cottonwoods. We might weave some together and make a sled of sorts. Then we can drag her home."

"A sled?" Cora could barely speak through her racking sobs. "And how long will that take? The longer we wait—"

Hoofbeats sounded near the river, and the crows redoubled their fury. Nettie Mae and Cora both straightened on their knees, looking around in desperate hope. Clyde burst through a stand of brush, mounted on the big bay horse. The bay threw up its head, crying a shrill protest; white foam sprayed from its lips.

"Beulah!" Clyde's shout was thick with agony. He threw himself from the saddle and ran toward the girl, but Nettie Mae held up a hand to stop him.

"Don't touch her! We must carry her back to our house, but carefully. We can't afford to make her injuries any worse."

Clyde wrung his hands and paced restlessly along the trail—never so far that he lost sight of the girl. His horse danced nervously under the thunderhead of crows, and Clyde paused to watch the animal. Then he wheeled around and crouched beside Nettie Mae. "I know how we can do it! We'll make a sling from Tiger's saddle blanket."

Dazed, Cora shook her head. Nettie Mae felt none too certain herself.

"Wait here. I'll show you." Clyde scrambled up and caught the horse. The bay pawed anxiously as Clyde stripped the saddle from his back. He dropped the saddle at the foot of the grave, then he pulled the sweat-soaked blanket from the horse's body. Unfolded, the blanket was just large enough to cradle Beulah's body.

Nettie Mae leaped to her feet. "That will do the trick, by God!"

She helped her son spread the blanket next to Beulah's body. Cautiously, they shifted the girl onto the dirty cloth, an operation which caused Nettie Mae to hold her breath in fear. She could only pray they hadn't worsened Beulah's condition by moving her too vigorously. Clyde returned the saddle to the horse's back, then lifted the blanket by the two corners on either side of the girl's face.

"Take a corner down there, by one of her feet," Nettie Mae said to Cora. "I'll hold the other side."

In that manner, they shuffled together along the trail, silenced by the urgency of their task. The bay horse followed, whickering now and then. As the clearing dwindled behind Nettie Mae's hunched and straining back, the crows subsided to their roost, and the gentle singing of crickets replaced that terrible noise.

The sun had set and twilight had already begun to encroach upon the prairie by the time they reached the sod-brick house. Nettie Mae's back and shoulders ached; she stifled a groan, but together they carried Beulah up the steps and into the sitting room.

"Don't try to take her out of the blanket," Nettie Mae said. "Let us simply lay her out on the sofa, blanket and all. It's a filthy bit of cloth, and it stinks like the corral, but there's nothing to be done about it now. Cora, fetch that lace cushion from my rocker. We must support her head, the poor dear."

Only when she had seen Beulah settled on the sofa and covered with a clean quilt from her own bed did Nettie Mae allow herself to stretch the cramps from her back and shoulders. Clyde sank to his knees and took Beulah's hand, staring desperately into the girl's slack face.

"What ought we to do now?" Cora's small, dull voice was brutally loud in the stillness.

"She needs the doctor. Clyde, you must ride to town and fetch him. Luckily, the night is clear, and the moon is just past full; you should be able to find your way."

Clyde nodded. He watched Beulah for a moment longer, his face gaunt with despair. Then climbed to his feet. "You're right, Mother. Of course, you're right. I'll saddle Joe Buck right away. Tiger's a faster horse, but he'll be tuckered out by now, and I won't risk him going lame on the way to Paintrock. God willing, I'll be back with the doc before sunrise." He cast a final, lingering look at the girl before he left the house.

When Clyde had gone, Nettie Mae turned to Cora, summoning her old, brisk air. "You must stay here with your daughter. Take my stool—that one there, by my spinning wheel. Anything you need from my kitchen, anything you need in all the house, is yours."

Cora clasped her hands at her throat. "Where are you going?"

"Back to your house, of course. I'll check on the children and put them to bed." Nettie Mae hesitated then, tapping her chin with one finger. She couldn't bring herself to meet Cora's eye. "On second thought, perhaps I ought to fetch the children over here. Maybe it's for the best if we keep them close tonight, in case . . ."

She didn't finish the thought, but went to the kitchen for a lantern. Moon or no moon, the children might be frightened of the long walk in the dark. Nettie Mae tossed a shawl hastily around her shoulders and was about to leave the house when Cora appeared at her shoulder. She halted Nettie Mae with one trembling hand upon her shoulder.

"I . . . I can't pay a doctor's bill. I haven't any money. I don't know how I'm to afford this, unless the doctor will take the president's china in payment."

"Don't you fret about money," Nettie Mae said. "I'll pay the bill."

She left her kitchen before Cora could argue.

13

WHEN WE WOKE FROM DREAMS

I passed that night in a kind of sleep, and I dreamed all the while, but the dreams were like none I had known before. I've had dreams that linger—the kind you can't help but dwell on, even after you've wakened, the kind of dreams whose strength you feel long after their visions have faded. There are dreams that go on tumbling through your head for hours after waking, and sometimes they remain just beyond reach, beyond your power to recall, and all that's left—even in the moment after waking—is an impression faint as bird tracks at the edge of a river.

The visions that came to me that night, as I lay once more under Nettie Mae's roof, were creatures of a different breed. I remember every bright moment of those dreams—I still do, to this day—every shadow and nuance, every clear, chiming note of certainty that came to me that night, while I walked the edge of the spiral.

I saw a flock of blackbirds rising from a field of corn. The flock grew and grew as more birds took to the wing—so many birds, I couldn't conceive of the number. They turned the twilight sky to gray, then black, and my head filled with the beating of their wings—wings so numerous they sounded like a hailstorm or the rain that brings the flood. The blackbirds called to one another as they flew. Their voices were harsh, a great clamor of sound that drowned out all the other songs of the prairie. But though their noise and their numbers were great, they soon moved on—the whole great flock twisting and flowing in the air, the cloud of their vast society dwindling as it moved away across the plain. I turned and looked back at the cornfield once the birds had vanished. I expected to find it picked clean, stripped of all life by the hungry flock. But the corn was growing straight and tall, and between the husks of the ears I could see the corn seed shining. Golden and multiplying, seed after seed formed along countless ears. Then the seeds fell to the earth and new life sprang up at once, green shoots that reached toward the sun. It was then I realized that one bird had remained. She perched atop the highest corn plant, swaying with the long silks in the wind. I asked her, Ain't you lonely, now that your flock has gone? But she looked down at the new life rising, her eyes bright and glad. Then she opened her beak and sang—sang up to a purple sky, a song so sweet and grateful, I wept with joy to hear it.

I dreamed of the low places, the dense green coolness down among the roots of the garden. A chorus of insects sang all around me, filling me, so it seemed that the music came from within my body. I crept among the great, fat stalks of plants, for I was the size of a moth now, delicate and light, and my skin glittered in the moonlight, dusted with powdery scales. As I pushed through the dense forest of the garden, I recognized the plants I had sown from seed. I greeted each one by name, for now I knew them all, just as they knew me, and they were glad of my presence.

But as I slipped among their hairy stalks and climbed over the stout ledges of their roots, I heard a sawing, rasping sound high above. I looked up and found a cutworm busy at the leaf of a beanstalk. It bit into the yielding green flesh, and the bean plant wept its fragrant sap. I could feel the beanstalk crying out with pain, in helpless offense. Then the leaf fell. I had to step quickly to avoid it. I called up to the worm, Don't hurt it, please. Don't hurt the plant. But where the leaf fell, the soil rose up to meet it, stretching tiny hands—white, threadlike hands that caught the leaf and held it down and drank its sap so the leaf went down into the soil, just as rain soaks into the cracks of the earth, with a whisper and a sigh. Then I could hear the soil breathing out as if in relief, a deep satisfaction, and every plant around me grew a little taller. Even the beanstalk the worm had bitten grew. It reached up for a distant sun, yearning for the light's embrace. The worm moved its terrible jaws and spoke. God is said to be great, the worm told me, so great you cannot see Him. But God is small, with hands like threads, and they reach for you everywhere you go. The hands touch everything—even you, even me. What falls never falls; what grows has grown a thousand times, and will live a thousand times more. Wherever hand touches hand, the Oneness comes to stay. Once God has made a thing whole, it cannot be broken again.

And last, just before I woke, I dreamed of the sheep in Clyde's arms— our miracle, the two made one. Clyde was standing on the hillside, circled by sage, lit by a round white moon. The pear tree was in full flower, and a wind came down from the Bighorns to scatter the blossoms. Petals filled the air, light as cottonwood seed, and when the lamb saw the petals flying, it opened its two mouths together and bleated with joy. And I looked into Clyde's face and found him smiling.

I woke with the sound of the lamb's call still ringing in my ears. Only it wasn't the lamb at all. There was a crow out in the orchard, croaking and clacking its beak, calling to the morning sun. Pale-yellow light glowed along the edges of the curtains—white curtains, cutwork. That was the first I knew that I had returned to the Webber house.

Don't try to sit up, a man said.

For a minute, I thought maybe it was my pa. I squinted and moved my head feebly on my pillow, trying to make out who had spoken. I didn't recognize the voice.

The man said, She's wakened, Mrs. Bemis.

A moment later, I heard a wordless exclamation from my ma, then her eager step coming from the kitchen. I was in Nettie Mae's sitting room, I realized, and my head ached something awful.

My eyes were blurred and kept insisting that they should see double. Nevertheless, I made out my ma's familiar shape. I could even read the worry on her face—the pretty frown, those blue eyes luminous with fear. When she saw that my eyes were open, relief stepped in to replace a little of her worry. She knelt beside the sofa and took my hand.

The man said, Your daughter has suffered a nasty blow to the head. She will have some pain and a sizable goose egg for days yet to come. There may be temporary effects, too. Memory loss over the short term—nothing serious or lasting. Confusion in her speech, perhaps, or some slowness of action.

With a fond little laugh, Nettie Mae said, Slowness of action—that's nothing unusual for our Beulah.

She must have plenty of rest, the man said. No strenuous work for two weeks at least, and all the hearty, nourishing foods she will eat. But she'll recover, with time. Now, young lady, you must tell us all what happened, if you can remember.

I blinked at the man. He was indistinct, his edges furred, but I could make him out a little better as the minutes passed. He resolved before my eyes, and I saw that he had dark hair shot with gray at the temples, a thick mustache that bent down around the corners of his mouth, and a monocle pinched against one eye, which made him look very serious and grave. He smelled of sharp, stinging smells—alcohol and bitter herbs.

Clyde said, This is Dr. Cooper, Beulah. I brought him down from Paintrock.

I turned my head sharply at the sound of Clyde's voice and regretted it at once, for pain flooded my skull, but I couldn't help it. My eyes would have sought Clyde out and followed him no matter where he went. I could as soon have looked away from Clyde as the lamb could have looked away from its twin.

Clyde was sitting in Nettie Mae's rocker—slumped there, bent with weariness. He was holding a bowl of something hot in his hands, steam rose from the bowl in slow curls, but his shoulders sagged, and he looked tired enough to drop.

I rode all night to fetch Doc, Clyde said—proud and not afraid to show it, now that he knew I would recover.

The doctor said, You've got a right brave son, Mrs. Webber.

Then he patted my hand briskly. Tell us, Beulah. Can you remember what happened?

I blinked. Then I blinked again, and would have rubbed my knuckles hard against my eyes if I'd had enough pep to lift my hands. It seemed all I could do just to speak—to think.

I . . . I fell from my horse, I said.

Memory returned to me piecemeal, a patchwork with sloppy stitches. Recollection of the fall seemed less real to me than my dreams had been, but I struggled to retrieve it, and did my best to sew the moments back together.

I said, I went riding down from the foothills. I should have gone straight back to the corral, but I wanted to stop and visit Substance's grave—see if I couldn't coax him to talk, and urge him once more to give up the futility of his own confined and angry ghost. But when I got there, the crows took flight, all calling at once, and Tiger spooked. That's all I know. Guess I don't remember actually falling. I only remember Tiger rearing up—and that's the last of it. Guess I must have lost my hold and hit the ground head first.

That's good enough for me, the doctor said. No more riding horses, young lady—not until you've thoroughly healed. When your memories are no longer impeded, nor any other functions, you may ride again, if your mother permits.

Your mother does not permit, said Ma.

By and by, the doctor left, and the Webber house settled back into its daily routines. Clyde took himself upstairs to catch a little sleep. I closed my eyes, but sleep evaded me. Rather, I listened—to the crow out in the orchard, the first cicadas of the season thrumming out in the grass. I listened to Nettie Mae singing softly under her breath as she went about her chores in the kitchen, and I heard the rhythmic creak of my ma in the rocker by the window. I could hear her embroidering, too: the faint tap of her needle breaking the tension of the cloth, the slide of thread into linen. It was a contented sound—settled, in no hurry to up and leave.

Tuckered by the long night's journey, Clyde had surrendered at once to slumber. But I could feel his dreams as vividly as I had felt my own.

What did he dream? A ring of white flowers like a halo, and bats among the lilacs. He dreamed of the calls of his flock, and the feel of his horse's neck, warm beneath his cheek. He dreamed a coyote trotting through the brush, swift and alive. He dreamed a pale circle, and from that circle his future flowed like the river, certain and strong.

When he woke from his dreams, he knew exactly what to do.

CLYDE

When he woke from his dreams, Clyde stared up at the slope of his ceiling, trying to recall the visions that had come to him in sleep. But though he still felt the great weight of import bearing down on his chest, he remembered nothing but a few stray scraps of imagery, fleeting glimpses of knowledge or fate, more hidden than revealed. He had seen an animal slinking through the sage, and he had been glad of its presence. What sort of creature it was, Clyde couldn't say. He had seen something pale and round—luminous, hanging against a dark sky. But whether it was the moon or the pear blossoms framing Beulah's face or something else entirely, he couldn't decide. The lack of certainty disturbed him, sickening him with a sensation of something left undone, something grave and crucial but still incomplete.

Sleep had been necessary, but it had also left him groggy and slow. He sat up on the edge of his bed, groaning at the slowness of his thoughts, the dense stubborn fog that occluded all sense. He stared out the window. It was still bright outside—still day. How many hours had he slept? The sun was tending toward the west, the light mellow and full. He shuffled across his small bedroom, staring through the glass at his farm. Animals were grazing contentedly on their pasture. Even the hens were going about their business without the urgency of hunger. His mother and Cora must have seen to the most pressing chores for him. It was kind to allow him his rest, for the night had been a long one, the ride to Paintrock daunting. Fear had chased him all the long journey, but Beulah was safe now—safe and well. The time for fretting had passed. There was work yet to be done, and this task would wait no longer.

Clyde found the house abandoned. Even the sofa where Beulah had lain was empty now, brushed clean. Cora and Nettie Mae had moved the girl upstairs to a more suitable bed, Clyde supposed—now that the doctor had declared her fit to walk. He was glad he wouldn't disturb Beulah's rest with his comings and goings. Let the girl gather all her strength back to herself—that strange and glorious power, the seeing and knowing that were hers alone. The sooner she had recovered, the happier Clyde would be.

He saddled Joe Buck and rode to the river, then up into the foot-hills, all the way to the deep gully and the felled tree. There would be no work for Clyde to do till evening, when he must bring in the flock and the cattle. He could spare an hour or two for leisure—and for his thoughts.

Clyde ground-tied Joe Buck and left the gelding to graze in the blue shade of the pear tree. He climbed up onto the red boulder and tucked his legs Turk-fashion, settling his hat low on his brow against the sun's glare. Clyde remained that way for some time, thoughtful and still, looking down on the land below. It was one farm in truth now. Two houses, but one land, any boundaries swallowed by grass, the lines erased by the softening of the year. They had made that farm together, made it one—Clyde and Beulah, working side by side.

Joe Buck whisked his tail, lashing away the flies. The gelding's yellow hide twitched, and patches of shadow and light rippled along his flanks. Clyde watched as Joe Buck browsed along the floor of the gully, searching for his favorite grasses, patient and serene. Far below, a wind stirred the pasture in green-golden ripples that moved like waves across a pond—like the rings that spread, endlessly rebounding, when you

463

drop a rock into water. Clyde could hear his ram calling to the ewes, a distant, sleepy call.

He reached into his trouser pocket and withdrew his carving knife and the chunk of white bone. It was coyote bone; Clyde knew that much, for it was one of the fragments he had gathered at the riverbank a few days before. He held up the broken, porous thing and turned it over in the sunlight, considering the shape and its proportions. Somehow he had forgotten this piece in his pocket, and hadn't discovered it till he'd reached Paintrock the night before. Then, aching from the ride and shouting outside the doctor's door, Clyde had chanced to slip his hands into his pockets, cringing against the cold. The bone had fitted itself in his hand; his fingers had closed around it, and Clyde had promised himself that he would put it to good use if Beulah survived.

He set to work, scraping with his knife, chipping away shards of white little by little. Joe Buck flicked his ears at the sound and raised his head now and then, watching Clyde inquisitively. The sun settled lower in the west, but Clyde worked on, till a blister had raised on his thumb and his fingers bore tiny garnets of dried blood in the places where his knife had slipped and nicked him.

Joe Buck moved toward Clyde, blowing gently, bobbing his head. Clyde folded his knife and slipped it into his pocket.

"You're right, old Joe. Time we got back home. Time we brought the sheep in, too. Night will be here soon."

He scrambled down from the boulder and stretched. Joe Buck waited patiently by his side, but Clyde didn't mount up yet. He held what remained of the bone between his thumb and forefinger, held what he had made up against the sky. A little white ring, perfectly round, and just about the right size to fit Beulah's finger. Clyde was sure of that.

He reached into his saddlebag and found the small wooden box Mr. Bemis had sent him from the Paintrock jail. Clyde dropped the ring inside. Then, on impulse, and blushing a little over his own sentimentality, he plucked one of the last blossoms from the pear tree and put it in the box, too. The ring needed more work—smoothing and polishing. By and by, he'd see it done. It would wait in the inlaid box till it was finished—till Clyde knew the time was right to ask Beulah for her hand.

He didn't stop at Substance's grave on the ride back home. There seemed little point in stopping. He passed the low mound at an easy lope; red earth, carpeted in growing things, blurred under Joe Buck's hooves. The coyote's skull was half-buried in tender leaves of bindweed. He could hear the ram calling again, summoning the flock, and Clyde urged Joe Buck on till they broke out onto the flat expanse of the pasture. The cottonwoods had shed their feathery white seeds; a haze of captured light hung above the grass, bright and pure as stars. The seeds drifted lazily around him as Clyde rode among his flock. The animals greeted their shepherd with deep, guttural calls. The ram fell into step beside him, and Clyde led the flock home from their pasture.

When he had closed the sheep in the fold and returned Joe Buck to the paddock, Clyde stopped at the well pump to splash his face with cool, bright water. He let it run down from his nose and chin and fall to the earth between his boots.

"I'm glad to see you're out and about. I hope you rested well."

Clyde looked up, wiping the last of the water from his eyes with damp fingers. His mother stood beside him. She had brought a ewer for wash water, and began to fill it as soon as Clyde moved away from the pump.

"I feel fit enough," he said. "But nothing worse than tiredness troubled me; I was never in any danger. How is Beulah faring?"

"Very well." Nettie Mae didn't look up as she spoke. The exertion of lifting the stiff pump handle made her voice flat with concentration. Clyde couldn't read her mood.

"I'm glad to hear it," he said, and paused, wondering what he ought to say next, how to find the right words, the definite words—how to assert himself absolutely without hurting his mother's heart.

The ewer filled, and Nettie Mae let the pump handle fall. A final gush of water spilled from the spout, tumbling into the thick green growth below.

Clyde touched his mother's arm as she lifted the ewer to her hip. Nettie Mae stopped, met his eye, and held it. Her dark brows fell—not into a frown, but into an expression of resignation. She said nothing, but waited for Clyde to speak.

"Mother." The words came slowly, cautiously. But he knew they must come. He wouldn't hold these words back any longer. "I'm going to court Beulah someday—when she's ready for it. Even once Cora has moved everyone up to Paintrock. I'll find a way, for I intend to marry that girl, if she'll have me."

Nettie Mae shifted—a small gesture that might have been a shrug. "Cora isn't going to Paintrock. Not anymore. At least, not this year. She and I talked about it at length last night, while we watched over Beulah, waiting for you to bring the doctor. We'll spend the winter together again under one roof. God will grant us a happier go of it this time, I think."

She turned and glided a few steps toward the house, careful not to spill any water from the pitcher. But then Nettie Mae stopped again and glanced at Clyde over her shoulder. "As for courting Beulah," she said, "you'll get no objection from me. Now hitch up your float, if you will, Clyde. I must send you over to the Bemis place on an errand, and it must be done soon. Supper won't cook itself, and night is coming on."

Nettie Mae swept across the yard, as straight backed and tireless as she always was. The cottonwood seeds glowed around her.

NETTIE MAE

She had never known such relief as she felt that morning, when Beulah woke from her dreams, released from a harrowing darkness that had held the girl in its grip all the long night through. Nettie Mae had no inkling of her own fear, no real understanding of how desperately she wished for Beulah to live until that moment, when life had returned to the child. Life had returned to Nettie Mae, too—life like a sunrise, warm with promise—and she had wept with joy and gratitude, trembling with the knowledge that Beulah would survive.

The moment of waking seemed to visit Nettie Mae again and again, as if eager to impress her with the sweetness of the memory. Stepping into the sitting room; watching the girl's eyes flicker and open. The doctor calling for Cora. Beulah blinking at the window, turning gingerly toward the sun. All through the day—long and weary, after that terrible, sleepless night—Nettie Mae revisited the memory, strengthened and consoled by the joy it brought. Happiness buoyed her spirit and fortified her body, so she went about the business of tending the animals as easily as if she had slept like a babe all night through.

Nettie Mae sang to herself as she diced carrots and turnips into her big Dutch kettle, as she scored the fragrant skins of spring onions. The onions stung her eyes and the gathered tears made her laugh, for it seemed absurd to weep while she sang, but she couldn't stop herself from singing any more than she could stop the tears from flowing. Her joy was too great, a round bursting warmth in the center of her chest. How long had it been since she had sung? Nettie Mae couldn't recall the last time she had done so. She must have been a girl, singing with the church choir. Years before her marriage. How strange and yet how sweet, to find words and tunes she had thought long forgotten rising to the surface of her memory, little larks taking to the wing.

She tucked a freshly killed rooster into the Dutch oven, sprinkled it with salt and cracked pepper, then fitted the kettle's lid and eased it down into the coals of the fire. A good chicken dinner was just the thing for a celebration. There would be more, too. Stewed greens, brightened by the precious dried lemon peel Nettie Mae always bought on her annual trip to Carbon. Mashed turnips and carrots, flavored by the bird's rich fat. Snap beans in onion cream. And a bread pudding sweet with cinnamon and dried apples—the cinnamon another delicacy Nettie Mae usually kept to herself.

She would keep nothing to herself now. Her heart had opened with Beulah's eyes, and gladness had flooded in. She could feel it rising, threatening to overspill its banks.

Let joy run out of me. Let it soak the barren ground of this house—my home—and let something new and bright grow up from the field of my past bitterness.

Nettie Mae heard Beulah's voice upstairs, speaking softly to her mother. She paused to listen. She could make out none of their words from where she stood in the kitchen, but their contentment was like music, and Nettie Mae rejoiced to hear it.

Cora hadn't left the girl's side since they had found her on the riverbank. Nettie Mae hoped Cora had stolen a few hours of rest; the woman must be worn ragged from fretting. *A good supper will be just what she needs, too—what we all need. As much hearty food as Beulah will eat, that's what the doctor said.*

Nettie Mae chuckled aloud over her own thoughts. There was a time when she couldn't force herself to say Beulah's name, nor even think it. "That girl," she had been, or sometimes "the Bemis girl." Nettie Mae was a sensible woman and harbored no delusions. She had no reason to believe Beulah's tumble from the horse might have cured her of her strange ways and her eerie habits. Rather, the fall had cured Nettie Mae—the shock of having nearly lost the girl, the threatened revocation of Beulah's mysterious promise. *You will have a family again someday. I've seen it; I know.*

She stirred the pot of greens, then stepped away from the hearth and pulled the kerchief from her sleeve—linen freshly embroidered with two pink flowers, Cora's gift. She smoothed the kerchief on her palm and traced one of the flowers with a fingertip. Then she tucked it away again and used the edge of her sleeve to dab the sweat from her brow.

Cora had given the kerchief to Nettie Mae the night before, as they had sat hand in hand beside the sofa, watching Beulah's too-still slumber, counting every faint rise and fall of the girl's chest.

"If we're to be parted," Cora had said, reaching into her apron pocket, "then I would like you to have this, with some hope that you might remember me fondly . . . one day."

Nettie Mae had accepted the kerchief without a word. She never could have found the strength to speak, even if she'd had some idea of what she wanted to say. No words, but Nettie Mae had thought, *Haven't I prayed for a chance to begin again—a chance to let go of my old pain and start anew without hate?*

Minutes had passed in the silence of the sitting room, with no sound but the murmur of low flames on the hearth. Finally, the great hard knot of emotion had dissipated in Nettie Mae's throat, just enough that she trusted herself to speak.

"Perhaps it's best if you don't go to Paintrock after all," she had said. "Winter isn't so terribly far away, after all."

"Winter is never far off," Cora had agreed.

They'd said nothing more on the subject, but by her flush of fragile happiness—by an upwelling of sisterly affection in her breast—Nettie

Mae had understood that the matter was decided. The Bemis family would remain, and Nettie Mae was glad of it.

She went to the kitchen window and pressed her palm against cool glass. She could see Clyde's float, rippled and distorted through the window, returning from the Bemis farmhouse with its cargo. Nettie Mae smiled, then tightened her apron strings. She was weary, but there was still much work to be done. She opened the door and called to the children, who were playing around the feet of the lilacs.

"Come inside, my darlings. Come on, hurry up. I'll need your help setting the table."

The children sprang up at the sound of her voice. They ran across the yard, laughing, with lilac petals clinging to their hair.

CORA

When she woke from her formless dreams, Cora lay still beside her daughter, careful not to move lest she tear Beulah from sleep and deprive the girl of healing.

It's a wonder I slept at all, Cora thought, *frightened as I've been.*

Frightened for her child—afraid the doctor and his reassurances would prove nothing more than a vision, a cruel trick of the mind conjured by despair and wild hope. Slowly, she turned her head on the pillow, half-convinced she would find the mattress empty beside her. In place of Beulah, there would be nothing—and the hard, heavy blow of loss would strike Cora, leaving her crumpled and weak, helpless as before. But no, the girl lay easy at Cora's side, breathing steadily, her eyelids twitching now and then as she wandered the paths of her dreams.

Thank goodness, Cora thought. *She is truly returned to me, then, and she is whole. I've been more fortunate than I've deserved.*

Cora's back began to ache from her stillness. Cautiously, she rolled onto her side, watching Beulah all the while. When she settled again, Cora faced the bedroom window over her daughter's body—looking north, toward her own home. The little gray farmhouse was just visible, the point of its steep roof peeking above the windowsill, sharp among the green blur of the foothills despite its distance and the bubbles in the glass. Cora slid her hand beneath her cheek, staring at her home above the gentle rise and fall of her daughter's chest.

We can wake the land, Beulah had told Cora once. *Wake the farm. Make it grow again.*

Perhaps Cora could do it after all. Rouse the world and guide what grew from the soil. Nurture and protect, instead of making ruin.

She shifted again on the mattress. The letter in her apron pocket crackled faintly. It was time to be rid of that note, she thought. When she rose—when Beulah finally woke and left Cora free to get up from this bed, too—she would cast the old letter into the fire. Write a new message for Ernest and send it with Clyde the next time he drove up to Paintrock for supplies.

I have woken the land myself, she would write. *I have kept your land alive, my dearest—our land, still living, as I hope our love still lives. I wait for your return, if you wish to have me, if you haven't decided to cast me from your heart.*

Cora's fingers twitched, remembering the outline of the two hearts in the bottom of the wooden box. The feel of wood scored so deeply by her husband's knife. Two hearts made permanent, intertwined. She thought, *All will be well. By and by, all will be well.*

Beulah sighed and stirred beneath the quilt. Cora peered anxiously at her daughter's face, but there was no cause for concern. Her color was good, and a soft smile graced her lips. Then the girl yawned. Her body went rigid, quivering as she stretched where she lay. She opened her eyes.

"Ma."

"I'm here, darling."

Beulah turned on her pillow as carefully as Cora had done, mindful of the great, tender knot that had risen on the back of her head. She squinted at the window. "What time is it?"

"Evening, almost. Time for supper, soon enough. Now that you're awake, I suppose I should head back across the fields and see to feeding your brothers and your sister."

Beulah grinned. "Ma. Nettie Mae is fixing supper. Can't you smell it?"

Cora's cheeks burned. She could smell it now, of course—had been smelling it all along, the compelling sweetness of roasted onions, the rich enticement of chicken cooking on the bone. But she hadn't noticed until now. Her thoughts had all been for Beulah and Ernest, for Nettie Mae and the winter to come. For the future.

Cora sat up, rubbing sleep from her eyes. "Are you hungry, dear?"

"Just about starved. Help me up, will you, Ma? I don't trust myself to do it on my own—not yet."

Cora guided Beulah upright and pushed a few pillows behind the girl's back. Beulah leaned against the headboard, blinking, swallowing hard.

"Are you well?" Cora asked.

"Felt sick for a minute there, but it's passing now. The longer I sit upright, the better I feel. My head aches, but it ain't too bad. I've had it worse, when I sweated too much in the summer, out there in the field." Beulah held her silence for a moment. She stared out the window toward their own home, just as Cora had done. At length, she said, "We ain't going to Paintrock." It was not a question.

"No. We aren't going to town after all."

"We ain't going to Saint Louis, either."

"How did you know I—" Cora stopped herself, shaking her head in curt dismissal. How did Beulah know? How did Beulah know anything—everything? There was no use asking the girl. Even if Beulah understood her strange power, her perfect sight, there was little hope she could explain it.

"And you're glad about it," Beulah said. "Happy to stay here."

Cora breathed deeply, considering her response. "I don't know if I'm glad, precisely. I suppose that remains to be seen. But I am committed. I will see my work through."

Cora kicked the quilt away from her feet, crawled over Beulah's legs, and stood. She stretched, driving back the cramp and fog of daytime sleep. Her dress was wrinkled, her apron askew. Why hadn't she thought to shed them both and sleep in her chemise? Cora clicked her tongue and shook her calico vigorously while Beulah looked on with a drowsy, tolerant smile.

"I look a proper mess," Cora said. "I was so fretful over you, I never stopped to think about bedclothes."

"And you were tired. Up all night, watching over me."

"Yes." So the girl had seen that, too. Or perhaps she had merely guessed. Cora was her mother, after all; no mother could sleep soundly while her child was in danger. "At least I removed my boots before I crawled into bed. Thank God for small mercies."

Cora slid her feet into the old brown boots, all soft leather and familiar creases. She laced and tied them quickly. The haze of slumber was lifting now, and an industrious energy had taken root inside her. Work called—the land outside, eager and companionable, warm and growing beneath a strengthening sun. How long would it take her to wake the Bemis land, she wondered, and where ought she to begin? The prospect would have filled her with dread once, or at least a shrinking feeling of inadequacy, for the farm was vast and hectic and she was but one woman. Now, she felt merely curious. Interested and ready.

"If Nettie Mae has been kind enough to fix us supper," Cora said, "then I truly ought to run back across the field and change into something more presentable. It won't do, to go to table looking like a dirty dish rag. Your dress is hung up there on the peg; you may put it on when you feel strong enough to stand. Nettie Mae brushed it out for you; the back was red with sand after you'd lain on the riverbank."

"I feel strong enough now." Beulah swung her legs over the side of the mattress. She clung to the bedpost and pulled herself to her feet. She remained at the bedpost for some time, holding tight, experimenting with her balance. Then she stepped away and walked easily across the room. The clean calico went swiftly over her head, and Cora helped her with the back buttons. Beulah reached for her pinafore. Then she paused and stepped back. She left the pinafore hanging on its peg.

"I'll help you down the stairs," Cora said, "to be sure you don't tumble. You must be careful about such things for a few more days, at least. Then I'll go and change for supper. You're to remain near this bed—doctor's orders—but I'll take Benjamin and Charles back home tonight. They can help me unpack our most pressing necessities. I suppose we're behind on our planting and our fence mending; we must all work hard this summer to catch up with our chores before the autumn comes."

Beulah put on her boots, then stood and faced Cora. "I'm ready."

How tall the girl had grown. She could scarcely be called a girl any longer; Beulah was poised on the edge of a new season. For a moment, one brief, trembling heartbeat, Cora wished for the power to stop time, to halt the turning of the wheel. Where had the child gone—silent in Cora's lap, transfixed by the prairie, staring in wonder at the grand, wild possibility of the world? She tidied Beulah's hair with her hands, tucking loose locks behind her ears. Gently, Cora laid the tip of her finger against Beulah's lip, just where the seed head had brushed it years ago.

Then she kissed her daughter's cheek. "I'm ready, too."

As they descended the staircase, Beulah clung to the banister with one hand and held tight to Cora's arm with the other. They went slowly, one step at a time, but Cora could already feel strength returning to her child's body—strength, vitality, and exuberance as lush as the summer that lay waiting just ahead. There was nothing left to fear on Beulah's account. She would be well, she would thrive, here in the place where her roots ran deep.

"Supper smells delicious," Beulah said. "Nettie Mae is a fine cook, but I never smelled anything like this from her kitchen before."

Halfway down the stairs, the sounds of cheerful work reached Cora. She could hear Nettie Mae directing the children in a voice both light and warm. "Benjamin, dear, can you carry that pitcher of water to the table, or is it too heavy for you? Don't drop it. Charles, we need one more plate. There, now. Doesn't the table look pretty? Oh, Miranda, what lovely flowers you've picked! Let me fill a cup with water, and you may set them on the table. Right there, in the center, so everyone may see."

"Flowers," Cora said, quietly amused. "Nettie Mae has made an occasion of it."

Then they reached the final steps and the kitchen came into view. Cora's feet froze on the stair. Her breath caught in her chest; she pressed a hand there, staring in shock, and felt the rapid beat of her heart. Nettie Mae had laid the table with the president's china. The mellow light of evening struck its gilded rims with sweet fire. The pattern of cobalt-blue vines and flowers glowed against a fine white tablecloth. The little ones hurried to their seats, faces shining as they looked up at Cora. Nettie Mae pulled out a chair. She lifted a hand in a summoning gesture—that imperious manner was as much a part of Nettie Mae as her wits and determination—but she smiled.

"I . . . I need to change my dress," Cora said.

"Nonsense," Nettie Mae replied. "You'll take too long, and we're all famished. Aren't we, children?"

Cora went to the table and sank into her chair, trembling. She stared down at her plate—that implausible treasure, too fine for a prairie woman—afraid to touch the china, convinced it would vanish under her hands and dissolve like a dream.

"Come, Beulah," Nettie Mae said, and helped the girl to her chair. "I've already called for Clyde; he'll be in shortly. He is putting the sheep in their fold. I hope you don't mind, Beulah, if I seat him next to you."

Nettie Mae presided over the table a moment longer—arranging the covered serving dishes just so, fussing with the placement of her saltcellar. Then she took the empty chair at Cora's side. Clyde stamped up the steps and swung the kitchen door open, calling greetings to Miranda and the boys. Then he went at once to the drain board, washed his hands and face, and took the last remaining chair. Cora noted the sideways dart of his eyes, the tiny, pleased smile when he found Beulah at his side.

"Let us say grace." Nettie Mae reached out, and Cora responded without hesitation. Their hands fit easily together.

BEULAH

Her ma did go across the field that evening, taking the little boys with her. Cora had spoken the truth: there was much work to be done, lost ground to regain before the seasons turned again, and the sooner they began their labors, the easier next winter would be. Beulah sat on the back steps of the Webber house, resting her back against the sod bricks, watching as her mother led Charles and Benjamin through the pasture. Night was coming down in that slow and careless way it has when springtime is fading, and summer rolls in to take its place. Summer is never in a hurry; it lingers and stretches and savors the light. Beulah meant to do the same. Evening songs of crickets and roosting birds filled the air, calling to her from the line of the cottonwoods—as did the distant scent of the river, all warm spice of leaves and slow water in its eddies.

Nettie Mae and Clyde were seeing to the dishes and to Miranda. There was no one about to check Beulah, no one to plead with her to be cautious. For her part, Beulah knew she was well enough for a stroll. Her legs felt sturdy, and though her head still ached a little, the ache didn't pound as terribly as it had done on waking. It was a small thing now, no more trouble to bear than the itch of a mosquito's bite. She slipped quietly from the steps and made for the river trail, whispering to the sheep as she passed their fold.

The deep red glory of sunset was fading by the time Beulah stood over Substance's grave. The clearing was still, save for a rustle of wind through the undergrowth. Beulah turned in a slow circle, face tipped up toward a purple sky, listening, waiting. The river spoke between its banks, repeating the tale it always told of high, cold places and endless snow, of the tumble of stone and the great, eternal wearing away—a story Beulah never tired of hearing. A few frogs still called among the cottonwoods, and high in the branches, one last thrasher whistled and paused, waiting for a distant reply. A white curve—the sickle of the moon—hung faint and waning above the slope of the foothills. Otherwise, the place was abandoned.

Beulah tipped the coyote skull gently with the toe of her boot. Its teeth had sunk into the red soil, leaving impressions just where Clyde had placed it. She could all but hear the words Clyde had said to his father when he had come, at last, to the grave—those words he had whispered in his heart.

"The world has passed to us now," Beulah said. "To Clyde and to me. We'll make of it what we choose."

No one spoke from below the earth, or from the space just above. Substance had stretched himself thin and wide, till the world took him back into itself and made him anew. He was somewhere down the river now, merging his great forceful self with the surge of the current, or perhaps he was among the crows on the barn roof—waiting within their bodies to become the egg in the nest, and then the fledgling, meek and small, and then a black bird winging across the fields. He was the seed in the seed head, fat and full with root and stem, or the pale, small egg secured to its leaf. The coyote slipping through shadows.

"Gone," Beulah said, and sighed, and smiled. She bent over his grave, straightening the coyote skull among the white-starred vines that surrounded it. Then she turned and headed back toward home.

As she walked the river trail, something small and pale caught Beulah's eye, lying in the dust. She picked up the corn seed, rolling it in her fingers, admiring the secretive flecks of scarlet dotting the hard yellow coat. She put the seed in her mouth and sucked it while she walked, swallowed down the clinging dust with its blunt taste of dry earth. When she took the seed from her mouth again, it was shiny and bright as a jewel, even in the dim shade of twilight.

Something small and lively crackled in the brush beside her—a rat, perhaps, or one of the ground-dwelling birds that hopped and pecked among the undergrowth. She peered into the tangled hedge but never saw the creature. Instead, she found an animal track pressed into the soil. She crouched to examine the track—the round fleshy pad, the four toes, the elegant symmetry of the whole arrangement. She could see how the dust had shifted at the rear of the pawprint, stirred by the animal's speed. A coyote, moving at a rapid trot along the verge of the trail.

Beulah pressed the corn seed down into the coyote's track, pressed till the soil gave way and the earth took her offering, and the red dust closed over the place to hide the seed while it dreamed.

"Grow," she whispered.

Then she stood, brushed her hands together, and left the cotton-woods behind.

AUTHOR'S NOTE AND ACKNOWLEDGMENTS

One for the Blackbird, One for the Crow was an unusual work for me. I've grown used to writing historical fiction that cleaves closely to true events, and although the bare bones of this story are based on a real chapter of my family's history—one I found too intriguing to resist—I gave myself the freedom to bend and twist reality to suit a larger artistic vision. But my readers have come to expect detailed notes at the ends of my stories, delineating facts and explaining where and why I deviated from the truth. Some readers have even said they find my notes almost as interesting as the stories themselves. So I feel I must tell you, in brief, the true story of the Bemis and Webber clans, and how this novel came to be.

After *The Ragged Edge of Night* was finished and safely committed to the editing process, I spent some time considering what theme I ought to explore in my second book with Lake Union Publishing. For reasons I still don't entirely understand, I was certain I wanted to write about death—my relationship to the sacred end, my private thoughts on the endless cycle of life. Perhaps the theme of death called to me so strongly because I'd spent several months researching the horrors of World War II for *Ragged Edge*. Maybe it was because my old cat Tron, who had been my dearest friend for the whole of my adult life, was rapidly failing in health, succumbing to cancer of the kidneys. Whatever the cause, I felt called to share with the world a different perspective on death—a consecration of the great unknown. I wanted to set death in its rightful place: not as a thing to cringe from with superstitious dread, but a natural process that unites all forms of life.

When I considered death—and considered it from my own reverent perspective—I fixated on my great-grandparents Clyde and Beulah Webber, for aside from family pets, theirs were the first deaths I ever knew.

Clyde and Beulah were my great-grandparents, the mother and father of my maternal grandma, Georgia Grant. I have the most wonderful memories of visiting Grandma and Grandpa Webber throughout my childhood. My mother would load my sister and me into the car and drive from Seattle to Eugene, Oregon, where my great-grandparents lived in their later years, as often as she could manage, for she had been close to her grandparents all her life. I loved those visits, especially at Christmastime. My great-grandparents' home was a wonderful time capsule, full of historic wonders like the player piano into which my sister and I would feed scroll after scroll, mesmerized by the old-fashioned music and the automatic dancing of the keys.

Clyde was witty and mischievous. He gave every member of our family a nickname—mine was Squeaky—and would refer to them by no other name. I remember, at the age of eight or nine, standing with my feet on the bottom rail of Beulah's garden gate, swinging slowly back and forth amid her lovely flowers, while Clyde leaned against the fence, teasing me good naturedly. "What are they teaching you in school, Squeaky? I hope they ain't told you the earth is round, 'cause it's flatter than a pancake."

In his youth, he had been a sheep rancher and a brilliant horse trainer, and after he and Beulah married, they lived in a tiny wagon—the kind Romany Travellers called home—out on the Wyoming plains. But when modernization caught up to him, Clyde adapted to the times.

He trained and sold a matched pair of Percheron draft horses and used the money to buy a Ford truck. He became a long-haul trucker from then on, and eventually settled with his young family in Eugene.

Beulah was as far removed from her portrayal in this novel as it's possible to imagine. She was a busy, fluttering, anxious woman, a meticulous housekeeper and gardener who never ceased to talk. (Clyde nicknamed her Windy for her prodigious gusts of speech.) She had a habit of placing little stickers on the undersides of every object in her home, labeling everything with a name: who was to receive that item after she died. Beulah left me her beautiful cranberry-glass candy dish, which she always kept full of old-fashioned ribbon candy, and which I raided eagerly every time my family came for a visit. That candy dish is among my most treasured possessions to this day.

Clyde and Beulah certainly loved one another deeply and lived to a ripe old age in one another's company. Their love, and their origins on the Wyoming frontier, are almost the only fragments of truth in this novel, though the general premise sprang from a true event—an event I uncovered by grilling my grandma Georgia and her cousin, Mona, about our family's history.

You see, one of the relics Beulah handed down was a gorgeous carved wood box, its lid decorated with a checkerboard pattern and her maiden initials: *B. B.* The sticker on the underside of the box bore my mother's name, along with the cryptic note *Daddy carved it while in jail.* I had to know how Beulah's father, Charles Ernest Bemis, had ended up in jail. Grandma Georgia readily supplied the details.

"He stole a wagonload of apples from a neighbor's orchard," my grandma told me, "because his own crops had failed that year, and he was afraid the kids would starve."

That sounded like a pretty good incitement for a novel, but Grandma had still more juicy familial gossip. She went on, "The real bad thing about it was, once he ended up in jail, his wife and the neighbor lady had to move in together. It was the only way they could get through the winter with two farms to run between them. But they hated each other's guts by that time, because Cora had caught Ernest and the neighbor lady fooling around in the bushes a little while before. That neighbor lady turned out to be my other grandma—Clyde's mom."

Ahh—now I had the bones of my story!

As I sifted through more conversations with my grandma and her cousin, and as I scoured genealogy sites for more facts about my family, the picture of my novel grew clearer. By the time the real Ernest Bemis ended up in jail for stealing his neighbor's apples, Nettie Mae's first husband had already died of unrelated causes. (His name was Benjamin, but his father was called Substance, and I couldn't resist using such an unusual name for my character.) However, the enmity between Cora and Nettie Mae was real—as was their distress at finding themselves forced to cooperate for the sake of their respective children.

I can well imagine that the year they spent living together was difficult for them both, given the sordid events that had transpired between the Bemis and Webber clans. But when these two women merged their households together, Clyde and Beulah had occasion to grow closer, and soon fell in love.

That settled it; the juxtaposition of love and hate beneath the same roof was too tempting for a novelist to resist. With these scraps of my family history, I set about constructing a plausible scenario to tell the story that was tugging at my heart.

As I researched the Bemis and Webber families—delving deep into genealogical records, squinting at scans of handwritten journals, and poring over old photographs of sod-brick houses—I learned of Cora's origins and the existence of the president's china. She was indeed the illegitimate daughter of Samuel Grant, brother to Ulysses, and the president did gift Cora a beautiful and expensive china set long after he'd left the White House. I believe the china set was intended as a heartfelt gift, not a bribe to buy Cora's silence, but I realized that if I rolled back time and set this story a couple of decades earlier, during Ulysses

Grant's actual presidency, I could leverage the china as a point of tension between Cora and Nettie Mae—a symbol of Cora's illegitimacy and the unforgivable stain on her soul (unforgivable from Nettie Mae's perspective, at least).

Once I'd settled on 1876 as my setting, the other pieces of the puzzle fell into place: a Wyoming frontier that was far less colonized by white pioneers than these ancestors truly found, the vast distance between most homesteads, and Cora's helpless fear of the wilderness. The setting seemed an appropriate backdrop for my exploration of nature and death.

This book came together far more easily than any I'd written before. In fact, *Blackbird* almost seemed to write itself, pouring out of me in an ecstatic rush whenever I sat down to work on the manuscript. The setting and the characters—and the mostly fictitious dilemma I'd created for them—carried the theme without any fuss. But midway through the book, doubt began to nag at me. Yes, I was writing the book easily enough. I hadn't yet run into a frustrating day when the words just wouldn't come, when I struggled to trudge through a chapter or a scene—common enough experiences for all writers, and a malaise that typically settles on me at least once per book. But still, I felt the novel was missing something critical. There was more I wanted to say about death and the great miracle of life, the sacred connectedness of nature. I couldn't put my finger on what exactly the missing piece might be.

I was beginning to despair, even though the book was still coming together with amiable ease. I gave myself a few days off and decided to spend that time out on the west side of San Juan Island—my home—reading poetry and listening to the voices of nature.

I walked out to my favorite spot for privacy and meditation, a soaring overlook above the nineteenth-century relics of the lime kilns, vast stone chimneys that were once used to process limestone, back in the days when San Juan Island had depended on economies other than tourism. There I sat, staring across the Salish Sea toward Vancouver

Island, listening to birdsong and the murmur of the waves far below. I took my phone from my pocket and pulled up a poetry site, one that displayed a poem at random every day.

My scalp prickled when I saw the poem; my breath caught in my throat. It was "The Two-Headed Calf," written by the late Laura Gilpin, a piece that carries special significance for me. It was the first poem I read after learning that my father had died in his sleep in 2003, when he had been only forty-nine years old. I have associated "The Two-Headed Calf" and its haunting imagery with my father ever since—and now, sitting among the wind and stone on my lonesome overlook, I felt the significance of that poem and of my father's early death throbbing in the center of my chest.

In an instant, I understood what was missing from *Blackbird*. I didn't know why the two-headed lamb belonged in the story; I only knew that it did. And as soon as I returned to my office, I emailed Chris Werner, my editor at Lake Union, to tell him the manuscript was getting a surprise addition that hadn't been included in the proposal.

The book came together rapidly from that moment on. *Blackbird* is still the only novel I've written that never became onerous for me, not even once.

On July 4, 2018, I took a few days off from writing to celebrate the holiday with my family, who had come up to the island to enjoy our fantastic view of two fireworks shows. My dear old cat Tron took a sudden turn for the worse, and I was obliged to track down the only available veterinarian at her home and bring her to my house to end Tron's suffering. His was not an easy death, but I was grateful to hold him while he made the inevitable journey, and glad I could alleviate some of his suffering, at least. My niece and nephew, Agatha and Henry, were visiting for the holiday. I was initially sorry that our planned weekend of family fun had turned so somber; and Agatha was upset, for she had known Tron all her life, and like me, she has a special fondness for cats.

While Paul dug a grave under our beautiful old pear tree, I asked Agatha to help me cut cornflowers in the garden—blue flowers for my blue cat—and, together with my mother, we had a nice conversation about death.

"You aren't crying much, Auntie," Agatha said.

"I know," I replied. "I guess that's partly because I've known for a long time that Tron was going to die soon. But also, it's because I know that death isn't anything to fear. It's very special; it's sacred. Think about all the animals in the world, and all the plants, and everything else that lives. All the millions of different kinds of life in the world. We're all so different from one another, but there are two experiences we all share. One is birth—or hatching from an egg, or sprouting from a seed, or however life begins. The other is death. Whatever kind of life we are, we all begin and we all end. In the beginnings and the endings, we can understand each other, and that makes a great connection among us all."

We took the cornflowers to Tron's grave and lowered his body inside.

"This is the worst part," my mom said ruefully. "Burying someone you love."

But I said, "I think this is the best part. Now Tron will become everything else we see all around us—the grass and the lilacs, the fruit on the tree. Every time we eat these pears, we can think of him, and remember how much we loved him."

I placed one flower on my old friend's eye, and Agatha and my mother helped me decorate his body with two circles of blue—circles for the endlessness of life, the unbroken hoop of our connection. As I tucked Tron into the soil and returned him to the earth that made us all, I thought of this book, which I was partway through writing. I thought of the story I wanted to tell.

I hope you have enjoyed reading it as much as I loved writing it.

I am grateful to so many people for their support and help during the creation of this novel.

Chris Werner, my acquisitions editor, has shown such enthusiasm for this project from the day I first proposed it. I hope we will continue working together for many years to come. Danielle Marshall, Lake Union's editorial director, has also been a champion for my work, and I am so grateful for her support.

I have had the privilege of working yet again with developmental editor Dorothy Zemach, whose sharp eye and wise suggestions helped make this book all it could be.

Valerie Paquin was my copy editor, and the work she put in to this manuscript astounded me in its detail and thoughtfulness.

I must thank my grandmother Georgia Grant, for sharing with me our family history—and Aunt Mona, who is my biggest fan.

Thank you to Tim, who has promised to keep a close eye on the Duke.

My gratitude to Laura Gilpin, one of the greatest American poets, for inspiring me all these years.

And most of all, my bottomless thanks and endless love to Paul Harnden, my husband. Every word I write is for him.

Olivia Hawker

January 2019

ABOUT THE AUTHOR

Photo © 2018 Paul Harnden

Through unexpected characters and vivid prose, Olivia Hawker explores the varied landscape of the human spirit. Olivia's interest in genealogy often informs her writing: her two novels, *The Ragged Edge of Night* and *One for the Blackbird, One for the Crow*, are based on true stories found within her own family tree. She lives in the San Juan Islands of Washington State, where she homesteads at Longlight, a one-acre microfarm dedicated to sustainable permaculture practices. For more information, visit www.hawkerbooks.com/olivia.